Miles away

N J Edmunds

BEAR PRESS

ISBN
Softcover: 978-1-739-63670-8
eBook: 978-1-739-63671-5

A CIP record for this book is available
from the British Library

For Bear Press
Editor: Andrew Jackman
Art Director: Sarah Joy

Set in 11/15pt PT Serif

1v00

For Helen

The Perthshire Advertiser

12th June 1970

GRIM FIND AT CITY HARBOUR

Girl, 17, Strangled and Dumped

Police too shocked to comment on horror

As we reported on 9th June, Carol Hosie, a shop assistant at McEwens of Perth had last been seen leaving work on Friday 5th. Last night Police swiftly sealed Perth harbour where the shocking discovery of Carol's body was made. Detective Inspector Malcolm Struth said she had a leather belt tight round her throat but added, 'Further details of injuries too shocking to reveal are being withheld.'

David MacRitchie of McEwens told me Carol worked in the haberdashery department, and that staff and management wished to send sincere condolences to the family.

A family heirloom might hold a clue to catching the butcher, D.I. Struth told me. A gold ring was not recovered with Carol's remains. Made by her grandfather, the ring (see picture) is unique, and Carol had worn it since her grandmother died. Carol's mother is under sedation.

Chapter 1

Late October 1976

"Why are you so fucked up, Dacre?" Spiny grinned and Dacre knew to expect more of his new friend's searing, engaging wit. "You can't say your own first name and now you're not even able to go upstairs on a bus, ya lanky spad."

They were on the No. 20 to town, and Dacre had taken a seat downstairs. Spiny thought it would be fun to try to make him climb the spiral steps to the upper deck.

It had been David Thom's idea to head for the Dungeon Bar. Dacre had been there once before and remembered enjoying the six-deep bar, the energising music, sweet smoke and a girl he had watched lustily over his pint glass. He had thought about her since and convinced himself he had caught her eye.

Occupying the basement, the Dungeon was painted black and lit only by the lights above the long bar. Some of the gig posters had changed, but the music was every bit as loud as he remembered. They had to shout to keep their conversation going. Spiny was in his usual stained suede jacket, Dacre wore denim, and David his old RAF overcoat. The three had gone out drinking together several times and Dacre was comfortable and glad he had made friends.

After a couple of rounds, and with ringing ears, it was Dacre's turn to shoulder his way through the throng for the next pints. Approaching the heaving bar was not for the faint-hearted. He'd learned quickly that if a square inch or two of space opened up between braced shoulders in front, it was crucial to push in quickly. When someone at the front had been served, there was jockeying to be done as two or three pints were held aloft like a prize, and deferentially allowed passage. Spilling beer was a crime. Dacre had honed his skills at the Royal Hotel disco in Auchmoor and took every slight advantage available. His next goal would be to gain the attention of the bar staff.

In front of him, a girl was taking her change from a sweating barman. Under the glaring bar lights, her brown hair was like shining dark chocolate, and he almost lost his concentration for a moment. She turned away from the bar cradling two drinks and Dacre deftly tried to slip his shoulder forward. At the same time though, a long-haired hulk in a black T-shirt pushed for the same space, and the girl was jolted forward. Dacre bumped her hand and tipped brown beer down the front of her top. He had seen the zigzag blouse before, its white bits catching the strobe lights. It was the girl he'd thrown hopeful glances towards on his last visit to the Dungeon, and he froze as his cheeks burned and the loud music was drowned out by the pulsing in his ears.

"Haha! Just as well I have my Friday night top on!"

The girl smiled brightly at Dacre, who barely managed to blabber, "God! I'm sorry!"

"Och, it was fatso's fault, not yours. Happens every week when I go to the bar. That's why I only ever carry two drinks at a time!" Dacre now noticed three other drinks stood on the bar. Left unattended for long they would be claimed by someone else, and adrenaline helped him think quickly.

"I'll carry those for you," he said, deftly grasping the three glasses.

"You'll lose your place at the bar—"

But Dacre led the way, clearing a path through the throng triumphant, gallant, and terrified. He turned round to face her and leaned close, shouting over Blue Öyster Cult, "Where are we going with these?" He could smell her hair, and she beamed greenish eyes at him, smiling and taking his breath away. He had forgotten about Spiny and David.

"I've no idea, they're not mine!" she giggled. "I only bought these two, it's just me and Marie here tonight."

Horrified, ashamed and excited, Dacre tried to look nonchalant. "These will do me and the boys, then!"

"That's theft! I'm going to report you." Her stern face cracked into a wide grin. "Or you could try persuading me not to I suppose."

"Do you come here—?"

"Often?" she finished for him, almost stumbling with laughter. "You'd better practise chatting up!"

He thought he'd blown his chance but she went on excitedly. "I come here every Friday, the music's brilliant. I'll look out for you next week, in case you give me another soaking. See you." With that, she moved off behind a pillar covered in band posters. Dacre returned to his pals and wished he'd been brave enough to follow her. He hadn't even asked her name. An hour or so later, when he was sure he'd seen her moving towards the exit, he told Spiny he was going to the toilet. He raced upstairs to the foyer but couldn't see her amongst the criss-crossing students. He was returning dejectedly down to the Dungeon when he heard her voice coming up the stairs, laughing with her friend. On the landing she almost collided with Dacre, and giggled, "You again! Watch him, Marie, he'll pour drink over you!"

"I'm sorry."

"Oh stop it, it's fine. He's really shy, Marie, he hasn't even told me his name."

"You haven't told me yours!"

"Come on, Isla, we'll miss the bus back to Hillhead," called Marie, already at the top of the stairs.

"You're in Hillhead?"

"Yes, I've seen you around. You're in Esslemont, aren't you? Tell me your name and I'll invite you for a coffee, we can do it formally, 'Come for a coffee sometime.'" Her sing-song mimicry of the freshers' ritual ice-breaker made him laugh as he extended his hand. "I'm Dacre." He was flattered that she had noticed him.

"Well, formal Mr Dacre, I invite you to Adam Smith House, room T21. Call in some evening, not too late or the porter won't let you in."

"Isla! Come on! The bus!"

Dacre had a spring in his step when he crossed the Dungeon floor to rejoin his pals. He was falling behind and guzzled from his pint to catch up.

"We thought you'd gone, got off with someone," said Spiny.

"Nah, just been to the bogs and stopped to read the band posters," Dacre replied, coolly. He was elated, but equally sure he had already been forgotten by the girl called Isla with the chocolate hair and the zigzag Friday top.

Chapter 2

Summer 1976

Dacre had drifted towards the science faculty at Aberdeen University in the same way he had drifted towards science subjects at school. His mother had hoped he would do medicine, and he knew she still believed he might be able to transfer to the medicine course later. He knew his dad didn't care.

It was late July when he had finally disclosed his disappointing exam results. The flapping sole of his left boot had seemed louder as he approached the door but there was no point trying to be quiet. She'd be awake and waiting. It was past midnight again, and he was home after another hot day trailing up and down seed potato fields: roguing. A good way of earning cash, and the pub at lunchtime broke the hard, boring day. This was their second roguing season, four teenagers in a Mini together with wellies, filthy hessian sacks, and waterproofs. The heatwave was continuing, but tonight he was muddy, wet, and cold. Spake had thought it would be fun to push him into a burn.

He had dumped his bag inside the front door, a corner of the mud-smeared brown envelope poking out to taunt him, and kicked off his boots before padding through to the kitchen to find food.

"Gordon, is that you?"

"Who else would it be?" he shouted back up the stairs.

"Why are you so late this time?"

"The farm was in Angus, Brian arranged it. Took us nearly two hours to get back, and we didn't stop until it was too dark to work."

"Brian? Who's that?"

Jeezusss! She asked me that last night!

"One of Spake's brother's friends, Mum, they've got the

car."

"Are you dirty?"

Fuxake! Is she stupid? Of course I'm fucking dirty! And muddy and cold and stinking.

"A little, Mum, sorry."

"Did you open it?"

"Oh Mum!"

"Your dad needs to know about your accommodation. You should be interested. You must want to know!"

How can I tell her?

"Mum, I'm only just in the door!"

"I don't know why you didn't open it yesterday, and why you had to take it to those filthy fields. We asked you last night. I wish you'd opened it and told us."

I did open it; that's the problem.

"I was tired, and then I had to leave at seven this morning. I opened it at lunchtime." He braced himself.

"In a field? Did you get it dirty?"

"Well, in the end rigg. It's a bit muddy but what does it matter? It's crap anyway."

"Gordon! You don't use that sort of language. You're going to be a doctor."

No I'm bloody not.

"I didn't get in."

Silence.

Oh, god.

After a moment, he heard her sniffing. "Gordon? You mean St Andrews? Edinburgh? You have to go to Glasgow?"

"None of them."

That'll be her for the night. Fuxake, I don't sleep anyway, but now she'll be wailing at me.

The bedsprings and the landing floorboard told him his mum was coming downstairs. His dad was away overnight again, at least.

The next few weeks had been awful, but Elinor Dacre

eventually accepted his going to Aberdeen. When his dad was at home he would dutifully respond to her prompts by grumbling his disappointment. By now, Dacre saw little interaction between his parents, and his dad always seemed irritable, his mum edgy.

The question of accommodation was contentious. His parents wanted him to move into a flat with his cousin: his mum to annoy her snobby sister, and his dad to save money. Dacre avoided the subject until Campbell offered his (shared!) room to another jerky law student.

Thank god! Imagine living with Campbell? Speccy git!

Dacre preferred the idea of having his own room in a flat shared with a group of strangers, and he accepted a place in a hall of residence. His only worry was about moving away from his ground floor bedroom. It wasn't the thought of leaving home, but the chance that he might have to face going upstairs again. The university brochure showed Esslemont House to be a modern three-storey block.

Bad dreams became more frequent and disturbing as his move approached. He discussed some of them with Spake in the Auchmoor Arms one night.

"You always fancied James, eh? Always knew you were a poof, Dacre. Dreaming about wee boys!"

"Piss off Spake, this is serious. It's as if I'm falling into a cellar or something. And James fucking Robb is in it somewhere! It's hellish. There's loads of blood. Someone's fallen, fuck knows who, and there's loads of blood. I didn't bleed when I broke my arm, so it wasn't me. What the fuck's that all about? And why Robb?"

Spake gulped his Skol and smirked. "You're just weird, Dacre. You're needin' tae see yer Dr Freud again." Dacre knew, though, that Spake's ribbing was not unkind. They had been close friends since primary school.

Spake had more important things on his mind. "Did you get enough spondoolies for another round?" They usually both tried to cadge a couple of pounds from their mothers to go to the pub, with empty promises to pay it back at the end of the roguing season. Roguing pay was good but the season was short, and cash didn't change hands until the seed potato crops had passed official inspection. An evening course at Elmwood college had taught them how to spot 'rogue' plants and purify the crop. If a crop failed, farmers didn't pay.

"I told you I got two quid. Your turn to feed the jukebox." As usual, he chose the B-side of an Andy Fairweather-Low single, 'Grease It Up'. After the coin had dropped and the buttons had been pressed, the jukebox whirred and clicked before the needle scratched the 45, and the two pals were ready to play air keyboards to each other as the music started. It had become their track, and they were the only ones who ever put it on. Objections only made them play it more. Their tastes in music were varied, including Dylan, Queen, and John Lennon. After a few lagers or when trying to impress girls in the Royal disco, they had been known to admit that 'Abba are not bad sometimes'.

Dacre went to the bar, where Mutch, the latest owner of the pub, smirked his usual tired jibe. "Ah! It's Dacre and Baker! I'm a poet and I didn't know it!"

Every bloody time! It's like he thinks he's just made it up!

"Two Skols please, Stuart." Mutch swiftly fizzed the lager glasses full. "That's fifty-six pence." There were four ten-pence coins in the change, more for 'Grease It Up'. Spake was back at the table trying to look cool, tapping his feet in time.

"You really not sleeping? What's bugging you? Still wanking about Sheila Henderson?"

"Piss off! I told you I keep dreaming I'm falling; I'm not joking. It's a nightmare."

"You been missing wee James since he left school? Dreaming about him! Ya big poofter!"

I wish he'd take this seriously. These mad dreams are scary. Christ! And Sutton said I'd get over it all!

Spake was now chatting to a guy at the next table, and Dacre sat brooding. On reflection, sometimes he thought maybe Dr Sutton hadn't been too bad after all. Sometimes his confidence ran high, and deep down he was proud he'd managed to survive school at all. Although his phobic anxieties were never far below the surface, he had become practised at coping with them. Burying them deeper.

"I'm going for another round." Spake was on his feet.

"Not for me, I want to catch the Volcano on the way home."

"Aw, come on, you don't need chips. Lager!"

"If I eat sometimes I sleep better."

"Have another pint, ya dobber!"

"It just means I'm up for a pee in the night."

"Poof! I'll call you Gordon if you don't."

"Piss off." He relented though, as usual. Spake bought more Skol and returned to the table triumphantly, gulping down a third of his pint in one go.

"We could fit in another after this!"

Chapter 3

Late September 1976

On the Saturday Dacre moved into his Esslemont student flat, he made two new friends. By the time his parents had helped him carry his case and bags up to the third floor, Dacre had been keen for them to leave. His mother had embarrassed him by crying when they collected his room keys, and his dad had been in a mood. When they had finally gone, he mooched about in his tiny room, wondering where to start.

After he had unpacked his stereo and LPs, the books his mother had bought him, and a box crammed with cups and teabags, he knew he would have to explore the flat. He had heard someone in the kitchen, and when he slouched in he smelled coffee. On a chair at the white table sat a boy in a checked shirt. His jeans had darker V-shaped patches inserted from the knee down to widen the flares. Dacre had done the same to his Wranglers, his mother having refused to ruin a perfectly good pair of trousers. The stitching was a bit uneven, but not bad, he thought, for an amateur.

The boy was slim and pale, with short fair hair, a high forehead and a very short fringe. He was smoking and had a coffee in a plastic mug. "Hiya."

"Hiya," replied Dacre, immediately wishing he hadn't used the same greeting.

The guy'll think I'm copying him.

"Want a coffee?"

"Aye thanks. Are you from Aberdeen?"

"A teuchter? Christ, no! Glasgow. You?"

"Auchmoor."

"Where the fuck's that?"

Dacre was surprised. At primary school, Auchmoor had seemed a huge place, and when he went to secondary, everyone knew it was the centre of everything.

"Fife, in between Edinburgh and Dundee. Are you David or Norman?" Dacre had seen the name tags that had been pinned on the doors of the flat rooms.

"Spiny."

"Spiny?"

"My brain hurts!" said 'Spiny', in a deep, slow drawl, delivered in attempted cockney.

"Monty Python?" asked Dacre.

"Aye, remember Spiny Norman? I've been called Spiny since the day after that episode. I hated being called Norman anyway. Poofy name, my ma's idea."

"Magic nickname, though."

"Better, anyway. What's your name?"

"Dacre."

"So you're Gordon Dackry?" Dacre was used to the mispronunciation, and his response was automatic.

"It's Dacre, rhymes with baker. And I don't answer to Gordon, I hate the name."

He wished he could change the subject. He started getting anxious with the sweaty palms and prickling hairs on the back of his neck he was so familiar with. It had all started with his name, the teasing about being a 'flasher'. The taunts of his primary school classmates when he had boasted that his dad called him Flash Gordon. Now all comic book heroes made him queasy and using or hearing his first name meant he risked vertigo, fainting and further humiliation.

"What are you doing later then, Mr Dacre?"

"I told you it's just Dacre. I'll call you Norman if you don't stop." He remembered Spake using that tactic on him and felt a pang of homesickness.

Spiny grinned, stubbed out his cigarette and said, "Beers? It's Saturday night, and our first day away from home. We'd better do something."

"Yes, but where? I don't know anywhere."

"They're having a cheese and wine party in the Hillhead

dining hall after the meal."

"I don't like wine. I puked at New Year and haven't touched it since."

"They just call it a cheese and wine party 'cos they want to be sophisticated. There's a bar as well. Come on, let's get fed first."

Dacre and Spiny wandered between the sprawling blocks of student flats and residences as they made their way towards what they hoped was the right building.

Other students were arriving with carrier bags, cases, rucksacks and boxes of LPs. Some had come on the bus laden with what they could carry. Most appeared to have parents in tow, but Spiny was pointing at someone their age unloading a small car by himself. Dacre was amazed.

"That guy's got a car of his own!"

"Must be an Agri student. Or a fuckin' lawyer." The ease with which Spiny could simultaneously appraise and disparage amused Dacre.

They found the vast dining hall downstairs in the main Central Building and had to show their flat keys to prove they were entitled to meals before joining a straggle of queuing students. Some seemed to know what they were doing, but he saw others uncertainly inspecting the steaming trays of food and seeking guidance from the white-hatted serving ladies. He decided they were the freshers. Several times confused-looking students returned to the servery having forgotten to pick up cutlery. Spiny said, "Tossers!" as he and Dacre swiftly grabbed theirs, pretending they would never have made that error.

After mince and mealie – "What the fuck is this sludge?" was Spiny's verdict on the oatmeal – the two went back to their flat. As Spiny opened the door, Dacre saw a neat, dark-haired boy moving two cases into the room opposite his.

The boy followed Dacre and Spiny into the kitchen. "Hi," he said, "I'm David. David Thom." He spoke quickly, in a strange accent Dacre thought sounded Irish.

Spiny grunted. "I'm Spiny. You just here?"

"I got here this morning, but my mum made me go straight out shopping for an anorak" – he pointed at the orange garment thrown over the table—"and then we had a fish tea at the beach." Dacre barely understood.

Spiny had picked up the newspaper with its headline about Rhodesia.

"Fucking colonists!"

Dacre shrugged. At least it made a change from bloody Vietnam for a while. He was getting tired of news from places he would never go.

"Come on," said Spiny, "let's go to this funky party they're putting on. I might even try the wine!" Looking at David, he added, "You coming?"

"Aye," said David. "Give me a wee while to empty my bags and I'll join you."

As David was at the door Spiny said, "Mind yer flashy new jacket. You'll need it tonight."

"Christ no, I'm not wearing that!"

After idling nervously in his room for half an hour, Dacre joined his two new and confident pals as they left to make their way back to the dining hall at 7:30. Porters in grey overalls were still arranging chairs around a low stage they had brought out. At one end of the room he could see three older students, two women and one man, who were opening bottles of white wine and chopping up orange cheese into squares. On a trestle table was a single keg of McEwan's lager connected to a Guinness tap.

"Some bar!" said Spiny. After three plastic cups of warm lager and an interminable two-minute speech delivered by a bearded senior student with greasy hair, Dacre wished he was back in the Auchmoor Arms. It seemed as if every one of the twenty or so mumbling freshers at the gathering was a complete spare, except him and his two new pals. There were girls he wouldn't look twice at and one or two he stole glances at. When he thought about it, other than Greasy Beard he couldn't see any males.

"Are you enjoying this?" he asked Spiny.

"Fuck, no. Lager like pish and no decent women. Have you noticed there are no other blokes here?"

David saved the day. "I know a good pub just down the road." Or that was what Dacre thought he said. The three agreed to go and find somewhere that had normal folk. They made for the door as bravely and coolly as they could, remarking loudly 'This crap's not for us' and 'What a load of spares!' The room was hushed as they exited, and they heard a feeble voice: "But you've missed the cheese—"

"Fuck, that was close! We nearly had to start talking to those dobbers." Again Dacre admired Spiny's way with words.

The pub was not far from the sprawling Hillhead Halls of Residence. Esslemont House was just one of multiple blocks housing well over a thousand students. It was on the walk to the Donview that Dacre first disclosed his acrophobia to his new flatmates. The bar stood on the north side of the River Don and reaching it meant crossing a high bridge. Dacre raced ahead, staring straight in front of him, and not responding to his friends as they tried to keep up with him and asked what the hurry was. Safely on the other side, he waited for them, still looking away from the bridge.

"What the fuck, Dacre? I want a beer but even I'm not that desperate!" Spiny's pale, smiling face was orange under the glow of the street lamps. It was late September and the nights were drawing in.

"Sorry, I had to get over quick. It's the bridge. Well, the height, not the actual bridge."

"You are fuckin' weird, Mr Dacre."

After a couple of pints Dacre felt confident enough with his new friends to explain a little about his problems.

"I was hoping room T29 might be on the ground floor.

When I got here I realised 'T' was for Top, and it was two flights up." He didn't tell them how much he was dreading having to sleep upstairs, something he hadn't had to do for years. Drink usually helped to dull his fear of going to sleep, but tonight was going to be a test. Getting up the stairs had been made easier with the boxes to carry and the irritation of his parents to distract him. Even spending time in the room had not been too bad, as long as he only looked at the sky when he faced the window. It was what tonight was going to bring that worried him.

He decided to change the subject. "Not a bad pub. How'd you know about this, being as you're Irish?"

"Irish? Who?"

Dacre blushed and hoped he hadn't insulted his new friend. David grinned widely and said, "Ah'm frae the Broch, min."

"Fuck, I hope you've washed your cock, ya sheep-shaggin' teuchter!" Dacre was shocked but amused by Spiny's humorous put-down, but still hadn't a clue what country David came from.

"Fraserburgh. Up the coast from here," David translated.

"You're Scottish?"

David and Spiny laughed loudly and good-naturedly at Dacre's faux pas and the three continued in a similar vein throughout the evening, periodically reminding themselves bawdily of Dacre's ignorance. By the time last orders were shouted, Dacre had worked out that David was half Scottish and half German, his father having worked on fishing boats. Initially from Hamburg, via Denmark, Norway, and Shetland, his father had ended up on a Fraserburgh boat. At the start of World War II, he had been interned, and once free after the war, he had married 'a quine frae the Broch'. The surname had been changed from Tomasz.

The rain had stopped but it was cold as they made their way back to Hillhead. The drink helped Dacre cross the bridge and he even unsteadily tight-roped along the kerb stones. They joked, laughed and discussed the others in the flat. None of them had encountered M. Davidson, the name on the door of room three. David had briefly met Andrew, a third-year student, and they decided he was too old for them to be seen with.

Dacre wished they had been able to find somewhere with a late licence. As they approached the flat he felt sick.

Here it goes, another night of it.

He'd remembered to shut his curtains before going out, at least, so he wouldn't have to face that. Trying to approach the second-floor window at night would have been unbearable.

As usual, the lager meant falling asleep was easy. It was what would come next he was worried about.

***

He hung like a bat, suspended, head swinging. Below him a whirlpool whipped and threw fleshy tentacles to grasp up at him, lashing and spitting. A silent scream echoed, scorching his eardrums as he fell. Face first, face crushed, teeth smashed. The taste of blood and spit.

As always Dacre woke choking and gulping in rubbery air when his jaws released the moist foam pillow. The familiar terror receded to make way for a rational fear. Fear that his screaming had been heard. As usual, though, he could only hear silence beneath his rasping breaths and his banging ears. The clock said ten to eight; he could hear it tick now. It was getting lighter outside, and if he stayed awake he knew he wouldn't go through it again.

His fear of heights was as bad as ever, but he was almost proud of how good he'd become at avoiding the triggers. Dr Sutton's advice had helped with that, and he was mostly able to live round the problem. But at night the acrophobia took back full control, and he would wake trying to recall his dreams, and then trying to erase them. Living on the top floor of Esslemont was going to be bad.

Chapter 4

In the week before the first term started new students were treated to a glimpse of the world they were entering. Evenings in Freshers' Week meant parties and drinking, and during the day there were guided tours of lecture theatres and a civic reception hosted by the City's Lord Provost. There was also the Societies Fair. Or Fayre. When they saw the alternative spelling on the posters, 'Wankers!' was all Spiny could say.

Dacre and Spiny went together to the Fayre. In a hall at Marischal College they found dozens of stalls, decorated with garish posters and manned by students dressed in wacky clothes. They threw flyers like confetti and told freshers how exciting the History Society or the Rock Climbing Club would be. Spiny said they were all oddballs who just wanted the joining fee funds or the chance to make passes at young students.

Spiny seemed to like starting arguments. First to experience his repartee was a bloke in a brown suit. He wore a Federation of Conservative Students badge and appeared taken aback to be spoken to by such an upstart. When Dacre drifted away Spiny had moved on to berate a long-haired Marxist for wearing ironed jeans. It was a relief to run into David at the Hockey Society stall.

"Our school had quite a good boys' hockey team," David told him. "Some of our teachers travelled to Aberdeen to play as Former Pupils at their old school, and they kept hockey going. Great fun. Fast." He was holding a hockey stick and turned to speak to a red-haired bloke with a beard. Dacre was intrigued but felt he couldn't join. At Auchmoor hockey was strictly for the girls. David signed up and the pair wandered on. As they passed the GodSoc stall David muttered "Jeeeezus noooo!" much to the amusement of Dacre. He was pleased that he had something more in common with his friend. They gathered numerous flyers, and David seemed to be a magnet for girls. The Archaeology, Potholing and Zoology societies all offered memberships to both of them, but it was always David the girls approached first. Their paraphernalia ... the tickets, leaflets and free biscuits, apparently pepped their confidence to giggly, gushy levels. Dacre was content to play second fiddle. Spake had had a similar effect on girls they met out of school, at concerts or the Royal disco. Spiny caught up with them as they escaped from a keen, red-faced girl in a camouflaged army cadet uniform.

"Guinness Drinking Society!" he announced triumphantly, waving his membership token. Dacre had tried Guinness once and just wanted to forget about it.

"I quite liked the idea of the Metaphysical and Supernatural society," said David.

"Poof," said Spiny.

"You can talk! You're a member of GaySoc."

"Piss off."

"You are! I signed you up." David pulled a pink card from his pocket, with Spiny's details neatly filled in proving he was a member.

"Bastard!" he smirked at David, as he tore the card up, and the three were still laughing at David's trick when they reached the pub.

***

By the second week of his first term, Dacre had begun to worry he might have been wrong to come to university. Freshers' Week had been okay, if exhausting and frenetic, but he'd begun to miss Auchmoor and his friends there. He wished at times he had gone to Dundee so he could go home more easily. His new friends Spiny and David seemed a bit like him: fresh from school, not sure what to do and trying to be cool about it. There were two others in the flat, Andrew from Inverness who was older, and M. Davidson who had barely been seen out of his room.

Saturday 9th October was Dacre's eighteenth birthday. He'd

been officially underage for the first part of the term, but no one had challenged him in bars. The week before his mother had sent him a five pound postal order and a note saying she would keep his cards at home. When he telephoned her on the day, it twigged that she had meant the money to be for a train fare. He didn't tell his new friends it was his birthday, even later when he used the fiver in the Dungeon Bar. That night had been good, though, a turning point. The atmosphere, the music and the developing banter between the three new friends seemed to lift his mood, and there was a good-looking girl. From then on there seemed to be fewer bad dreams.

It was on his second visit to the Dungeon, a couple of weeks after his birthday, that he had his chance encounter with the girl with the chocolate hair. The next day he had been barely able to contain himself. He kept visiting the kitchen to scan crowds of students going to and fro, and looking towards Adam Smith House trying to guess which window lit Room T21. He was desperate to make his 'Come for a coffee sometime' visit, but didn't want to appear too keen. 'I've seen you around. You're in Esslemont.' He seesawed between pride that she had noticed him and gloomy certainty she would have forgotten. He worried he might have misheard her friend call her name in the noisy foyer. It would make it easier when it all came to nothing if he tried to forget 'Isla'.

Unable to concentrate on chemistry, he reached for a book David had dumped in his room one evening. 'Introduction to Clinical Psychology, a Guide for Undergraduates', he read on the glossy cover. He was intrigued by the black-and-white photographs and the diagrams outlining primitive brain functions. The decerebrate cat and the anencephalic baby were gruesome, and when he saw the photo of a young child displaying 'Cri du Chat Syndrome' he had to close the book. He could almost hear the feline mewing and imagined it would be piercingly loud.

He went back to the kitchen and tried to find a clean

enough cup in the mess of dirty dishes. It wasn't his turn to wash up, he knew that. "I'm bored with chemistry." Spiny was in the corner smoking.

"Try economics! I thought doing Land Economy was supposed to be easy."

"At least you don't have nine o'clock lectures every day, though. You weren't even up when I came back at lunchtime on Friday."

"Aye, but Thursday night was good. I was wasted."

"Too much beer?"

"Errr … sort of." Spiny looked guilty, sly and conspiratorial. Dacre suspected he had a story he wanted to tell.

"What did you drink?"

"Nothing. I ran into Dermot; you know, the guy from my school. We dropped acid."

"You did what? Acid?"

"Yeah. LSD."

"Jeeezuss! Have you done that before?" Dacre was shocked. He had heard of some cannabis being passed round when he was at school, and there had been a story of someone's big sister taking Valium, although he had no idea what that was. LSD, though, always seemed to be in newspapers.

"No. First time. It was amazing. I could still feel it on Friday night." Thinking back, Dacre had noticed Spiny was a bit vague and odd in the Dungeon.

"What the hell was it like?"

"Weird, scary, like a mad dream. People's faces were melting. We played darts and Dermot thought we were fighting off pygmies."

Dacre had met Dermot in Freshers' Week, when he visited Spiny on an old bike, whizzing around with his long black coat flaring behind him. He brought Pomagne, spoke very quickly in a strong Glaswegian accent, and was very funny. Everything Dermot had said made Dacre laugh, although he hadn't quite been sure whether he liked or feared him. He'd certainly enjoyed his patter though, especially his tale of the drunken priest and a bucket.

"Dermot has done it loads, and gets it from a guy in a flat in Seaton," explained Spiny.

Dacre was uncomfortable and didn't want to hear more. He took his coffee and made an excuse about finishing his chemistry.

He slept fitfully over that weekend, but instead of the usual vortices and sweats, he was comfortable each time he woke, deliciously satisfied but with little memory of his dreams. He didn't think the broken, bleeding boy on the slabs had featured, and James Robb's chattering hadn't annoyed him. A familiar fragrance filled his head, but what was it?

Chapter 5

With a pounding in his chest, he entered Adam Smith House and turned left past the porter's desk. Unless they were residents, males had to be signed in, but the fat man in the overall didn't even look up from the Evening Express. Dacre was pleased to be inside and felt less exposed. His excitement was mixed with a feeling of being watched, as if he was on a secret mission. Perhaps the girl was watching for him.

T21 was on the top floor and in his state of nervous arousal climbing two storeys was even harder than usual. Gritting his teeth and staring at the stair treads, he closed his eyes to pass each draughty half-landing window. Finally reaching the top floor, the noise of his footsteps on the linoleum made him cringe. Approaching T21 at the end of the beige corridor, he realised he had no idea what to say. Uncertainty overflowed, and he walked on past the girl's room. At a fire door, he paused and shook himself. He about-turned almost purposefully and back at T21 he gulped, inhaled and knocked.

"Go away! I've told you!" The voice from within shocked Dacre who froze, staring at the glossy door. He was surprised by his own voice echoing loudly.

"Sorry, I didn't know when to come ... I—" He had started to turn away when the door opened. He could hear David Bowie.

"No, come back, please, I thought it was my boyfriend again. Sorry, please, come back, oh god! I didn't mean you."

Dacre was embarrassed, wanted to escape, and now sure he had misread the situation. "Sorry. You're busy, I'll go," he mumbled, his throat dry.

This is awful, I've made a terrible mistake, fuck, shit, boyfriend.

"No, you're fine, honestly, I was hoping you'd come." She was smiling, beckoning him in. "God, I'm glad that's over!"

Dacre thought she meant his awkwardness and went back to blabbering. "Sorry, I don't mean to be like this; it's the stairs."

“No, I didn’t mean you, silly. I’m glad you’re here. I meant I’m glad I’ve got rid of my pest of a boyfriend. He hasn’t come round tonight, so far anyway; I hope that means he’s got the message. What do you mean, the stairs? You don’t look that unfit.” She smiled at him, an appreciative grin. But Dacre was whirling.

Pest. Boyfriend. Got rid of? What? Has she finished with him? Oh god, I shouldn’t be here! I knew she was too nice.

“Boyfriend?” he managed to blurt.

“Ex-boyfriend. Good riddance.” She was beaming. “I only met him in Freshers’ Week and he wouldn’t leave me alone. I told him at the weekend that I had met you and to get lost. Sorry to take advantage of you, but I had to say something. And anyway, I hoped you might like me enough to let me off.” Dacre’s head was spinning with disbelief and the faintest hint of hope.

While Isla filled her kettle at the sink, Dacre looked around him, still unsure. The cassette case lying beside a radio-cassette player was Aladdin Sane, and there was a Diamond Dogs poster above her bed. A full-sized Rod Stewart adorned the wardrobe, though, and even with palpitations, Dacre registered his disapproval. He decided that he would be able to excuse Isla ... he could use her name now, he thought. All of these distracting thoughts raced round his head in an instant, barely holding back the growing need for him to say something.

“I wouldn’t have come if I’d known about a boyfriend.”

“That’s another reason I had to chuck him. Sit down, for god’s sake, you’re not going anywhere.”

He perched on the edge of the desk chair, which had clothes draped over the back. She reached behind him to lift them away, and as her hair brushed his shoulder he recognised a familiar fragrance. He was slowly adjusting to the idea that he was in the room of a good-looking girl and that she seemed to want him to be there.

She said on Friday she had seen me around! She chucked a boyfriend!

"I like Bowie, but I don't like Rod Stewart." He knew he had to keep talking.

"One out of two's not a bad start. I saw Rod last year in London, he was amazing." Dacre had never met anyone who had travelled so far to see a concert and had only been as far as the Caird Hall in Dundee. He was relaxing, welcome relief loosening his muscles. The pair chatted on and soon Dacre was talking effortlessly. They discussed music, school, their courses and childhoods. Isla was from Edinburgh and he thought she was joking when she said she'd been at an all-girls school. He was so at ease he even explained about dropping his first name. Isla laughed delightedly, promising to keep his secret.

"I won't call you a flasher. Unless you are, and I might like that if you only flash for me." Dacre blushed deeply but was proud and elated.

After an hour and a half, he realised it was getting late. "I should go, I suppose."

"Scared the neighbours will talk? I'm not. I'll come and visit you next time, though."

"OK, that would be good."

"What floor are you on?"

"The second floor, like you."

"How do you manage that? All those tiring stairs to climb!" She had a wicked smile.

"I'm fit enough; it's heights I don't like." Dacre cursed himself. *She'll think I'm a nutter.*

"Well, next time you come here I'll just meet you at the bottom and hold your hand."

As he was turning to say goodnight at the door, she leant forward and kissed him on the cheek. He could smell her hair when he woke the next morning.

***

Isla came to see him in Esslemont a few nights later. His mood had dipped as the nights wore on, and he had almost given up hope when she knocked on his door.

"Thank god!" she said. "I tried to come and see you two nights ago. The main door to the block was locked. And last night. I'm glad it was open this time. I didn't want you to think I wasn't trying."

Why didn't I think to check that? She's been trying to see me!

It was only a few minutes later that they embraced, and he accepted this was really happening. As the term progressed, Dacre thrived. His confidence grew and his problems seemed to matter a bit less. He and Isla quickly became close, meeting between lectures at times and spending evenings together, their embraces growing more passionate.

One evening in November, they were discussing his other flatmates. Isla had met Spiny and had heard about David, but remained curious about Shy Guy, as M. Davidson had become known. Still no one knew what the M stood for. They were in her room this time, listening to some Faces, which Dacre had begun to enjoy.

"He must come out sometimes. I'm going to knock on his door tomorrow night. He could be dead."

They both laughed wickedly at the thought, but Dacre said, "No, I see him in the morning sometimes. He has to go to the bathroom at some point. He still hasn't spoken to me, though."

"They must have decided to put all the weirdos in one flat, what with you and the heights problem."

He knew she was joking. They had discussed his trouble a few times, and although she had struggled to take it seriously at first, when he opened up about the bad dreams, she listened sympathetically. She had also noticed his curtain habit. "Seriously, though, do you think you're getting over it? You don't seem to mind coming to my room now."

"Look at the reward waiting for me."

"Smooth-talker! You'd better mean that!" He kissed her as well as he knew how. Dacre had had one nervous fumble after a school disco, and an older girl had snogged him after the Royal Hotel disco one Friday, but he'd only had sustained connection with Isla. He was delighted that she seemed to welcome his advances. He thought they were both learning, and wondered whether she would know what to do if things went further.

Coming up for air, he ventured, "Did you do this with your last boyfriend?"

She pulled away, and said, "Don't remind me. He wasn't a real boyfriend. He thought he was god's gift. Kept saying he was 'experienced'." She screwed up her face in disgust, and went on, "I only went out with him because he seemed charming and grown-up at first, but he was a creep. You rescued me." Dacre had still thought the other guy might be a threat and felt a glow when she said this.

Shaking inside, he felt he had to ask. "Are you, err ... experienced?" He regretted it immediately.

Isla paused, looked at him askance, and countered, with a cheeky smile, "Are you Jimi Hendrix, or just asking inappropriate questions of a lady?" Dacre panicked, fearing he had offended her, but she leant forward and kissed him hard. He relaxed even more a few minutes later when, pausing for breath, she whispered, "I didn't let him."

Buoyed, Dacre felt confident enough to let go of Isla and change the record. He chose a Hendrix LP and she giggled.

Chapter 6

Isla and Dacre's first proper date was watching a stage hypnotist humiliate willing volunteers. It had been Isla's idea, some of her friends having seen The Great Romano's show in Edinburgh. They queued on a freezing November evening with a mix of students and Aberdonians, the line stretching from the front of the palladian Music Hall on Union Street right round the corner into Golden Square. By now Dacre could understand some of the Aberdeen accent and listened to those around him as he and Isla tried to stay warm.

"Ah heard he gave a loon a richt red face, made him prance aboot like a gype. The loon thocht he wis a ballet dancer. Didna ken fit was goin' on!"

"Really? Ah canna wait!"

After the show, he took Isla to The Red Lounge, another of the Union's sticky-carpeted dens. They managed to squeeze into a booth in the corner where the red velour seats dampened the noise enough to allow them to discuss the show. The air was thick, sweet and smoky.

"I thought it was awful; what a shame for those people." Isla sipped her half-pint.

"Funny, though! And Shy Guy! His name's Miles! Wait until I tell Spiny, he'll have a field day."

"Poor guy. Are you sure it was him? I thought he didn't go out?"

"Definitely him. I saw him leaving afterwards. He looked a bit angry, really, but you have to admit, it was really funny."

M. Davidson had been one of the first to climb to the stage. Each victim was asked their name by the short, fat man dressed like a circus ringmaster and given an instruction. For the rest of the show whenever Romano said 'Sergeant Miles!', M. Davidson would obediently don a policeman's hat and sing 'The Laughing Policeman'. The audience cheered and laughed every time as he hollered, "Ha! Ha! Ha! Ha! Ha! Ha! Ha! Ha!

Ha! Ha! Ha! Ha! Haaa! ... Ha! Ha! Ha! Ha! Ha! Ha! Ha! Ha! Ha! Ha! Ha! Ha! Haaa!" At a snap of the great man's fingers, he would stop abruptly and sit down, his helmet tilted.

"Were you tempted to go up on stage? You looked weird when he made everyone grip their hands together."

"I must admit I was feeling drawn forward. I had to stop myself standing up."

"I had to stop you, you mean! I grabbed your arm!"

***

Sunday mornings in the flat were usually quiet. Doors occasionally opened, a toilet flushed and doors closed. Dacre stirred, and lay thinking about last night's fun, his mind wandering between the Music Hall, thoughts of Isla and the laughs on the last bus home as some of Seaton's characters entertained the students. The locals, having caught a late bus along King Street for years before Hillhead was ever built, had gradually developed a tolerance for students, at least on Saturday nights when they were bleezin' enough. Last night a tiny old man sang beautifully to anyone, especially the young, embarrassed girl beside him. His serenade had begun as soon as he slumped into the seat. Rum and Doric meant he was completely unintelligible, but that didn't matter except to the poor girl he was leering at. The little man's large wife had been forced to squeeze herself up the tight stairs, from where she loudly berated him. "Leave the poor quine alone, you feil gype."

Dragging himself up to go for a pee, Dacre padded along the corridor in his Y-fronts and was surprised to see Shy Guy, or Miles as he now knew, doing dishes and humming to himself in the kitchen. "Hi!" said Shy Guy, breezily. "I saw you in the crowd last night. At the Music Hall. Magic, wasn't it?"

Shocked at hearing his reclusive flatmate speak, Dacre was only able to utter, "Err ... magic, yeah."

"What are you doing today? Anything interesting?" The mysterious hidden flatmate of three months was now all smiles and chat.

"I've got loads of botany stuff to do."

"Ah well, never mind, if you fancy a break later, and a coffee, just chap at my door. See you later." When Miles had squeezed good-naturedly past him and back into his room, his door wedged open, a bemused Dacre managed to complete his toilet visit. By the time he returned to his room, he was wondering if he had imagined the whole encounter. He tried to concentrate on his botany, but Maud Jepson's biological drawings merged into each other as his mind wandered back and forth between plant anatomy and Shy Guy's sudden bloom. Back in the kitchen again making toast for his lunch, he heard Miles call out from his room, "Having a break, Gordon? I'll make the coffee."

Ten minutes of breezy chat later, Dacre was in Miles's neat room with a coffee and a biscuit. Miles asked why he preferred to be called Dacre and smiled knowingly on hearing the Flasher story. Dacre realised it had suddenly become easy to talk with Miles.

"I know what you mean. I was teased at school for my name. They called me 'Michael Miles', but because we didn't have a TV back then I didn't know what they were on about. 'Open the Box! Open the Box!' I can hear them now. It was that sort of thing that led to my problem."

"Problem?" asked Dacre, not knowing what to say.

"I saw a specialist who called it social phobia. Sort of extreme shyness in a way." Dacre was intrigued and still puzzled at the sudden change in Miles, who certainly wasn't shy today. "You might have noticed I don't mix much."

Now that's an understatement!

"Umm, I thought you were just busy studying."

"Last year I was lucky to get through at all, I missed so many classes. I had to get help to get to the exams."

He's not a fresher!

"Help? From the university?"

"No, Mum found someone. Like before when the psychologist gave up on me. It was brilliant for a while but it's just as bad again now. That's why I forced myself to go out last night. I've been reading up about hypnotherapy."

"Hippo what?" Dacre was beginning to wonder if Miles was on drugs.

"Hypnotherapy. It's hypnosis done by doctors, not just to make you laugh. The doctor I used to see at home was a GP in Kilmarnock, and he told me stage hypnosis like last night should be banned. Abuse, he said. Dangerous, even. I have been reading about autohypnosis." Miles was in full flow, and not at all chary. His enthusiasm drew Dacre in and he listened intently.

"Autohypnosis?"

"It's when you induce a trance in yourself. The doctor I saw up here in Aberdeen was going to teach me, but we couldn't afford any more sessions."

"You had to pay a doctor? Does that happen?"

Miles went on to explain that hypnotherapy wasn't part of doctors' training, and not many understood it, or even believed in it. Hardly any doctors used it, and because it wasn't standard medical practice it could only be used for their own patients. "If you're not on their list, they have to do it in their own time, and that means paying them. It was just really lucky for me that Dr Dave had started doing it and we didn't have to pay."

"Dr Dave?"

"Everyone calls him Dr Dave 'cos his father's in the same practice and two Dr McLennans was too confusing."

Dacre was trying to keep up.

"Dr Dave tried it on me, but he didn't know much about it yet and he asked me to see a more experienced doctor, but we'd have to pay. It was good my mum could afford it." He looked out of the window, adding, "After my dad died."

Dacre could scarcely believe Miles was so effusive. He spoke calmly and confidently, but with barely a pause even after disclosing that his father had died. "We had to go to Kilmarnock to see Dr Kirby, he'd been doing it for ages. He liked doing it for his patients, but my mum had to take me in the evening. But when I came away to Aberdeen, I had to find someone else to do it, or at least my mum did."

Dacre thought he should say something. "There can't be that many people that need it, are there? For shyness I mean."

"No, I suppose not, but they use it for all sorts of other things as well. People who are scared to go on a plane. Or who pull their hair out. Scared of heights, or just anxious all the time."

Heights!

"Does it always work? For anything, I mean?" Questions queued in Dacre's racing mind. Telling his Flasher story had been easy but he was still reluctant to expose more weaknesses. He couldn't have got a word in edgeways, though. Miles continued in full flow and went on at length about some people being very susceptible to hypnosis and others not at all. He had expected to be susceptible to Romano because hypnotherapy had worked so well in the past.

"But, err, you're still shy."

Miles smiled. "Yeah, that's just it. It doesn't last. I had to keep seeing Kirby to have top-ups. Short sessions like a booster, to kind of remind you. I want to learn autohypnosis so I can top myself up."

"That's when you do it to yourself, right?"

"You've got to learn how to do it. If you're susceptible that is." Miles stared back at Dacre, his speech pressured, and continued earnestly, "That's why I went last night. It was hard to get there, and I was in a real state. Did you see the crowd, the queue? I was desperate, I sort of tried the autohypnosis on myself, to see if it would get me there. I kind of had to get there, I was sure The Great Romano was going to help me, take me out of myself, even if he is a bloody charlatan. My mouth's dry, the talking."

As Miles gulped water from a red mug, Dacre took his chance to try to get a word in. "It certainly took you out of yourself!" He couldn't help laughing and blushed, continuing quickly, "Sorry, it was just so funny, in a scary kind of way. My girlfriend didn't much like it at all." Dacre hadn't described Isla as his girlfriend to anyone before, and it felt good.

Miles was looking at the floor now, shaking his head. "I didn't like it either. Even though he kept making me laugh like that, I was kind of screaming inside." He looked up, wryly. "Still, it's certainly had the same helpful effect on my problem. I hope it lasts a bit longer this time. I'm still hoping to teach myself properly."

Within a few days, though, it was as if Miles had disappeared back into Shy Guy again.

The Sunday Magazine

June 24, 1973

HIGHLAND HORROR

Special Report by Senior Reporter Caroline Stockley

This Tuesday will mark exactly one year since the tragic discovery of the body of 16-year-old Mhairi Cullen. Mhairi's mutilated body was found weighed down in the fast-flowing waters of the River Dochart, in an otherwise idyllic spot, but one which will forever be remembered for one of the most disturbing crimes in recent memory. A crime that remains unsolved.

Five hundred miles from London, sixty miles from Glasgow and a million miles from anywhere, misty and magnificent Glen Dochart is the last place you might expect to find horror. But horror visited the Cullen family last year after an angler snagged his line in the River Dochart. His catch wasn't the brown trout he expected and what was eventually retrieved from the river bed was what remained of Mhairi Cullen. A full year on and Mhairi's grieving family still don't know how she ended up in the river, or who dumped her there after surgically removing her right leg.

Mhairi's mother Johanna agreed to tell me her story in the hope she can help someone remember something that might help Stirling and Clackmannan Police, the responsible force. In Johanna's words, 'The police have got nowhere, even with their roadblocks and searches.' All enquiries so far have come to nothing, and although the case remains open, my investigations suggest the police retain little hope of ever catching the brutal butcher who brought young Mhairi to her end.

Continues on page 7

Chapter 7

Tuesday 4th January 1977

As the train pulled out of Inverkeithing, Dacre began to sweat, his chest pounding. Nausea rose as the little boy opposite him stood on his mother's knee craning his neck for a better view of the rust-red girders of the Forth Bridge and the tiny boats far below. He was trapped in a window seat by the snoring, tattooed giant beside him, whose outstretched arm still gripped a lager can. Earlier Dacre had been stealing glances at the Lager Lovelies on the empty cans. Turning to look to his right, past the rigger, he was met by a cheery, beery stare from the man's friend across the aisle.

"Want some?" the man slurred, proffering a fresh can from their stack.

Dacre felt the bile rise. He mumbled something intended to convey polite refusal, and turned away quickly with a gurgle in his throat, only for the grimy window to fill his view. The whitecaps of the grey Forth were hundreds of feet below him.

The generous drinker's rambling and laughter ceased suddenly when Dacre, pallid and limp, crumpled heavily into the man at his side. The sleeping monster stirred, snorting, "What the—?"

Coming to after Dalmeny, Dacre became aware of the hulk beside him wiping vomit from his shoulder and arm.

"Sorry son, I've had too much. Just as well you were asleep. Bet you're glad I missed you, eh?" Dacre could taste vomit but was too confused, drowsy, and embarrassed to correct the man. His pal across the aisle was laughing helplessly.

The oil rig workers from Aberdeen took their kitbags and unopened cans off the train at Haymarket. Dacre was still feeling faint when he followed his fellow passengers onto the platform at Waverley a few minutes later. Isla was waiting and as Dacre passed through the platform gate she rushed forward, smiling broadly and throwing her arms round him.

"Oh, Dacre! I've missed you! Are you OK? What's that smell?"

"I had to sit next to a drunk who was sick," he lied, guilty for being dishonest and proud of his quick thinking.

"Oh, how awful, you poor thing!"

Dacre had been ecstatic when Isla had invited him to visit her in Edinburgh. The Christmas holidays at home in Auchmoor had dragged, and on every hushed phone call he had waited for her to tell him she had met someone else. When he had asked his mother to lend him the train fare she'd been vacuuming again.

It's New Year's Day! No one ever comes, anyway. Even Aunty Janet now.

When she finally switched the screaming machine off, Dacre took his chance.

"Mum, d'you remember I told you about my friend Isla from Edinburgh? She wants me to visit her on Tuesday."

"I knew it! You've got a girlfriend! Is that who you are always on the phone to? What's she like? Ooh, how exciting!"

Fuxake, I knew it would be like this!

He told her only what he had to, only enough to ensure she would fork out for the travel.

"Yes, she's doing history and English ... somewhere in Edinburgh, I'm not sure where ... she's going to meet me at the station ... yes, she's a first-year ... I think she has two sisters ... I don't know what he does ... Alexander—"

Jeezuss! She wants to know more than I know!

For the rest of the day, Elinor was all smiles, singing along to the radio and interrupting her TV programmes with more questions. Dacre was glad when Tuesday morning came but a little guilty when she slipped him ten pounds, whispering conspiratorially, "Don't tell your dad." Ten pounds was a fortune, more than he needed for bus and train fares.

Off the train and now with Isla, Dacre's confidence

recovered. He enjoyed her excited chatter and plans to show him her city. He would tell her about the bridge later, he thought. He was already planning to arrive early for the train home and find a seat near a toilet to cross the Forth in.

The pair walked through Princes Street gardens hand in hand, telling each other once again what they had done since they had parted at Hillhead. Isla took him to a café at a busy road junction, opposite a huge clock. Dacre could vaguely remember its Roman numerals from his only other visit to Edinburgh, when he had trudged the huge Binn's department store with his bickering parents. The café was below street level and dimly lit. Dacre gazed happily into Isla's eyes while they shared a huge ice cream dessert. He paid the bill as gallantly as he knew how, and with his mouth now suitably sweetened he pulled her close to kiss before they climbed back to the pavement.

Isla led him through the traffic and along a road in the shadow of the castle. Some distance away from busy Princes Street, the street widened into a cobbled open space where there were a few bars and a very grubby-looking guesthouse. "Once we pass through the Grassmarket, we'll go up to the High Street and I'll show you the whole city," she explained.

"You can see the whole city from there?"

"Onlee weeth the Great Isla's special powers." Her mock Italian cum Spanish impression of The Great Romano was not good, but Dacre loved it. Now, drifting into an awful sitcom German accent, she continued: "I vill lead you up zee stairs, ant ve vill haf none of zee vorrying, OK?" Dacre hadn't expected stairs and began to feel uneasy. Isla shook her head. "You'll be fine, just imagine you are going up to T21."

She led him up a dull cobbled street and round a curve, before turning up steep steps. "Close your eyes ... I'll lead you up, it's quicker this way." After more cobbles and a left turn, he could see the castle up ahead. Presuming that was their destination he was surprised when, with a jaunty "Here we are", Isla stopped abruptly outside a narrow, tall building sandwiched between other tenements. Entering through a nondescript door, she led him to a small desk where she paid their entry fees. A cool, flagstoned hallway led to a stone, spiral staircase. Try as he might, he found it hard to liken the place to Adam Smith House. She led him on up and round, chatting all the time and not letting him stop. He looked straight ahead and concentrated on watching her climbing ahead of him.

"I wish I could stare at your bum every time I had to climb stairs," he said, "I'd never have any trouble."

"I'm glad you like the view." She laughed and turned to hug him when they reached the top landing. Dacre was hardly aware he had just climbed several storeys.

The Camera Obscura fascinated Dacre. He had never heard of it before, and was surprised how much easier the device made viewing the world from high above. Isla laughed at his attempts to explain what he understood of the physics. "I don't care how it works; it's still just plain old-fashioned magic to me," she argued. "Don't spoil it for me by trying to explain it."

"I don't understand it anyway, to be honest," admitted Dacre. "I was just trying to impress you."

"It's not the best of chat-up lines. Anyway, we're way past chatting each other up, aren't we?"

***

Dacre emerged from the reeking toilet cubicle on the train back gagging at the smell from the overflowing porcelain bowl. At least I haven't puked, he thought, returning to a seat. Holding on to the sink, eyes shut and facing away from the tiny opaque window, he had braced himself until the train had stopped and pulled away from what he guessed was Inverkeithing. There had been only one try of the toilet door handle, followed by grunted swearing and retreating footsteps.

Staring at the back of the worn, tweedy seat in front of him,

Dacre thought about his day in Edinburgh. It had been wonderful and awful, joy with Isla marred by flash memories of vomiting on the bridge and growing dread as the return journey threatened.

This is mental. I've got to do something. That bastard goatshagger Sutton said it was all going to settle once I got over the fall. What a load of pish!

Remembering Isla's kisses and smiles at Waverley helped. "It's only six days 'til we're back in Hillhead," she'd said as the train began to pull out and Dacre leaned further out of the pulled-down, filthy window. "I love ... it there."

By the time he was on the bus back to Auchmoor, Dacre had decided to do something about his problem. Otherwise, he would lose Isla.

***

By the end of January Dacre felt like his life had leapt forward. Lying beside Isla in her bed in Adam Smith, he was dozing when she rolled onto her side and raised herself on her elbow. "How do you think it all started? The heights thing, I mean."

They had discussed his problems again earlier after they climbed the stairs to her room. He had managed to change the subject, and now in a sleepy bliss, his thoughts had returned for the umpteenth time that day, that hour, to their first time alone together after the Christmas break. Barely minutes after he had spied her seeing her parents off, she had knocked at his door. As soon as he had unlatched the red door of his Esslemont room, she had been in the room hugging and kissing him. Before side one of The Royal Scam had finished, he had overcome his clumsy fumbling and felt that sudden, moist warmth envelop him as she had sighed and muttered into his neck, "Aah ... Dacre ... that's ... it ... mmm ..."

Now, reluctantly, he turned his mind to his predicament. They'd had to take a detour to avoid the high bridge over the Don on their walk to the beach earlier that day. She was patient with him, but he wondered how long she would put up with his acrophobia.

"The psychologist I saw said it was all to do with my broken wrist. I fell but I don't even remember it. But there's more to it, I know there is. Some of the dreams I have, they're mad. I'm always falling, but madder stuff too. A wee boy bleeding, for fuck's sake! And my mum has something to do with it." He lay on his back and spoke until he was exhausted, explaining details from his childhood he didn't know he remembered.

Chapter 8

1960

She heard moaning from the other room again. Wearily she mopped one more time at the little boy's red, wet forehead, whispering "I'll be back to you in a moment, pet", before trudging back along to check on his sick baby brother.

"Mummy ... hurt ... head hurt."

The woman came back in after a few minutes holding a teaspoon, her other hand pulling her dressing gown around her against the cold.

The heat from the boy's body was no comfort. "Here you are, special syrup, to make you all better." She proffered the spoon and waved it under his nose. His eyes streamed pus from their swollen red rims. Between his coughs, she helped the spoon between his cracked lips and something primitive in him made him suck in the warmed syrup and crushed aspirin.

He lay still now. Stock still as if dead, but for his shivering. She pulled his pyjama top down to hide the rash on his scrawny belly, his wrinkly skin maroon against the grey, damp sheet. The street light shone through thin curtains, and as they waved in the freezing draught the dim room shimmered yellow.

Once again the pitiful cries called her back along the cold hallway, and once again her slipper caught on the splintered, bare boards. "I'm coming, Baby."

The boy now looked into the yellow light. It no longer hurt his eyes. Nothing hurt, and now there was no itch. He stood on the launch pad, his bare toes curled over the edge. The warm breeze filled his wings, lifting him to soar freely and swoop through the air, shrieking with delight. I can fly!

The mother woke in silence, her baby's warm body peaceful against hers, his breathing comforting her. Silence from along the corridor. *He's settled.* Dutifully she padded along the hall to check. The shocking, icy wind roused her as she reached his door.

The empty bed. The open window.

She screamed.

***

1963

The Spitfire swayed in the draught as it soared across the cracked magnolia sky. Cloudy curtains filtered orange light, paling in the dawn. Over the silence the boy became aware of rhythmic grunting, then moans and shrieks.

Out on the landing, the familiar floorboard creak guided the boy's little cold feet towards the summoning sounds, louder now, drawing him on. When the door swung past the cold brown lino it caught on the edge of the rumpled rug, and he had to push with both hands.

Mummy was sitting up, gasping, grasping the sheet, shushing. There was hushed, hurried ruffling of the hilly, candlewick landscape beside her.

"Daddy? Daddy home?"

Mummy sighed, clutching her nightie tight to her neck, and rose awkwardly from the bed, in pink woolly bedsocks. "Come on, back to bed. Dreaming again. You won't remember in the morning. Just a dream." He heard her voice croaking. Then her kind hand was on his back, guiding him around the creak, tucking him in.

The Spitfire soared, throwing darker shadows as the sun broke through the curtain clouds.

***

October 1967

The bus was cold and the man in front of Elinor had the sliding window open. The draught lessened the reek of sweat and smoke. On her knee was her shopping: some new gym shoes for Gordon, and new curtains for the living room. She was glad the walls were finished at last. Alun must have done some extra work to pay for curtains and the paint. He's a good man, she told herself.

It was one of the older buses they still used on the rural routes, and the door had been jamming at every stop. Near the ice-rink, the bus driver sighed and started to get up once more from his seat, but a figure ran along the pavement and climbed on.

"Thanks, I thought I'd missed it again." The man's voice and accent caught Elinor's attention and despite the cold, she felt heat rising over her breast and neck. Her pulse raced and her throat dried. Reflexly she lifted her head briefly just as the man turned to find a seat in the busy bus. Their eyes met and he uttered, "Ellie—" before she turned pointedly towards the rain-spattered window. She heard him make his way past to the back of the bus, her gaze fixed on the passing blur of damp grey walls and dim windows.

She watched his broad back when he passed her to leave the bus near Glenrothes. It was dark by the time the bus reached Auchmoor.

***

Elinor turned carefully, fearful she would wake Alun again. Her neck ached, and as she slowly turned her head she shut her mouth tight against the pain. Painting the ceiling last week, that's what caused it, she rehearsed. It would soon be time to get Gordon up.

The bed felt cold beside her and she couldn't hear his breathing. Relief when from downstairs she heard the back door scraping open. As it banged shut the bed shook a little, and she heard footsteps, tuneless whistling and his van doors creaking open. His tool bag clanged into the back, and she heard muffled cursing, the motor starting and the van pulling away.

Only rain pattering on the window broke the silence and her tension eased. She sat up painfully to see the clock. He had left early and she must have slept after all. The pain receded slowly and sleep reclaimed her.

***

His voice echoed. 'Ellie ... Ellie ... Ellie.' That tenderness, and the comfort of his arms. His voice. Comforting me. I don't want it to stop. So warm.

"Mum. Aren't you getting up?" Startled, she sat up, her dreamy comfort melting away as pounding fear and guilt flooded over her. "Gordon! Coming, I'm sorry, I overslept. I'm coming."

Elinor rushed Gordon into readiness for school, her dream and familiar guilt never far from her thoughts. She knew it was ridiculous, a result of the chance meeting on the bus the day before. She would never be able to speak to him again. That much was clear. For the first time since his last letter she had wept silently in the darkness last night. Alun hadn't noticed, at least.

***

On his way to Nairn, Alun Dacre's mind wandered. Anger had receded by the time he passed Perth, and the A9 always lulled him. After Dunkeld he settled in behind a truck as the road snaked slowly through villages and small towns. Pitlochry was a bottleneck, then it would be on into the Highlands. Beyond Aviemore, he would turn off through the hills and forests with fewer lorries but more pootling Land Rovers and tractors. The slow way to Nairn would take him the best part of the day, justifying expenses for an overnight stay and avoiding Inverness. He'd have to go back via the highland capital, though. Dod had picked up a contract servicing escalators in a new shopping centre.

Dod was trying to branch out towards escalators. The old lifts they had specialised in for years were becoming outdated. In the last couple of years, Alun had visited a diminishing number of sites with increased frequency, as the old machinery needed ever more maintenance. That suited him, but his boss didn't like the trend towards newer American elevators, which came with installation and servicing packages.

Alun had serviced the lift in the Golf Links Hotel for years now and was there two or three times every year to try to keep it going. He knew the elderly owners were eagerly anticipating retirement. Several times, over late-night whisky Alun had listened as the morose man, drinking only water, explained that he would sell up if he could. Alun thought their only chance of attracting a buyer would be if an American chain took over, and that would mean investment and a new lift, if not a total rebuild. It was much more likely the building would instead continue to decay, alongside its despairing owners. Although a golfing town, Nairn didn't yet interest investors. During his time in Fife, Alun had seen the golf at St Andrews attract more and more American visitors and the money that followed them.

Alun was thirty-nine and had been servicing lifts for over five years. For twelve years before that, he had been an engineer in the RAF at the base in Leuchars. As a civilian with a son of three and a liking for the betting shop he had needed work, and after a short spell in the gas works in Methil he took a post at George Lambie Specialist Engineers. Dod Lambie had left the RAF a couple of years before Alun and had soon used his meagre engineering skills and considerable entrepreneurial instincts to establish the business. He travelled widely promoting GLSE and took contracts all over Scotland, the maintenance of lifts developing into his most successful income stream. Alun was dependable and a good engineer and Dod funded overnight accommodation to allow for round trips taking in multiple jobs. Soon Alun was spending two or three nights each week away from home and had grown to like it. There were still the smaller jobs, repairing cookers and washing machines and anything else Dod thought he could make a few pounds from. He always takes his cut, thought Alun as he finally accelerated north out of Pitlochry.

As always, the further he travelled from home the more Alun relaxed. By the time he drove into Nairn, thoughts of Elinor, Gordon and the old trouble were replaced by pleasing anticipation of a fry-up and a couple of beers after he finished the job. He was able to tell himself things were better since he had sorted Redbond out. *I warned him off good and proper*, he thought, smiling in self-congratulation. And he knew how to cadge a free meal in the hotel and keep his allowance for beer. *Serves Dod right, with his 'Working hard, or hardly working?', every bloody time he sees me!*

Chapter 9

Not long after he'd dropped his first name to escape teasing, Dacre broke his wrist. The two events were unconnected, but both had lasting effects on him. It was after the injury that he began to fear heights.

He knew it had been in the Easter school holidays of 1967, and he thought it had happened in a fall, but he wasn't sure. He had woken in the cottage hospital with no memory of the events of that day.

Dr Mackie and a nurse were washing their hands in a deep white sink using a red bar of the same hard cracked soap that they had in the toilets at school.

On the wooden worktop next to them was a roll of thick white bandage, in front of a Marathon Chocolate Bar Easter Egg box. He could see some white stuff in Dr Mackie's hair, and more on the collar of his brown shirt. Dacre's head hurt, and when he tried to sit up, he realised he couldn't move his left arm properly. It wasn't sore, but heavy and hot.

He could see his arm wrapped in white plaster from his elbow to his knuckles, and he reached over to feel the warm cylinder.

His mum leant in from the side of his bed. She looked like she had been crying, but when she saw him moving she smiled at him and stroked his forehead, holding his right hand tightly and adjusting her paisley-patterned scarf.

"Oh, thank goodness, Gordon," she said. "Dr Mackie, Gordon's woken up!"

Don't call me that! It's Dacre.

"Is your arm awful sore? Dr Mackie says you're fine but you've got concussion."

"What's a con cushion?"

Dr Mackie turned round, drying his hands on a green-and-white stripy towel. There was red writing at one end of it. He came across the squeaky floor and stood at the end of the bed.

"How old are you, son?"

"Eight."

"Yes, the anaesthetic's wearing off. You'll be fine, son," he said, smiling kindly, "but you won't be getting up to your mischief for a while. That stookie's staying on for six weeks."

He was kept in hospital overnight because he couldn't remember anything. Dr Mackie said he must have had quite a head knock, but his head didn't hurt at all. He was picked up by his dad the next morning.

"Dad, one of the boys got ice cream for breakfast!"

Alun seemed to take little notice of what his son said, and Dacre thought he had made him angry again. His dad often seemed to be angry. At home, his mum was waiting and crying. His dad didn't go to work that day or the day after and spent a lot of time in the telephone box along the street. Each time he returned he seemed to be more and more annoyed.

"I've had to rearrange all my work, and I'll not get mileage payments or expenses. It's all your bloody fault! And his, of course!" Dacre tried to cover his ears but, with his plastered wrist, he could only try to bury himself in a pillow. He had never heard his dad so angry and every day there were arguments, shouting and his mum crying.

That school holiday was awful, and he was kept off for an extra week. When his dad went back to work he was still in a bad mood, and Dacre knew it was all his fault. Every time the van drove away he worried his dad wouldn't come back. Twice his dad made Dacre go to work with him and there was frightening silence in the van until they were miles away from home. But it was better than his mum's crying.

***

On one trip his dad stopped the van near a row of lock-up garages in Perth. "Wait here. I need to get something out of the freezer."

Dacre watched his dad walk over a messy, muddy yard to the door of one of the lock-ups. He returned quickly and threw his keys through the van window. "Bugger it! I've got the wrong set of keys!" He yanked the van door open to get back in, hammering the steering wheel with both hands. As his dad's anger flared, Dacre felt tears collecting, but after a moment Alun opened the van door and got back out. He crouched in a gap between the lock-up wall and a high fence and lifted a brick from amongst the weeds. Minutes later he emerged from the lock-up carrying a blue box and replaced the brick in the long, wet grass. Shaking drips from his hand he climbed back into the van. "Thank Christ! I'd forgotten about the spare key."

Dacre stayed silent until he was sure his dad had calmed down. He looked behind his seat to where Alun had stood the blue box. "What's that, Dad?"

"Just some stuff out of the freezer."

"Daddy, why is there a freezer?"

"Because I sometimes store things in it."

"What things?"

"Meat."

"What meat? Are there sausages?"

"You don't need to know."

"Why not?"

"Because it's a bloody secret, that's why!"

After a few minutes, Dacre went on. "Secret meat? I'm going to ask Mum if she wants some secret meat."

"Don't you bloody dare!"

Dacre knew he should be quiet, but he couldn't contain himself. "Dad, is it meat like at the butcher's?" He pictured blood on the butcher's apron and sides of beef hanging behind the counter and could feel sawdust under his feet.

Sighing, Alun stared at the road ahead as he said firmly, "Listen, it's a secret only me and Charlie know, something we do to make a little extra money."

"Mr Younson? The one with the stuffed animals?"

"How did you know that?"

"When you had to drop something off for him one time I saw them, through the window, there was a stuffed stoat on his windowsill, and a deer's head on the wall. Do you know the difference between a stoat and a weasel, Dad?"

"What? Listen. This is a secret. Don't talk to your mum about it, or anyone, right?"

"Is the meat from the animals Mr Younson stuffs? I want to see!"

"Shut up. Don't say anything about this to anyone. Charlie does a bit of poaching. Deer, the odd sheep. But you mustn't tell anyone."

"Alright, Dad." Dacre was silent, excited about Mr Younson and the stuffed animals. Charlie Younson sometimes borrowed the van and Dacre had once seen a big book on the passenger seat. It had a red cover and the gold lettering read 'C.J. Maynard, Manual of Taxidermy'.

He had one more go as they were approaching Auchmoor.

"Dad, is Mr Younson learning to drive a taxi?"

His dad sighed. "What the bloody hell are you on about? Taxi? He's still RAF."

"But why is Mr Younson's meat in your freezer in Perth?"

"Oh, for god's sake! Sometimes I let him store some of his animals in the freezer. He gives me a cut when he sells them to a butcher we know and that's how I pay for your bloody football boots, alright?"

"He cuts you?"

"Oh, Christ! He gives me some of the money he makes. It's a secret. You'd better not tell anyone, OK? And don't tell bloody Dod Lambie either, or he'll expect a cut. He makes enough."

Dacre was silent for the rest of the way home, excited and honoured to be taken into his dad's confidence. That night he dreamt of stuffed animals coming to life.

***

The night before he was to go back to school his dad came home very late. From his bed, Dacre could hear arguing through the wall. The next morning, his mum had red eyes when she brought his school blazer and helped him get his plaster arm in the sleeve. As they walked towards school, Dacre started crying.

"No one is going to laugh at you because you have a plaster on." He clung to her arm for as long as he could, only letting go when he saw some of the boys in his class near the open school gate. It wasn't a bad day, though and he managed at school without crying. He almost enjoyed his school dinner and was quite a novelty with his arm in plaster. Steven had asked, "Can I write my name on your stookie?"

"What?"

"Everyone does it. My big brother had one on his leg and everyone in his class wrote on it. His pal Michael wrote 'pish' on it and they had to scrub it off!" They both sniggered and Dacre felt better. He had quite a list of names on his plaster by the time it was cut off, a few weeks before the summer term ended. His parents seemed to be arguing a bit less, and his dad was back to his usual pattern of being away from home two or three nights each week. Dacre began to hope that they would forgive him for breaking his wrist. He still didn't know how he had done it. And he didn't dare ask.

Chapter 10

1968

School was very different in Primary 6. The order imposed by the new, strict teacher contrasted with Miss Berry's compassionate, mothering approach. Dacre liked Mr Smart straight away. He was a tall man in a suit and a small moustache, and instead of big splayed feet like Miss Berry he had polished brown shoes and marched like a soldier. He told his new class that after the war, he had stayed abroad managing a rubber plantation in Malaya. Best of all, Mr Smart called all the boys by their surnames.

For a few weeks, he enjoyed the new rules and routines. No two pupils could speak at once, and all had to file in and out of class in line. On the first day of term, Mr Smart said, "Boys and girls! Please all find a seat; you can choose to sit where you like, for now."

Miss Berry had arranged the boys and girls in pairs, the alphabet placing Dacre next to Steven. They sat together again, Dacre choosing seats near the front of the classroom near the door. It seemed right, somehow. There was some toing and froing, and a stand-off when two girls tried to sit behind them. Steven farted to make them back down and ushered two boys to replace them.

Mr Smart stood watching the Brownian motion gradually become ordered, like a random game of musical chairs. As the last of them found a seat, the noisy chatter and shuffling of chairs on the wood floor died down. Still, the teacher stood silent, arms folded, observing. The children soon hushed and looked at him guiltily as they realised that a playground rammy had been permitted inside the classroom.

"Thank you, boys and girls. That is the last time you will speak to each other without asking my permission by putting your hand up. When the bell goes you can talk." Miss Berry had tolerated discreet whispering between pairs, except when they were doing tests.

Three hands had gone up. James Robb, a small boy with dirty knees, was first to speak up. "Mr Smart, can I go to the lavvy?"

"Ask properly, Robb."

"Can I go to the toilet?"

"Robb, please say, 'Please may I?' instead of 'Can I?'"

"Mr Smart, please may I go to the toilet?"

"No."

"But I'm needin'!" The subject was closed, though, and the other hands drifted down. Mr Smart's class was very different. By break time, they had each read out loud in turn from copies of a difficult book, *William Tell* by J.H. Fassett. They had also done some arithmetic, copying from the shiny, clean blackboard upon which the teacher wrote neatly in yellow chalk. He carefully cleaned the board with a wood-backed duster which he then replaced in its tray on the corner of his desk. There had been almost complete silence except for the stilted reading, interrupted by Mr Smart's assistance with long or difficult words, and by one more request from James Robb who clearly felt hard done by.

***

On the fourth Monday of P6, the situation changed. When they filed into class, they were all handed a piece of paper. Dacre's had 'C1' written on it.

"Please all proceed to your new designated seats."

There were numerous pleas of 'But, Sir!' and 'But I sit here'. Mr Smart stayed silent and solemnly the class shuffled around each other to find their new places. Dacre was dismayed to find that he was no longer sitting beside Steven, and instead he was at a double desk by the window with Graeme, a tall, clever boy with glasses who was useless at football. He felt uneasy in his new position and looked around for Steven who now sat in the back row next to James Robb.

Mr Smart spoke at last. "I have been observing all of you and I have now decided where you will sit. Some of you are with children you don't usually mix with at playtime, and some of you are with your chums. I have matched you up in pairs I think will be good for you. We all have different strengths, and I want each pair to support each other."

Dacre and Graeme glanced at each other suspiciously.

How can I support him?

As the morning went on, Dacre felt less and less happy. He and Steven had enjoyed sitting together but now he felt lost and alone. Graeme could do long division much more quickly than Dacre could, and wrote his figures down in a different way. At break time, they filed out to the playground and Dacre asked Graeme why he didn't do sums the way they were supposed to be done. "My mum's a teacher and she showed me. Mr Smart said it's okay to do it her way, as long as I get the right answer." More than one right way of doing something was a new concept to Dacre, and it unsettled him a little.

After break time football, they returned to class, dripping rainwater as they took their new seats. Dacre's spirits had lifted when he scored with a header, and he had a muddy tennis ball stain on his forehead. But then the reality sank in of having to sit in his new position for the whole school year. The milk arrived, and Dacre found it unusually hard to swallow. The delicious cream at the top of the bottle made him queasy. Normally, removing the foil bottle top was a simple highlight of Dacre's school day, but today his thumb drove right through and cream spilled over onto his desk. He drank his milk slowly, unable to enjoy it.

When it was his turn for reading practice, Dacre became unusually nervous. He stuttered over the words until Mr Smart interrupted. "What's wrong with you today, Dacre? You're a good reader, one of the best in the class." Dacre blushed, squirmed and felt sicker. "Sit down. You'll do better tomorrow." He wanted to cry.

"Look! Twa coos shagging!" It was Robb, of course, who was always first with new swear words.

"Who said that?" Mr Smart barked. But the damage had been done and many of the class sniggered and looked out of the window. Down below, in the field on the other side of the wall, one of the Friesian bullocks had mounted another. Dacre looked too but quickly turned back to the room, briefly aware of the world spinning, black and white on a vivid green background. A nasty taste rose in his mouth and he vomited milk and cornflakes on the floor between him and Graeme.

The Janny was called to shovel sawdust on Dacre's mess, Robb was belted with three lashes of Mr Smart's tawse, and Dacre was taken to Nurse Battle-Axe. None of the pupils knew the school nurse's real name. A huge woman with a massive chest, she wore a dark blue uniform with metal buttons. Everyone was scared of her, especially the boys: she had counted their testicles. Now she made Dacre lie down for half an hour, and he felt silly, embarrassed and worried about what the boys would be saying.

However, when he returned to the class, it was as if no one had noticed he'd gone. James Robb being belted had restored order, and every pupil was obediently copying out a poem from the blackboard. They were to learn it that night and be prepared to recite it out loud the next day. Homework was something they were getting used to.

After his desk was moved near the window, Sunday nights were worst. He slept little and was often sick in the morning. Two Mondays in a row, his mother kept him off school, sending a note with him the next day explaining to Mr Smart that he had picked up a tummy bug over the weekend. Dacre's crying and stammering continued. Some of the boys stopped talking to him, and a few made fun of him, but most simply ignored him, as if he were an ill dog cast aside by the pack.

***

"Gordon has had a wee chat with me and now he's going to

join his friends." Dacre pushed past his parents and ran to join the group of boys playing football in the playground after school. He could tell from his mum's face they'd been arguing again. Ever since she'd told him about Mr Smart's letter he'd had an empty churning in his tummy, sure that being sick in the class had been very bad and meant his parents would be taken away.

Now Mr Smart had explained the real reason his parents had been summoned. He'd been embarrassed and a bit angry that his teacher had discovered his problem with heights. And he didn't believe him when he'd said lots of other people were the same. It was his problem. His fault. But Mr Smart hadn't seemed angry at all. Perhaps he was going to make everything all right.

"Thank you, Sir," said Alun, when Mr Smart welcomed them into the classroom.

"Mr Smart is fine, thank you. It's the pupils who call me Sir," said the teacher, smiling genially. "I have put chairs here for us to sit." Three full-sized chairs had been arranged in a space beside Mr Smart's desk. They dwarfed the pupils' little wooden seats.

"OK, Sir." Authority had mattered in the RAF.

"Anyway, thank you for coming. Do you know why I invited you here?"

"Not really, Mr Smart, except that Gordon is in trouble. Has he been fighting again?" Elinor was nervous and her voice was louder than she meant it to be. Alun glowered at her.

"He's not in trouble at all. He's very well behaved. I have noticed, though, that he seems to *be* troubled *by* something. I moved the children round recently, put them at new desks, and he has been very unsettled since then. He's not seeming to listen and he's struggling. He's gone backwards a little." Elinor's hand covered her mouth. 'Backwards' was a word no parent wanted to hear. Smart continued, "I've watched him at playtime and he's quite a leader when at play with his chums.

It's in the classroom. I wanted to ask you if he has been all right at home?"

The Dacres looked at each other briefly and Alun turned to the window, keen for his wife to speak instead of him. In the silence, Mr Smart helped out.

"The day he was sick, I take it he was fine that night? No more vomiting, I mean?"

"Sick? When?" Alun looked at Elinor. "You didn't tell me."

"I didn't know he had been sick. In the playground?" Dacre had been scared to tell his parents.

"No, he threw up all of a sudden in the classroom. He seemed to have suddenly been upset and I think it's since he moved near the window." Mr Smart wiped his glasses on the end of his tie, and Alun spoke up.

"We thought he'd been in trouble. He's been okay at home."

"How would you know? You're always away." Elinor blushed, turned to Mr Smart, and said, "I'm sorry, Mr Smart. I just find it hard sometimes."

Alun went pale. "That's none of his business!" Suddenly ashamed, it was Alun's turn to blush. "Sorry, Sir, I just mean that's for us to worry about, not you."

All three were silent for a moment. Mr Smart cleaned his immaculate glasses yet again, and the Dacres looked away from each other until Elinor spoke rapidly. "Gordon has been having trouble going to sleep at night. It's as if he doesn't like his room anymore. Last winter he was getting all grown up and going to bed himself. He likes to play with his Airfix models before bed. Now he has brought them all down to the living room, and I'm forever having to tidy them away."

Mr Smart looked sympathetically at Elinor who was near to tears, but Alun broke in, "I thought he was sleeping well; his curtains are always shut when I go to work in the morning. He used to be up waving out at me."

Mr Smart interjected. "Do you mind if I ask, does Gordon sleep upstairs?"

"He does, and he's staying there. Sorry, Sir, but he's at it. He wants the box room downstairs. He's always on about it. But I keep my tools in it."

Elinor ignored her husband. "He makes me close the curtains before he goes in his room, even when it isn't dark yet."

"He's at it, I tell you! He's got you round his little finger. You pampered him too much after it happened. Afraid he'd blame you, were you?"

Sensitive to the Dacres' discomfort, Mr Smart spoke quietly with authority. "Might I be able to venture a suggestion? Is it possible that Gordon has become upset by heights?" He pointed behind the Dacres. "As you can see, the windows in the school are quite large, and he does seem troubled by sitting on that side of the room. I think I may move him back across to see if he settles."

"Maybe that's why he has to have the curtains pulled. Perhaps we *should* move his bed down to the box room." Elinor wiped at her eyes and sniffed. "Hay fever, sorry."

"But my tools!" said Alun, before quickly blushing and looking away. After a pause, "I suppose they could squeeze into the back of my van."

There was a little less tension in the weeks that followed. The tools were moved out to the shed. "The garden will have to wait if I have to decorate the box room. And I can't get the mower out without moving my tools now, anyway."

"I know, Alun, but it'll soon be winter. And you said yourself some of your tools don't fit the new machines, and there are better ones at work."

The box room was surprisingly big, even with Dacre's single divan in it. Dacre's model Spitfire and the Lancaster were carefully hung on a wire above his bed, with room for more models after Christmas.

Chapter 11

November 1968

In late November, Elinor's sister Janet and her family came to the Dacres' for Sunday afternoon. Dacre knew he would be forced to play with Campbell. It was always cold, but the house was too small and the boys were asked to have fun outside. Campbell was much more confident than Dacre, like Janet. Uncle Douglas had come too, and Dacre remembered his dad saying Douglas would rather be on his fancy golf course and that he only came so Janet could show off her posh lawyer husband and his fancy cars. It was always Uncle Douglas who said it was time to leave, he had something called 'cases to read'. Dacre wasn't sure why he wondered if his mum liked Aunty Janet. She was always busy and moaning in the days leading up to the visit, but when Janet and Douglas arrived she gave them fairy cakes and spoke in a funny voice.

Dacre and his cousin hardly knew each other. Campbell was only seventeen weeks younger than he was, but didn't play the same games or even say the same things. His mum had told him it was because he had an older sister.

"My god, they've got another car! They only had the Cortina for three years." Alun turned away as the Bishops drew up outside the house in their burgundy Austin 1800.

"Jan! How lovely to see you. And Campbell, aren't you tall?" The sisters went through the front door followed by the two boys. Campbell had a yo-yo. The men joined the others in the cramped living room, where Jan's shortbread offering was already open. After the boys had been given a piece each, Elinor took the packet to the kitchen, and switched the kettle on, placing it on the checked Formica worktop.

Janet called loudly, "Oh, Ellie, you've decorated the lounge! How lovely! Is that magnolia? We've had the drawing room done again this year. Good wallpaper's so expensive now, isn't it?"

"What's a drawing room?" asked Dacre.

"I'm sorry Alison couldn't come; she's at the gymkhana," Janet announced. "Douglas says he might buy her a pony if she is still as keen next year."

The kettle began hissing, and Elinor called through from the kitchen, interrupting her sister's flow and distracting from Alun's scowling. "Gordon, why don't you show Campbell your Spitfire? He's getting good at camouflage paint, Campbell." In Dacre's room, Campbell squeezed along beside the bed and looked up at the wire across the ceiling with the two models waving gently in the draught from the window.

"Your bedroom's minuscule."

"What?"

"It's tiny. Weren't you in a bigger room upstairs? Mummy, come and see Gordon's teeny-tiny bedroom!"

"Why don't you boys go and play outside?" Elinor suggested as she passed back to the living room with a tray. Alun was looking out of the window at the Austin and Douglas was reading the *Sunday Post*.

"I haven't seen this rag in years! Same old drivel," he said.

In the kitchen where she was pouring tea, Elinor was joined by Janet, who pulled the door closed behind them, and whispered, "You're not pregnant, are you? Decorating and moving Gordon down to a smaller room." She smiled conspiratorially.

"Good Lord, no! Perish the thought! Gordon has been a bit unsettled since he broke his wrist, and his teacher thinks he has a problem with heights. It's a bit of a worry. I think he's lost a lot of ground at school, although Mr Smart is very kind."

"My friend Catriona's daughter had to see a psychologist about strange behaviour, and she wouldn't eat."

"Jan, he's not strange."

"It's nothing to do with that awful Bugsy, is it? He's a bad influence; I've always said that. Common and crude. I know he's good looking, but … you know." Janet had met Bugsy once at New Year and had not been impressed.

Elinor supported her right arm on the corner shelf as she poured the tea, and said, "Don't be silly, he was harmless, just fun; he used to cheer me up, that's all." She put the pot down and rubbed her arm through her cardigan.

"He seemed to spend a lot of time here, though. What's happened to your arm?"

"Oh … nothing … I had to scrape ice away from the path the other day. Alun's away so much, you know, and I don't want Gordon hurting himself again."

"Did we mention we're thinking of sending Campbell to George Watsons? The fees are definitely worth it, such a good education. Douglas will be a partner by next year and we'll move into the town a bit. Probably Colinton."

When the Bishops were gone and the dishes washed, Elinor closed the living room door, having made sure Dacre was in his room. "Thank god they've gone for another year," said Alun, and then sneered, "Still, you know, it's nearly Christmas isn't it, a time for goodwill."

Ignoring his facetious manner, Elinor said quietly, "Gordon's moping in his room again. I wonder if we should ask the doctor if he can be seen by a psychologist."

Alun looked up from the *Post* and sneered. "You don't even know what a psychologist is. You're just saying that because your posh sister suggested it."

"Were you listening at the door?"

"What?"

"How do you know Jan said that?"

"I guessed she'd said it to you when she suggested it to me. Interfering posh bitch! She seems to have decided our son 'has a problem'." Alun parodied his sister-in-law in a whiny voice.

"Mr Smart thinks he has a problem, Alun, and he's a clever man. And Gordon won't even go upstairs now. I know they've stopped making them sit the 11-plus exam now but he's at an important stage."

Alun went back to his paper and the football reports. The *Sunday Post* was the only paper he ever read. East Fife had lost again at home. Not halfway through the season and they were already near the foot of the Division Two table. Turning the page, he focused on the horses.

***

Campbell was lying along the back seat of the Austin. As the car pulled away from the toll booth on the Forth Road Bridge, he roused to his parents' chatter. "I'm telling you, I think something is going on. And Gordon used to call him Uncle Bugsy!"

His dad said, "I've cases to read, remember, I'd rather not consider anything like that. I don't want to know."

No more was said by the time they arrived back in Currie.

Chapter 12

He waited in the office, swinging his legs under the hard chair, the silence broken only by the secretary's clacking typewriter. When his mum came, shaking the February sleet from her overcoat, her scarf was pulled up high round her neck, as usual. They set off and Dacre's teeth chattered as he held his mother's chilled hand. His legs were chapped, and on the way up to the clinic the sleet stung the redness between his grey shorts and his soggy sock tops. When Mr Smart had announced to the class that he was to go to the school office to await his mother, Dacre had felt a fierce heat in his face, and thought he was going to be sick.

"Mummy's come for him!" Inevitably it was James Robb mocking him.

"Robb! Quiet!" Mr Smart hushed the class and ushered Dacre out.

When his mum told him she had spoken to Dr Mackie and that he would be seeing a specialist, Dacre had protested. By the time Christmas had passed, he had decided it had just been a threat to make him behave. Mr Smart had moved the class around again and hadn't told everyone why. Dacre learned to hold his breath on stairs, counting the steps to himself. He told Steven this was a game he had invented. Steven tried it once, found it boring, and didn't ask again.

Then the appointment letter arrived. "But I don't need to be put on a Special List!" His school had a class of children who were kept separate from the rest. Dacre was scared of them but knew it was wrong when boys called them names. They were officially known as The Specials.

The day of the appointment came some weeks into the spring term, when the clinical psychologist held his monthly clinic in the cottage hospital. Ten minutes of the appointment passed before Dr Sutton said a word. While his mum shuffled silently on her hard chair, Dacre stood looking at the skeleton poster on the wall. Faded by the light from the window behind him, the bones were dusty yellow on a cream background, each one outlined by a black line. Tiny writing along the length of the longer bones gave their names. A fine dotted line joined small bones to a name printed to one side. He couldn't believe there were so many bones.

Eventually, the silence was broken. "Are you interested in anatomy, Gordon?" Dr Sutton pushed his gold-rimmed glasses up onto the bridge of his nose and looked at his papers. His long hair straggled over the collar of a worn green corduroy jacket with pale brown elbow patches.

"What?"

"Gordon! Don't be rude! Answer the doctor." His mother apologised. "He's shy, Dr Sutton."

"Anatomy, Gordon, is the study of the structures of the body. Doctors have to learn human anatomy very carefully to know how to find out what is wrong with people."

"Listen to the doctor, Gordon. You could be a doctor one day."

"Gordon, can you tell me what your first word was?" Dr Sutton was looking expectantly over his glasses. Dacre turned away to the poster again.

Elinor Dacre moved in her chair and cleared her dry throat. "Umm ... he—"

"It's OK, Mrs Dacre, it's a question I always pose first to the child. Sometimes they know and sometimes they don't, and I find it tells me something about the interactions between parents and child."

Elinor's speech was juddery as she rushed out her words. "But we don't talk about ... I mean ... we've never ... it's not his fault ... he doesn't know ..." Sutton quietly watched and listened until she paused, managing to regain some composure. "It was Dodod."

"Dada?"

"We thought it was Dada or Dad, and he just had got it

wrong. Then later Alun's, I mean my husband Alun's boss visited with some worksheets one time a few months later and Gordon called him Dodod. His name was Dod. It's just that … sorry …" Dacre was staring at her, with a puzzled look. He had never before heard about his first words.

"It's OK, Mrs Dacre. And that sort of thing happens very commonly, especially when there has been a regular visitor to the home and—"

"Oh! No, he was just here every day for a while when Alun's van was off the road, around the time Gordon was babbling. Just a funny … a sort of … coincidence."

"Gordon, would you go to the shelf behind you and bring me something you like. A toy, or a book, or one of the models."

Dacre stared steadfastly at the poster, not moving. "Gordon, do what the man says!" Elinor was blushing and crossed her legs, the chair creaking. Dacre blushed but didn't move. Dr Sutton stood and reached out, inviting Dacre to take his hand.

"Gordon, go with Dr Sutton."

He tried, but he couldn't approach the window side of the room. They were on the third floor in a dormered attic that had been converted to accommodate visiting specialists. The window overlooked the town down the hill. Dacre felt sick.

"I … I … don't want any of the things," he stammered.

"It's OK, Gordon," Dr Sutton said. "Come to the door with me instead." Dacre meekly followed him, glad to face away from the window. Dr Sutton opened the door and ushered Dacre out onto the landing. He had no choice but to stand near the top of the steep stairs. He was confused, now, but pleased to be away from the window, and by staring upwards, he managed to control the spinning.

"Come back into the office and sit back down where you like, please, Gordon."

Dacre returned to examining the poster. He liked the bones of the hand best.

After the appointment, Dacre waited with the nurse while

his mum stayed talking to Dr Sutton. It seemed like hours he had to wait with the silly toys and the nurse before Elinor eventually emerged red-faced and holding a handkerchief.

"Oh, it's hot in there!" she said when the receptionist waved at her. She sat down beside her son, facing away from the reception desk.

"That nurse gave me baby toys to play with!" His mum shushed him, and there was more waiting until the receptionist called out to his mum that a note was ready to take back to Dr Mackie. Dacre ran to the desk, followed by Elinor, trying to smile.

"Bye, Dr Sutton, see you next month." The receptionist smiled and turned back to Elinor as Dr Sutton lumbered across the reception area towards the exit. "He's wonderful, isn't he?" she said.

"Err ... yes, very good." Elinor became calmer after another endorsement of the specialist. She had known Sadie the receptionist at school.

"I've hardly seen you in years, Ellie! I wondered if you'd moved away."

Elinor squirmed, always shy. "I don't go out much, busy with Gordon, and Alun's away working so much." The excuses were easy, rehearsed. Dacre watched his mum hesitate before she turned and made to go.

"I still meet up for a cup of tea with some of the girls sometimes, in the afternoon, before school chucks out. You should come. It's a laugh."

"Sorry, I've got to rush, Alun's tea."

Elinor clutched the envelope Sadie had handed her as she hurried through the heavy swing door and out towards the small car park. Dacre sauntered along behind her. Heading for the bus stop, they were just in time to see Dr Sutton trundling out in his Morris Traveller, a huge, black, hairy dog almost filling the back. As the car turned out to go down the hill towards the main road, the wheels gripped well despite the wet slush. Dacre knew his dad had always dreamt of having a Traveller. 'Most reliable car there is. Practical and stylish. Because it's good old British-made.' Dacre wanted a Triumph Herald because his toy Corgi model was pale blue. He didn't dare mention Ford or Vauxhall, which his dad said were flashy, American and not made to last.

On the way to catch the bus, he told his mother about the carpals, metacarpals and phalanges. As the bus pulled away, Elinor relaxed and loosened her scarf a little to let herself speak. "Didn't you like Dr Sutton? He was nice wasn't he?" Elinor was in awe of doctors.

"I didn't want to play with toys in there. And he smelled of jobby and had spots on his chin."

"Gordon! Dr Sutton was clever, and Dr Mackie said he's very good. He just wanted to see you play; it's part of what he does. And I'm sure the smell was just something on his shoe."

Dr Mackie's detailed referral letter, and his private talk with Elinor, helped Sutton reach his formulation. He reported that Dacre had developed a fear of heights, but suffered most when he looked down and through a window. It was a reaction to the trauma of his fall, the broken wrist and his parents' arguments. "We call his fear of heights 'acrophobia'," he had explained to Elinor. "Your son now associates heights with falls, pain and his parents fighting. The fear of heights ... the acrophobia ... it always annoys me when people make the mistake of calling it '*vertigo*' for goodness sake ... anyway, sorry, I digress." He was cleaning his glasses. "It is a reaction to the trauma, though he barely, if at all, remembers the incident. Perhaps it is just as well he is too young to process what happened, but subconsciously he fears the family will break up, although he's not capable of expressing such a thing or even imagining it happening."

Elinor had been unable to take in much of what Dr Sutton was saying. She had been horrified at herself for talking about private things with the doctor. Somehow Sutton had led her to discuss what she would never talk of, even with Janet. She had quickly found herself talking about the rows with Alun, and she'd cried at the kindness and concern Dr Sutton had shown her.

The consultant made it clear in his letter to Dr Mackie that he thought the family had taken absolutely the best possible action in moving Dacre's bedroom downstairs. Elinor was pleased to be proved right by such authority. The suggested remedy was for the school to continue to accommodate Dacre's problem by allowing him to sit away from any windows. Sutton also suggested moving P6 to the ground floor, but the Headmaster decided this would be too disruptive.

Mr Smart was pleased by the improvement in Dacre, and his classmates got used to him. His problem was rarely mentioned, except by James Robb.

***

Autumn 1969

He was bobbling up and down gently, floating along on a warm stream banked by waving palm trees. Uncle Bugsy's laughing face suddenly loomed huge against the bright white sky. He fell into Bugsy's gaping mouth, then over the back of his tongue into a steep helter-skelter, whirling down and round and down towards a blackness racing up at him. Impact. He plunged painlessly into nothing and gulped huge, sweet lungfuls of candy-floss air before floating back up, safe again on the lazy current.

Such dreams dominated Dacre's sleep as his eleventh birthday approached and the trees began to drop leaves. He remembered little, but woke unsettled and thinking of Uncle Bugsy.

***

"Is Bugs coming for my birthday this year? He didn't come last year." Bugsy Redbond, his Uncle Darren, had always been there in Dacre's early childhood. His dad's friend from the RAF rather than a true uncle, he featured in Dacre's earliest memories. Now nearly eleven, he was embarrassed to admit to himself that there had been a time he had thought his family was Mum, Bugsy and himself, and Alun was the visitor. With Alun Dacre away through work so much, Bugs had often played with him and taken him out in his pushchair. To Dacre, he had been an adventurer, an explorer, a scientist, a footballer. He had idolised him as a hero until quite suddenly when Dacre was in Primary 5 Bugsy had seemed to fade out of existence.

Now in Primary 7, he hadn't seen or heard of Bugs for two years. Although at birthdays and Christmas he still half hoped his uncle might appear with a present for him, Dacre had developed some mixed feelings.

The thought of his erstwhile 'uncle' could make him a little uneasy, even queasy. He didn't know why.

"No, he will not be coming," said his dad. Elinor came into the living room and picked up Alun's teacup from the floor.

"Christmas?" asked Dacre, looking from one parent to the other. Bugs always used to give Dacre great presents ... a blue football one year.

"I don't think he'll be able to," said Elinor, hurrying out to get on with her cleaning.

"Ohhh ... but why not? He always used to come. Why does he never come now?"

"He's got a real job now. And he lives in Kirkcaldy, anyway," his father barked.

"We go to Kirkcaldy sometimes. Can we visit him?" There was no answer. Bugsy had had lots of jobs since he and Alun had left the RAF together. He had worked in Woolworths in the storeroom and used to bring pick 'n' mix sweets. At one time he drove a van like Dacre's dad, but Bugsy's truck was open at the back and had big tools and buckets in it. Bugs wore dungarees, not boring overalls like his dad.

Dacre thought back to the last time he had seen Bugs in the flesh. It had been the first Christmas after his broken wrist. He had saved Bugsy a piece of his plaster cast and had been looking forward to presenting him with it. It had been a quick visit, though, and his 'uncle' hadn't even come in. Dacre had seen his mum answer the door, but before he could come in from the garden where he had been cleaning his bike, Bugsy was already heading towards his Ford Anglia, his mum holding a bag. He could remember his excitement but now felt childish for having wanted a hug from Uncle Bugs.

But when Christmas had come there was no present. As P7 progressed, and as the move up to Big School approached, Dacre forgot Bugsy.

***

Any anxiety about the move to secondary was soothed by the excitement, for the boys at least, of the World Cup. Pocket money went on Anglo bubblegum, hastily chewed and discarded while the prized cards were saved and exchanged. Dacre learned to spell Czechoslovakia: that card took pride of place in his collection. Esso promotional coins were rarer, and despite Dacre's pleas his dad only brought home three. Steven had shown Dacre his coin album.

"My dad always gets Esso. I only need four more to have a full set."

It was Sunday evening. Dacre had been allowed to stay late at Steven's to watch the football. West Germany knocked England out in the quarter-final, and after the match they had gone up to Steven's bedroom to try to decide which team to follow now. Tommy McIntyre had started saying only traitors support England, and Dacre was secretly pleased for the Germans. Steven was distraught though and suddenly threw his Esso coin album on the floor. He stood up and stomped round his bedroom, declaring, "I wish it was me had my hand chopped off instead of that stupid girl in the harbour!"

"What?"

“England should have easily beat the jerries! It’s not fair! German cheats!”

Dacre thought his friend was going loony.

“What did you say about your hand?”

Steven threw himself face down on his bed, scattering football cards and crushing his prized Shoot magazines.

“My big brother’s pal’s brother joined the police and said they found a dead girl in a harbour with her right hand cut off. There were bones sticking out. It’s all a big secret. Not in the papers. Michael’s pal’s brother’s like a spy!”

10th June 1970

In fading twilight, he saw steam rise in the still summer air. Hot urine was wetting his thighs. His head swimming, he clung to a bollard fearing he would follow her over the side. The loud splash had shocked him. He had dreamt of slipping her gracefully underwater, but the tide was low. Now instead of her blood, he could only smell diesel. *She deserved better*, he thought, as he started to walk away.

A man was following him, with a dog. Thumping panic competed with his arousal. Suddenly uncertain, he walked on when he reached his car. The barking was louder now, closer. Turning a corner, away from the harbour, a grim castle loomed ahead, until its familiarity dawned on him. He followed the high fence grinning at his good luck: in all his excited planning he'd forgotten the lock-up was nearby. He ducked into the clearing in front of a row of garages and slid in to hide between two of them. The man was shouting as the yelping dog was dragged away. Fear had added spice to the thrill and he stroked the weight in his pocket.

Safe in the lock-up his eyes grew accustomed to dim light penetrating the dirty skylight. He smiled and shook his head as he realised how lucky he had been: *that dog could smell her!* His breathing was gradually slowing, and his mouth felt as if it was lined with carpet backing.

He crept to the back of the lock-up and opened the fridge. Out-of-date milk and a half-empty bottle of Irn Bru. There was barely a hiss as he unscrewed the top before guzzling the sweetness.

Opening the freezer compartment under the small fridge he drew his sticky prize from inside his jacket. It felt surprisingly heavy and he could feel its perfect little fingers through the wet linen wrapping. *Safer to leave it here. And I didn't even think of the lock-up!*

Chapter 13

17th June 1970

Dacre wished his mum hadn't had to go to another appointment. It meant he had to spend another day of the summer holidays in his dad's work van. His dad had hardly spoken, but now he'd stopped suddenly and Dacre looked up.

"We've been along here before, Dad. That's the prison."

Alun ignored him and was muttering. "Still a lot of police around." They turned left into a road lined by high fences and Alun stopped the van opposite a clearing. There was a blue police transit van parked at the end of the road, and several uniformed police near the river's edge. One of them left his colleagues and approached the open window of Alun's van.

"Sorry to bother you, Sir. Can I ask what you are doing here?"

"I just stop here sometimes to write up my job sheets." Alun indicated the sheaf of grubby papers held in a bulldog clip on the bench seat between them.

"Did you happen to park here last Wednesday, Sir? See anything going on?"

"No, I haven't been here for weeks. Only occasional trips this way, you see."

"OK, Sir. Sorry to have bothered you."

As the policeman walked away, Alun muttered, "Too risky."

"What, Dad?"

"You wait here. I'll need to find a phone box. Give me that notebook from the floor, I need Charlie's number."

The van door slammed and Dacre watched his father walk back towards the main road. He'd been in a bad mood when Dacre had arrived home from school and was made to go with him in the van. It was the second time Elinor had gone to meet Sadie and some old school friends. "You're old enough to look after your bloody self!" his dad had said. "I've got to go to bloody Perth. Get in!" Dacre decided not to bother asking if he could stay up late that night to watch the World Cup semi-final.

His dad had said he had to stock his van up from the lock-up, and Dacre now looked across the road into the clearing where the row of garages stood. He remembered his dad bringing him here when he was little, seeing the prison in the background and his excitement about the animal parts in the freezer. His curiosity pricked at him until he got out of the van and walked over the rough ground to the lock-ups. There used to be a hidden key, he thought, and kicked through the long grass and weeds between two of the lock-ups until he felt something wobble under his foot. Under an old brick was a brass key.

***

As Alun started the van and pulled away, he spoke quickly, grinning. "Bloody stupid police! They nearly got me! Christ! That was lucky. Charlie says fine to leave it in the freezer. He'll pick it up next week." Dacre realised his dad was talking to himself. "I'm going back the long way. There are police everywhere round here, I'll go back towards town instead, and back round by Dundee."

Dacre had managed to put the key back and return to the van before Alun had come back. His mouth was still dry and he was staring at the grimy dashboard. His dad reached across and punched him playfully on the arm. "What's wrong with you? You look like you've seen a ghost."

Dacre swallowed. "I felt a bit dizzy when you were away at the phone."

Alun ignored him and started humming 'Take Five'. To leave Perth they crossed a bridge over the Tay in heavy traffic. Dacre looked to his left from the van window and saw over the parapet the wide, black river down below. He had to look away quickly. An hour later they pulled up the slipway onto the Tay Bridge and Dacre felt his stomach churn. The bridge wasn't as high as the Forth bridges, but Dacre knew it was a mile and a half long. He felt he had to shut his eyes tightly as they pulled away from the toll booth and out above the river, but visions of the lock-up and the freezer filled his mind. Nausea rose, and his breathing quickened. He had to open his eyes, and the rolling waves of the Tay down below him made his eyes rock and the world start spinning around him. He heard nothing after his father shouted, "What the hell? Not that again! You stupid …"

His mum was helping him out of the van when Dacre came to. "Oh, you poor thing. Was it the height on the bridge?"

"Little bugger heaved all over my van! Passed out. I thought the great baby had got over all that!"

Elinor supported him into the house and lay him down while his father went on cursing. Dacre dreamt that night about Steven and the girl with her hand cut off.

Chapter 14

1972

Dacre found the move up to secondary school easier than expected. He knew to avoid heights when he could and a discreet report from Mr Smart meant his teachers knew to place him away from windows. By the end of second year, even upstairs classrooms were OK if he held his breath on the stairs.

In the summer holidays between S2 and S3, he spent most of his time on the golf course with Steven Baker. One morning on the first tee as the sun melted the mist and the dew glistened, Dacre was surprised when Steven turned up with Tommy McIntyre. They were whispering and stifling giggles, and Dacre immediately felt left out. He didn't really like Tommy, but recently Steven had been with him quite a lot, and they'd disappeared early after golf the day before. "Where did you two go yesterday?"

More giggling and Tommy said, cruelly, "You wouldn't like it, you poofter."

Steven couldn't resist telling him, though. "Down at the rushes." 'The rushes' was an area of uncontrolled reeds and long grass near the river, on the other side of the common. Older boys met there, and sometimes even girls.

"We go there all the time," explained Tommy casually. Dacre knew Steven had never been there.

"Come this afternoon," said Steven. "The rope swing's magic."

"He won't be getting one of my fags." Tommy strode to the tee. Dacre played badly, worried about cigarettes and cancer, and even more about the rope swing. His golf was no better in the afternoon, and he followed Tommy and Steven sulkily as they hurried to get to the rushes. Making their way across the common, the path through long grass led along beside the railway embankment. In a marshy area shaded by tall trees, feathery-topped reeds waved in the wind, and a muddy trail led to a clearing that had been trampled flat. Two older boys were lying in the shade, puffing on cigarettes.

"Yes, children?" the smarter-looking one with the long hair said.

"Fuck off," said his smoking buddy.

"Hi," said Tommy, hopefully.

"Fuck off!"

"I've got cigarettes."

"How many?"

"Five Park Drive. Have you got a light?" Tommy looked embarrassed.

"Give us one each and you can stay."

Long Hair said, "What have you other two got for us?" He grinned expectantly at the two boys standing behind Tommy.

"The fags are Tommy's and mine," said Steven, moving forward to stand at Tommy's side.

Steven you rotten shite!

"And you, young fellow? What delights do you bring to the party?"

Dacre felt four pairs of eyes boring into him, and was very much the outsider. He now remembered Long Hair's name was Robert, and that he fancied himself. Steven turned away from Dacre's silent, pleading gaze, looking sheepish and guilty. He couldn't bear to look at sniggering Tommy.

The grubby-looking older boy took one of Tommy's Park Drive and said, "The wee shite can only stay if he gets the rope swing down." He pointed to tall trees thirty yards away. A thick rope hung down through the leaves, but someone had thrown the lower end of it up into the tree and it had wound itself around a branch. The resulting loop hung about fifteen feet from the trodden, dry earth below. The two older boys now grinned and walked towards Dacre, making him move closer to the tree.

“Get up the tree and get the rope back and we’ll let you stay,” said Long Hair.

“If you don’t, you can piss off, you wee wanker,” said the other.

Dacre had little choice but to walk in front of them towards the tree. He glanced behind, where Steven was glum and sheepish, and Tommy smoking and grinning. Forced up to the wide trunk he tried another pleading look back but his two captors had him penned in. “Get the fuckin’ rope!”

Steven had turned away, and Dacre knew he had to make his futile attempt. With moist hands, sweat on his brow and sick in his gullet, he made himself face the tree trunk and tried to scramble up. Even three feet off the ground was too far. His head spun, his heart pounded and he knew it was hopeless. Shafts of sunlight pierced the thick leafy canopy and shone on him like a spotlight. Turning, he shrieked, “I can’t!” He slithered down the rough trunk, knuckles grazed and jeans green with algae, and pushed past the two laughing boys. He couldn’t bear to look at Steven as he ran through the reeds, tears welling.

The next couple of weeks were miserable. He couldn’t bear to go to golf. Steven kept his distance, and he knew Tommy would be revelling in telling everyone about his humiliation. He moped around the house, dreading the new school term. The news of his cowardice would have spread.

Steven knocked at the door in the week before school restarted.

“Oh, hello, Steven, we haven’t seen you for a while. Have you been on holiday?”

“Hello, Mrs Dacre, umm … no, I’ve just been doing other stuff.”

“I wish you’d take Gordon to do it with you; he’s never out from under my feet. Gordon, Steven’s here for you,” she called over her shoulder. “Gordon! Where are you?”

Dacre appeared at the kitchen door, and Elinor ushered

Steven in. “Show Steven your Airfix models.”

I hate bloody Airfix; she thinks I’m still a kid! It was Dad that liked them, anyway.

The two went silently to Dacre’s room and soon patched it up.

***

“For god’s sake! I thought the little baby had got over all that! Bloody interfering teachers! Think they know our kid better than we do!” Elinor knew better than to argue with Alun. Dacre’s acrophobia worsened after the rope swing incident, and two of Dacre’s subject teachers had noticed him struggling. The Deputy Head checked Mr Smart’s primary school report on Dacre and a review by Dr Sutton was requested. When Elinor showed Dacre the letter from Dr Sutton, he grumbled a half-hearted protest but felt a stirring of hopeful relief.

His mother went with him to the appointment but Dr Sutton made her wait outside. It was a ground floor room this time, and Dacre was alone with Dr Sutton throughout, except when a nurse excused herself to take something from a cupboard. “Whatever happens, Gordon, don’t worry that anything is your fault.” Dacre now he began to feel guilty. He had been trying to blame Tommy McIntyre, and sometimes even Steven, for the recurrence of his problems. Dr Sutton’s words unsettled him, and he began to feel the old sensations returning: the beating in his chest and the spinning.

“I hope you had a nice birthday last week, Gordon. Do you remember seeing me before, Gordon, back when you were in primary school? You were just eight then. You came here with your mum and we talked about your problem with windows. That’s why we’re in the nurse’s room downstairs this time.”

Of course I fucking remember!

Dacre’s main recollections were of bones, a Morris Traveller and the smell.

“Have you been having more trouble with heights again?”

Dacre looked at the floor.

Stupid tosser, why does he think I'm here?

He was surprised at how angry he felt all of a sudden, but couldn't speak. Images flashed before him of Uncle Bugsy, his dad, Dr Mackie with white powder in his hair and his mum with her paisley pattern scarf pulled up high.

"Is your wrist still sore, Gordon?" He looked up and realised he had been rubbing his wrist.

"Er ... no, it's fine," he managed to mumble.

"Has your mum or dad told you why Mr Cochrane suggested I see you again?" Dacre didn't respond, and Sutton continued. "Your school attendance has not been good this term. Have you been worrying?"

"I was sick and had headaches."

"Have you any hobbies, Gordon?"

What?

"I remember you like model aeroplanes. Do you and your friends all like those?"

Bloody Airfix! I'm fourteen!

"My hobby is my smallholding." Sutton looked out of the window and pointed. "My car is always a mess, what with the goats and chickens, but it's tremendous fun to have a hobby, Gordon." Dacre looked out and just outside the window was the same old Morris Traveller. He could see the top of a bale of hay behind the front seats. "My kids are in the back. If you stand up, you'll be able to see them."

He keeps his children in there!

"Goats are wonderfully satisfying to keep. Their milk is so good for us and they help fertilise the crops. You should taste my radishes!" Dr Sutton was standing beside Dacre now, and if he stood on tiptoe, Dacre could see the top of three small heads with waggling ears. He could also smell Dr Sutton.

That smell! It must be goat shit!

Relieved now that Dr Sutton was just a weirdo and not a total nutcase, Dacre relaxed a little. He managed to relate a little of the story of the rushes and the rope swing, and the consultant soon decided that the recurrence of Dacre's old problems had been brought on by the humiliation of being bullied into exposing his acrophobia. Sutton told Dacre he didn't need to speak with his mother, and he would be advising the school once more about ensuring Dacre could avoid upstairs classes.

When Elinor told Alun of the outcome, he appeared pleased. "I told you it was just the baby in him, nothing wrong with him; he just needs a telling. Bloody cheek them interfering. I told you."

The school took note of Dr Sutton's advice and he was allowed to change his subjects a little. He no longer had to endure Religious Education on the third floor, and instead was allowed an extra period of PE with Mr Dunlop, which suited him well even though he had to join with an S2 class.

PE had sometimes triggered anxiety in Dacre, but Mr Dunlop was sensitive to his problem and always seemed to manage to excuse him from rope climbing. He was always put in one of the other groups, circuit training or cross country, and when the groups rotated no one noticed it was never Dacre's turn to climb.

He liked Roy Dunlop, or Randy Roy as he was known. Athletic, fashionably dressed and humorous, he was a role model to most of the boys, and a focus of adolescent desire to girls. A year later, when Dunlop left the school suddenly over a Christmas break, there was considerable heartache. The rumour mill spun with wild ideas for a few days until the next piece of gossip took over. By that time it had become accepted wisdom that Dunlop had run off with George Best's wife.

Dacre was allowed to drop Music altogether, replacing it with Biology, which meant he was in two different classes but had the same Biology teacher. His problems receded to a tolerable level, and to reach his few first- and second-floor classrooms, he perfected joining a huddle, unnoticed.

The Press and Journal

18th April 1974

TRAGIC INGA FOUND DEAD NEAR GRAVEYARD

Police refuse to reveal horrific details

The body of Inga Sabiston, 14, was discovered yesterday, bringing to a tragic end the hopes of her anguished parents. Inga was last seen on Thursday 4th April when she left her school bus a short distance from her home in Crimond. After extensive searches hopes of finding her were already fading when Inga's remains were found.

Farm grieve Peter Maitland thought he had come across a dead animal. Unconfirmed reports suggest one or more of Inga's limbs may be missing, but police sources have refused to reveal the gruesome details.

Police are understood to be interviewing construction workers at the planned power station at Boddam, near Peterhead. A Scottish North Eastern Counties Constabulary spokesman refused to comment further but temporary workers living at the Boddam site are known to attend stock car racing at Crimond Racetrack.

Inga's mother Janine Sabiston, 38, is said to be under sedation.

Chapter 15

1975

"You boy! Down! Prefects! Take control!" Mr Blair glared around the room and Dacre and Spake shrank back, but as the only prefects present, they knew they would have to intervene. They climbed the wooden steps at the right side of the stage and stood looking up at Billy Robb, who jeered down at them as his mates cheered him on.

It was one rainy Friday while discussing the genius of Peter Gabriel's lyrics, high on air thick with wet serge blazers, sweat and tomato sauce crisps, that Dacre's acrophobia caused more trouble. By Fifth Year, music had become important to Dacre and Spake. Their hair was getting longer, and they wore flared jeans. Spake's tastes were influenced by his big sister Denise who was at university in Edinburgh, and sophisticated. Dacre studied *Sounds* and *Melody Maker* and read album sleeve notes in Woolworths. Parents had given up playing Mantovani, Humperdinck, or Sinatra, as record players were moved into teenage bedrooms. A loosely formed club of like-minded older pupils had been allowed to play LPs in the assembly hall some lunchtimes.

A gang of third and fourth years had become fed up being forced to listen to Genesis, and had taken their protests to the stage shouting 'put Slade on, ya wankers'. Billy Robb, a wily, wiry version of his big brother James, had the reputation of a hardman and had climbed up the left-hand stage curtain. He was hanging from the lighting gantry, spitting on anyone who passed below, when Mr Blair, Head of English, happened to pass the entrance to the hall and stopped. The prefects knew Big Kenny had to be obeyed.

"What the fuck do we do?" muttered Spake, before heading straight for the ladders to the stage lights. "We could each go up one side and walk across the gantry." Before Dacre could move, Spake was halfway up shouting, "Aye, Robb, I'm coming for you, you wee shite!"

Robb was now swinging enthusiastically from the lighting rail, pausing only to aim his spittle at sheepish Dacre below. Sweating and palpitating, Dacre walked reluctantly to the left-hand ladder and managed to climb three rungs before freezing, his limbs cramped and his lips tingling.

"Go on, boy!" roared Big Kenny.

Robb hollered "Gerrrronimoooooooo" and swung forward from the rail before launching himself forwards, arcing twelve feet down to land on a gaggle of his pals and collapse into them in a swearing tangle of college jerseys, Doc Martens and crew cuts. When the giggling rabble had untangled itself, somehow there appeared to be no injuries. Robb was led away over the polished parquet floor to be belted and Spake jumped down the last five feet from the ladder to join Dacre.

"Wee bugger! I nearly had him. You weren't much help though." Spake passed Dacre to sit down on the steps from the stage, and grinned up at his fellow prefect leaning against the wall beside the curtain. Dacre let himself slide down to sit on the floor, but the collar of his blazer caught on a tarnished brass cleat. He shuffled awkwardly to free himself but the jacket started to pull up under his oxters. The cleat tore through his collar and he slumped heavily onto his elbows.

"Fuck!" Dacre looked up anxiously to check for teachers, but the music was loud enough.

"Not your day, eh?" Spake was laughing.

"Aw fuck! I couldn't climb up there. Shite!"

"Did you see that Robb kid though? Wee tosser could have killed himself. You'd think he'd be careful of heights, not being able to fly like his big brother!"

Dacre was puzzled. "James? Fly?"

"Nah, not James. The other brother, died when James was really wee. Fell out of a window, right on the concrete slabs. Head smashed to fuck. Blood everywhere. D'you not remember?"

"Really? Christ, I'd no idea!"

"Aye. I remember James used to claim he had a big brother who could fly, said his brother'd flown away to live in the sky. Fuckin' dobber! My mum told me what really happened."

"I'd never heard that."

That night Dacre slept badly and dreamt of falling.

Chapter 16

January 1977

"Go on."

"I thought you'd got bored and gone to sleep."

Isla raised herself up on her elbows and turned to look at him. "No, I've heard every word."

Dacre was drained. He had been lost in his childhood and felt like he had been talking for hours. "So, if you leave me now because I'm a total nutcase I have no excuse." Isla had lain quiet through most of his account, squeezing his hand at times and asking occasional questions. Now she lay back.

"I'm not going to give up on you." After a pause, she asked if something had happened on his visit to her in Edinburgh. "You just seemed a bit … sort of … not there at times."

He owned up to what had happened on the train over the Forth Bridge.

"It was *you* who was sick! Eeuch!" She rolled away from him.

"I've got to do something about it. Remember Miles said hypnosis might help? He said some doctors do it."

"You didn't tell me he'd told you about that." After her reaction to Romano he thought she would go on to dismiss the idea, but she turned back to him. "I do think you should ask a doctor about hypnosis. Ask at Student Health."

"Student Health?"

"Didn't you read any of the pamphlets before you came? One of the first things you had to do was register with the doctor. In case you need one during term time."

Dacre pushed himself up onto his elbow and reached over to pick up the green packet of pills from the chair beside her bed. "That where you get these?" he grinned.

Isla reached up to take them back from him. "Hey! Leave those, they're private." The white sheet slipped down off her chest and he knew she could feel him growing against her thigh. "Don't try to change the subject," she murmured, half-heartedly.

***

Dr Stones was a little old man in a white coat, with some remaining white hair at the sides. As Dacre looked down on him, the strip light in the clinic room reflected off his shiny pate. When the GP sat down behind his cluttered desk, he looked even smaller. Dacre sat on the other side feeling embarrassed and awkward.

"Well? I haven't got all day."

"Err, it's difficult, I don't know what to say—"

"You'll have to tell me; I can't guess. Is it a sore throat? Piles? Or an itch?"

"There's nothing wrong with me, it's—"

The doctor cut him off with a sigh.

"What do you mean? Why are you here? I hope you're not wasting my time. I had three students this morning claiming to be depressed and wanting to be excused from exams."

Fuxake! This is a waste of time.

"I was going to ask if you could hypnotise me."

"What? Whatever for? No. I don't do that. You'll have to go to someone private if you want that sort of tosh. A GP would never do that."

Dacre could tell the doctor wanted to finish for the day and wasn't interested in helping him. He rose to go, but Stones said, "Wait, I'm sorry, it's been a long day." It was four o'clock. He went on, "I'm better in the mornings, and some of the other GPs here are younger and more inclined to take on the psych stuff."

"Forget it," said Dacre, and left.

***

He knocked lightly for the third time. He knew he was in there, even though there was not a sound from behind the red door, now that the muted radio music had been silenced. “Miles? Can I come in for a minute? It’s me, Dacre.”

He was about to give up when there was a shuffling sound, the door cracked open and a pallid profile murmured, “I’m busy.”

“Please, Miles. I need your advice.”

After a pause, “I have to go out.”

That’ll be right!

Dacre said nothing for a moment. “I’ll walk with you if you like. Going to lectures?” The door opened and Miles ushered him in. They both knew Miles was going nowhere and managed a wry smile to each other.

The room had changed. Newspaper cuttings and posters covered the walls, all very red, with black-and-white banner headlines proclaiming, ‘ALLY BACKS MILLER’, ‘NEW CAPTAIN, NEW ERA?’ and ‘PITTODRIE EXCITEMENT RISES’.

“I didn’t realise you were a football fan,” said Dacre, aware as everyone in the city that the Dons were having a good season. Thinking back to the only other time he had been in Miles’s room, the morning after the Laughing Policeman show, he remembered the walls had been bare.

“I saw Dr Dave at home at Christmas. He said I need a focus.” Now that the door was shut Miles appeared less tense, but still didn’t look Dacre in the eye.

Dacre said, “It’s advice from your doctor I was going to ask you about.” He turned and studied the Pittodrie fixture list to avoid facing Miles’s window. Miles was silent. “I’m having trouble with something and I thought I could see a hypnotist.”

“Hypnotherapist.”

“Sorry, yeah, that.”

“What’s wrong?”

Sharing his problem with Miles was easy. Easier even than with Isla. Miles seemed to relax and managed to smile knowingly when he heard the lengths Dacre had gone to trying to live with his problems. He even related some of his own experiences with social phobia. “A psychologist I had to see said I had to confront it. He wanted me to stand in front of a class of strangers and read a poem out loud! I would have passed out.” Miles was talking quickly and explained that he had refused to see the specialist again, which was when his GP Dr Dave tried hypnosis. “He had just been on a course to learn about hypnotherapy.”

Dacre remembered Miles telling him this before, but didn’t want to interrupt.

“He knew the basics but he didn’t know what to do next so he passed me on to his friend. Dr Kirby was brilliant.” Dacre noticed again that while he remained animated, Miles’s speech slowed a little when he talked about hypnotherapy.

When Dacre described the bad dreams about falling, Miles smiled and nodded. “Dr Kirby would be able to help with that; it’s a simple phobia. Trouble is, he’s in Kilmarnock. That’s why I had to find someone up here. Dr Dave and Dr Kirby had both joined some sort of society for hypnotherapists and my mum had asked him if there was anyone in Aberdeen.”

“Who did you see?”

“A man called Kinghorn.”

Dacre went to find the Yellow Pages in the Central Building.

***

There was a satisfying crunch underfoot as Dacre made his way across Hillhead. The curving path was a glistening river, its surface broken by footprints of all sizes which increased in number as tributaries flowed in from nearby residence blocks. Students too lazy to stick to the path left melting prints in the grass as they joined the main flow towards the Central Building. Most were heading for the dining hall or the 20 bus.

The sun was breaking over Adam Smith as Dacre reached the cobbled turning circle. There was a single set of tyre tracks in the frost, made by the first bus of the morning. Skirting round the medics waiting to get on board, he followed the breakfast-bound stream but veered off in the Central Building foyer towards the line of payphones on the wall. Each one was under a useless perspex dome, designed to afford privacy but in the echoing hall having the opposite acoustic effect. He'd found the graffiti and the plethora of sticky label adverts a helpful distraction when he had stopped listening to his mother's wittering.

"Hilton Road Surgery." The officious voice wasn't welcoming.

"Hi, can I speak to Dr Kinghorn?"

"Four fifty-five today."

"Err ..."

"Do you want the appointment or not?"

"Yes, please." Dacre, like all students, was free on Wednesday afternoons.

"Your name?"

"Gordon Dacre."

"Address?"

"Errr ... home, or Hillhead?"

"Which GP are you registered with?"

"Dr Mackie."

"We don't have a Dr Mackie. Are you a patient here or not? Are you wasting my time?"

"I'm sorry. I want him to hypnotise me."

"Oh, you're one of those. He arranges that himself. It's nothing to do with me."

Dacre was beginning to regret calling.

"Can I speak to him?"

"Oh, give me your number and I'll leave a note for him. Bloody cheek, him getting me to arrange his private work."

"I'm in a call box."

"Oh, for god's sake, ring back in the afternoon." She hung up.

***

After morning lectures, Dacre and Isla met up in the Central Ref. After the initial chatter about their respective lectures, and after David had turned to speak to a girl at the next table, Isla whispered to him, "How did you get on with the phone call?"

Dacre was hungrily devouring his pie, chips and beans, having missed his breakfast to make the call. Swallowing, he wiped pastry from his cheek and grunted, "Waste of time. The woman wouldn't listen."

"I thought the doctor was a man?"

"You have to get an appointment first and you can't speak to them. Besom told me to phone back later."

"Besom! My granny used to call me that!" said Isla smiling. "Still, you should call back like they said."

"What's the point? She'll just make it difficult again."

***

"Good afternoon, Hilton Road, Kath speaking. How can I help you?"

Isla had told him that her GP practice at home had several doctors and lots of staff, and that someone else might be more help. Dacre had thought they would all be like Besom but now felt himself relaxing.

"Oh! Thanks. I was hoping to speak to Dr Kinghorn about hypnosis."

"Let me see. He likes to call hypnotherapy patients himself and make their appointments. Now, when will I ask him to call you back? Let's see ..."

"Sorry, but I don't have a phone."

"That's OK, if you're having to use a telephone box, Dr Kinghorn lets me arrange for you to call him at the end of his afternoon surgery. He usually finishes about five thirty. He's always running late, he's meant to finish at five."

Having expected another brush-off, Dacre was pleased he would be able to tell Isla he had arranged to speak with Dr Kinghorn that evening. But when Isla knocked on his door at half-past nine he was despondent.

"He was nice about it, but said he could only see me

privately 'cos I'm not a member of his practice. I asked him if I could join, but he said no because his practice doesn't cover this area and it wouldn't be allowed. I didn't know what he was on about really." Dr Kinghorn had said he would have to charge twenty pounds just to see Dacre once, and that he expected to see all hypnotherapy patients at least three times. "I can't afford it. I told him I'd have to forget it."

"Oh, that's a shame!"

"And I remember now Miles said anyone you get hypnotised by would charge you unless your own GP does it, and my GP is that idiot at Student Health, so I'm stuffed!"

"Didn't you say Miles was learning to do it himself? Maybe you could learn?" The record had finished and Dacre absentmindedly lifted the lid and flipped it over to play the other side, dusting it briefly with the felt cleaner. "You always play this when you're pissed off," commented Isla as 'Meet Me in the Morning' began.

"Do I? 'Blood on the Tracks' is just the best album ever, that's all." Dacre smiled at last. Isla nuzzled into him and they were both quiet for a while. Before they parted for the night, Isla had persuaded him to think about self-hypnosis. One of her history tutorial group members was doing psychology and had told Isla enthusiastically about the subconscious mind and how fascinating it was.

"I'm sure she'll know something about hypnosis. I'll ask her."

"Hmmm. OK." Dacre was still doubtful, but keen to please.

Chapter 17

February 1977

"I have a present for you, but you'll have to wait for it." Dacre and Isla were walking through the park on the way back to Hillhead. The crocuses were coming out, and the park was brighter than it had seemed for months. It was Friday afternoon and they had met by chance in High Street. He had just cashed a cheque when Isla came over the cobbles towards the tiny bank. Despite the spring-like sunshine, Dacre shivered while waiting for her to withdraw money for the weekend. They walked hand in hand along The Chanonry to reach the park.

"I haven't got you anything." Dacre was intrigued and a little embarrassed she had thought to buy him a present.

"It's OK, I didn't pay for it. And I won't be able to give you it until Sunday, anyway."

With confusion tinged with excitement, Dacre gripped her hand. "I'll buy you a Tom Collins tonight, then."

On Sunday afternoon, Dacre's listening to Annie Nightingale was interrupted when Isla knocked on his door and came in with a Woolworths bag, smiling and offering it to him. "I told you I had a present." Inside the bag was a heavy paperback book, which Dacre suspiciously drew out. The back of the book told him it was a textbook of some sort, and he was a bit disappointed.

"Turn it over," prompted Isla, "it's only a book. Jill said it's fascinating."

"Jill?" said Dacre, turning it over. He smiled as he read '*Hartland's Medical & Dental Hypnosis*'.

"Ahh, I see."

"I asked Jill if she knew anything about hypnosis and she went on for ages about it. I didn't understand what she was on about, but she's dead interested in it." Her hand went to her mouth. "Oh, god! I've just thought ... I hope I haven't upset you! I didn't tell her anything about you."

"Err, what? Sorry? What did you say? There's a whole section here on doing it yourself." Dacre had gone straight to the index, and found 'Self-induced trance' which directed him to 'Autohypnosis'. He was already flicking through the pages, and quite distracted.

"Is it OK?"

"Sorry, thanks, yes, this is magic! I'm going to speak to Miles about it when I next see him."

Dacre read well into the night after Isla had gone. By the time he drifted off, he had covered the history of hypnosis and some of its applications. He was very keen to ask Miles how he was getting on with self-hypnosis.

***

Dacre tentatively knocked on the door. It was Thursday afternoon, and he knew Miles was in. "Miles. Can I ask you something?" The faint music from inside stopped and there was silence. He knocked again. "Miles. It's me, Dacre." Eventually, light footsteps approached and the door cracked open.

"Can you come back another time?"

"It's OK, I just want to ask you if you want to borrow this." Dacre held up Hartland to the gap.

"You've got Hartland's book? I have that, I've read every page." Miles opened the door a little further, and Dacre knew Miles was going to let him in. This had become the usual routine. Once inside, Dacre noticed even more red decorations and P&J cuttings. His eye was drawn to the spine of Miles's copy of Hartland, between the maths textbooks and folders of notes crammed on the bookshelf.

"I wanted to ask if you had managed the self-hypnosis? I want to try it myself."

Miles sat on the edge of his bed, his eyes on the floor. "Your heights thing?" He spoke very quietly.

"Yes, it feels like it's never going to get better."

Miles looked up and straight at Dacre, with a sorry expression. "It won't. You're stuck with it if you don't get help. It'll only get worse. You're lucky though; it's only a single phobia." Miles blurted this out almost in one breath and continued staring at Dacre, who looked away, acutely aware of Miles's apparent anger and antipathy towards him.

"I'm sorry, I didn't mean to ..."

But Miles suddenly lay back on the bed with his clenched fists pressed into his eyes, the veins engorging along his rigid forearms. Dacre now couldn't look away, the red and white duvet cover, the pallid arms and Miles's red T-shirt merging into a sickening whirl, inducing vertigo as if he were on a cliff edge. He couldn't remember being so affected without the stimulus of altitude. He lowered himself down on the chair, his turn to stare at the floor until the whirling slowed and nausea receded.

Miles managed to speak through tears. "I'm just so angry at myself, that's why self-hypnosis is difficult for me, I really need someone to put me into a trance. I just can't do it ... get there myself ... it's no use." He sighed noisily and began drying his face on his pillow.

"I'm sorry, I didn't mean to upset you." It was all Dacre could think of saying.

Miles slowly pushed himself up and managed a weak smile. "It's OK, I know you didn't. I just get so frustrated at myself."

"I'll go."

"No. I'll be OK. I thought you were going to see Kinghorn?"

"I tried, but there's no way I could afford it."

"I'm sorry, I should have told you that's why I stopped seeing him. My mum could only afford a few sessions. He charged more than Dr Kirby and she'd already spent too much. I started feeling bad about her spending it all, and I told her the treatment was finished and I was doing better. That's why I was trying autohypnosis, but I just can't do it. I don't like lying to her. Especially ..." He paused. Dacre remembered Miles's father had died, and thought he was about to break down again, but Miles sobbed once, quietly, before inhaling deeply and straightening up. He lifted his head, and asked Dacre, "Have you tried to do it?"

"Self-hypnosis? No, I wouldn't know how to start. The book gives you ideas, but I don't know ... well, I want to ask how you'd got on." Dacre stood up from the chair. "It's OK, I'm sorry, I shouldn't have ... I'll go—"

"I could be your therapist. That would be something, eh?" Suddenly animated, he reached out and grasped his Dons toorie bunnet from the floor beside his bed. Pulling it on and stretching it down almost to cover his eyes, he said, "This can be instead of a doctor's white coat." Miles was looking up from the bed with a wry grin, tears drying on his cheeks. It was the first time Dacre had heard humour from Miles, and he managed to smile back.

"I could maybe do you in return?"

"I'm beyond help," said Miles quickly. "No, let's concentrate on you first."

***

Miles talked quietly and calmly, with a confident authority Dacre had not expected. He felt compelled to obey the slow, clear instructions.

"I want you to look at the very tip of this pencil. Look at the point. Focus on it. Don't take your eyes off it." Dacre was fixed on the graphite tip. "Now start counting backwards to yourself. Start at 300 ... 299 ... 298 ... that's it ... keep going ... counting down ... never taking your eyes off that pencil tip—"

Miles went on and on and Dacre could see nothing but the pencil suspended in mid-air above him, and hear only the numbers he counted down silently. There was nothing else.

"Your eyes are now getting more tired ... you may want to blink. Those eyelids are heavy ... your eyes scratchy ... you want to blink. It's okay, you can blink ... let your eyes close ...

feel the relief. Keep counting … keep counting … slowly … downwards. The pencil is out of focus now … as your eyes get heavier … and close. Eyes now tight shut … you couldn't open them if you tried." Dacre's eyelids were glued together. "Now … I want you to take a very, very deep breath in and hold it."

Without trying, Dacre felt his lungs filling and his chest expanding.

"Hold it … hold it … now let go! Breathe out. The delight. The relief. Your chest is emptying. Your body is sinking into the chair." Miles was commanding. "Now another deep breath … go on … deep … deeper … the deepest breath you have ever taken. Hold it … hold it … let go!"

Deep in the trance Miles had induced, Dacre was fully aware of every sound. Miles reassured him that he could wake up and go anytime he wanted, but Dacre wouldn't have moved for anything. He was so comfortable, and everything Miles said was so perfect, he just wanted it to go on. Miles told him he was strong, confident and fearless, and Dacre knew it was true. He could do anything he wanted to. Every time Miles repeated and repeated his calm instructions, Dacre knew they were more significant.

"Now I'm going to count slowly from five back towards one, and with each number, you will feel lighter, less asleep, and more alert. Five … feeling lighter … four … coming up … three … slowly waking from refreshing sleep … two … coming to … eyes beginning to open … one. Now wake up, eyes open."

Dacre had no choice but to follow the path upwards and out of the trance. He opened his eyes and stretched as if he had been asleep for hours. He could recall every word Miles had said and he had even heard the volume of Spiny's music rise when he padded along and made coffee. Jethro Tull's flute had enhanced his dreamy pleasure. But only Miles's words had mattered.

"Miles, that was amazing! I feel great. How did you learn to do that?"

Miles looked pleased and relaxed. "I've read it all over and over, and I tried to do exactly what Dr Dave used to do with me. You induce the trance and then use deepening techniques to enhance it."

Miles was different—speaking very freely and confidently.

"You seem better as well. Sorry, but it shows in how you talk. You're not ... err ... so jumpy."

"Dr Dave said he always felt great after using hypnotherapy on his patients. So did Kirby. That's the first time I've done it for anyone, and I must say I feel great, almost like I did when I was the one being treated."

"So why can't you do it to yourself? Autohypnosis I mean?" Dacre was elated and keen to learn himself if it worked as well as this.

"That's the trouble, I just can't seem to get there properly, into a trance I mean. I go through the motions but nothing happens, and I feel worse instead of better, angry and frustrated. A failure again."

"Could you teach me? If I get good at it maybe I could help you?"

Miles looked sceptical and eyed the floor. "It'll never work for me. Unless I give up and go back home, I mean, and my mother would be furious, even if it made me better. I mean if I gave up on university, you know. Dr Dave would understand though. He'll be more experienced now, and he could carry on where Kirby left off." Miles's words flowed faster and faster, and Dacre thought he was going to lose control again.

"I could try, though," he said, trying to steer Miles away from his troubles, and keen to learn to treat himself. He kept them on the subject of trance induction, and they consulted Hartland to find a self-induction script. By modifying Miles's technique a little, Dacre found that by lifting his eyes to the ceiling and focusing on a small dot, he could make his eyes want to close. Counting backwards from three hundred and taking slow, deep breaths helped him approach the state of waking sleep that Miles had induced. A short time later, he counted himself back awake and looked dreamily at Miles.

"It looks like it's working for you, you lucky bugger." Dacre had never heard Miles swear. Looking despondent he went on, "I just can't, I don't know why, but every time I try, I get nowhere. I can feel myself getting angry right now. I hate myself."

Dacre in contrast felt very positive and enthused. He was elated at the thought that self-hypnosis was going to cure him of his problems, and impatient to get on. But his success was making Miles worse. "I'd better go. I've got botany to do. Thanks, Miles."

***

The botany could wait. Dacre couldn't resist trying to get into a trance again. He lay on his bed and stared at the ceiling, and soon he was drifting down, sinking into the bed as he breathed deeply out. Miles had suggested that later on when he'd learnt more he could try visualising looking down into his room from the ceiling as he entered trance. He thought this might be a way of starting to tackle his acrophobia. But Dacre couldn't resist trying it now, and soon found himself floating up and looking down on himself, lying peacefully far below. The Dacre on the bed was smiling and sleeping like a baby, and he gazed down protectively feeling calm and in perfect control. He could have stayed there all night, but gentle knocking on the door helped him rouse.

"Dacre. It's me, let me in."

He dreamily opened the door to Isla.

"You didn't go for your meal. I was about to give up on you," she said, smiling and pulling him towards her.

"Sorry, I was miles away."

Isla kicked the door closed behind her with her foot as they embraced.

Half an hour later Isla pushed herself up on one elbow. "Why are you getting up? Dacre, come back."

"I just feel great. I want to go out. Let's go to the Union." He was pulling on his jeans.

"But it's nearly nine o'clock. We'd need to get a bus, and the bar shuts at eleven."

But Dacre was already half-dressed. "Come on, let's go." He pulled her up and hugged her. "Get dressed, come on, I'll beat you to the bus stop."

"What's got into you?"

On the way out, Dacre stopped and pointed out of the landing window. "The bus is just pulling through the main gate. Come on!" After running for the bus and climbing breathlessly up to the top, they sat in the front seats, and Dacre was counting the money in his wallet. "I've got four pounds and thirty-eight pence. I'll treat you."

"Dacre, do you realise what you've just done? You looked out of the upstairs window, and now we are upstairs at the front of the bus. Are you OK?"

"I feel great. I don't know what I made a fuss about."

"What's happened? Why are you better?"

Dacre smiled, gripped her hand, and pulled her close. "From now on, call me Romano. I am a hypnotist!"

Chapter 18

March 1977

"Oh, who's David? I don't think you've mentioned him before."

Fuxake! She's got to know everything!

The pips went and Dacre reluctantly pushed his last ten pence into the slot. "He's just a guy in some of my classes, Mum, he's from Fraserburgh."

"Oh! Mr Lambie had a contract in Fraserburgh and sent Dad there a few times. A power station or something. I wonder if he met David's dad? It's a small world, you know, you should ask David what his dad does."

Dacre had almost forgotten to phone home, and Isla had made him leave her a little earlier than usual to do his duty. Promising to phone again next week he put the phone down with a shake of his head. He didn't care about his dad's work or his boss, and no way was he going to ask David.

It was past eleven o'clock and the path was icy. By March the porters had stopped spreading salt, and a spring frost had caught them out. After he had slithered across the Hillhead complex to Esslemont, the usual sensual joy as he hypnotised himself to sleep was replaced by irritation and frustration after his mother's wittering. He lay in the dark, distracted from his usual induction. His mother's words intruded like a broken record.

***

A sickening kaleidoscope of stuffed animals, labelled bones and a bluish-white hand gradually stopped circling, out of focus now. A voice boomed … "refusing to release details, but unconfirmed reports suggest both her arms had been severed. Police are questioning the many temporary workers accommodated at the nearby power station where extensive building works are underway." A camera moved from a green road sign reading 'Fraserburgh 8m' to a man with a microphone. He stood near a poster. 'MISSING' was its heading, and under a picture of a girl bold letters read 'INGA SABISTON'. A siren started blaring.

"Turn that fucking thing off!" Spiny's loud banging on his door was more successful than the wailing alarm clock next to his head. "Thank fuck!" came from the corridor when Dacre eventually found the clock switch. He lay in the sudden silence, pleased he had had such a long and peaceful sleep.

Under the hot cascade of the shower, he froze motionless when the soundtrack to his dream began and a vivid film played on a screen in his head.

Did I dream that? A horror film? What the fuck? Oh, fuck!

***

"Shut it, Spiny, I'm not joking, it was bloody scary. I can't get it out of my head."

Dacre had hardly touched his chips, and Spiny smirked. "Put you off your food? I'll have it!" His hand flashed out and grabbed at Dacre's plate. Dacre went on mumbling at the floor while Spiny filled his face. The Central Ref was emptying and the noise of scraping chairs drowned the thump of the jukebox. Two porters were clearing the floor getting ready for a Friday night disco.

Dacre picked at a couple of chips Spiny had left him, and looked up to realise David was sitting across the table. Their last lecture of the week was about to start. "You not going to physics?" said Dacre, reaching for his bag.

"Can I ask you something?" Dacre felt David staring at him.

"Sorry, I've not been good today," he said, standing up. "Let's go, we'll miss physics."

"No, wait a minute, Dacre, I want to ask you what you were saying to Spiny. I didn't hear it all."

Dacre managed a sheepish grin and stayed standing. "It's OK, it was just one of my stupid dreams, I think I need a straitjacket."

It was David's turn to stare at the floor. "Did you say Inga? The girl with no arms?"

"What? Just a stupid dream, c'mon ... I mean ... why?" Dacre's mouth dried as the film of his dream began again.

"What did you say she was called? It's just that it's weird."

"Inga."

"Jeezuss! Did you know about that?" David was still staring at Dacre and he sat back down.

"Out boys, I've got to clear these chairs away." The porter's grey overall had a splash of tomato sauce along the left sleeve. David ignored him and he shuffled away muttering to himself.

"Look, tell me what you said to Spiny. This is fuckin' mad!"

When Spiny had asked what the hell was wrong with him on their way to lectures Dacre had recounted his dream. It had felt good to tell someone but Spiny had tormented him relentlessly since. He was reluctant to tell David and expected the same treatment, but David was adamant. He spoke quietly, hesitating to gauge David's reaction. "It was horrible, I was seeing all sorts of hellish stuff, gory stuff, y'know, a cut-off hand for fuck's sake, and then this film played, or like TV, the news, a girl with her arms cut off. Her arms ..." He looked away, clearing his throat. "And she was called Inga, I saw the name, printed, on a poster, the guy was pointing at it, Inga, Inga Sabiston. I tell you, I need a straitjacket. I know it was a dream, but I'm sick in the head making something like that up—"

"You didn't make it up."

Dacre stared at his friend, who was looking down at the floor and fiddling with a toggle on his duffle coat. "You didn't make it up. It happened. Inga was at my school. In Fraserburgh. She disappeared, then about two weeks later she was found in a ditch. Rathen, near Crimond, I think. She'd had both her arms sawn off at the shoulder. Like you said to Spiny." David looked up. "How did you know about that?"

"It was a dream!"

"She was in my year at school. Fourth year I think it

happened." He stood up abruptly. "I'm going back to the flat. Fuck physics. I haven't thought about that for years." Dacre followed meekly, numb and a little foolish. He suspected this was one of David's practical jokes. Spiny must have told him about the dream and they decided to take the piss.

Dacre dreamt about Inga Sabiston again that night, but the second time around it didn't have the same effect, and the next morning it was his hangover he had to deal with. Spiny had dragged him out to the Red Lion. When his headache cleared, he made a start on some chemistry. On his way to the dining room when at last he thought he could eat, he smiled to himself at his pal's excellent piss-take. David had been out when they tried his door last night, or Dacre would have got him back somehow.

After their evening meal, Dacre and Isla went for a short walk. It was light until after eight o'clock now that the clocks had changed, and they strolled down to the park and took the track along the Don which curved round the sprawl of Hillhead. "Did I tell you about the awful dream I had?" She looked at him quizzically. "It was mad. Stuffed animals, human bones, somebody dead, meat in the butcher's shop—"

"Stop. I don't want to hear any more."

"No, but it was funny, I told David and—"

"Funny? Disgusting!" Isla dropped his hand.

"No, I mean—"

"That's awful, laughing at something like that." She turned and walked away from him, back along the muddy path. Running to catch up with her, he slipped on the mud and fell forwards onto his knees and hands. Isla stopped and turned when he yelled.

"Serves you right!" But she was laughing as she helped him up.

"I meant what David did was funny, not the dream! He pretended the dream was real, that it wasn't a dream. He said it really—"

"I don't want to know."

"Sorry. It was a dream, just one of my stupid nightmares. I think it's the hypnosis that causes the dreams."

"Don't stop the hypnosis. You've been much better since you started it and you were getting weird before."

Chapter 19

April 1977

Dacre was right about the cause of the dreams. He realised he could avoid dreaming at all if he made himself bring himself out of trance before trying to sleep. With this careful self-hypnosis routine, he thrived and in the mornings he was raring to go. His confidence grew, lectures were interesting, and exams were easy. From the top of the 20 bus as it made its way up to Hillhead he now enjoyed looking down at the crocuses on the verge as they were gradually replaced by early daffodils, and when he marched smartly up to Isla's room he could look out of the window on each landing to take in the view. In his positive frame of mind, even the tower blocks of Seaton were majestic. As the Easter holiday break approached, he looked forward to going home, keen to tell his mum how well he was. He knew he would be able to visit Isla without fear of the Forth Bridge.

***

Spake drained the last of his pint and looked pointedly towards Dacre, proffering his glass.

"Sorry, I was thinking about the time with the rope swing. You remember?"

"Guinness, please."

Dacre went to the bar, returning with a Guinness and a pint of heavy. "On the way home, let's go to the rushes. For old time's sake."

Spake looked up with foam on his top lip. "What? It'll be dark on the way home, for god's sake." It was half-past six on an April Saturday, and the two pals had cadged money from their mothers and met up for the first time since Christmas. Elinor had looked disappointed when Dacre dumped his washing before quickly leaving for the pub. The Arms hadn't changed, but they had both expressed nostalgic fondness for it as if they'd been away for years.

"Well, let's go now then, then back for more beer."

Spake protested but raced his pint to keep up with Dacre, and they made their way in the direction of the common. Spake laughed along with his pal but it was clear he thought they were wasting pint time.

"But why the fuck?"

"I just want to climb that tree."

"Aye, right!"

"You'll see."

The common was still pocked by puddles of dirty brown floodwater. The tree that had humiliated Dacre was leafless and seemed smaller. Running the last few yards Dacre launched himself at the trunk, using the lower branches to haul himself upwards. Soon he had easily conquered it and the algae-covered rope hung down below him. With the fraying knot of the old rope between his feet, he stood on the old branch looking down triumphantly. Spake stood in disbelief on the soggy, rotting reeds.

"How's that? Nae bother!"

"That's barry!" said Spake. "How come you can do that now?"

"Barry?" Spake had picked up some of the Edinburgh lingo, and Dacre reflected that their worlds were expanding as horizons stretched beyond Fife.

Spake went on, "But what's happened? You OK now? Heights, I mean."

After shinning down the trunk, Dacre turned and grinned, slapping green powder from his jeans. "I've got magic powers now."

"You on something?"

"Nah. Just learned a new trick. Hypnosis."

"Really? Like on TV? Don't do it to me."

Dacre explained on the way back to the pub.

***

Back at Hillhead for the summer term, things continued to go well for Dacre provided he continued his nightly routine. That was the problem: sometimes he didn't bother and went straight from trance to sleep, and he started to dream again. Nothing shocking like the Inga Sabiston nightmare, but vivid snapshots of mundane scenes. He would wake gradually, dreamily relaxing as a gently rising conveyor belt brought him slowly up through warm surf to lie on a warm and sunny beach. Then fleeting memories of his dreams would come. But there was none of the terror and vertigo of his old nightmares, and now that he had cured his acrophobia, he became complacent. The new dreams were benign and tolerable.

After some weeks, though, he would wake with a nagging feeling that he was almost, but not quite, remembering something. Something important, but just out of reach. He became distracted and frustrated, and the elusive meaning of the images in his dreams caused new anxiety.

Isla tried to joke him out of it one Sunday morning in early May, while they sat together in her room with their books open. They sometimes found it refreshing to study together away from the library. Barely speaking, they could concentrate on their essay writing or revision, sometimes forgetting lunch or coffee breaks. But this time, Isla had noticed that each time she looked over at Dacre he was staring into space, looking puzzled and troubled, instead of deep in thought. "I bet Einstein had moments when he couldn't understand his physics," she said, smiling broadly.

"Ach, I can't concentrate today; I'm going to stop. I've hardly taken anything in."

"Are you not sleeping again?"

"That's just it, my sleep's magic, but the bloody dreams!"

"But I thought you'd managed to ... you know ... control the dreams. You said if you were careful to wake yourself up properly you were OK?"

Dacre leant back in the desk chair and stared at the ceiling.

His arms were outstretched and he gripped the desk edge, his knuckles white. He said through clenched teeth, "Sometimes I'm too tired and I just trance myself. That's when it happens."

"Nightmares?" Isla came across from her bed and stood behind Dacre. His books were spread around, and only a few lines of an essay were scrawled on his lined paper pad. She crouched down and stroked his shoulder, her head close against his.

"Tell Dr Isla about your nasty dreams," she whispered in his ear.

Dacre's face and arms relaxed a little. "But that's the problem, it's nothing nasty. Not scary stuff. Things I know ... I think. But I just can't remember. And there's something I feel more and more I ... kind of ... I dunno ... I *need* to remember! Really, it's important, but I just can't get what it is, you know? Round and round in my head all the fucking time."

He could feel his frustration building again but was glad he'd been able to tell her. But then she said, "I knew something was wrong. But if it's just dreams, it doesn't matter, surely?" Dacre tensed again and pushed himself upright, flinching away angrily out of her embrace. He turned round in the chair as she stood back up. His eyes were moist.

"I've got to get this bloody essay finished for tomorrow, and all I can do is go over and over a fucking dream I can't even fucking remember! And you say it doesn't matter!" Isla sat down on the bed. He thought she looked shocked and hated himself.

"Just don't give up on me," he said more quietly, gathering his books and stuffing them into his khaki kit bag. He reached for the door handle and wiped tears away with the back of his other hand as he looked back at her.

"Don't give up on me."

***

Half an hour later Isla knocked at Dacre's door. He knew it had to be her, and waited as long as he could before pulling himself up off his bed to open the door, ushering her in without a word. They sat in silence until eventually, he said, "It's the hypnosis. It's changed my dreams, and it's ever since then."

Isla took his hand and squeezed it. "I'm trying to help you; don't walk out on me. Please!"

"I'm sorry. I've got to know what it is, though. In the dreams. It's getting more and more like I can see it, but when I wake it's just a blur."

Isla stood up and parted the curtains just enough for her to see the early spring sunshine on a bank of daffodils rippling in the breeze. "Have you had that awful one again, about ... you know ... animals, and meat?"

"No, I almost wish I fucking had! At least then I'd know none of it was real. When David took the piss like that I knew it was all crap I'd made up. I wish the others ... the other dreams I mean ... were just someone fucking winding me up. But the people are so real. I know them, I think. Fuck!"

Isla sat back down beside him on the edge of the bed. "You mean it's people you're trying to remember?"

He sighed, his shoulders dropping. "Two people, I think. In a frame. And ... Jeezuss—," he was shaking his head, "a paintbrush ... and brown gunk in a jar. I'm fucking loony!"

"A frame? Is it a picture? Someone painting a picture, you mean?"

"I keep wondering if it's a window. And they're always down below. Looking up at me."

They were quiet for a moment.

"Are you still doing the hypnosis every day?"

He looked up from the floor and turned his red eyes to her. "Yes, and at first I only got the dreams if I'd been too pissed or knackered and not brought myself out properly. But last night it happened anyway, and I'd been really careful. And I want to know who I'm dreaming about, but I don't really. Oh, fuck! I'm rambling a lot of shite again!"

Isla managed to smile and took his hand. "It's OK, I think I know what you mean. Go on."

"And now I'm scared I keep getting it even if I do everything properly. For fuck's sake, I wish I hadn't started doing hypnosis! But then I'd be fucking useless because of the heights thing."

Still holding his hand, Isla reached out to the desk and pulled Hartland's book towards her. "Do you think there's something in here? It might say something about dreams."

"It does. It talks about dreams and revealing memories you've hidden away. Calls it regression. It needs an experienced therapist to do it, though." They discussed it for a while and Dacre relaxed, less worried that Isla had lost patience with him. When she went back to study she took the borrowed copy of Hartland with her, and he'd promised to ask Miles what he knew about regression.

***

He hadn't seen Miles for a few days, but that was nothing unusual, and it was no surprise when he didn't answer Dacre's knocking on Monday morning. But he'd slept better, and even though he'd dreamt of the window people again he was more hopeful.

The Daily Record

5th July 1976

DUTCH LINK TO OBAN SLAYING

Limbless Lady had Football Tattoo

Strathclyde Police are working with Dutch forces to identify a murder victim. The body of a woman, thought to be about 20, was found on 8th June in a culvert under the Gallanach Road two miles south of Oban.

DI Sam Sprake told me "This is a murder enquiry, the left arm of the deceased was deliberately removed, and while we have not yet located the arm, the hand was found discarded further up the burn.

"The deceased has a tattoo on her left shoulder which we believe to be the logo of Dutch football side FC Twente (see picture inset).

"With no clues from any of our missing persons lists we are releasing this information in the hope that members of the public might recognise the tattoo. We are now considering the possibility that the deceased was a Dutch tourist."

Chapter 20

May 1977

Dermot was hungry and spaced out. And lost. In the dark, Hillhead's blocks of flats all looked the same and in trying to find his flat, he had stumbled into several parties. He could remember leaving when his flatmate started speaking Martian. He hadn't liked the way his face kept melting. The stars had been winking at him, inviting him out to play, and he'd gone looking for the old gang he ran with back in Maryhill when he was still in shorts and gutties.

In one flat he'd wandered into some girls making toast, and their terrified screaming at him made him run away. He now sat on a wet tarmac path, propped up by a lighting bollard.

"Fuck are you doin' there? C'mon, I'll take you back to my bit." He became aware of Spiny leaning over him and pulling at his sleeve.

"Get yer ane jaikit, Tony! There's one in the box. Mammy! He's tryin' tae tak ma jaikit!" Dermot was still in Maryhill. He could still smell the toast and was suddenly hungrier than he had ever been.

"Got any midget gems?"

"Jesus, Dermot! You've done acid again." Spiny, drunk himself, unsteadily helped his rubber-legged friend up and huckled him towards his own flat, across the landing from the girls making toast.

"They girls can cook! I saw them. Toast! Smells good … let's go in there," said Dermot as Spiny roughly dragged him in the opposite direction.

"Fuck me! What's that smell?" When Spiny pulled him through the flat door, Dermot lurched straight past and started retching into the kitchen sink.

Spiny and his flatmates had noticed a smell in their flat and had eventually told the porters. The duty porter had decided someone had blocked a toilet.

"It's the toilet. It's getting fixed tomorrow," shouted Spiny over his shoulder while he took a noisy pee.

"Christ! One of you's got a problem, stinkin' bastards. A shunkie shouldnae smell like that."

Dermot, his appetite having dissipated, wandered off into the night.

***

On Saturday morning Dacre woke to loud knocking on his door. Isla was in Edinburgh, her grandmother ill. The noise didn't stop and he got up.

"Fa's room is 'at?" asked a man in a boiler suit. "The reek's from in there." He pointed over his shoulder with an adjustable spanner.

Guessing the man meant the room opposite, Dacre smiled and said, "Miles. But you can't go in there. He's gone home to Ayr, left last week."

"Dis he keep beasts?"

"What?"

"Animals, loon. Pets. It's nae nattral, that reek. Somethin's rotten in there. It's nae a plumber yer needin'."

The second knock on Dacre's door that Saturday morning was made an hour later by the duty accommodation officer. "I'm sorry to interrupt you, but I understand you told the plumber Mr Davidson had gone home. How do you know that, exactly?" She seemed nervous, Dacre thought. She was out of breath, and the large bunch of keys in her hand was jangling.

"Errr ... he shoved a note under my door. I found it last Wednesday when I woke. I was in a hurry to get to lectures and I didn't pay it any attention."

"This Wednesday?"

"The one before. I didn't see him all last weekend and found the note again on Sunday afternoon."

"Can I see the note?"

Dacre found it on his bookshelf. "Is there a problem?"

The woman was pale, and her words shook as she rushed them out. "I don't know. It's just when the plumber said he had gone home, I thought I would phone and see if I could ask what he'd left in his room to make that smell. But his mother says he hasn't been there. He hadn't phoned home either since last week and told her he was going away on a field trip."

"A field trip? He does maths."

The note, in neat longhand, read:

I have to go,
Ayr is so nice in the Spring.
My Mum will be missing me.
Thanks for talking to me.

Miles.

"So no one's seen him for ten days?" The accommodation officer was now shaking.

"Not me. And why would he say he's away to Ayr if he's not?" Sensing the woman's anxiety, Dacre began to feel uneasy. "You don't think he's in his room ... I mean ... ill?"

She didn't answer and turned away with the keys, her hand trembling. She had a master key selected but couldn't insert it into Miles's door. Dacre stepped out of his room and stood beside her at the door. She looked at him helplessly, her lip trembling. Dacre felt sick.

"David!" he shouted. "Spiny!" He knew they had both gone out and he was the only one there. He knocked loudly on Miles's door. "Miles! Are you in there? Come on. Open up!"

The accommodation officer had one hand over her mouth and nose, her eyes on Dacre. The plumber had asked about animals. "Miles, have you got animals in there?" he tried, his voice weakening. But he knew he was going to have to open the door. The woman meekly let him take the keys. He held the door-pull and with his other hand he inserted the Yale key, paused, and turned it. As he cracked the door open the smell intensified. The bright red door creaked as he pushed it inwards, revealing more bright red splashed over the white emulsion wall.

As the accommodation officer gagged and sobbed, Dacre hesitated, turning uncertainly. She managed to nod back to his questioning expression, both hands over her face, one wet, red eye visible against her pallor. His heart pounding, he turned and pushed the door a little more.

Miles had been busy with his scissors. Every inch of wall seemed to be red. Cuttings from the P&J had been pasted over with glossy pictures of his team. On the desk was a hardback book, a Dons annual or testimonial biography. Scissors and paper scraps showed how the walls had been decorated. Along the top of the wardrobe and the bookshelf over the desk were red and white scarves. The mustard yellow curtains were festooned with red crepe paper. He noticed how neatly it had been attached using paper clips.

There was no visible sign of Miles. The smell was now overpowering, even with the door wide open. The accommodation officer was weeping with hopeful relief. "He's not in here. Thank god. I thought—"

Dacre was retching into the wastepaper bin. At the bottom of the wardrobe, there was a moist patch on the purple carpet, and he had become aware of a hum. Wiping his mouth on his sleeve, Dacre pointed at the wardrobe, mumbling, "In there."

"Oh god! Don't open it! Wait! I can't!" The accommodation officer turned away, her head still in her hands. Dacre forced himself to crack the wardrobe door open and the humming became a loud buzz. Flies escaped into the room, and Dacre shrank back as the door swung slowly open.

Under hanging clothes was a near-naked, white and purple corpse in the foetal position, its head obscured by plastic. Vomit had seeped under the red string securing the bag and dried on a wrinkled, pasty shoulder. Faeces and urine had leaked out of red Y-fronts, soiling the floor. A blue-white hand wearing a gold ring fell out of the wardrobe. It was like ice when it touched Dacre's bare foot. He passed out.

***

Saturday had been spent between his flat and the Central Building. When he had come to, Dacre was propped on a kitchen chair with a policeman standing over him. He was told screaming had alerted students and porters, and the police had been called. When she calmed down, the accommodation officer had explained that Dacre's presence in Miles's room was not suspicious. He had soon repeated the same story to three ranks of policemen. The first pair of young constables had been as distressed as he was, and one of them escaped to take the accommodation officer home. A sergeant with a large chevron on the arm of his tunic had then arrived. He avoided going into Miles's room but took Dacre's statement again, concluding that the CID was required.

He had been allowed to retrieve some lecture notes and then his flat had been locked, and he was ordered to stay in the Central Building. A friendly but tactless porter had given him free coffee, but insisted on telling him details of other suicides he had witnessed at Hillhead. By the time the CID man had turned up in his grey raincoat, Dacre had been pleased to escape to give his account once again.

The police were then satisfied. Spiny and David had been tracked down and had nothing to offer about Miles except that they hadn't seen him for ten days either. Andrew was away seeing his girlfriend. Miles's mother had been informed and was making her way to Aberdeen.

By evening, Dacre was allowed to return to his flat, where he found Miles's door had been taped over. A sign read 'Police, No Entry', and the smell was just as bad, even though men in overalls had loaded a stretcher into an unmarked van. As it had driven away, Dacre had seen gawping faces at several nearby windows.

By now he was tired and feeling sick. He hadn't eaten since

breakfast but wasn't hungry. After lying staring at the ceiling for an hour, he realised he wasn't going to settle and rose to stand at the window. The curtains were wide open, it was dark and windy, and the trees in the distance were swaying. It was some weeks since he had been affected by heights, but now the lamp posts began to spiral round like giant corkscrews, and the ground and buildings wavered. Holding onto the window ledge, he tried to steady himself. He closed his eyes and lowered himself back onto the bed. He had to get out.

***

Dacre put two ten-pence pieces in the call box when the pips stopped. "Hello. Can I speak to Isla, please?"

A woman answered, "And to whom am I talking if you don't mind?"

"It's Gordon, is she in?"

"Isla! There's a boy on the phone for you. Hurry! He's in a telephone box." The phone was put down noisily, and after a pause, Dacre heard soft footsteps.

"Hello?"

"It's me, I'm sorry, I wanted to speak to you."

"Dacre? Is that you? Oh, I'm glad you called, how are you, what have you been doing?" Isla's breezy chatter was a tonic, but he had to tell her what had happened.

***

Sunday

Isla ran to Dacre and hugged him on the platform. "Oh, Dacre, I'm sorry I was away. God, you look awful! You shouldn't have got up so early, I told you I'd see you at Hillhead. Have you been waiting long?"

"I'm fine ... sorry ... I only just got here. The buses don't run the same on Sundays." He didn't want to tell her he had been sitting in the station for two hours, after walking aimlessly for much of the night.

Isla had caught an early morning train back from Waverley. Her mother had excused her from visiting her grandmother again and driven her to catch the early train. On the bus back to Hillhead, she held Dacre's hand tightly as he related the story again. "It's so awful! Why did he do it? Was he so ill? It's so awful." She began crying and he squeezed her hand back, unable to reply. They were silent until the bus turned through the main gates of Hillhead.

"I can't go back to my room, I'm sorry."

"We'll go to mine. Have you eaten anything?"

"Nothing since yesterday morning. I tried a biscuit but I just felt sick."

Isla's mother had given her a fruit cake and when they reached her room, she cut him a slice with a knife she'd taken from the dining room. Dacre managed to eat it slowly while going over the previous day's events, jumping back and forth between the police interviews and the discovery of Miles's body. Adrenaline-fuelled, he rose and paced, wearing a path round Isla's little room as he repeated ever more pressured accounts of his Saturday. Eventually, he sagged on the edge of her bed, red-eyed but tearless, and she helped him drink tea until he fell asleep lying across her bed.

Her alarm clock said two am when Dacre stirred, disorientated and mumbling blearily, "Where? Isla? Why are you sitting there?"

"Shhh. It's okay, I let you sleep. I couldn't move you anyway; you've been flat out since about tea-time." She was at her desk in near darkness, the lamp turned towards the wall. "I've managed to read up for next week's English Lit. Tutorial."

"I'd better get back," said Dacre, sitting up and stretching.

"If you're sure? I'll come with you."

"No, you'd have to walk back alone. I'll be fine."

As he approached Esslemont he saw lights on in Spiny's room. His room door was wedged open when Dacre entered the flat. "Christ! I heard what happened. What the fuck?"

Dacre was glad not to be alone, and they talked. Spiny said he wasn't going to be able to sleep and insisted on opening some lagers. After a few cans, Dacre was drowsy again and managed to go into his room, without looking at the taped-up door opposite.

Chapter 21

Dacre's acrophobia resurfaced after Miles's death. He had been sure hypnosis had caused Miles's deterioration and suicide and he immediately stopped self-treating. Climbing stairs became more and more challenging, and several times the vertigo was so bad he nearly vomited in the library. His broken sleep was marred by the return of awful, vertiginous nightmares. Again and again, he would fall endlessly to his death before waking with a vivid image of Miles's blue face screaming silently to him through plastic. He began to realise he faced a choice.

It's either the heights thing with the crazy half-memories or I let hypnosis fuck with my head until I top myself like Miles.

He knew he had been moody with Isla, and his old fear returned she would go off him or find someone normal. One evening he went to her room earlier than usual determined to apologise and explain how bad he was feeling. He'd told himself that if she chucked him at least that would be one less thing to worry about. When she opened her door to him, she had just been for a bath and seemed surprised to see him. He wasn't sure if she was pleased.

"Shut the door, please, I'm half-dressed."

"Sorry, it's just ... can I talk to you? I'm sorry. I'm—" He kicked the door closed behind him and stood looking at the carpet. "I feel hellish about Miles. I didn't even go and see him once. After he taught me the hypnosis I mean. I just got on with it. I was supposed to try to help him. Now the hypnosis has killed him." He was breathless after hurrying up to her room. "Sorry, I mean it's messing me up. Help me." She said nothing and he went on trying to explain that his guilt over Miles was made even worse by his dilemma that if he didn't restart hypnosis his life would be hellish and if he did the remedy might make him kill himself.

He was surprised at Isla's blurted reply. "Oh, please just

start the hypnosis again. You were so much better! I have hardly seen you smile since it happened, and you're even worse with the heights thing. I don't know how to help you but you were better when you were doing it." She was facing away from him, brushing her wet hair at the mirror over the sink. She was crying when she turned and looked at him.

"D'you think it's safe, though? Look what happened to Miles. I can't stop thinking about him trying to distract himself, all that football stuff, the red everywhere, you know. Christ, I thought it was blood when I opened the door! He was so desperate, and I was doing so well—"

"Look. Miles couldn't do it properly. He told you that. It's not your fault, Dacre. It was a therapist he needed because he was more difficult to put into trance. You were good at it. Susceptible, that's what Hartland calls it. That's not your fault." Dacre had forgotten Isla had borrowed Hartland from him. She went on, "If you get the strange dreams back but fix the heights thing, you'll be better overall, surely? And maybe you could look into regression. You know? Work out all that funny stuff about people in a window?"

"It wasn't funny."

"Sorry. But you know what I mean. You can't go on like this. You should *try* to work out the meaning, then maybe the dreams won't bother you."

"I'll think about it."

They lay together for a while on the single bed, silent and still. It felt good and she held him tightly, neither of them aroused. After a while, he raised himself on his elbow. "I'm going to get on with hypnosis and let the dreams happen. Just bear with me if I'm mad."

They kissed and he left to go to his own bed.

***

Isla's willingness to help had given Dacre the push he needed, and hypnotising himself again was surprisingly easy. Like riding a bike, it felt natural to focus, breathe and sink into the conveyor belt his mattress became. Gently down ... down ... peace ... peace ... sleep. The induction script was already an old familiar poem, each line anticipating the next and guiding him down his gentle, meandering slipway to perfect peace. He noticed quickly that the effects of the trance seemed even stronger. He was exhilarated afterwards, ready for anything and joked he could fly let alone cope with heights.

On a Sunday morning, the new Dacre bounded up the Adam Smith stairs after breezily calling "Morning!" to the surprised night porter, who was preparing to go home after his shift.

"Aye, fit like?" was the tired reply.

He knocked on Isla's door until she woke. "What? Who's that?"

"It's me, let me in. We're going for a walk."

Isla eventually opened the door holding her alarm clock and trying to see the time through sleepy eyes. "It's only ten to eight! What—?"

"It's a fine morning, come on, the beach will be magic."

"Back to bed would be better." But Dacre won, and after pulling on her jeans and a sweatshirt, Isla pushed her feet into clogs.

"You'd be better putting on your baseball boots for the beach."

"My god! *You're* organising *me*. That's a change!"

As the two walked on the cobbles of Brig o' Balgownie, Dacre jumped up onto the parapet of the old stone bridge and walked across in the early morning sunshine as if he was unaware of the long drop to the deep, dark water of the River Don. Isla stopped and stared, amazed at the change in her boyfriend. They missed breakfast and after their walk, Dacre bought crisps and chocolate digestives. They had coffee back in Esslemont until Dacre decided it was time to study. He wanted to go over his whole year's botany in preparation for the degree exam.

Things continued to go well for Dacre, and if he kept up his nightly routine he found he could top himself up in just five minutes each morning. There were very few falling dreams, and in his positive frame of mind, he almost welcomed the re-runs of what he called half-memories of the obscure but familiar couple in the window. Hartland knew a thing or two, he told himself. Ego-strengthening should be taught in schools.

The pair in the dream emerged more clearly as the re-runs continued, and Dacre came to enjoy seeing the embracing couple emerge from obscurity. After all, he was beginning to suspect they were his parents.

***

Paddling in the warm surf, he turned to wade a little deeper. He floated up to walk on the water which evaporated into a fluffy, spongy cloud. The cloud melted into mist and he peered through as it dispersed. Far below him, a door swung open on a homely room. A woman was sitting up in bed, wrapped in a sheet. Before his eyes misted over, he saw someone writhing under moving blankets beside her.

Dacre woke abruptly, his duvet askew and his heaving chest bare. His ears were pounding and beads of sweat moistened his brow. The drawn curtains of his room came into focus, a corner of his desk cutting a dark triangle against the mustard fabric. Reality slowly dawned and his fists slowly unclenched and his palpitations slowed.

This had been a new dream, but just like the embracing couple in the window, the two protagonists had faded into frustrating obscurity. Just out of reach.

***

Dacre had a bad day. He missed the crucial slide in the lecture, and made just a few meaningless notes on his pad. His mind would drift back to last night's new dream, but it faded into a little less detail in each version he tried to replay to himself. It had to have been the same couple, he told himself, but something was very different about them. Something which made him uncomfortable. Something he shouldn't be thinking about, but which disturbed him and preoccupied his thoughts.

He couldn't bring himself to explain his disquiet to Isla. He'd mentioned to her a few nights ago that he had been dreaming about seeing his parents embracing, and they had both laughed about it. Now, after he had picked at a rubbery dollop of macaroni cheese on his plate, not edible even under a sea of ketchup, he excused himself, standing up languidly from the long table in the Hillhead dining room.

"I'm not feeling too good tonight. I might go and just lie down."

Isla looked up from her plate, a sliver of lettuce at the corner of her mouth. "I thought you were a bit quiet. Headache?"

"Something like that." He was walking away but turned briefly. "See you tomorrow."

"No goodnight kiss later?" He smiled wanly and was gone.

An hour later, Dacre was back in the Central Building with two twenty-pence coins. He dialled the number. Waiting for her to answer he rehearsed his question again. 'Mum, when I was wee did I come into your room a lot when you and Dad were in bed?'

"Hello." His dad never answered the phone, and Dacre's throat dried.

"Hello ... it's me." He could hear himself croaking, and his anxiety slithered up the middle of his back.

"Oh. Run out of money?"

"No, I just ... where's Mum?"

"She's got a migraine." Dacre knew his dad hated using the phone.

"Oh, right. How are you? Where were you working today?" It was all he could think of to say to his father.

"What? Usual places. Dunfermline, then Perth, had to pick stuff up from the old lock-up. Why?"

"It doesn't matter, just chatting." Dacre felt the familiar awkwardness of talking to his dad. This was more than they had said directly to each other for years. His mum usually did the talking. "Tell Mum I'll call again as usual."

"As usual?"

***

During the night he briefly woke in a serene daze to a fading echo of his mother's comforting voice. She had risen from the bed and shepherded him back to his room. The mound under the blankets was surely his dad. But when he drifted back to sleep, he was under the high walls of a prison, and in his hands was an ice-cold, severed hand. A cartoon image of a girl floating in water imprinted itself on his mind, a zigzag line graphically indicating where her missing hand should be.

***

"Feeling better this morning? I missed you last night."

Dacre managed to force a smile for Isla. He swallowed his toast and drained his teacup before speaking. "Aye, well, no, not really. A bit better, but, ach I canny really tell you here, I don't know what's going on with me."

"'Ach I canny tell you?' What sort of a way is that to speak to me? I'm a posh girl, remember!"

Cheered a little by Isla's easy humour and friendly teasing, Dacre relaxed and agreed to meet her after morning lectures. He had decided to dismiss the latest nightmare, and by the time they met again he had settled himself enough to tell her he had recognised his mother in the dream.

"It's basically the same dreams as before ... well ... different but the same two people ... and it's definitely my mum and it's got to be my dad." Isla listened as he told her about the couple in bed and that his mum had spoken to him. "I'm not going to let it bother me any more. And I'm never going to mention dreams again."

"Yeah? That'll be right!" She grinned and shook her head.

"Well, one more, but it's just too mad. A dead body, and a frozen hand, weird stuff."

"That's poor Miles again, his hand when it fell out of the wardrobe against your leg." He didn't tell her the hand was small like a girl's, or of the bloody bones protruding. Suddenly distracted, Isla stood up quickly, gathering her bag of notes and leaving some of her fruit-slice uneaten. "God! I forgot, I'm supposed to meet my history tutor at one o'clock, she wants to talk about my last essay. Sorry, I need to go. I'm glad the dreams are getting better." She waved and rushed out.

***

"You're still upset by dreams, aren't you." Isla had left the library to meet him after a day of lectures and they were walking through Seaton Park on the way back to Hillhead. Dacre's plan not to let his dreams bother him hadn't worked, and he now realised his preoccupation must still be showing.

"Sorry. I thought I'd got it all OK. In my head, I mean. I was trying not to say any more. Fucking dreams!" He told her that every night now he heard his mother yelping before the door swung open to reveal her in bed with the obscured figure beside her. "It's like a short scream. I still don't know if it's my dad in the dream but now I almost hope it isn't."

"You mean in bed with your mum? Oh, no! I didn't realise that's what you were worried about." Isla was quiet and they walked on.

Eventually, Dacre said, "I'm sorry, I'm not a nutter, I'll get this sorted out."

She smiled sympathetically but they said nothing else about it. He knew she was revising hard for degree exams, and he was trying to do the same. Later that evening, though, Isla returned to the subject. "D'you think your mum might have been yelping with pleasure? I mean ..." Her words trailed off and he saw her face redden deeply.

"Oh, Christ! No! Oh jeez." He smirked and squirmed and they both cracked into laughter. Dacre said, "It really *had* better be my dad then!"

"But really, you need to work this through. Understand the dreams, I mean, or they'll drive you mad."

"Madder."

"I mean it. Do the regression thing. The ego-strengthening went well, you're good at hypnotising yourself."

Dacre could tell she had been giving it a lot of thought but worried she wouldn't put up with him much longer. He desperately wanted to try regression, but he was terrified of finding out something he didn't want to know. And he hadn't told Isla the awful dreams about dead girls. Why did he know about them, and what if regression proved he knew more? Hartland made it clear that regression was only for experienced therapists and might not be safe. What if he made himself worse, and just before his exams?

Isla was persistent. "You've got to do something. We can't go on like this. Listen, I'm sorry but I'm going to read some more history, then I'm going to bed."

Whether or not Isla was giving him an ultimatum he didn't know, but she'd brought him to a decision. He would lose her if he didn't sort himself out and answer the questions in his dreams, and the only way was through self-regression. He had no idea how to start but chance came to his assistance that night.

***

He needed to read some more revision notes before bed. Unable to concentrate, he blamed hunger and sauntered along to the kitchen to check the cupboards in case a flatmate had left some food. Passing Miles's door was becoming easier now the police tape had gone. It had remained locked since being emptied and cleaned on the Monday after his death.

It was the first time he had been alone in the flat in the four weeks since Miles's death. In the immediate aftermath, they had sat every night making toast under the grill or eating packets of biscuits. It was better than going to bed. None of them had attended Miles's funeral. Miles's mother had not wished to see her son's room, and the boys were told she had returned south quickly after identifying his body. They'd discussed sending flowers but none of them knew how to, and the card Spiny had bought was still lying on the kitchen windowsill. Miles's shyness meant none of them knew his address. Gradually, their old routines had returned. Dacre hadn't told Spiny or David that he felt especially guilty.

Tonight, Dacre was out of luck: there was no food in any cupboards and only some out-of-date milk in the fridge. He stood for a moment at the kitchen window and looked out into the late May gloaming. There were lights on in some bedrooms in the other blocks. He could see clearly into some and below him, to his left, a boy and girl appeared to be shouting at each other. He found he was unable to look away. Somehow he felt drawn into their presence. The girl suddenly turned and pulled the curtains shut, but the scene remained imprinted on Dacre's vision. He shook himself awake and realised he had almost been in a trance. Back in his room, he still couldn't concentrate on botany and went to bed, two deep breaths sinking him rapidly into a deep trance. Framed by the window, a vivid picture of the arguing couple was imprinted on the back of his eyelids.

The following morning, Dacre surfaced to welcome contentment. Wispy curtains had parted to reveal the two familiar figures in his old dream. His mum faced the window looking up at his dad who held the little paintbrush and the jar of cream. Somehow it all made sense. Dressing, he realised his left wrist was aching.

***

"You're chipper this morning."

"Chipper?"

"Bright and cheery. My dad says it. You've not been like this in the morning for ages." Isla was beaming at him over her cereal.

"I feel good." He leant forward and spoke softly so the students next to him wouldn't hear. "I know who they are, in the dreams. I saw them. I found a way of regression, by accident. It worked, and they're getting clearer, and I feel OK about them. Funny thing is, I think it's got something to do with my broken arm. It was aching like mad when I woke up. Weird."

Chapter 22

June 1977

"Mmmmm—" Isla stretched luxuriously and pulled herself out of Dacre's arms. She handed him his jeans. "I've done enough revising tonight, and I'm just going to sleep. Last exams tomorrow! You should go back and just go to bed as well. There's no point staying up all night, you must have done enough by now."

"Aye, you're right, but it's just ... well ... chemistry's my weakest subject, and—"

"Stop it, you'll need some sleep. I'm going to bed. See you at breakfast." She kissed him once more before almost pushing him out of the door. On the way across the dry grass towards Esslemont, Dacre decided to set his alarm earlier and do his extra reading first thing, so it would all be fresh in his mind.

His nightly routine now included a few minutes staring down out of his window at a well-lit ground floor window. There were always plenty to choose from. He would then close the curtains and lie back luxuriously on his bed, already on the way to a deep and pleasant trance. The same scenes would play, his parents in bed and or embracing with the jar of cream, and sometimes the scenes played together. His dad was always obscured, either by the riffling pale curtain or under the blankets, but the misty pictures were clearing into focus. He knew his dad's face would soon sharpen. He had decided the yelp of pain he had heard was his own, as he fell and broke his wrist.

He lay yawning, wondering if he should risk going straight to sleep. His mind was full of chemistry, though, and he had been drinking a lot of coffee. After a second trip to the toilet, he opened his curtains, had a good, long look down at a window and was quickly miles away.

***

Aeroplanes zigzagged silently across the sky, multicoloured vapour trails drifting down as confetti on the wheat field he lay in. Peace was rudely interrupted by the phone ringing loudly downstairs.

Why doesn't Mum answer it? Why is it so loud?

He pushed himself up on his elbows, he called out, "Mum! The phone!" Forcing his eyes open showed him the dinging noise came from a vibrating alarm clock beside his bed.

But why's Mum put that there? And why's she down there with —?

Dacre sat bolt upright, his heart pounding and his mouth dry as dust. Struggling to breathe, and with the jangling of the alarm shivering through him, he tried to see in front of him through a sudden snowstorm as his head swam and cold sweat beaded his forehead. He collapsed back onto the bed, his wrist throbbing.

Timeless unconscious hours later, loud knocking on the door rattled him. "Dacre! Dacre! It's me. Wake up! Why weren't you at breakfast?"

Isla's frantic knocking brought him round. He peered at her when he cracked open the door.

"You've slept in! It's quarter past eight! Your exam is at nine, isn't it? Hurry!"

Still dazed, he stood still, staring at Isla. "I know who it was —"

"There's no time. Come on!"

Isla forced him to get dressed and raced him through Seaton Park. All the way, he was mumbling about his mother and Isla was worried. Her exam was at eleven, and she had intended to revise for an hour before heading off, but when Dacre hadn't turned up at breakfast, she thought he must have slept in after studying late. She was surprised at how dazed and confused he seemed, but she knew he had to get to his exam.

"Come on, and stop going on about your mum! She can't

help you." Isla was laughing nervously now, and Dacre seemed to wake up as they reached the top of the steep path out of the park.

"Oh my god! I've got an exam, what time is it?" He looked through trees trying to see the clock on St Machar's Cathedral.

"It's ten to nine. Hurry, you'll make it."

"It was Bugs in the dream!" Dacre had stopped, and was ashen.

"Oh, Dacre! I don't know what you're talking about. You haven't got bugs. Shut up and come on!"

Somehow, she helped him to make it to the exam, and the now-familiar setting of the exam hall at the Butchart Centre seemed to bring him to himself. Ten minutes into the allotted three hours, he was able to plan how to answer the questions.

***

At lunchtime, Dacre waited for Isla in the Central Ref. until her exam was over. She found him sitting alone near the jukebox. Freebird was blaring and he didn't hear her approach. "How was the exam?" she said cheerily, putting her hand on his shoulder to attract his attention. "Mine was better than I expected."

Dacre looked up at her and made room on the bench seat. "I can barely remember anything about it, but I managed to write loads. The chemistry seemed simple, somehow, almost unimportant, but not hard."

"I'm surprised, the state of you when you eventually woke up. I've never seen you like that."

He interrupted her laughing and pulled her close, though the loud music meant he wouldn't be overheard. "I know who it was. In the dream. It was my mum, but she wasn't with my dad."

"You mean ...?" Isla covered her mouth.

"He was ... they were ... oh Jeezuss ... I—"

The record finished and they sat in silence until Bad Company started, loud enough to drown anything. "Oh, Dacre!

I think I know what you mean."

"The bastard!"

Isla took his hand in hers, "Who was it? With your mum, I mean. Did you know him?"

"Friend of my dad's."

"That's awful. But are you sure?"

Dacre looked up from the floor. "Yes. It's real. I know it is."

"But it's a dream."

"It's real. He was always around when I was wee. Then he just stopped coming. Now I know why. My dad chased him off. And I used to like him! Bastard!"

"What are you going to do?"

"What do you mean? What the fuck do you think I can do?" Isla stood up and walked to the serving counter. When she returned, Dacre stood up. "I'm sorry. Sorry. It's just …"

She sat down with her tray. "You don't need to say any more about it. Get something to eat."

Dacre wandered off to look at the food but came back empty-handed. He sat down, silent and rubbing his wrist. Eventually, he said quietly, "I'm going to tell her I know. About her and that shite Bugsy."

***

Dacre was quiet as they walked back to Hillhead. When they reached the path outside Adam Smith, he didn't seem to know what to do or say.

"Let's forget going for a walk. Let's go to the Kirkgate Bar, then have our last Friday night in the Dungeon until next term."

Dacre looked surprised. It was usually him who prompted trips to the pub. He brightened and Isla smiled. "I thought that would cheer you up."

"Meet you at the bus stop in fifteen minutes." Dacre ran off towards Esslemont. Isla watched him for a moment, shook her head, and turned round to walk to her room, almost bumping into a girl carrying two open bottles of wine. They had overtaken her as she staggered along through the Seaton Park. Isla now made room for her to pass, and the girl stopped unsteadily, slurring, "Is this Johnston Hall?"

Isla laughed. "No, Johnston's back in Old Aberdeen."

"I know it is, I live there ..." The girl wandered merrily off, humming to herself. It seemed to be the thing to do when your exams were finished.

The Kirkgate was packed, its bar three deep. After two pints, Dacre had relaxed and was telling Isla animatedly about Bugsy and what he was going to do. He would confront his mother and tell her what he now knew. "But, Dacre, it was a dream. You can't be sure it's—"

"No. One thing I do know ... it *was* real. I know it was."

Isla decided to try to steer away from the subject. "It's my round."

She fought her way to the bar, and by the time she came back with the drinks and two packets of crisps, Dacre was talking to a boy from his botany class. There was general excitement, and most in the bar had finished their exams, or no longer cared about them. The few locals were squeezed at the far end of the bar.

They didn't talk about the dream or Bugsy again until Sunday, both having needed a quiet day to recover on Saturday.

Packed to go home, they met up at breakfast, sad at the prospect of the long summer break. Isla took his hand as they walked back to his room. "Are you *really* going to speak to your mum about it?"

"I don't know. But I know it's real. It's not just a dream. It was the same again last night, but clearer than ever. I was looking out of a window with no glass in it, I was in the house next door to ours, and I could see them in our living room. The paintbrush and jar again. And his arms round her." He didn't mention he had also dreamt again about Perth and the gruesome cartoon.

"But what are you going to say? I think you should be careful."

"God knows."

***

While he packed his bags before his parents arrived to take him home for the summer, Dacre wondered how to confront his mother about her and Bugsy. And he was disturbed that his subconscious had connected dismembered girls with two places his father had been. He was dreading going home.

Part II

The Inverness Courier

Friday 25th June 1977

MAN FINDS BODY IN TREE

A man from Culloden had a horrific shock yesterday when walking his dog in woods near the Nairn Viaduct. Alec Tainsh, 63, came across a body hanging in a tree.

"I thought it was an old sack, but then I saw a hand. I haven't seen anything like that since the war," said Mr Tainsh, a former Corporal in the Seaforth Highlanders.

Inverness Police released a statement: "Incomplete human remains have been found between Culloden Moor and Dalroy. It appears the deceased became entangled in tree branches overhanging a burn and was left hanging there when the recent flash floods in the local burns receded. A search of the area is underway to locate the lower right leg which appears to have been removed, possibly by animal activity. The local doctor who confirmed life extinct estimated the death may have occurred two to four weeks ago. A full post-mortem is underway."

Chapter 23

1977

Having changed out of his uniform at the end of his shift, PC Craig Masson sat upstairs on the bus into town. After finishing probationary training at Tulliallan Police College, Masson had thought the Police National Computer was the key to his future. Now after nine months at Oxgangs Police Station, he had realised his crusty older colleagues were less convinced. He'd tried again that afternoon.

"But don't you see, Sarge, the PNC will mean we can catch criminals from Glasgow. Even Fife!"

Wardrop had looked up from his *Evening News* shaking his head. "Change the record, son. You're not at Tulliallan now. It doesn't matter how much you go on about your bloody computers, they'll never catch on."

The bus seemed even slower than usual, and by the time he reached Tollcross he was tired and hungry.

"Where've you been, Luggy? I've been here twenty minutes." Phil Moffat was good-natured as usual, grinning at him over his pint.

"Bus was slow as hell again. I can't wait to get a car."

"It's OK for you, on your big polis pay!"

"You get plenty of tips from the tourists, and it's the Festival in a few months. And you get to play Space Invaders when it's quiet."

"I'm fed up with that. I've been trying to write a program for stock control, and I'm trying to persuade the bar manager to get a digital cash register."

When he met up with Phil every Thursday, it was never long before their conversation turned to computers. They'd both become absorbed in basic programming at Napier College and they spoke the same language.

"So you still haven't got far with the PNC?" said Phil as he sat down with Masson's pint and tomato sauce crisps. They had both read papers on the national network linking all police forces in the UK when it was introduced in 1974.

Tearing the crisps open, Masson said, "Bloody dinosaurs're just not interested. I thought my job was all going to be databases and solving crimes at a desk, but I never even see a keyboard. There's one computer in the corner of the office and it's never booted up. I don't think they know how to."

"You'll be jealous of Jack when I tell you what he's doing, then."

"Jack? I haven't heard from him since we left Tulliallan. Have you seen him?"

"Aye, I ran into him last weekend when I was visiting my parents. He's in Dundee, and guess what? He's working on the PNC. He says they use it all the time in Tayside."

"Lucky bugger! How come he landed on his feet again?"

"He wants to meet up. I know I'm not polis like you two, but I thought the three of us could play about with ideas, networks and stuff. Maybe a job for me'll come up sometime?"

The two friends talked on and agreed it would be good to meet regularly with Jack, and for all three to keep in touch about their ideas by post and phone. Masson was excited by the thought of actually using the PNC if the police ever entered the computer age.

Chapter 24

June 1977

"What's wrong with you? Are you hungover?"

Dacre grunted a denial towards the car window and closed his eyes.

"There's something wrong. Are you ill?" His mother's probing questions dried up by the time they were past Montrose. His dad was distracted by the novelty of FM radio, and couldn't conceal his envy of Charlie Younson who had lent him his car again.

In the evening Dacre was no less moody. He mumbled thanks for the roast dinner and left much of it uneaten. The three sat watching a nature programme on TV, in silence. By half-past nine Dacre made his escape to bed.

"He wasn't much company." Alun put his newspaper down and stood up to reach over to the TV. Pressing the channel button he muttered, "We missed most of *The Palladium*. What he wanted to watch that rubbish for I don't know. Thinks he's too clever for the rest of us, he does."

"I don't think he was listening anyway." Elinor lowered her voice. "Give him a break. I think he might've broken up with his girlfriend."

"Girlfriend?"

"Haven't you spoken to him at all? You never pay any attention."

"Shut up. I've told you before." Elinor left and went to bed herself.

At the end of his first week at home, Dacre was still ignoring his mother. From her sympathetic attempts at conversation when he had emerged for toilet breaks or to make himself coffee, he could tell she knew he was upset, but she seemed to have no idea she was the focus of his contempt. She seemed to appear whenever his bedroom door opened, and he caught her eye once as he clicked down the telephone. He knew she had been trying to listen to his call, and before disappearing into his curtained room he had thrown a glare at her, hoping she couldn't see the tears wetting his cheeks.

"Oh, Gordon, can I—?" He closed the door quietly, ignoring her appeal.

***

Speaking to Isla had helped but Dacre could tell she didn't know what to say. He thought she had been near tears herself, and he was beginning to worry that over the long summer she would lose patience with him if he didn't find the courage to confront his mother. Or she might be lured away from her weak and pathetic country bumpkin boyfriend.

He lay for hours in silence, staring at the toys and treasures of his childhood and yearning for Aberdeen. Hypnosis was no help ... he couldn't concentrate on his induction. At night he roiled and sweated for what felt like hours, and if he did give up and switch on the bedside lamp something about his room made him uneasy. The distorted cartoon shadows thrown on the wall by the old Donald Duck shade hadn't scared him since he was tiny, and he didn't care that his parents had taken his Airfix models down. His eyes kept returning to the lampshade until one night he felt a thump in his chest as it dawned on him ... Uncle Bugs had given him that lampshade one Christmas. He sat up, switched the light off angrily, and held his head. Tears stung his eyes. After a while, he lay on his side with his legs drawn up, his fists tightly clenched. *That bastard with my mother!*

If sleep did overtake him the nightmares would roll, day or night. Every screening was more vivid, and a theme of building sites, diggers and boyhood games was cruelly terminated by the same shocking climax. And every time his mother's affair was more real.

***

April 1967

"Geronimoooo!" Steven disappeared out of the window. It was Dacre's turn, and he stepped from joist to joist over the void below. The Geronimo house was being built back to back with Dacre's home, which added to the daring excitement. The pile of sand below them was just outside the fence, but they knew they would be briefly visible to his mum as they launched themselves like commandos. It was the best game the three boys had come up with that Easter holiday, and each jump meant conquering an obstacle course of ladders and skinned knees to reach the unglazed upstairs window.

"Go on! Jump! I want my turn." But Dacre had frozen, staring at two embracing figures over the fence. Tommy impatiently pushed him and he toppled over the window ledge, his foot catching on a ridge of rough, hard mortar. He swung sideways, limbs flailing as the sand heap moved out of reach and hard, stony ground raced up at him. Impact. Blackness.

***

Drenched in sweat and dry of mouth, his drumming heart damped all sound and his left wrist ached. Dacre was filled with horror. Images flashed on the screen of his eyelids. The bedroom; a rainy window; his mother turning quickly away; another figure beside her, materialising as Bugsy holding a little paintbrush and a jar of beige paint. Dreamy fog clouded over to obscure the figures before his mother emerged from the mirk, now sitting up in bed. A figure scuffled under the bedclothes beside her.

Wrenched again from wretched sleep, he knew he had to confront her. Gradually his dreams had revealed his fall and broken wrist were results of witnessing her affair with his 'uncle'.

He now recalled it had been Bugsy who took him to the cottage hospital in his van, not his dad. A pillow in a yellow pillowcase, taken from his parents' bed ... the marital bed, he now thought with fury ... had been under his twisted arm on the van's bench seat. The gear stick had vibrated against his right thigh. His mother must have followed once his father had come home—he now remembered them arriving just before the black rubber mask had been placed over his nose and mouth. He had been gassed to sleep to have his bones straightened.

He was beginning to make sense of things. He knew from Hartland that extreme emotional shock could cause memory loss, the brain's way of coping. He now knew there had been no concussion, and his child brain had simply refused to accept what he had seen. Hypnosis had now re-exposed to him what his mother had done.

His dad had fallen for her story and rushed home to his injured son, but had later discovered the affair somehow, and sent Bugsy packing. Dacre now hated Bugsy Redbond and the pathetic gifts he had brought which he could see now were barely-disguised advances on his mother. He now understood his morose father's cool and dismissive treatment was just what his mother deserved. She had betrayed his dad, and let her son grow up believing his fall and injury were behind his parents' icy, unhappy relationship. The bitch.

Chapter 25

Spake returned to the bar stool. "For fuck's sake! We've got to go tomorrow. If we don't get off our arses, we won't get any contracts. It's the end of June, we need to—"

"I know: 'Get Up Them Fucking Dreels!'" Dacre finally managed a smile. For last year's roguing season they had been joined by Brian and Donald, two friends of Spake's older brother. Brian had decided he was the gaffer.

Dacre had finally left his room when Spake had come looking for him. Seeing his friend lifted his clouds a little, and he watched Spake returning with more lager. "Fuck's been wrong with you, anyway? You wouldn't even come to the phone. Pining or something?"

"Something like that." Dacre was keen to change the subject. "Let's go and speak to that fool Harrison first, then out to Burnturk. It's a long cycle but we need to get on with it."

Spake grinned. "We don't need to cycle. My mum says I can take her car this year. All season. She's off work all summer."

"Brilliant! We can organise our own stuff and keep all the spondoolies between the two of us."

They had joined up with the older boys last year because Donald had a car. The year before they'd had to ask Spake's mum to drive them round the farms to make contracts. Mrs Baker taught at the agricultural college and had been glad to help her son and his friend negotiate with wily farmers. But they'd then had to cycle to the fields each day, and the use of a car would help them earn much more. They looked forward to working as a pair and enthusiastically spent the evening making plans, facilitated by Elinor's willingly donated tenner.

Guilty bitch!

***

Gradually his anger focused on Bugsy, and Elinor's endless patience with his moods and silences made confronting her even more difficult. He could tell his parents continued to tolerate each other, and began to understand his mother's cowed deference. He admired his father's forgiveness, but Alun still didn't pay much attention to him, and there was still tension.

He made himself discuss things with Spake one sunny lunchtime. They were eating their piece in the end rigg, lying on the dry earth in the shade of a hawthorn hedge. Sparrows were taking dust baths.

"Christ, that's hellish! I thought there was something wrong with you. Are you sure?"

"Yeah. The dreams are so realistic and they're the same every time, always the same stuff going on, kind of mixed up. In one the bastard's cuddling her and in the other he's fucking hiding in the bed. Bastard!" He threw the remainder of his sandwich at the hedge, scattering the sparrows. It hung on the hawthorn, dripping salad cream. "It's the hypnosis. I reckon I have regressed myself and got to the truth, or at least what I had forgotten, 'cos I don't think anyone told any lies, they just didn't tell me what happened."

"But do you reckon your dad knows, I mean about her being with him?"

"He's got to. It explains a lot. Bugsy suddenly disappeared and I think my dad must've warned him off."

"Bastard. Your dad should've battered him."

It was good to tell someone else other than Isla, and telling Spake was letting him pour out some of his fury. He stood up and kicked a dry ridge of mud left by a tractor tyre, baked hard in the dry summer. Dust and dry earth showered over Spake and his lunch.

"Fuck's sake, Dacre! My fuckin' piece!"

Dacre continued stomping along the end rigg. "Bastard! Bastard! Fucking shite! I've been guilty for years thinking it was me breaking my wrist made my dad a miserable bastard. They argued all the time after it happened, and I thought it was me. But he was angry at her, the fucking cow!"

Spake scraped some of the dirt from his sandwich with his filthy hands, and ate it anyway, spitting out grit. "At least your parents stayed together. It must have been hard for your dad."

The afternoon passed slowly, and both were quiet bar the usual moaning about the heavy sack, and Spake shouting in disgust when his hand sank into the mush of a rotted seed tuber.

"Ach! Fuck! That's honkin'!"

In the Mini on the way back, Dacre appeared to have cheered a little. "We did a good fourteen acres today."

Spake looked straight ahead. "Are you going to tell your mum you know? About ... well ... you know? Or just go on pretending you don't know?"

The silence resumed until Dacre turned to face him and said, "I've been trying to put it off, but I've fucking got to. It's driving me nuts letting her get away with it. It's just how do I do it?" There was more silence, then, "I want to get that bastard Redbond. It's all I've been thinking about for days. But, somehow I sort of owe it to my dad to have it out with my mother first."

"Let's get pissed tonight."

The Arms was full of youngsters that night, and they went to The Royal instead. On the way, they talked about tennis. Dacre was for Jimmy Connors while Spake was hoping Borg would win Wimbledon.

"Connors's such a child. He won it last year but he's just being a right tosser this year. Borg's just so cool."

"Connors is moody, but just 'cos he's determined." Dacre tended to side with an underdog, especially if the press disapproved, and Connors had made himself unpopular by ignoring the Wimbledon protocol. Dacre had already had a good argument with his father about it.

As they walked, Dacre thought about his friendship with Spake. "Remember 'Mamzelle', Spake?"

"How the fuck could I forget a body like that? And those

stockings and suspenders!"

"You imagined that, Spake."

The visiting Mademoiselle, a young assistant French teacher whose exotic accent made her Mamzelle, had been a source of adolescent fantasy and desire to the boys. Present for one term, the buxom young student had one day mistakenly referred to S. Baker as 'Sbaker'. Her intense blushing at the ensuing laughter and her gallic apologies to Steven had filled him with lusty pride. He had willingly accepted his new nickname.

The Royal was quieter. "You get a more mature punter in here," Spake said, surveying the old men in the corner and the scattered groups of boys, most of whom they had been at school with. "Hiya Tich!" he called towards a young man barely five feet tall, who was two years older than them. He wore an oily, green boiler suit with double turn-ups, and pulled a packet of Kensitas from his breast pocket as he dropped a butt on the bar floor. Lighting his next cigarette, he turned away.

"Fuck off, we don't need snobs in here."

"You'll stunt your growth, Tich." Spake grinned at Dacre and pulled a fiver from his back pocket. "Heavy?"

"Aye, the lager's pish in here."

"Everything's pish in here, but at least there are real people."

Dacre grasped the money to head for the bar, and grinning over his shoulder, said, "Aye, Spake, and Edinburgh's not full of posers, I suppose?"

"As if 'Aiberdeen's' any better! Get the bloody bevvy."

Dacre was glad to be out with Spake instead of confronting his mother.

***

July 1977

Dacre had still not tackled his mother about Bugsy Redbond

when on Saturday he travelled to visit Isla, the first time he had seen her in three weeks. The journey was easy this time and Isla met him at Waverley. She had taken a job in a hotel near her home where her father knew the owner. She had to work mornings cleaning rooms and evenings waiting on tables. This had meant their phone calls had been limited to once or twice a week.

"Oh, it's lovely to see you! I've taken the whole weekend off." She hugged him tightly.

"Aye, it's been a while." She took his hand and walked him excitedly up out of the station into the sunlight. As they walked along past the Scott monument, she chatted away about work, her friends, and her mum's change of car.

"Do you like my new outfit?" she asked as they passed the steps of the National Gallery. Pulling away from him and standing expectantly for him to appraise her, she pouted extravagantly. Posing with one arm crooked against her hip and the other reaching out to him, she waited for his approval.

"Aye, nice," he responded, turning to go. "Come on, I want to go to Bruce's."

Isla caught up with him and took his hand. "What's wrong? I thought we had all day."

"Aye, I suppose." They walked on in silence. A man had sold packets of seed to some children who were now feeding pigeons nearby. Dacre kicked angrily at a group of the birds on the cobbles in front of him, scattering them in a flapping rammy until they regathered quickly to peck more seed.

"Dacre!" Isla let go of him. She stopped, and when he turned she stood facing away from him.

"I … em … don't want bird shit on my shoes," he mumbled. Isla turned, crying, and said something he couldn't hear over the traffic noise, the birds' warbling and the children's babble. "What?" he asked, impatiently.

Isla marched past him and screamed, "You have dried mud all over your fucking boots!" He had rarely heard her swear before.

He caught up with her at the traffic lights. "Sorry, I should've —"

"What's wrong with you! You've been horrible. Why don't you talk to me?"

"Can't you just talk to your new boyfriend instead? What is he, a barman? A waiter?"

The people around them started crossing the road. "That poor girl shouldn't have to put up with a grubby, common brute like that," a woman wearing tweed said to her paisley-patterned companion.

Isla reacted quickly. "I heard that! Keep out of it, you awful, snobby witch!" Dacre stood speechless, as Isla flushed, looking furious, embarrassed and drying her eyes. They walked back from the pavement, up the steps between the ionic pillars fronting the gallery.

"What do you mean?" Isla hissed. "How dare you? New boyfriend? What?"

Dacre stared at the ground. "I'm sorry, it's just—"

Isla wasn't stopping, though, and when she glared at him he had to look at the ground. "We're not all like your mother! You need to think before you accuse me." Dacre had nothing to say. He looked up at last, and Isla was staring at the pillar he was leaning against, tracing her fingernail down the fluted sandstone. "Did you ask your mum about it?"

"Not yet."

"Well, don't take it out on me!" She walked off and strode back to the traffic lights, crossed and stopped on the other side, looking into a shop window. Dacre followed with the next change of the lights and stood beside her. Isla continued to stare at the shop display. Eventually, she said, "I don't want a new boyfriend, but if you say that sort of thing again—" Taking his hand, she led him up Hanover Street and down the steps into Milne's. "Buy me a drink. I've worked every day for nearly three weeks. I thought I was going to enjoy today!"

As he returned from the bar with a pint for himself and vodka and lime for Isla, she managed to smile, wiping her eyes dry in the shady booth. "What a start!" she sighed. "And I haven't had a vodka and lime since school discos."

He grinned sheepishly. "I'll need to face it, and speak to Mum."

"I know. You've been a nightmare. I was wrong; you were more fun when you couldn't climb stairs!"

"I'm sorry—"

"Shut up. Don't say anything else. We've only got this afternoon."

Dacre looked at her over his pint as he took a draught.

"But, yes. Face it. Sort it out. *Please*, Dacre!"

On his way back towards Auchmoor, Dacre was deflated. He was disappointed in himself for his outburst and disconcerted by Isla's quietness. They had separated for a short while when he had been engrossed in the records in Bruce's. When they met up later outside Marks and Spencer she was distant, and their chat was stilted until she mentioned "I just met your aunt."

"Aunty Janet? How?" Dacre was confused.

"She was in M & S with Campbell. I didn't know he was your cousin." Hairs stiffened on Dacre's neck and his ears pounded. "It turns out we've been neighbours for years. They live just a few streets away in Colinton. See? We have more in common than you think!"

Dacre became even more threatened when she went on to explain that she had met Campbell a few weeks previously. She had been out for a drink after work with one of the other waitresses and bumped into an old school friend who was on a date with Campbell. He'd looked familiar and she wondered if she had met him before when she'd been at school. When he'd spoken of Aberdeen, she realised she had seen him around Kings College.

"He's doing law. Did you know he was in Aberdeen? You

never told me."

He'd wanted to say Campbell was a snobby, speccy git. "I didn't think to mention him. I hardly know him." When he heard that Janet had whispered to Isla that Campbell had split up from his girlfriend, Dacre felt sick with fear.

"And your aunt knows my mum," she'd continued, "it's a small place, really, Edinburgh. You should have told me your cousin was in Aberdeen. We could all get together next term." Dacre's mood slid from then on and he'd struggled to stop himself lashing out again. As they parted at the station, Isla had hugged him and kissed him lightly. "You will phone me, won't you? We've hardly spoken all holiday."

His journey home was miserable, but he did smile ruefully when the train pulled out of Aberdour and he realised he hadn't noticed crossing the Forth Bridge. His fear of losing Isla, worst of all to bloody Campbell, was worse than his fear of heights had ever been. He just knew bloody Janet was trying to get Isla and Campbell together.

'We're not all like your mother!' Isla had said.

How do I fuckin' know that?

On the bus from Kirkcaldy, he decided if he didn't tackle his mother, Isla would ditch him for someone else. If she hadn't already.

He said out loud, "Yes. Face it. Sort it out." A woman across the aisle looked at him before gathering her bags and moving to another seat.

Chapter 26

Anticipating the confrontation was sickening him. He climbed to the toilet, then back down heading to the kitchen. For once it wasn't last night's beer that dried his mouth. As he reached the foot of the stairs, the Sunday Post dropped onto the doormat. He'd forgotten it was Sunday. His father would be at home and never did anything on Sunday except read the *Post*. Dacre smiled as he returned to his bed with a dimple glass full of water. He could put off facing her again.

Normally Elinor got up early to start housework and Dacre would angrily pull the blankets up over his head. This morning, though, it was Alun who clattered around before eight o'clock. He heard him make tea, but only silence from his mother. Assuming Alun would take tea upstairs, Dacre marvelled again that his father could forgive her. But then steps thudded along the short hallway and the door slammed. The rear van door creaked and a bag of tools crashed onto the metal floor before the van started up and pulled away. Dacre threw the covers off and lay back. The ceiling was bisected by the bare wire his plastic aeroplanes used to hang from.

Oh god. He's gone out.

He toyed with leaving it until another time until the thoughts of Isla with Campbell stung him again. He sat up, deafened by his pounding heart.

Face it!

In the kitchen, he lifted the kettle by its worn Bakelite handle, refilled it and clicked it on at the wall. He felt a shiver as he waited for it to boil and remembered how his comical reflection in the chrome pot used to scare him. The house felt cold, and when he parted the kitchen curtains the back garden was dull under a grey and threatening sky. He wandered into the living room ... the lounge, his mother now called it. (*Fucking Aunty Janet!*) The bulb was gone in the big light and he pulled the brown curtains open. His dad's van really had gone.

Fuck.

The lump in his throat was making him sick.

Face it!

He had spent most of the night mentally writing his script and learning his lines, but this wasn't in the plan. Instead of marching into the kitchen to give it to his mother straight, he now found himself sitting alone, waiting nervously for her to get up. At last, there was movement upstairs. He heard the bathroom door, a tap running and the medicine cabinet opening. He had helped Alun build it one summer holiday.

At last. Oh god. Fuck.

Opening the living room door quietly he looked up just in time to see the back of Elinor's pink quilted dressing gown disappear back into the bedroom, the door closing quickly. He stood waiting at the foot of the stairs holding on to the handrail. He thought he was going to vomit. He heard no more, and eventually pulled himself up to the landing.

"Mum. I'm making tea."

No sound.

"Mum?"

"Wait a minute. I'll come down."

Back downstairs the kitchen was full of steam and the kettle lid rattling. When Elinor entered the living room she was wearing Janet's old sunglasses. She sniffed. "Hay fever. It's been really bad."

Dacre hadn't noticed her suffering yet this year. When he was a toddler, sometimes the whites of her eyes had been so swollen with clear jelly he had been scared. When he brought the tea in she was dabbing with a handkerchief, and she winced when she gripped the mug, changing hands carefully.

"Hot! Thanks. Nice day yesterday? How was Isla? Did you —?"

"Mum, I can remember my fall. When I broke my arm. I know about you and Bugsy. How could ...?"

Elinor stiffened as he spoke, and putting her tea down on the hearth, she stood up and went out of the kitchen and back upstairs before Dacre could finish. The bedroom door closed sharply. Dacre followed her up and stood outside, unsure what to do, but determined.

"Mum. Mum?" Silence, until he heard sobbing.

"Bitch." He turned and went down to his room. As he lay, he could hear summer rain bouncing noisily on the shed roof. He wished his dad would come back. If she wouldn't talk to him about it, he would tell Alun he knew. He and his dad might get on better then. *Bitch.*

There was no sign of Alun, though, before Elinor knocked at his door and entered, tear-stained. "Gordon, I'm sorry. It wasn't —"

"Shut up. Get out." He stared at the wall beside her.

"Gordon, please, you don't know—"

"I fucking do! I saw you and Bugsy cuddling. That's what made me fall. You—"

"No, Gordon! It wasn't like that." She sniffed and wiped her eyes. He saw she had one of his grandmother's embroidered handkerchiefs.

"Oh, no? I suppose it was just him being friends? Dirty bastard!"

"I'm sorry, Gordon, you've got it wrong. Don't tell your dad. He'll—"

"Fuck off!" Elinor seemed to shrink into her dressing gown. She turned and crept upstairs, sobbing loudly.

"Bitch!" Shouting felt good.

***

Alun didn't return until mid-afternoon. Dacre mooched about downstairs. He turned the television on. James Stewart and some Red Indians. He turned it off, but the silence made him turn it back on. Twice he heard his mother in the toilet and froze until he knew she wasn't coming down. What had happened had thrown him off balance, and he had no idea what to say next.

She didn't even deny it!

The back door banging and the tool bag dropping to the floor startled him. He hadn't heard the van drawing up. His father breezed into the living room, with four cans of Tartan in a plastic bag. "The bloody thing took longer than I thought, but I got it going at last. Where's your mum?"

"Err ... upstairs. She hasn't got up."

"No lunch? These'll have to do, then, eh?"

"What? I mean where have you been? It's Sunday."

"Charlie Younson said he would pay me two quid to get his twin tub working again. It was the spinner belt. A bugger to free up, but I did it. It took me so long he gave me these as well. Want one?" He opened two cans and set one down in front of Dacre. Glad of the respite from worry about his mum, Dacre gulped some beer.

"Ta, Dad. Who was he, again? Is that the bloke who used to borrow your van to go poaching?"

Alun paused and looked taken aback. "Yeah, that was Charlie. I'd forgotten I told you that. Not a word, eh?"

"And he always scrubbed the van with Domestos afterwards. I could always smell it."

His dad looked away without replying, and Dacre looked out of the window for something else to say.

"Nice day, eh?" Bright sun had dried up the earlier rain.

Now chewing on a heel of dry bread, Alun gestured above with his thumb. "She often does this nowadays. Says it's migraine."

"Says it's hay fever today."

"I haven't heard that one for a while."

Dacre smiled and relaxed, still pitying his father. But at least he seemed to have had a good day, he thought. It must be easier for him to be out. "Want a chippy for tea, Dad?"

"You paying, I suppose?" Alun smiled and pulled his wallet from his overall pocket as he reached for another can. "Shame we can't get some more of these. Off-licence is shut on bloody Sundays!" he said, throwing the remaining can to Dacre. He thought of the Arms, but couldn't be seen in there with his dad. Foam spewed when he opened the beer and they both laughed, and later Dacre went to the Volcano for suppers, one fish and one steak pie. As they shared them with Scotsport in the background, Alun told him he had taken a cup of tea up to Elinor.

"She doesn't deserve you."

"Don't be daft, your mum has a hard time, what with the housework and all."

Dacre didn't know if that was a joke or not.

***

"Hello, may I speak to Isla, please?"

"Is that you, Gordon? She's out, I'm afraid. She called saying she wouldn't be home for dinner." Dacre knew Mrs Alexander's voice. "Shall I ask her to call you back later?"

"No, err, no, thanks, it's not important, thank you. I'll try again tomorrow."

She's out with that bastard Campbell.

No, she's at work, you fool.

Bastard fucking Campbell.

He called Spake and they met in the Arms.

"You're bein' hellish slow with that pint. I'm going for more. C'mon, catch up!"

Dacre didn't look up. "I had two cans already."

"Half-pint, ya poof?"

Dacre managed an ironic sneer at his pal. He felt guilty for his mood.

"You confronted your mum, then?" said Spake when he sat back down with a fresh Guinness.

"Aye. It was a nightmare."

"Is it true?"

Dacre was staring at the floor. When he looked up his voice was breaking. "My dad's put up with a lot."

"Christ. Fuck, Dacre, that's hellish." The door opened and a group entered, noisily heading for the bar. "Tommy McIntyre! Ya wee wanker!" Spake stood up and clapped Tommy hard in between his shoulder blades.

"Who the fu—? Spake! Ya lanky, hippy wanker!" Their traditional greeting honoured, the two stood facing each other, trading light punches to the arms. When Spake sat back down with Dacre, he brought two more pints, courtesy of Tommy. Spake beamed, proud of his achievement.

"Tommy is a bookie's clerk."

"Oh, right. What's that mean?"

"No idea, but he's earning. Took pity on us poor students. Said he'd seen your dad a bit recently, by the way."

"Well done!" Dacre reached for his pint, cheering at last as the jukebox blared Bad Company. He wouldn't have to talk any more.

Fuckin' women! The new barmaid's alright, mind you.

***

When Isla finally returned home, there was a note from her mother.

'Gordon called, he had no news, said he'll call you tomorrow.'

Isla was tired after being asked to stay late at work. A twenty-first birthday party had meant the bar needed extra staff to distribute drinks. She was glad not to have to call Dacre. He hadn't plucked up the courage to tackle his mother, and she couldn't bear another row. As she climbed the stairs to her bedroom, she wasn't sure if she was crying with exhaustion or sadness.

***

One of the fields failed its inspection. "Apparently, we missed some rogue plants. Bastard! We'll have to re-rogue it." Angry, Spake was driving fast on the narrow roads. The early morning sun on the windscreen hurt Dacre's hangover, and he had his eyes shut. "Harrison phoned last night, and my mother took the fucking call. Fuck!"

Dacre didn't care. "We can do it this afternoon. It's only six acres."

"I wanted to watch cricket this afternoon. Viv Richards." Spake was full of surprises.

"Cricket? Fuxake, when did you start watching cricket? Posh rounders, you always said."

Spake grinned at his pasty, halitotic passenger. "One of my flatmates watches it all the time, and I sort of got into it at the end of term."

"Christ! You've got a telly in your flat?"

A tractor pulling a silage cart suddenly shaded the windscreen, and Spake braked hard, veering onto the low banking. There was muffled whumping as the Mini's small tyres bumped over the verge then a slowing rasp as it grated into a hawthorn hedge. The tractor didn't stop.

"Shit. Is it scratched? My mum'll kill me."

"I can't get out to see, you daft git." Dacre couldn't help laughing. The car was deep in the hedge, and they climbed out of the driver's door to push it out. It was too muddy to see any scratches. Dacre was still laughing when they reached the field.

The extra six acres meant they didn't get back to Auchmoor until early evening, and once again when he tried phoning Isla he missed her. After a bath, he dressed quickly and went straight to the front door.

"Aren't you going to eat something? Please, Gordon." Elinor spoke from the kitchen.

He banged the door shut behind him and sat in the park eating a bag of chips until it was time to meet Spake in the Arms.

Chapter 27

August came. The roguing season was over and they'd been round collecting money from reluctant farmers. Dacre had almost given up trying to speak to Isla. She seemed to work late every night, and he had tried calling so many times he began to suspect her family was becoming fed up with him.

He spent most of his time with Spake until near the end of the month Spake left to spend a week on the farm in Dumfries where his sister Denise was working. It was still weeks before he could escape back to Aberdeen, and Dacre shut himself in his bedroom, pretending to be asleep when Elinor made sporadic attempts to talk.

"Gordon, I've made some soup." After a few days, she stopped her gentle tapping on his door.

One morning he was up and dressed by the time Alun came downstairs to go to work. "Christ! You frightened me. I haven't seen you for days."

"Where are you going today?"

"Crianlarich. Why?"

"Can I come?"

Alun picked up his piece bag and turned to go. Dacre noticed he left his overnight bag which meant it was just a day trip.

"To Crianlarich? Are you still drunk from last night or something? I'm only going 'cos bloody Dod's desperate to keep the contract." Over the summer, Dacre had noticed Alun was away overnight less often. Envious of his employer, Alun often scoffed cruelly about Dod's business not doing well, but still complained about reduced pay and expenses. His dad seemed to have little respect for his boss, and Dacre had realised Dod was a bit of a chancer.

"No, Dad, I mean it. I need to get away."

"There's nothing in Crianlarich. I'm only going to service another bloody hotel lift. And I need to go to the workshop on the way, so hurry up, if you're bloody coming."

After twenty minutes, they pulled up on a weedy, gravelled area outside a corrugated iron hut near Falkland. "Is this it? Headquarters?" Dacre sniggered.

"Yes, and bloody Dod's here already." There was a metallic blue Ford Escort next to Alun's van. "Fucking *'company car!'*" he muttered through his teeth, "knows all the dodges, he does." Dacre got out and followed his father to a metal door at the end of the Nissen hut. It opened with a screech. Three bare bulbs hung in a row along the apex, and a dimly lit passage led between wooden crates and RAF oil drums to a door at the far end. A hand-painted sign read: 'George Lambie Specialist Engineers'. Underneath was a sheet of paper with 'OFFICE' scrawled in red felt pen. Dacre left his father rooting in boxes and picked his way along to knock on the door.

"Dod, can I come in?"

"Who's that?"

The door swung open. The office was little more than a narrow cupboard boarded off across the end of the main hut. Dod was sitting on a stool with a catalogue open and turned to wave Dacre to come in, putting the black phone down with a clatter. The receiver's coiled cord was brown and frayed.

"Finding cheaper supplies, Gordon." He raised an eyebrow. "What are you doing here?"

Dacre stood in the doorway of the tiny office. Above Dod's head hung a framed display of insects and some pictures of Fife landmarks.

"Just bored. I came out with my dad for a change. Why the hell are those bugs on the wall?"

Dod looked behind him, and said, "Just something I used to do when I was a kid. A hobby. Y'know the sort of thing."

"Weird!" Dacre couldn't help staring at the frame.

Dod smirked. "You were the weird one, seeing bloody psychologists. Waste of space, that lot. No idea. No use."

Dacre bristled, annoyed that his dad must have told Dod

about him seeing Dr Sutton.

"Piss off!"

Dod's phone jangled and he grinned at Dacre as he turned away.

***

Alun looked along the van's bench seat. His son was snoring with his face against the van window. He shifted down a gear to begin the winding climb out of Lochearnhead. With each left-hand bend, Dacre's head lolled away from the grimy glass, only to recoil back on the right-hander. Roused by the impacts of his face against the window, he snorted and muttered "Goal!" before shaking himself awake.

"Some company you've been." Alun stared at the road. He pulled hard at the heavy steering. "I hate this run. Give me the A92 any day, much straighter."

"Yeah."

"Like you'd know! Your breath stinks, d'you know that? Drink too much, you do." From time to time, Dacre noticed his father's Welsh intonation.

"A lot on my mind," he managed to reply.

"A lot on your mind? A lot in your bank, more like." Dacre was on a full grant and knew Alun was jealous of the free government money. "Bloody students. Spongers, you are, the lot of you."

"But the rent, and the meals. And the bus fares."

Alun resorted to moaning about the road. "Typical! One straight bit and there's a bloody bus holding everyone up."

"Where are we, anyway?"

"Glen Dochart. Be another half an hour to Crianlarich, at this bloody rate." Dacre closed his eyes again. At least now he knew why his dad was always miserable. A few minutes later, though, as they passed a white hotel near the road, Alun chuckled, "Remember camping here? Down there by the river. Bloody soaked, we were! You were about twelve, and I'd only just started trips up here. Didn't know it always rained."

"Thirteen."

Dacre thought for a while and then said, "That was here? I thought it was much further away." It might have been the last time they'd spent much time together, and he smiled recalling trying to put up the flimsy borrowed tent in a gale and driving rain. Soaked, they'd soon given up, and when his dad took him into the nearby Luib Hotel he'd thought they were going to stay the night. But after warming up by a huge log fire, while Alun had some beer and he ate crisps and watched his clothes steam, they'd driven home and he was back at school the next morning.

A few miles on Dacre asked, "Is this where the police stopped us? A big line of cars?"

"I don't remember that."

As they pulled into Crianlarich, Alun reminded Dacre he couldn't take him inside the hotel. "Spoil my chances of the free lunch, you will. I go through the kitchen round the back." He winked and tapped his nose.

"Just drop me anywhere."

"There's nothing here, you know. Only the hotel and a few houses, and I'll be hours. They installed a lift a few years ago, but a second-hand one. Trying to get coach trips to stop here. The old codgers need a lift, see? So where are you going, eh?"

"Oban." Dacre had seen the name on the road signs.

"Why? Got another woman there?"

Dacre didn't know what to say. He didn't know if Alun even knew about Isla, let alone could suspect him of two-timing her.

"No. I just need to get away."

"Why? You've got nothing to worry about, except your next beer. Get away from what?"

He hadn't intended to ever tell his dad he knew about his mother and Redbond. She was the guilty one. But somehow, he couldn't deceive his dad.

"Mum." It was all he could make himself say.

"What's wrong with her?"

"Well, you know ..." Dacre's guts were churning.

But his father was grinning. "Yeah, she's a moody bitch at times, isn't she? She's OK, though. Just needs kept in line now and again when she misbehaves. That's what they all need, women. Kept in line."

"Dad. I know ..."

"You don't know the half of it, son. Find a good one like I did, and you won't go wrong, though. Live and let live, eh?"

Dacre didn't know where to put himself.

***

It was nine forty-five by the station clock. It didn't matter though: Dacre realised he had only thirty-six pence in his pocket. "Is there a bank near here?" he asked at the ticket office window.

"Nae on a Thursday, son."

He didn't bother asking if there was a Cashline machine. There were only two or three in Aberdeen. Dacre had used the one in Union Street once instead of writing himself a cheque, just to try it, and kept the card in his wallet in case he ever saw another machine.

"You can get a bus at one o'clock. Mind you, it's gone up to over five bob now."

Decimalisation hasn't reached this far, then?

He sauntered a few hundred yards in drizzling rain, and after nearly an hour he gave up trying to hitch-hike to Oban. As the sun tried to poke through he trudged back to the hotel, damp, cold and dejected. There was no sign of his dad's van in the car park, and he hung around the hotel reception for a while hoping to ask someone if Alun was still there. Half an hour later there had been no sign of life, even in the plastic, wood-effect Saloon Bar. Eventually, he decided to head towards home and walked along into the shadow of what a sign told him was Ben More. Soon he was in the front of another van, and the man smoking at the wheel was heading to Callander. When he was dropped at Lochearnhead, Dacre had dried out and warmed up a little, and the sun had appeared. He hitched by way of Crieff to Perth, where a bag of chips and a can of Kestrel lager made the day almost worthwhile. He waited with his thumb out near the shaded high walls of Perth prison.

It was early evening by the time he made it back to Auchmoor. He pondered having another go at his mother, but his dad seemed to have forgiven her and he didn't want to make things worse. Elinor was in the kitchen and tried to talk to him again. "Where've you been all day, Gordon?"

"Crianlarich, with Dad. Not that you would care." It was the most civil he'd been to her for weeks.

"What? In his van? You've never done that before. Oh, Dacre, I'm sorry. You've hardly spoken to me since ... well ... you know. I'm sorry, I really am. But it was all a long time ago. It'll be better now. And he hasn't—"

"I don't want to hear anything about Redbond! Shut up, OK?"

"No! I meant your da—"

"Shut up! Please, no more!" He slammed the door and walked out. It was too late to call Isla.

She's probably with bastard Campbell anyway!

Luckily, Spake was back from Denise's and had some money. When Dacre returned from the pub, Alun was unloading some tools into the shed. "Hi Dad. You didn't spend long in Crianlarich."

"What do you mean? I've had a bastard of a day. It took me until three o'clock, no lunch, then I had to go to another job in Stirling on the way back. Bloody Dod tracked me down, phoned the hotel."

"But your van was gone in the middle of the morning."

"I had to move it round the back, hotel was expecting a coach party, see?"

Dacre lay in bed later wondering if hypnotherapy would

help him get through this. If his dad had learned to forgive and forget, he could do the same. He tried to reach the safety of trance by thinking back to happy times. As he drifted off, his dad was giving him a half set of golf clubs bought from a friend, while he played hide and seek with his mum. She had always let him win.

Chapter 28

The following morning Dacre woke feeling sick. The cartoon of the dead girl with a severed hand had appeared in his dream again. This time there was a long traffic queue and a policeman with a big red moustache questioning his dad. There was the same prison, Perth, but the setting was Glen Dochart. Long after his dad left for work and his mother started hoovering, he lay fretting. Was he now going to dream up a third dead girl? Near Crianlarich, somewhere else his dad worked? He spent another day mooching about in his room and was still distracted that evening.

"What's eating you this time, Dacre?" Spake was grinning, and Dacre could barely hear him in the noisy pub.

"What?"

"I thought you said last night you thought you were going to get over the stuff with your mum."

Dacre tried to ignore Spake and pretended he couldn't hear over the din. When Spake had phoned he'd been glad to escape home, but still felt guilty for continuing to snub her. He wanted to break the ice but the new dream, and its ridiculous connection to his dad, had stirred his mind. And he definitely couldn't tell Spake about his mad ideas about his dad and dead girls.

After a pint standing at the bar, they managed to find seats at the end of a table where some older men were sitting smoking. "What have you been doing today?" Dacre felt if he kept himself talking he might not drift back to thinking about the dreams.

"I played golf with my dad, one of his friends pulled out and they had a tee booked on the Jubilee Course."

"St Andrews? Brilliant."

"It was crap. The course was great, but I haven't swung a club in over a year, and only just broke 100."

"Christ! Duffer!"

The easy chat didn't last, though, and after a while, Spake leant forward and said quietly, "Fuck's sake, Dacre! You're at it again, drifting off to wherever you go all the time, in your mad fucking head, I mean."

Dacre tried to smile. "Aw, fuck, Spake! It's hellish." He told Spake about the trip he had made to Crianlarich.

"Very nice! A road trip with your old man. What a bore. At least I got a round of golf."

"Shut up, Spake." He had to tell someone. "Listen, I keep thinking girls have been murdered all over the place. And now Glen Dochart."

Spake was grinning and shaking his head. "Fuck's sake, Dacre, you're a head case. Is James Robb in this one?"

Ignoring his pal, Dacre went on to disclose some of the bizarre dreams, and his growing feeling that he should believe them. Spake said confidently, "It's obvious, Dacre. A girl was killed in Fraserburgh, one in Perth and the other in Glen Dochart. Solved! I should be a detective."

"But the Fraserburgh one was made up, it was the dream that started it all, and a pal who lives there made stuff up to take the piss out of me."

"I'm not surprised if you spouted that sort of shite. For fuck's sake, get more pints in!"

When Dacre returned with two more lagers, his face was still burning with embarrassment at how stupid he had been. Thank god he hadn't mentioned he'd connected the dreams to his dad.

But Spake said, "Did you say Glen Dochart? On the way to Oban?"

"Aye, but forget it, I'm—"

"I've been thinking. Big Alick Stewart used to live in Crianlarich, or just outside. His dad was an estate worker or something. If there was a murder near there, he'd know, and if there wasn't we'll just take the piss even more." He pointed over Dacre's shoulder. "He's over there. Come on." Before

Dacre could put the pints down Spake was on his feet, threading his way through the crowd towards Big Alick.

Dacre didn't know Alick Stewart well. He'd only come to Auchmoor High in third year and left after fourth. He was a nightly fixture in the Arms, though, in his oily John Deere overalls. Filled with dread of certain humiliation, Dacre gulped some beer and squeezed through the crowd towards the end of the bar. Spake was already in conversation with Big Alick.

"So, fixing tractors, eh?"

"Aye, guid work, guid pay. Not like you spongers!"

"Listen, I heard a story 'bout a girl from Crianlarich getting murdered, a few years ago. Is that not where you used to live?"

"Aye, ah mind that. Grim! Rumour wis the lassie had her leg sawn aff! They found her in the Dochart, the burn, like. Polis never got naebody for it." Alick looked pleased with himself. "It wis at the end o' ma second year, 'cos ah mind when ah heard, on the bus hame after the school sports. Ah canny mind her name ... maybe it wis Mhairi ... I think that wis it. She was a couple of years older than me, but she wis on the same school bus to McLaren High. Until she wisnae, like." He was grinning proudly.

Dacre felt the blood draining from his cheeks, and Spake pulling him through the crowd by his jacket sleeve. As he sat down he heard Big Alick shout, "Fuckin' poofy students!"

All Spake could say was, "Fuckin' hell!"

Dacre couldn't face another pint and left Spake talking to Tommy McIntyre. He trusted Spake not to say anything about Dacre's dreams. Deep in thought, he didn't stop for chips on the way home. He couldn't doubt Big Alick ... he'd just answered Spake's enquiry. David Thom had heard Dacre relate one of his dreams, and played a sick joke about 'Inga Sabiston'. But Alick had confirmed the dead girl called Mhairi was real.

It was all too mixed up. Why Perth prison when the murder happened in Glen Dochart? He could remember the police roadblock, but it can't have been important because his dad had forgotten it. And Alick said the girl's leg had been sawn off. In his Perth dream, it was her hand. He shook his head.

I am just mad! The Perth girl was in a bloody cartoon!

He told himself it was just a coincidence that a girl had died in Glen Dochart, and had brightened up a little when he approached his front door. He would use his mental dreams to break the ice with his mum. He'd say that's why he'd been so nasty to her.

"Hi, Mum." She looked taken aback that he had spoken. "I was going to tell you about a silly dream I had. You should hear this."

"Oh, OK. I'll switch the telly off. A cup of tea?" She hurried off to the kitchen calling back, "I want to hear it but you'll need a drink and a sandwich."

It felt good to let his mum look after him. He ate toasted cheese while he told her how he had dreamt about a cartoon murder and managed to mix it up with his trip to Crianlarich. "Mad, eh?" He beamed at his mum.

Elinor was smiling. "You silly sausage!" Dacre didn't mind her going back to baby talk and felt this was just like old times. She put down her tea, shaking her head and grinning, waving her finger at him the way she had when he'd hidden in the wardrobe and made her jump. "But we shouldn't laugh. What happened to that girl was awful."

For a second, Dacre was confused. *The cartoon girl?* His mum went on, "I was so worried when you and your dad went camping up there. When I saw it on the news, I mean. I was quite pleased your trip was rained off and you came straight home."

There had been a roadblock. Elinor had seen the TV news report about a girl's body found in a river with her leg cut off. "You and I watched it again on the late news after your dad had gone to bed. Mind you, you were so tired after the long day, and what with getting soaked, you were nearly asleep. I don't know if you really saw it." She took his hand, and he let her. "That was about the last time my little boy let his mum help him get ready for bed."

When Dacre went to bed a short time later, he was happier than he had been for weeks. The TV news report he had watched with his mum explained why he'd dreamt about a murder after going to Glen Dochart again with his dad. Talking with his mum had helped. He might be able to forgive her after all. His dad was right, 'Live and let live, eh?' He tried again to introduce positive thoughts to his trance induction.

***

Shafts of white sunlight lit his bedroom the next morning as Dacre roused slowly from a long and deep sleep. He drifted off again, a tune playing in his head. Suddenly he sat bolt upright. Inga Sabiston had come back to him. Her name echoed in his ears above the background tune. Snippets of the earlier dream replayed, the TV newsman beside the Fraserburgh road sign and the 'MISSING' poster. This time the reporter spoke in his dad's voice: "Live and let live, live and—" But in the background behind the man with the microphone was Perth prison, as clear as Dacre had seen it two days ago. The poster faded in and out of focus, morphing between Inga's school picture and the bold lines of a cartoon. The cartoon was clearer. The girl with a missing hand was floating, and behind her was the outline of a boat against a high wall. The tune ringing in his head grew louder and louder: the 1970 World Cup team song. *Back Home ... They'll be thinking about us ... When we are far away—*

He sat up with the pulse in his neck pounding and his scalp tightening. Closing his eyes and shaking his head didn't banish the dismembered girls. His eyes were dry but stinging, his breathing deep and rapid. He lay back and forced his eyes open. The outline of the girl's body was etched in the cracks on the ceiling. The old wire where his Airfix had hung slashed through her wrist. Cartoon or not, the Perth girl appeared real. He realised with horror that his dad had worked near

Fraserburgh, in Glen Dochart and close to Perth prison where he now believed the cartoon girl had met her end.

Dacre needed to pee, and after he came back downstairs he went into the kitchen in his Y-fronts.

"You should get dressed," said his mum over her shoulder. She was cleaning the sink.

"Mum, did you say Dad worked in Fraserburgh? When was that?"

"Oh, did you ask your friend if his dad knew yours? Dad was up there quite a lot, some job at a power station they were building I think. I remember he was away a lot when you were getting ready for your O-Grade exams. When was that? Your fourth year, wasn't it? What does your friend do at university? Did you find out what his dad does?"

Dacre was feeling sick. He didn't understand anything any more, and anger rose in him as his mother went on and on and on. Pressure boiled up until he exploded, shouting, "Shut up! Always fucking nosey! Bitch! Fucking traitor! You don't deserve Dad. How dare you, you bitch!"

"Gordon! What has ..."

"Fuck off! Shut up you cow!" Dacre's mind continued to whirl with confusion, fear and fury. He ran back to his room and slammed the door, throwing himself on his bed and punching the pillow. He lay brooding in his room until gradually the thumping in his chest slowed. He felt bad about his outburst, but couldn't explain it to his mother. Being angry with his mother was easier than making sense of the maelstrom in his head. At least he knew she was guilty.

He ran a bath and lay until the water was nearly cold, ignoring his mother when she knocked on the bathroom door. Eventually, he put his dreams in some sort of order. He got out shivering and dripped downstairs in the towel. After slamming his bedroom door closed, he heard his mother passing the door. "Thank goodness, I'm desperate!" There was thudding as she ran upstairs to the toilet. "The floor's all wet!"

Serves the bitch right.

Half-dressed and with water still dripping from his overgrown hair, he sat on his bed and took a sheet of paper from the floor. On one side were some of his physics lecture notes, and with the satisfaction of knowing he wouldn't need them again, he turned it over and wrote notes about the dead girls.

1. Inga Sabiston.

Underneath he wrote *Fraserburgh*, then crossed that out, correcting it to read:

> *village near Fraserburgh. 1974. In a ditch. (Power station?) Arms cut off. He underlined FAKE. (David Thom!)*

Below, he wrote:

2. Mhairi (?)

Summer 72? Crianlarich, Glen Dochart. River. Leg cut off. *DEFINITELY HAPPENED*. (Big Alick)

He stared at what he had written. Reading backwards he could make out the word ENTROPY deeply imprinted on the reverse side of the sheet.

He hesitated, reluctant to commit to paper what the dreams had suggested about a third killing in Perth. Then, leaving a gap on the page, underneath he wrote in smaller lettering,

3. Name unknown.

> *Date unknown. Location unknown (Perth?) Hand removed. Floating. I MADE THIS CRAP UP??? CARTOON!!!*

He lay back on the bed and summed it all up. Only one of these so-called murders was real. He had to get this nonsense out of his head if he was ever going to concentrate on what mattered: the need to forgive his mother as his dad had.

Dacre finished dressing, grabbed his jacket from the hall and walked to the phone box outside the post office.

"Hello, can I speak to David, please?"

"Aye, hang on a minute," the woman he presumed was Mrs Thom said to Dacre. After a pause, the receiver was picked back up.

"Hello?"

"David? It's Dacre here."

"Aww! Dacre! How're you doing? Looking forward to getting back to Aberdeen?"

"Aye, I suppose. Can I ask you something?"

"Aye, what?"

"You remember I told you about that dream I had?"

There was a pause, and then Dacre's heart sank when he heard the sombre tone in David's reply.

"Inga Sabiston?"

"That wasn't true, was it? You were just taking the piss, right? There ... err ... wasn't really a murder?"

"Aye, it was real! Christ, why would I make up something like that? It happened just before the O-Grades."

Dacre couldn't listen any longer. He put the phone down without saying goodbye. At least two of the murders were real.

Chapter 29

PC Craig Masson stared at his glass.

"But what if there was a serial killer, someone going about in different areas, different countries even, and no one knows it's all been one guy. I mean every force thinks they're dealing with a one-off? That would get their attention."

Jack was shaking his head. "Nah. Come on, Luggy, we've got to start with something believable."

It was the end of August and they'd met in the Canny Man's, Craig after work, Jack on annual leave and Phil having been sacked for losing the rag with an American tourist who'd wanted ice in his beer.

"But burglaries? I mean they all tend to be local neds, always in their own area. We all know the usual suspects."

"You'd be surprised. There's teams from Glasgow doing jobs in the Borders, even the Highlands. High-end stuff. In, out, fence the stuff before the local CID even know it's gone."

"And you heard about this in Dundee?" Craig could imagine Sgt Wardrop's response if he mentioned sharing information between different forces. He'd given up trying and accepted that if he didn't get a transfer out of Oxgangs he'd never get a chance to see the PNC used.

"Do they take on any civilians in Tayside? I need to get out of bar work."

"You'll never leave Edinburgh, Phil, you know that. But I'll check the notice board next time I'm across at St Leonards, they post job adverts for backroom jobs there." Craig drained his pint and held the glass out towards Jack. "Your round, Jack."

While Jack was at the bar, Phil said, "You're right, Luggy, if you're going to get them interested in the PNC it needs to be something big. Something unsolved. Murders probably. There must be records kept."

"Aye, but it would mean them loading all the old stuff on

the system, in all the different force areas I mean, and that'll take years, especially if the bosses aren't interested."

Jack returned with pints and crisps. "Phil, did you say you were writing code for a stock control programme? Looks like they've got one here. Electronic till, the works."

"In the Canny Man's? You're joking! I'm going to look, mine'll be better." Phil took a slurp of lager and went to talk to the barman.

"That'll be him for the night. I bet he gets a job here," Craig said.

Chapter 30

"Listen, sonny. If you want me to call a doctor I will, but you can't come in here and tell me this rubbish. Away home and stop your nonsense, laddie."

"But I'm telling you! You check, Fraserburgh, Glen Dochart. And there's one somewhere else! Three of them. Girls, dead. With bits cut off! You've got to do something!"

The policeman came round the end of the counter and loomed over Dacre.

"I've warned you! You talk this rubbish and say your father's got something to do with it one more time and I'll go and get your father right now! Calm it, sonny! I never had you down as one for the hippie drugs and black magic. Are you sure you haven't taken anything?"

"Fuxake!" shouted Dacre, as he ran out of Auchmoor Police Station. He was followed by the lumbering man with the chevrons on his serge tunic who stood at the door and shook his head.

"Jeezus wept!" he thought, "bloody students and their drugs! Talking about being hypnotised! And he was one of the bright ones, supposed to be. What a waste!"

After ending his call to David Thom, Dacre had gone straight from the phone box to the police station, and now he headed for Spake's house.

"Hello, Mr Baker, I was looking for Steven."

"Are you OK, Dacre? You look a bit ... err ..." Even the parents of Dacre's friends knew not to use his given name.

"I'm OK, just been in a bit of a hurry," he replied, breathless after running.

Spake appeared and they went to his room. "I'm just about to have my tea. You that desperate for a pint or something? Fuckin' alky!"

"No. I just want to sit quiet a minute."

"Eh?"

Dacre stood looking out of the window. He told Spake about his call to David and that Inga Sabiston's murder was real.

"But what's changed? You told me you were dreaming about a TV reporter. You'll have seen that like you saw the Dochart one."

Dacre told Spake he had gone to the police. "I'm sure the other one's real as well. The dream was even clearer last night. Her fucking hand hacked off, floating in a harbour I think. And the cartoon had a boat in it. And it has something to do with the Mexico World Cup. I told the police it might be my dad that did it."

"Fucking hell! You went to the police? Dacre, you mad bastard, they were dreams! And a fucking cartoon for Christ's sake! And what the hell's your dad got to do with it? You mad bastard."

"Three murders, all with arms and legs cut off, and all of them in places he's worked!"

"You stupid tosser! No wonder the bobby thought you were on drugs!" Spake was shaking his head and grinning as his pal flopped down on the bed and punched the mattress.

"Hey! Watch my Dylan albums!" Dacre was lying on the open gatefold cover of Blonde on Blonde. "Listen, my aunt and uncle are here and my mum's made a meal. I'll have to go down. You can stay here if you like."

"Nah, I'll go out for a walk. Maybe I shouldn't have gone to the police, but I sort of panicked when it all came together."

"Daft bugger."

Dacre walked round Auchmoor. When the Volcano had opened, he sat in the park eating a sausage supper. He tried to call Isla from the phone box but again she was at work. When he guessed enough time had passed, he made for Spake's house again. His friend didn't take much persuading to come out and spend some more of his roguing money. They chose the quiet of The Royal. It was not long after opening time and only two old men sat at the bar.

“Thanks.” Dacre took the Guinness without protest and Spake sat opposite him. With foam on his lip, Spake looked sympathetically at his friend.

“I still can’t believe you went in to the police station babbling that load of shite! It sounds just fuckin’ mental.”

“The murders … I mean the dreams, they get more real each time. Sort of come into focus, you know? Like a film playing over and over again, but clearer. And two of the girls have turned out to be real.”

“But the other one’s a cartoon! Come on!”

“It’s important somehow. As if there’s something I can’t quite remember, but important. Connected.”

Spake was quiet, and Dacre wondered if he really believed him or not. When he came back with more pints, he tried to change the subject. “What courses are you taking next year?”

“Eh? Oh, electrical engineering, stuff like that. The course is pretty much laid out for you really. Not much choice after first year. But anyway, listen, if the hypno thingy is telling you more details, and some of them seem to have been proved right according to Big Alick and the other guy, maybe you should use it deliberately and get the full story? Pretty interesting.”

Dacre was glad of his friend’s encouragement, but said quietly, “What if I find out stuff I don’t like?”

“You mean about your dad? That’s shite, Dacre, I can’t believe that bit, it’s got to just be a coincidence, like you said yourself. But use the hypnosis. Get to the bottom of it or you’ll go really mad.”

Dacre was slow with his pint and when Spake had finished his he said, “You should just go home. You look fucking awful, by the way, shattered.”

“Aye, sorry, I’m not much use.” Tommy McIntyre had come in and was creeping up behind Spake. Dacre stood up to leave just as Tommy’s hand slapped the back of Spake’s head and he splurted Guinness. “Spake! Ya lanky, hippy wanker!”

Dacre started to saunter home, uncertain about Spake's advice. After the embarrassment at the police station, he had promised himself he was never going to enter a hypnotic trance again, but now his friend's advice had almost persuaded him to give it one more go. Spake's words repeated themselves to him as he crossed into Rothes Drive, and by the time he crept in the back door and went to his room with a pint glass of water a different plan was forming in his mind. He pushed the other two empty pint glasses aside with the full one, and smiled in self-congratulation at his agility when he caught the outermost one as it toppled off the edge of the bedside table.

He fell asleep without hypnosis and woke with no memory of any more dreams.

He knew what to do.

Chapter 31

He found the library on a corner of Kinnoull Street, not far from the station. As he entered between impressive timber doors Dacre realised that the Sandeman Library was much larger and grander than Auchmoor's. The single-storey modern block he had used as a child looked like the pre-fabs some of his friends lived in. This red sandstone pile with its tall, arched windows and clock tower seemed to confirm the importance of his mission.

To avoid his mother, he had left by the back door when she was upstairs. He was in yesterday's clothes and carrying his army surplus jacket. He took a bus to Cupar and two trains. Approaching Perth the train wound its way along the bank of the River Tay. He looked without interest at golfers on an island course, but his neck bristled when he saw a ship and a crane. A harbour.

Dacre had come to Perth's library to prove that the cartoon murder was just that: a figment of his crazy imagination. He knew two of the murders were real. He had seen a TV report on the Glen Dochart one, his Mum had confirmed that. And he guessed his dreams about the TV news report and the poster naming Inga Sabiston meant he had also seen a report of her death. But the third one he *must* have invented.

He told himself he'd seen Perth's prison and harbour on his trips to the lock-up with his Dad. He wasn't sure why the Mexico World Cup featured in his dreams but guessed he must have been to the lock-up around that time. And the cartoon had to mean the whole thing was imaginary. But he had to know that for certain before he moved on to the next stage of his plan: proving his Dad had nothing to do with the two real murders.

He found the library's reading room, unsure where to start. He was sure a place the size of Perth must have a newspaper, and that it was bound to have reported on any local murders.

He noticed a man in a denim jacket sitting at one of the tables chewing a pencil in between making notes on a pad. As Dacre passed behind him he saw 'Perthshire Advertiser' at the top of the man's paper. He was examining the Situations Vacant adverts.

Dacre quietly asked a tiny woman behind the desk if there were any back copies of the Perthshire Advertiser. She set down the four books she had been holding and smiled kindly at him.

"Are you a student? We have quite a few come in here when the re-sits are coming up," she whispered. Dacre realised she must have thought he had come to study, although why he would want to study old newspapers he couldn't guess. She led him to the back of the building and a room that was brightly lit by tall sash windows. The whispering woman was relating the recent history of the library, and Dacre soon knew all about the new young manager whose pet project had been to instal microfiche records.

"Here we are, I'll show you how it works." By now Dacre was attuned to her soft murmurs, and before long she had found the Perthshire Advertiser archive and showed him how to scroll through acres of newsprint reduced to the size of a stamp.

He knew the World Cup had been in June 1970 and thought that was a good place to start. He rolled innumerable images back and forth until he found 1970. The Advertiser was issued twice weekly and Dacre started by looking carefully through the 1st of June edition for any mention of a murder. It was difficult to move the magnified image slowly enough to let him read every line, small ad and death notice.

After an hour he had reached the 9th June edition. Rubbing his tired eyes he scrolled slowly as far as page 2 and sat up sharply. 'Concern Grows For Missing Shop Girl.' The pulse in his neck quickened. The paragraph below told of the strange disappearance of Carol Hosie, aged seventeen, who had not been seen since leaving work in McEwens department store on Friday 5th June. Dacre read the paragraph again and looked at the grainy image of a girl with long pigtails wearing a school uniform. An image of the harbour flashed across his eyes as if it was on the screen in front of him, and his mouth dried. Concentrating on the awkward and over-sensitive controls of the microfiche reader he continued to check every page of the paper. He knew he was stalling for time and that if he was to discover what happened to the missing girl it would be when he dared move on to later issues. When he forced himself to move on to 12th June he was dreading what he would read. He didn't have to look far. On the front page the headline 'GRIM FIND AT CITY HARBOUR' was followed by 'Girl, 17, Strangled and Dumped. Police too shocked to comment on horror.' The paragraphs below dominated the front page and surrounded the same school photograph. Carol Hosie had been found floating with a leather belt tight round her throat. A Police Superintendent was quoted: 'Further details of injuries too shocking to reveal are being withheld.'

Dacre sat back. The stark details on the screen confirmed all three murders he had been dreaming about were real. He still had no idea what the cartoon could mean, and wondered if he'd heard a radio report and let his imagination draw the gruesome picture. He stood up and pushed his chair back behind him, the scraping noise raising tuts from other library users. As he passed the librarian's desk she looked up, smiling at him.

"I hope you found what you ... ooh ... are you feeling OK? You look ... Let me get you a drink of water."

"Sorry, I was ... it's ok." His heart was racing like his mind, and he must have looked unwell.

"There you are. Is it too hot in here for you?"

The librarian handed him a tumbler of water and he drank it in one. Wiping his mouth, he replied, "Yeah, sorry, a bit hot. Is there anywhere I can get a copy of one of the papers?"

The woman beamed. "Mr McKay is here today. He's very clever with things. He can use the printer. It'll cost you forty pence, though."

Half an hour later he was on a train towards Dundee with the 9th June Perthshire Advertiser in his jacket pocket. There was over an hour between trains at Dundee and Dacre couldn't settle in the station. After ten minutes of pacing the platform, he left the station and headed across towards the city centre. Wandering, he passed the Pillars Bar just as it was opening its doors at five o'clock. He entered and ordered a pint of export, sitting down with his back to the bar to thwart the landlord's attempts to strike up a conversation. He was glad when the door opened and two regulars entered who were on first name bantering terms with the barman. He tore off the front page of the newspaper and folded it into his wallet.

He caught a later train and it was getting dark by the time he reached home. He was relieved there was no sign of his father's van, a sure indication he was working away. Elinor was already in bed, but there was a note left for him. Isla had phoned and wanted him to call her back if he was home by half ten. The clock read '11.15'.

He didn't need hypnosis that night. It was a shame it was too late to wake Isla's household with the telephone bell, but he was excited that she had called, and as he readied himself for bed he tasted her on his lips and smelled her in his clothes as if he had just returned from Adam Smith to Esslemont. The shock he had felt in Perth had gradually been replaced by resignation, almost contentment. All three murders were real, but it meant his mad mind hadn't dreamt them up. And tomorrow he was going to prove his Dad had nothing to do with any of them.

Chapter 32

"Falkland? What the fuck for? It's only quarter past nine! Dacre, you're a nightmare."

"Ach, Spake, c'mon, it'll do you good. I'll buy you a pint after. I'll be round in twenty minutes." He put the phone down and smiled, wiped toast crumbs from his cheek and grabbed his jacket.

Walking towards Spake's home in the late August sunshine, Dacre didn't need to go over his plan again. He waved when he saw Tich Lamont come out of the bakers and climb into a transit van parked half on the pavement. "Dacre ya spongin' wank! Get a job!" Tich wound up the window as the van pulled away, but not before Dacre called,

"Sit on a cushion, Tich, you might be able to see out the window!"

Spake was sitting in his mother's Mini when Dacre arrived. "I thought you'd still be in your bed," said Dacre, stooping into the passenger seat and trying to find the seat belt.

"My mum needs the car back by lunchtime. You still haven't told me why you've got to get to Falkland all of a sudden." Dacre explained his plan, and Spake, after a pause, said, "But, do you think Mr Lambie is going to let you go over his records? And what if your dad's there? He's going to want to know what you're doing."

"My dad's working away. And Dod's not got a clue, too busy trying to organise the next job, my dad says. Let's go, I'll think of something."

***

Dacre pushed on the main door of the hut. The radio he had heard playing inside became louder, and without entering he called inside, "Hi, Dod, can I come in?"

"Eh? Who's that? Alun?"

Poking his head in Dacre could now see Dod Lambie sitting with his feet on a wooden crate that served as a table in his tiny office. He looked up from the magazine he had been reading, and called, "What are you doing here?"

"Remember I was here with my dad last week? I think I left a sheet of phone numbers. My dad used it to write some notes on. I think it might be in the big work diary, and I'll need it for next year, for arranging roguing with the farmers."

"Aye, help yourself, the diary'll be on that shelf somewhere." Dod picked up the phone and pushed the battered door half-closed, shutting himself in. Dacre heard the dial turning and then Dod's muffled voice.

The job diary lay on an oily shelf outside the office. It was a thick blank book with handwritten entries in date order, the jobs separated by a line scrawled across the page.

Dacre had memorised the dates he needed to see. Crimond/ Fraserburgh April 1974 ... David had said it was just before the O-Grade exams; Perth 5th June 1970 from the Perthshire Advertiser, and Glen Dochart June 1972 from Big Alick's account of the school sports, which Dacre had calculated would have been the same year he finished S2.

It took Dacre only seconds to flip back through the pages to April 1974. He could see no entries mentioning Fraserburgh or power stations, and none of Alun's work appeared to have been north of Dundee. He flipped forward as far as July and an entry jumped out at him: 'Boddam – power station – Peterhead – service entrance gates (Saltoun Guest House Fraserburgh 1 night)' He smiled. Three months after Inga Sabiston was found dead.

He flicked back quickly through time and saw Crianlarich noted in the list several times, the earliest in September 1972 when Alun appeared to have done a 'First Big Service' on the hotel lift. Dacre was elated. He just had time to note that there had been no jobs in Perth through the whole of May, June and July 1970 before he heard the phone crash onto its cradle and Dod grunting, "Bastard! Fuck off then!" The door opened and Dod stomped through, muttering to himself.

"You still here? Sorry, bastard Americans, you see, taking all the work."

Dacre waved a scrap of paper and said, "Found it. Thanks, I'll get away." Dod was still cursing and Dacre was laughing when he joined Spake in the car.

"All OK then?" said Spake, starting the engine.

"Aye. Found the dates no bother, and my Dad wasn't there until months after any of them. The murders, I mean. It wasn't him. The pub opens at eleven, right? I'll buy you a pint."

"I need to drop the car off first."

Spake's lively humour, three pints of lager and two bags of crisps put Dacre in his best mood since leaving Hillhead. He walked home from the Arms in sunshine thinking of Isla. He was going to phone her that night, but the house was empty when he arrived home in the early afternoon and in his carefree mood he dialled her number without taking his jacket off. When the phone was answered after two rings, the surprise of hearing Isla's voice for the first time in weeks made him wish he'd gone for a pee and thought about what to say. They'd missed each other's calls for weeks.

"Hello, 3892."

"Isla, it's me."

"Who?" Her briskness put him on edge.

"Isla, it's Dacre."

There was a pause and an intake of breath. "Oh! Lovely to hear from you at last. What's wrong? It's afternoon, I'm about to go out. To work."

Dacre had to put aside the idea she might be going somewhere other than work. "Remember I told you about the girl in the ditch near Fraserburgh? In my dream, I mean. It was real, it really happened, and there were two more, I've been finding out about them. I went to Perth library, and Big Alick told me about the other one, all of them at places my dad worked, I actually thought it was him, but—"

"Are you drunk?"

"Eh? No, I mean ... just a couple of pints ... with Spake ... but —"

"You're rambling a load of rubbish, call me when you're sober—"

"It's true. About the murders I mean. But my dad didn't do them, I went to Dod's office and—"

"Dacre! Stop it! Have you spoken to your mum yet? Told her what you know?"

Dacre swallowed, before managing to go on, "Yes. Well, I did but she denied it. I think my dad's forgiven her anyway. I mean I don't really know that but ... it's difficult."

"And you've started having dreams about murders and you thought your dad was a murderer? Dacre, you need help. You've invented that murder stuff to distract yourself from what went on with your parents."

"Look, sorry, forget I said all that, I'm sorry, I know it all sounds mental. I just want to see you, it's ages since we ..."

There was a short silence, before she said, "I know, it would be good to see you. Talk properly. It's only a few weeks until we're back in Aberdeen, and—"

"I know! I can't wait. Oh, it's great to speak to you at last!"

"I know, it's a shame we haven't seen each other. I'll see you as soon as I get to Aberdeen. Listen, I've got to go, I'm late already."

He had to ask. "Late for work? Or seeing someone else?"

"Work! For god's sake!"

"I'm sorry, I just—"

"I know what you meant. Not all women are fucking hussies! I've got to go, I'll see you in Aberdeen." Her swearing was like a slap in his face and he walked to the toilet in a whirl. The joy at finally speaking with Isla had been smothered by how obvious it was she didn't want to speak to him. He peed noisily then soaked the sleeve of his jacket washing his hands. "Bastard!"

"Gordon! Shut the bathroom door! I could hear you from

here." As Dacre passed the kitchen, the back door was open and his mother was emptying shopping bags.

"Fuck off, bitch," he mumbled to himself as he closed his bedroom door.

***

A letter arrived for Dacre in the next day's post. 'Hello Dacre, we got cut off when you phoned the other day. My ma told me my aunt had kept bits from the newspaper about Inga. She knew the family. She gave me this, I thought I'd send it to you, from D Thom.' The cutting from the Evening Express, dated 18th April 1974, was headed 'TRAGIC INGA FOUND DEAD NEAR GRAVEYARD', with the subheading, 'Police refuse to reveal horrific details'. Paragraphs below told of the location near Rathen West Church, on a road near Crimond stock car racetrack. Dacre folded it up and stuck it in his wallet.

Blood on the Tracks was playing and Dacre stared at the ceiling. Isla's 'you need help' ran round and round his mind, drowning out Dylan's voice. He wondered where he had gone wrong. It had all been so good when he started the hypnosis. But then the dreams started as a side effect. First the stuff about his mother, then the murdered girls. Maybe Isla was right. Had he invented something worse than what his mother did to put off facing up to her? Except he hadn't invented it. The hypnosis had made him dream about murders, but real girls had been hacked up. And even worse he was hooked on hypnosis: without it, he could hardly function. And hypnosis had made Miles kill himself. What a mess.

He thought back to Spake joking about 'Dr Freud' and came to a decision. He could hear the TV through the wall and knew his mother would be distracted by Crossroads. He turned up the Dylan and after flushing the toilet to make double sure she wouldn't hear him he crept upstairs, avoiding the creak on the landing. In the top drawer of the chest at the end of his parents' bed were assorted cards, school reports and official letters. He soon found the appointment letter from Royal

Dundee Liff Hospital and scribbled the address on a scrap of paper.

His first name's Granville, for fuck's sake!

Chapter 33

Deciding to ask for help had helped Dacre relax, and he barely thought about Isla, murders or his parents. He was even managing to tolerate his mum.

After a bath and before going out to meet Spake, he was scooping warmed-up stew from his plate one evening when his mum joined him in the kitchen.

"I forgot. A letter came for you today." Elinor dropped a white envelope on the table beside him. The handwriting on the envelope wasn't Isla's, and a Fife postmark meant it was not from Liff Hospital. Anyway, it was too soon to receive a reply to his letter to Dr Sutton. He was intrigued to know who it might be from but his mother was hovering with undisguised curiosity.

"That'll just be from one of the farmers," he invented, before going to his bedroom to open it.

Motray Den
By Kilmany
Fife
6th September '77

Dear Mr Dacre,

I was delighted and intrigued to receive your letter to me, which has been kindly forwarded to me by my former secretary. Sadly I shall not be able to offer you a return appointment with me for several reasons, not least of which I am now retired from practice.

However, I was very interested to hear about your experiences with hypnosis, a subject with which I have made myself rather familiar in recent years. You alluded to disturbing dreams, and, if I am not mistaken, a suspicion of a special awareness you feel you may have. Those are areas of particular interest to me. If it might help you to have an informal chat about your situation we would be glad to welcome you to visit us. My telephone number is 0334 53973.

You were correct in your assumption, though, that I will not disclose to you anything your mother may have discussed.

I do hope you will consider making contact if I can help you at all, and it would please me to hear more about your hypnotherapy techniques.

With kind regards,

Granville Sutton

Spake spluttered beer down his cheesecloth shirt. "You did what? And he wants you to go to his home? You think he wants to seduce you?"

"He said go and see him and his wife, ya silly bugger."

"A threesome!"

It was clear Spake wasn't up for a sensible discussion of hypnosis and the subconscious.

***

A woman answered in a posh accent, "Hello, 53973."

"Hello ... err ... hello, may I speak to Dr Sutton, please?"

"He's milking at the moment, I'm afraid, and it's better not to stop and start, it upsets them, as you'll understand, but he won't be too long, can I take a message for him? Perhaps he'll call you back, or you could phone another time? What was it about?"

The woman's wittering on was putting him off his prepared

script, and he only had one ten-pence coin. "I was hoping to see him, he wrote to me."

There was a slight pause. "Oh! Are you the young man about the hypnosis? Granville's very excited, and will be so glad you have called! He's been in his study with his books and it's been so lovely to see him working again. Well, I mean bookwork instead of his animals. I'll tell him to come, can you hold on while he washes up?"

"I'm in a phone box. He said I could come to see him. Can I come this Saturday?"

"Yes, I'm sure he would be delighted. Are you coming by car? I'll give you directions."

"No, I'll be on my bike."

"Oh, a motorbike! How exciting! If you're coming from the West turn left just after Rathillet and before you reach Kilmany. If you're coming from the East, turn right. We're not far from there, just after the first bend. Come for the afternoon. I shall go to tell Granville now." The pips went and she hung up. Dacre shook his head as he left the call box. It was Thursday afternoon and he would have to get his bike out of the shed.

***

As he strained up the long slope towards Rathillet, a cattle float passed him and the wind which rocked him stank of dung. Dacre stopped to pull his bicycle onto the grass verge while a stream of cars passed. It was taking longer than he'd expected. Having not been on his bike for nearly two years, the twelve-mile run to Sutton's house was hard going.

He coasted down the slope towards Kilmany. A winding couple of hundred yards down a narrow lane he found Motray Den. A row of three single-storey cottages had been combined into one L-shaped dwelling at the end of a shady track. A layer of windblown dust and straw from the field opposite lay on the doorstep, piled up against the bottom of a sturdy brown door. An old blue Volvo estate car was the only sign of life. This can't be it, he thought, but then noticed a note stuck to the inside of a small window in the door. 'Round The Back.' An arrow pointed to his right and, walking round the end of the building, he saw outhouses in a large yard. Beyond stretched a small field, half of it fenced off to enclose five grazing goats. In the corner of the yard a small, grey-haired woman was filling a watering can. She looked up.

"Hello. You must be Mr Dacre. Come in, come in, I didn't hear you arrive. Where is your motorbike?"

Mrs Sutton was not what he had expected. She motioned him to follow, her tanned face with divergent white lines at the corners of her eyes making him smile back and relax. He followed her the few paces to the back door.

"I cycled, I parked my bike at the front."

"A pushbike? Goodness, you must be tired. Come in, come in, sit down." They entered through the low doorway into a room with small windows and an uneven flagged floor, pleasantly cool and dark after his long cycle. She gestured to a low, flowery sofa facing the sunny window.

"Hello, Mrs Sutton, thank you, I am sorry to invite myself," he said as he went to sit down. He was becoming less nervous and able to say his prepared lines. "I saw your husband when I was a boy and wanted to ask him some—"

"Husband?" She was laughing, as was Dr Sutton who had come in behind them and was standing in the doorway. In silhouette, Dacre thought he hadn't changed much, with only a little more grey hair. He wore the same glasses and looked like he had the same corduroy jacket on, despite the warm sunshine.

"Sorry, Gordon, let me make the introduction. Meet my mother, Morna Sutton."

Dacre was blushing deeply now, but Mrs Sutton came over and took his hand. "Oh, I am flattered, Gordon, what a charmer you are!"

"Sorry, I thought—"

"Not at all, Gordon. Mum, meet Gordon Dacre, as you know he's the boy ... sorry, man ... who I hope will tell me about hypnosis and his dreams." Turning to Dacre, he said, "My wife died three years ago, Gordon. My mother moved north to '*look after*' me."

"I had to. You still can't boil an egg."

Easy chatter followed, and Dacre relaxed. After tea and fruit loaf Dr Sutton led him through to his study, a small room with shelves of books and a pine table for a desk. He sat down in one of two armchairs, inviting Dacre to sit opposite. "I'm glad you wrote to me, Gordon. I'm not sure if I can help you, but subconscious phenomena have become something of a special interest."

"Everyone calls me Dacre, it's easier."

"Interesting, I noticed you signed your letter 'G. Dacre'. Do you dislike your name, Gordon I mean?"

The Flash Gordon story made Sutton smile kindly. "I grew up detesting my name, and the teasing I endured. The worst one was 'Granny'."

Dacre was soon at ease and impressed by the psychologist's recall of details.

"Did you keep up your interest in anatomy, Gor ... Dacre? I wondered if you might go into medicine."

"I like Biology. Botany's my favourite course. It was my mum who wanted me to be a doctor."

"Ah, yes. Your mum. Elinor."

Dacre bristled inside, fearful of what Sutton would say next.

"I can't talk about your mum. But she did help me understand your problems a little." He looked out of the window, silent. He swallowed, before going on. "Tell me about your dreams and the hypnosis. The dreams are repetitive, you say? And they give you a feeling of premonition? Well, it's not really premonition, is it? You dream of *actual* past events, I think you said in your letter. Fascinating! And you wonder if hypnosis has given you some special insight, I think?" He spoke quickly and Dacre guessed he was changing the subject from his mother. Sutton would keep what his mum had told him to himself, he'd said that in his letter. Anyway, Dacre had no intention of mentioning his dreams about her and Redbond. That was none of Sutton's business.

Dr Sutton's subtle questions helped Dacre express things from his dreams he had struggled to explain to himself. He spoke in detail of the three dead girls, their injuries and where their bodies were found. Sutton interrupted occasionally to clarify the timing and order of the dreams. When Dacre had described in detail his investigation to clear his father of the crimes, he sat back exhausted, and took a drink of his tea.

Granville Sutton cleared his throat. "Dacre, may I ask you a very direct question?"

"Yes." Dacre's mouth dried and his neck hairs stiffened.

"Why have you come to see me? I have read your letter very carefully and I am very interested in what you have told me about those horrid slayings. If I can help you with something I will, but what specifically did you come all this way to ask me?"

The leather seat squeaked as Dr Sutton sat back. Dacre had no prepared answer, but Isla's 'you need help' still echoed in his mind. He finally overcame his clamped vocal cords.

"Why me? I mean why do I know these things?" He had taken himself by surprise, and his hoarse words reverberated.

But Sutton appeared to have been anticipating the question like a student who had a sneak preview of the exam paper.

"Good. I hoped that was what we could talk about. As I said, I have become very interested in hypnosis as a tool to explore the subconscious. My reading has led me towards hypotheses that I was sure I would never test. However, your account suggests you may be a perfect subject. Ideal."

Dacre had exhaled some of his tension but felt himself reinflate.

"You mean you want to experiment on me?"

Sutton laughed. "No, no, Dacre. Don't worry. I am retired and my reading is a hobby now. I don't publish my work these days. Let me fetch some more tea." Dacre looked distractedly around the room until two more cups of tea were on the table and Sutton was back in his chair.

"Shall I tell you what I think? You are what I am beginning to describe to myself as 'super-susceptible'. What I mean by that is you are especially sensitive to hypnotic trance induction, and you have a wide channel open to the deepest reaches of your subconscious." He was polishing his glasses again. "On top of that it is just possible, though still very unlikely, that you may have what is often dismissed ... has often been dismissed by myself, I should add ... as bunkum: 'second sight'." Sutton's precise and considered words seemed to flow naturally and reminded Dacre of one of his physics lecturers.

"What do you mean? Second sight? Like thought-transference or something?"

"Well done! That is the kind of area I am interested in. Phenomena loosely described as paranormal and often derided, but which I am beginning to believe may have a basis in reality. What does thought-transference mean to you?"

"I have no idea. A sort of supernatural power, like in the comics, horror stories, that stuff?"

"Some certainly believe it to be supernatural, as you say, but it has been studied for many years broadly under the more usual term, telepathy. It means the transfer of thoughts from one mind to another. Whether it exists or not has been debated for many years. Do you believe it is possible?"

Dacre felt uncomfortable but flattered to be asked his opinion. He shifted in his chair and put his teacup down on the table. Looking without focus at the wall opposite, he said, "I think I know what you mean. If you are talking about it, well, I mean, it must exist, surely?"

"I'm not sure myself but I am very interested in the idea,

even more so since you wrote to me. Since the afternoon your letter arrived I have been reading about trance-like states. I hadn't thought before about the possibility of hypnosis channelling telepathy, or perhaps facilitating it, so to speak, and I am fascinated. I really would like to hear about your hypnosis, and how you learned to induce yourself so effectively. I think you said a friend taught you?"

Dacre described his struggle to find a therapist and how Miles had eventually helped him.

"And how is your friend? Does he find it as effective as you do?"

Dr Sutton was leaning forward in his chair listening intently, but sat back frowning when Dacre said, "He committed suicide. He couldn't make it work for him. I found his body, in a wardrobe, suffocated." He was surprised at how easy it was for him to tell Dr Sutton. He had taught himself to avoid thinking about Miles, and he could see it had shocked the psychologist, who was frowning and shaking his head.

"How absolutely awful for you! You alluded in your letter to fears about unwanted effects of hypnotherapy, and now I understand why. And the poor chap! Oh, Lord!"

In his letter, Dacre had meant his dreams might be side effects, and he'd tried to put aside what hypnosis had done to Miles. But the memory of the decaying body in the wardrobe was never far away.

Both were silent for a few minutes. "I must wet my whistle," said Sutton rising from his chair. "I'm very dry. Can I fetch you something while I'm at it?" He walked out before Dacre could reply.

Staring at the ceiling Dacre tried to find an excuse to leave. He didn't want to talk more about his dreams, or his guilt about Miles. But Sutton returned with two large glasses of whisky.

"I don't know about you, but I need one of these, and it is Saturday, after all." He smiled and put the heavy glass down beside Dacre, "And anyway, it's almost time for the football results." He switched on a small TV which Dacre hadn't noticed amongst the piles of books, and the teleprinter began shuddering across the screen. The taste of the whisky was not pleasant, but he liked the warming in the middle of his chest. By the time he had half-finished it, Sutton stood up. "Another? The only beer I have is homemade I'm afraid, but you're welcome to try it."

"Err ... yes please." Dacre wondered what he was letting himself in for.

The thick, cloudy beer went down surprisingly easily, and the two relaxed and talked football for a while until Dr Sutton took him outside. He had to see to the goats. A large jug of thick and creamy milk was soon handed to Dacre to take back to the kitchen, where Morna Sutton was busy baking.

"Oh, thank you, Gordon, here, I'll take it from you." She took the jug to a small side room, and he saw her straining to open the door of a tall fridge.

"Oh, my joints! Don't get old, Gordon." She smiled brightly and winked. She had retrieved the glasses and refilled Dacre's with beer. "I'm very glad you've come. It's a long time since I have seen Granville sparkle, enjoying someone else's company. He was awful after Trish died, although I was glad to see the back of her. She wasn't good to him. Played around, if you know what I mean." Dacre was struck dumb and took a long slow draught from his beer.

"Is dinner nearly ready?" said Sutton, shaking off a pair of clogs at the door.

"Leave those outside, I'm always having to tell you. And yes, nearly. Maybe twenty minutes."

"Good. Time for another beer. Come on, Dacre, I want to tell you something before we eat." He marched off quickly, with Dacre following.

"Dr Sutton, I had better get going before you have your tea. I need to—"

"Nonsense, you'll eat with us, and Morna will drive you back. She hasn't had a drink since she went on her new tablets. Come on, sit down."

"But my bike ..."

"Listen to me. I've worked it out, what's been happening to you, I mean. Sit down." Another whisky was poured to go with the beer.

***

It was after nine o'clock as the Volvo rolled along with Morna Sutton at the wheel, her son asleep in the passenger seat and Dacre's bike on the roof rack. They'd had slow-cooked lamb with minted boiled potatoes and homemade bread, followed by blackberries with sugar and a dribble of creamy goat's milk. Dacre stuck to beer, letting Dr Sutton have a bottle of red wine to himself. The conversation had been lively, easy and humorous.

As Mrs Sutton leant forward to concentrate on driving in the dark, Dacre went over again his new friend's summary, which seemed to explain his problems perfectly. Granville Sutton was convinced of Dacre's super-susceptibility, as he called it. Under the effects of hypnosis, he could delve deep into his subconscious and process memories. Dacre had been relieved when Sutton dismissed the possibility of him being telepathic.

"I don't think I want special powers."

"Rather like you didn't want to be Flash Gordon, I suppose."

Sinking back into the worn leather bench seat, Dacre breathed in the goaty aroma filling the car and remembered the first time he'd met Dr Sutton, the elbow patches and his kids in the Morris Traveller. Over their pre-dinner drinks, Sutton had gone on to suggest that Dacre might have witnessed traumatic events in childhood, possibly involving his parents. Patient confidentiality had prevented Sutton from spelling out anything he knew, but Dacre strongly suspected that his mother had confided her affair to him after the appointment. Dacre recalled Sutton's careful summary as he sipped malt whisky.

"The severe trauma of your fall, the injury, and your parents' issues conspired to induce your acrophobia. It was a defence mechanism you developed against admitting to your parents' problems, and one which remained relatively effective until the phobia impeded your love life. At this point, you chanced upon hypnotherapy as a remedy for the phobia, and your super-susceptibility awoke the old, forgotten, painful memories. Am I making sense, Gordon?"

Sutton was speaking clearly, despite the whisky. Dacre nodded him to continue.

"When your parents argued after your accident you became very frightened and blamed yourself. You buried those bad memories and concentrated on punishing yourself, with the phobia. But when you used hypnosis, much later, you uncovered those traumatic things and had a primal need to re-bury them and defend yourself and your family. I believe your subconscious dredged up other traumatic things you had heard about, but forgotten, like the TV reports you had seen about murders, to distract you from your parents' issues."

"But why did I think my dad was a killer?"

"You had uncovered unfortunate things about your mother, things you didn't like." Sutton had hesitated. "Your subconscious needed to balance your mother's ... er ... guilt, with something. It used the pure coincidence of your father's work locations to invent some guilt for him."

Dacre had to interrupt again. "But what about the cartoon murder? How did I know about that? I know it happened, it was real, I mean. But I can't have seen somebody draw cartoons about it."

"That's a little difficult to explain, I give you, but I'm sure there must be something. All in all, I think Ellie ... er ... I mean your mother, might deserve a bit of ... understanding."

Dacre had thought Sutton seemed unusually flustered for an instant, suddenly cleaning his glasses and losing eye contact. "I'm sorry about all the trouble I've given you, Dr Sutton."

Dacre's subconscious had falsely linked murders he'd heard about to his father. 'Joining the dots,' Sutton had said, in a sophisticated attempt to find a defence mechanism against his parents' problems. To help him avoid confronting his mother. Isla had been right!

***

Dacre went to bed happy that night. Dr Sutton had helped him understand his bizarre dreams, and why he had linked his dad to murders ... to shift his focus from his mother's guilt, and to excuse himself from stirring up trouble between his parents. He looked forward to telling Isla about the power of the subconscious mind, and that she had been right about it all.

He barely had to start his induction routine before he was deeply asleep. Dreams yet again replayed the film of his mother with Bugsy ... the same embrace, the same room, the paintbrush and the jar, and then his mother sitting up with her lover concealing himself under blankets. But instead of hatred of his mother, he woke full of admiration of his dad's forgiving nature. If he could forgive her as his dad had, things would stay fine.

Chapter 34

September 1977

Dacre was relieved his parents' marriage had survived. Now that he understood where his ridiculous ideas about his dad had come from, he found it easier to tolerate his mum and began to be civil to her. He was generally more positive, looking forward to returning to Aberdeen to patch things up properly with Isla. Her brusque manner on the phone was his fault. He shouldn't have phoned her when he had been drinking, rambling nonsense about his dad and murders. He tried a few more times to phone her and managed to shrug off his disappointment. She would never have gone out with Campbell. What had he been thinking?

A week or so before the start of the new term, he carried his washing to the kitchen.

"You're well prepared! I'll make sure that's all clean for you for next week," said Elinor over her shoulder. She turned off the tap and continued, "There's a letter for you."

He mumbled thanks and managed to smile back at her. This time it wasn't another brown envelope from the university, and he recognised the handwriting: his first letter from Isla. Brimming with joy he returned to his room to open it.

37 Kinlockhart Avenue
Edinburgh

14th September

Dear Dacre,

I am sorry. I have tried to talk to you. Since we finally spoke two weeks ago I have tried to telephone you lots of times, but just like all summer you are never in. I cannot take it any longer. As you haven't called me I know that must mean you still haven't faced up to your problem about your mum. I was already wondering what to do about us, but when you started going on about those totally crazy things about dead girls in your dreams it was just too much, and has made me decide. I am so sorry, but I don't want to go out with you anymore.

I'm not going to be at Hillhead next year. I'm moving to a flat.

I'm sorry, and I hope you can sort your problems out. Perhaps if you do, we can meet up again sometime.

Bye.

Love,

Isla x

A cold sweat broke, and heavy thumping in his chest.

She's moving to a flat! Not at Hillhead. How? I tried! I called. She was never in. Fuck! Fuck!

Lying back on the bed, tears flowed and a low moan escaped.

"Gordon? Are you OK?" Elinor knocked lightly at his door.

"Bitch!"

"Gordon, what's happened?"

"Fuck off! It's all your fault."

"Gordon!

***

The next week was unbearable. He couldn't wait to get away from his home and his parents, but Dacre dreaded being in Aberdeen. And he was angry. Angry at his mum, and when he admitted it, angry at Isla. *Why had she said she had tried to phone him?* He had asked his dad almost every night if there had been phone calls for him. *And why had she always been out when he called? Why was she lying to him? Campbell?*

His anger grew and grew, but as he read and reread the letter eventually some resignation to the situation grew alongside it. After a few days, he couldn't bear the sight of the letter and dropped it into the desk drawer amongst a selection of discarded tickets, leaflets, and notebooks he'd used as a child. Once he was back in Aberdeen he'd have Spiny and David. To hell with women. Even Isla.

One evening he had been leafing through botany books and returned distractedly from a visit to the toilet, intending to start packing. Alun was in his room, rummaging through the scatter on the desk. "Where did you put those old Bayviews?" Alun had collected East Fife match programmes for a while some years back, and when he had lost interest Dacre had taken them.

"What?"

"There's one with an advert in it for GLSE. Dod wants to keep a copy of it for some reason. I said I'd take it to work tomorrow. Where are they? What's all this gubbins?" He was scuffling through the desk drawer.

"I threw them out last year." Alun didn't hear, too absorbed in his search. Dacre went back out, annoyed at the intrusion and deciding to pack his things on Saturday. They didn't need to leave until the afternoon. When he returned to his room with a coffee, he saw his dad about to read Isla's letter.

"Hey! That's private! Give me it."

"I thought you had chucked that girl months ago. Still pestering you, is she?" He was smiling. Cruelly, it seemed to Dacre.

"Give me that!" He snatched the crumpled paper and screwed it up.

"I wanted to tell her to stop phoning. Every bloody night, bloody cheek! I kept telling her you were out. It was as if she didn't believe me. Bloody women, they're all the same."

"Fucking get out!" Dacre pushed his father to the door. He lay on his bed trying to make sense of what had just happened. Why would his dad think he and Isla had already broken up? And what did he mean about telling her he was out? When? Had she phoned? His mum had taken no calls.

Dacre was still angry and confused when he tried to get to sleep. It was difficult to reach trance, and in the end, he tried to empty his mind by reciting an East Fife team list. Had memorised them years ago from the old Bayviews.

***

'Dodod gone. Dodod gone.' His mum laughing. Echoing sounds. The van drawing away. He was looking out of the living room window in Auchmoor, just able to see over the sill if he pulled himself up to stand on the settee.

***

Drifting towards wakefulness Dacre mumbled to himself, "Christ! Dreaming about Dod Lambie! It must have been Dad mentioning him last night ..." He rolled over.

***

Walking barefoot on the landing, shivering cold, night-time. Someone crying. Or laughing? Squealing? Creaking floorboards under his cold feet. The brown Sapele door, his tiny hands pushing against it. Sudden quiet. Mummy sitting up in bed. Scruffling bedclothes beside her.

***

The dream was worse, better, more confusing, but clearer than usual. The squealing stayed with him. Pain? Or laughter? Ecstasy? He tried to piece together some sense from the dramas in his sleep. Dod Lambie? Was this a new dream suggesting it was Dod in the bed with his mother? But Redbond was the lover. She had admitted it.

Tears were collecting. He'd slept all night and he was

despondent and exhausted. To hell with hypnosis! He'd only started it to stay together with Isla, and it had caused their break-up. It had caused all his problems. He'd rather have the acrophobia.

***

Crossing the old stone bridge over the River Dee, the van came to a standstill in a queue of traffic. He glanced to his left, over the parapet, and caught sight of the river flowing underneath him. A fleeting sickness rose until he looked away. His dad engaged gear to pull away, swearing again at the traffic.

***

The journey with his dad had been OK at first. There was no room in the van for his mum and Dacre had managed to hug her before he left. Alun had stopped outside some shops in Dundee. "I'm getting some cans for tonight. It's always cheap here." He returned with four cans of lager, mint humbugs and a betting slip. The trip had been planned to take in some overtime for Alun. Another journey to Inverness, this time extended by a detour via Aberdeen. "Dod will never know," he had said. "He never checks the mileage."

The radio crackled and kept drifting off the station. Dacre found the distortion of the wavering signal even more infuriating than Radio Two. When they were past Montrose and crossing the old bridge over the North Esk, Dacre turned to his father. "I need to ask you something, Dad."

Alun stopped humming to 'Coward of the County'. Dacre noticed for the first time that his father's hair was thinning. The scaling bald patch reminded him of a pocked potato pushing through the side of a dreel.

"Don't tell me you need advice from your old man? I thought you were too clever."

Dacre ignored the jibe. "Did you say Isla had phoned? And you told her I was out?"

"You mean the posh girl? The one that kept phoning for

you?" Alun grinned. "I protected you from her. You didn't *really* want to get in with a posh lot, did you? Mind you, maybe you should, your bloody Uncle Douglas comes in handy. Anyway, your mum said you'd broken up. I just kept telling her you were out. Why?"

"When?" Dacre felt sick.

"Lots of times. A couple of times you were in the bath after work. Sometimes you were in the pub. I did you a favour, eh?" he said, winking conspiratorially.

"Mum said we'd broken up? When?" His voice was wavering, the lump in his dry throat swelling.

"Soon as you came back from Aberdeen."

What did the bitch say that for? Now, Dad has made things even worse. And he thinks he's helped me. What a fucking mess!

***

When Alun Dacre drove away from Hillhead he was unaware of his son's distress. Keen to get through the Aberdeen traffic on his way to Inverness, he drove off into the September gloaming with just a quick nod. Dacre trudged to Esslemont House with his grip slung on his back by the handles, lugging his heavy suitcase behind him up the gentle slope. He left the case at the foot of the stairs and made his way wearily upstairs to his flat. It felt as if he had never been away. Disinfectant and fresh paint didn't completely mask the familiar odour. Miles would never be gone. But he felt surprisingly at home until he remembered Isla wouldn't be coming.

He had hoped Spiny might be there, but there was no answer at his door. Someone called B. Sharkey was to have Miles's room, and the other three doors also bore new names. David had moved into a flat off King Street. The posters had all been removed, and his room seemed small, empty and cold. When he dropped his grip on the bed, it smeared some grease on the folded duvet. *Fucking van!*

Taking a step forward, he looked through the window, reflexly glancing towards Adam Smith House. Dejected, he looked down, and immediately the ground began to spiral sickeningly up to meet him.

Chapter 35

Dacre's resolve to forget Isla crumbled. Between morning lectures, he quickly made his way to High Street in the hope he might see her among the throng. Crowds of students weaved to and fro between classes; some were finished for the day already, some just arriving. He took a long way round between his chemistry and botany classes, but remained disappointed. New scarves and jackets were on show, with assorted distinguishing adornments of handbags, haversacks and LPs. Dacre had been late for a lecture one morning after lingering until he made sure a girl in a green jacket wasn't Isla after all. He was desperate to explain that he had been trying to contact her, his dad had got it all wrong. She still didn't even know he'd been to see Dr Sutton.

By Wednesday evening he was despondent. He was also finding second year more demanding. Only two subjects meant more detail, and evidence of research. Already he had a schedule of essays to complete, and he'd had to buy a pile of new and second-hand textbooks. Initial enthusiasm had waned as the year's work stretched out before him, and he felt overwhelmed.

Lying back on his bed, Dacre realised he was also very lonely. He didn't even know where Isla was living. He kept hoping it wasn't too late, and even that perhaps she had been testing him with her letter. It was irrational, he knew, but he had to make sure she was not, in fact, back in her Adam Smith room, waiting for him.

"Hi, Davey."

"Aah, you're back, are you?" The Adam Smith porter recognised him and waved him in. The flights of stairs were like old friends. He knew every crack in the pale green walls, but tonight he knew they were old friends who would mock him if they knew what a pathetic mission he was on. He knew she wouldn't be there, and even if she was she would spurn him. But still he crept on up, cursing his new shoes for their siren screech on the polished linoleum. A landing door below him crashed open, and he heard loud voices. He froze until he was sure they were going down.

He didn't even need to knock. A new name tag on the door of T21 told him Isla was gone. It was a relief, really: she wouldn't confirm his rejection to his face. Shoulders slumped, he sighed and made his way back to the stairs. Pausing on the top landing he leant on the white windowsill. With his forehead against cool glass and a strong smell of new paint catching his throat, he realised his hands were sticking to the wooden sill and almost smiled through welling tears. Way below him was the empty carpark and a grass border. He looked straight down the sheer grey wall at a row of huge, wheeled refuse bins, and a new path of concrete slabs. Against the bottom of the wall and directly below him was a large heap of builder's sand. *Geronimo!* As he watched, the sand began to roil and eddy and the ground around it spun. The birling sand seemed to reach up towards him and brought a tornado of vomit boiling up through his gullet to lash the back of his throat. The window he leant on gave way and he fell screaming towards the slabs.

***

The hospital trolley moved slowly. Each tiny bump under its wheels sent oscillating waves of dinging pain from his neck to his forehead and back again. Vomit and blood fouled his mouth and blocked his nose, but a smell forced its way through. A strange smell, not one he associated with hospitals.

The motion of the trolley rolled his head and his cheek touched against cool plastic. The reek became stronger. Refuse. Stinking rotten rubbish. Forcing his eyes open, instead of a hospital corridor, he saw an open sky. A staked sapling passed by and he saw a grey paramedic pushing his trolley. Another walked alongside him, laughing.

"Aye, the loon's fair fou, right enough."

“Yer nae, jokin’. And I never noticed when he came in!”

Slowly he processed his situation. The hospital trolley was a refuse buggy and the paramedics were porters, wheeling him across Hillhead. His moaning caught their attention.

“It’s alive! C’mon, son. Oot ye get.” The man pushing was done in.

“Some hangover tomorrow, loon.” The other one was still laughing.

“I’m not pissed,” managed Dacre, “I don’t know what—”

Davey from Adam Smith took over pushing. “You had a good shot at it, son. I was the one that found you, puke aw doon yer jacket.” Despite Dacre’s denials, the two porters had decided they knew better.

“The lassie that found ye was fair disgusted. She was going to report a prowler, then she saw ye’d fallen down drunk on the top landing.”

“Aye, she’d to step over ye to get down the stair.” Davey had found him slumped against the wall on the second-floor landing. He had caught his nose on the windowsill as he fell, and it was bleeding into his sick. The other porter was called from Fyfe House to help remove the unconscious Dacre, and the two had carried him down to the service exit. The bin trailer had served this purpose before.

“I ken you’re in Esslemont,” said Davey, “but which block is it?”

“T29.”

“Top floor,” said the Fyfe man. “I’m no carryin’ him away up there.”

Dacre was helped up off the oozing black bags and propped against the wall. Dacre thought Davey had always seemed to like students. “C’mon, son. You’ll manage. You’ll sober up by tomorrow. Haud on tae the rail on the stairs, mind.” His head was banging and he couldn’t face trying to explain. He didn’t know what had happened, anyway.

***

By the time next morning's lectures were over, Dacre's head wasn't hurting so much, and his nose didn't bleed when he blew it. He was glad when he saw a note on the tutorial room door: 'Two o'clock Chemistry Tutorial CANCELLED (Tutor held up).' As he wandered back through the park to Hillhead, he was still looking out for Isla. Back in his room, he gingerly pulled last night's clothes from the bottom of his wardrobe. He hadn't tied the top of the plastic bag properly and he retched at the smell of vomit. He hadn't expected to need the launderette so early in the term.

Watching the machine wobble on its base he chewed one of his father's sticky mint humbugs. He had known the acrophobia would come back, but last night had been bad, more intense than any attack he remembered. And it was only a week since he had stopped hypnosis. The first indicator of trouble was crossing the Bridge of Dee in his dad's van, and he'd tried to dismiss that as fury at his mother. And his dreams were still as bizarre. Last night he had heard James Robb insisting his big brother could fly. Had he remembered Spake telling him Robb's older brother had died in a fall? Or were more buried memories of his own emerging?

As the machine slowed and his tumbling clothes began to become distinguishable, the checked shirt, yellow Y-fronts and blue denims, so Dacre's thoughts focused on the choice he still faced. It was either live with the disabling phobia or restart hypnosis and reveal more horrors buried deep in his subconscious. It was as if hypnosis was a drug he was addicted to. He had proved again that if he stopped treatment the inevitable consequence ... the withdrawal effect ... was a severe worsening of the illness. He was hooked.

Dr Sutton had said he did not believe hypnosis itself was to blame for Miles's death. He suspected Miles had been so clinically depressed it made hypnosis unsafe. He'd said any clinically trained hypnotherapist would have refused to continue treating him when he had such a severe mental illness. Dacre wasn't ill in the same way, and hypnosis for the phobia should be safe, although it might make him remember other things he'd forgotten. Sutton didn't think being super-susceptible meant hypnosis wasn't safe.

Dacre decided to just deal with any new dreams that came along. He had no choice but to start treating himself again—if he was going to be normal. And there couldn't be much more in his past he'd forgotten. He wished he could explain it all to Isla, but he knew she had meant it. It was over. He emptied the machine and threw his clothes into the huge tumble dryer. He noticed the Adam Smith windowsill had left white paint on the heels of his hands.

***

It was easy to enter a trance that night, and the short time he had denied himself his drug seemed to make it even more potent. He slept well and felt altogether better the next day, his mind clear and focused. He chatted freely and enjoyed himself with his classmates, gladly taking coffee and lunch with them, instead of searching for Isla.

He continued to self-hypnotise every night. Soon his fear of heights was history and new confidence grew. The old dreams still reran nightly, but they were familiar and unthreatening now that he understood them. There was one new and very distressing one, but he managed to explain it away by reminding himself of Dr Sutton's advice. He modified his morning routine by adding a few minutes of light trance with ego-strengthening, and repeated to himself a script that blanked out any dreams from his memory, at least until the next night. Overall he was very pleased with himself.

When he did think of Isla, a refreshing nostalgia replaced the woe. He would see her some time, he knew, and he would like to know how she was getting on. It was a shame they had parted, but he would be fine.

Chapter 36

The pace and intensity of second year were still challenging, but Dacre enjoyed it and the time passed quickly. Within a few weeks, the heavy schedule of essays and tutorials meant he spent several evenings each week in the library. He worked well in the atmosphere, the swish of heavy swing doors and the hushed sounds made by other conscientious students.

One night when he'd gone to the library to check botany references, Dacre looked up when an autumn gale shook the building. Heavy rain lashed against the window, and a bright orange street light shimmered through rivulets weaving down the glass, splintering the late October darkness outside. He was reminded of The Great Romano's stage lights in the Music Hall, arranged in mesmerising strings intended to create an eerie backdrop. That all seemed years ago. It was that show, he mused with world-weary nostalgia, that had sparked his interest in hypnosis. He'd become resigned to his situation though, and thoughts of Isla or any other girlfriend had receded. The past was the past, and his parents could fix their own problems. His future would be to apply himself. He had even considered doing joint honours in his two subjects, unable to choose between them.

"What the fuck are you doing here? It's Friday night, for fuck's sake!"

There was loud tutting from the girl behind him. Reflected grotesquely in the wavy window in front of him was a mass of tight ginger curls raised over hunched shoulders and a broad back. Until then she'd been the only other student on the second floor.

"What are you looking at, Coco? Anyone ever tell you your head's like an explosion in a mattress factory?"

Dacre couldn't help laughing out loud at Spiny's cruel but hilarious insult. Under cover of the wind and rain, his flatmate must have wandered in through the doors, and now stood at the end of the large table Dacre had spread his books on.

"What are you doing in the library?"

"I just fucking asked you that! Come on! It's the weekend. You've been a boring shite. We're going out." Spiny grabbed at the piles of lecture notes and books, scrunching some of the Maud Jepson drawings Dacre was so fond of.

"Are you pissed?" whispered Dacre, loudly, trying to stifle more laughter.

"Fuck aye! Like you should be. C'mon!"

The girl, or Coco as she would now be known, tensed visibly, sighed loudly and threw a filthy stare at the reprobates. Guffawing and trying to retrieve his notes from Spiny, he clattered along behind his friend. The swing doors whooshed closed as the pals ran heavily along the landing. They whooped and banged loudly on the banister, stamping their feet like children all the way down to the ground floor. Dacre felt a welling rush of joy and anticipation.

"Dump that shite! You're not taking books into the Union."

Dacre obediently propped his canvas bag against the wall in the vestibule. Probably his last sensible thought for the night was that a porter might take it to lost property.

A beer in the Machar, and then a run in the rain to the Red Lion for a couple more meant it was almost ten o'clock when they made it to the Union. The Dungeon was stowed out, sweetly smoky, and wonderful. Dacre wondered to himself what he had been thinking. He hadn't lost his skill in threading himself to the bar, and bought a double round, passing the first two pints back over the heads of the jostling rows behind him. He'd supped an inch out of each of them for safety. Spiny was a closer, more valued friend with every pint, and by the time the volunteer stewards herded them up the stairs and pushed them out into Upperkirkgate, Dacre felt bonded to him for life.

The last 20 bus was pulling away down Littlejohn Street by the time they had organised themselves to try and catch it.

Spiny shouted, "Fuck you ya tossers, fuckin' buses are for tossers! Tossers!" The rain had eased, at least, and with no choice but to walk back to Hillhead, they wavered off singing and shouting. Spiny had a vague idea they might find a different bus in King Street.

As they approached the university sports ground, chattering voices from behind them drew Dacre's attention. A group had emerged from a taxi, laughing loudly. With horror, he recognised Isla was among them. All his mature promises to himself ebbed quickly away.

The four from the taxi turned left towards Kings College, the two in the middle holding hands. Isla was to their right, and a boy was on the other side by a hedge. As they turned, Isla caught sight of Dacre and called out to him.

"Dacre! Where've you been? I've been trying to see you. Oh, Dacre! Come here." He could tell she was a bit drunk. He was elated, but the lone boy stepped round the couple, who had started snogging, and stood beside Isla. As Dacre approached, the boy grasped her hand. She looked quickly at him and pulled away. The boy looked daggers at Dacre, who was shocked to recognise his cousin.

"We're going back to Campbell's flat for food. Oh, come with us, Dacre, please." Isla was delighted, giggling, and seemed to have forgotten Campbell's clumsy approach to her. Dacre hadn't.

"I haven't got enough food. Or chairs," Campbell interjected.

"Don't be silly, there's room for two more. Hi Spiny!"

Isla had rushed forwards and was holding Dacre's arm. She looked from Spiny to Dacre and back, grinning widely. "You two look like you've had as much to drink as us!" Dacre thought she looked lovelier than ever.

"Anyway, the flat's on the third floor. He'd never cope! He's always had a problem with heights. Come on Isla, leave him there, he's drunk." Campbell was pulling the other couple to encourage them to move off towards his flat.

"Dacre's over his heights problem, aren't you? He's cured it; he's a genius."

Through his beery haze, lusty distraction and anger at his cousin, Dacre managed to think to himself: *He's jealous, he wants Isla, the bastard! But she defended me! I love her.*

Campbell wasn't giving up. "That's a lie, he couldn't manage up a high kerb. Ever since his mum had it off with '*Uncle*' Bugsy!" Dacre shook himself free of Isla and ran at Campbell who dodged to one side, letting Dacre run into a low garden wall and fall over it into a shrub. "Ha! Watch you don't fall, Gordon! Careful that wall's not too high! Ha!"

Dacre was half-lying in the bush. He saw that over the road behind Campbell, and beside the Bobbin Mill where he had once taken Isla for a meal, there was a building site. Rising above the rooftops at forty-five degrees was the steel lattice arm of a crane. Yellowish in the street lights, it was swaying in the wind.

Dacre pushed himself out of the bush and suddenly ran over the main road.

"Dacre! Be careful! What are you—?" Isla was going to follow him, but Campbell pulled her back, as an approaching taxi driver honked and shook his fist.

Spiny had been dozing against a wall but roused in time to see his pal disappear into the shadows. "Where the fuck's he going? Needin' a pish, Dacre?"

Oil drums were arranged round the perimeter of the building site, with heavy wooden planks laid between them to form a safety barrier. Dacre leapt over and reached the crane. He turned back to call to the group over the road, "Just watch me, you lanky posh wanker!"

Grasping the handle of the crane cab, he hauled himself up onto the caterpillar tracks and gripped the underside of the lifting arm. Soon he was clambering up the shaft, still shouting towards King Street.

"Fuck's sake! Jeezus! What a fuckin' laugh!" was all Spiny could say over his laughter, as his pal waved at them from high above the roofs. Isla was not so amused.

"Dacre, please, come down! You'll kill yourself! Oh, please! God! What are you doing?"

Dacre was undaunted, fired up by anger, pride, joy and drink. He carried on climbing until he was at the end of the boom. "See, Campbell? Heights? Fuck off, you big posh speccy poof!"

"Hoi! You! Fuckin' geddoon!" The night watchman had woken up. Dacre scrambled down, leaping the last ten feet to evade the watchie, who tried to run under the crane's boom to follow him. Dacre was too fast, though, and crashed through the plank barrier to run up the lane beside the Bobbin. Soon he was back on the other side of the road, breathless. Spiny was breathless with laughter. Isla was shaken, and hugging him. The necking pair, oblivious, had grappled their way some yards along the road, impatient to find shelter. Campbell stomped past them unnoticed, towards his flat.

Spiny and Dacre each had an arm round Isla's shoulders as the three made their way to Hillhead.

***

On Saturday morning they lay in late. Stretching her cramped limbs and pushing herself up on one elbow, Isla looked at Dacre where he dozed beside her with a foot on the floor to stop himself falling out of the single bed. She sighed. "I thought you were never going to speak to me again. What happened to us?"

Stirring, Dacre murmured, "I didn't even know you'd phoned."

"But I kept phoning and you were never in."

He turned to look at her. "My dad got mixed up by something my bloody mum said. Then I gave up when I decided you were probably going to go out with Campbell. When I saw you with him last night, I nearly ran away."

"What? I was only there because I had gone looking for you again. Then we met Campbell and his friend. Marie said he might know where you were, and we should stick with him. But really it was his flatmate she wanted to stick with."

"That was Marie last night? They were pretty steamy, I thought they were going to do it against the wall."

"Oh, god! I wonder how she got home? I shouldn't have left her there."

"She looked like she could handle herself. I thought the guy was going to disappear down her throat."

After he had made coffee, Dacre came back in and sat on the edge of the bed in his Y-fronts and T-shirt.

"I did worry you would go off with Campbell. He always seemed to have everything I wanted when I was a kid."

"He's a creep. I wasn't with him last night. Not like that. He kept pawing at me in the taxi. That's why I told the taxi driver to stop where he did. Then when we saw you, he started trying to hold my hand."

They were quiet for several minutes. Both looked elsewhere sipping their coffee, and Dacre humming to the radio. Isla broke first. "Do you think he knew about your mum all along?"

"Fucking bastard. My mum must've told Aunty Janet. Bitch. Bitches!"

Isla squeezed his hand. "Come on. We've missed breakfast. Let's go for a walk."

"I couldn't eat anyway, I'd puke. Fresh air might be good."

They strolled hand in hand along the sand beside the Don estuary, the tide out and their feet making deep impressions in the sloping sandy bank. When they turned north to walk beside the crashing North Sea a stinging wind chilled their cheeks and deafened them. They climbed the steep dunes and sat on the sand in a quieter hollow amongst the dense tufts of marram grass. Dacre told Isla about going to her old room to look for her at the start of term, but not about his collapse.

"I didn't even arrive for the beginning of term anyway. I

had a bug and was laid up in bed. My mum said it was exhaustion after working all summer." She paused when the screams of gulls suddenly filled the air. "I didn't want to move into the flat, it just sort of happened. My mum heard that Sarah was looking for a flatmate. I knew Sarah all through school and Mum's friendly with her mum. I was really miserable when we seemed to be breaking up, and I'd rather have been back in Adam Smith, but I didn't have the energy to argue. They all seemed to think it was a good idea and my mum thought it would cheer me up."

"Was your mum glad you'd chucked me?" Dacre had worried his frequent phone calls over the summer were annoying Mrs Alexander.

"No, she's not like that. And she was disappointed when she saw the flat. It's freezing. You should have heard my mum going on about Freda. That's Sarah's mum. Freda'd made it sound like it was a palace. It's a dump. I was even more miserable. I wish I'd never written that letter."

Dacre put his arm round her shoulder and she leant in to him. "I've got to ask you, Dacre? Did you face up to your mum? I've got to know we aren't going to end up with you taking it out on me again." She hugged him tightly.

"I did and I didn't. I mean ..." He felt Isla loosen around his shoulders, and went on quickly, "Well, it's OK, I have sorted all that out. I did what you said, I needed help."

Isla sat back with a quizzical look. The wind was blowing sand around them. Dacre wiped her dark brown hair from over her eyes and smiled, shaking his head. "I went to see the psychologist, Granville Sutton, the one I saw as a kid. You were right about me. I had invented it all, sort of, like you said, to put off tackling my mother." Dacre described to Isla his visit to Sutton, and the psychologist's formulation of his situation.

"Your poor dad. And then he got it all wrong about us. I'm sorry I wrote the letter but I really had no idea you had been trying to call me."

Dacre held her hand tightly and said, “I’m trying to do what my dad’s done. Sort of forgive her. If I stir it all up it might make it worse for him. They seem to have worked it out somehow. I wish she hadn’t bloody told fucking Janet, though!”

Isla kissed his sandy cheek and smiled. Wind tears were drying around her eyes. “Come on, my bum’s getting wet from the sand. And it’s Saturday. Let’s go to the Union.”

As Dacre stood up to follow, he said, “I’m starving. I want egg and chips.”

Chapter 37

November 1977

"Your hands are freezing!" Isla drew back from him and smiled. "If you think you're coming near me tonight, you'd better warm up."

"Aye, it's brass monkeys, too early for white stuff even in Aberdeen." Dacre's teeth chattered as the snow on his hair melted down his neck. "Come here, warm me up." He reached for her again and she giggled and pulled back to let him into her flat.

"No chance! I told you last night, get some gloves."

"I've got some, it's just—" He paused, turning away to close the door.

"You said the same last night."

Dacre turned and took his dripping jacket off, hanging it on a hook. By the time he had turned back round, the coat was on the floor with the hook and some crumbly plaster. The Crown Street flat wasn't maintained like Adam Smith had been. It was now well into November and the hall was icy cold. They left the jacket where it was, quickly closing Isla's bedroom door behind them to stop more heat from escaping. Her mum had visited the previous weekend and taken her to the Electricity Board shop in Union Street. The fan heater she had bought struggled to warm the room much above unbearable, though, and they had continued to spend most evenings in Dacre's room. "You only want me for my radiator," he had joked. The shared single bed didn't seem so bad this year, and the evening visits soon required Isla to come prepared to stay over. Tonight they'd arranged to go to a new pub in Belmont Street, near her flat.

"Can we leave the heater on when we go out?" asked Dacre, hopefully.

"Sarah would kill me. She's immune to the cold. She goes

about half-naked."

"I know!"

"Keep your eyes off her." Isla laughed and grabbed him. "God! Warm your hands on the heater, please!"

Dacre had almost bumped into Sarah on his first morning in the flat. After a night spent concealing his presence to spare Isla's blushes, he had been desperate for a pee. Unable to wait any longer, as soon as he heard the front door close he'd run to the bathroom and forced his bladder empty, the noise of his cascade echoing in the icy little room. Coming out, he jumped when he heard a breezy "Good morning!" from the narrow hall behind him. "I didn't know we had guests."

Frozen to the spot, he had turned slowly round to see Isla's flatmate framed against a dark stained door, wearing only a red towel. Dacre had managed to stutter, "Sorry, I thought you were ..."

"You always leave doors open?"

"Sorry, I ..." He held his hands in front of his Y-fronts.

"No, I mean you might have closed the front door properly when you came in last night. I've only just closed it. I'm Sarah, by the way." She had walked towards him, an inch or two taller than Isla and a little heavier. She was barely concealed by the towel and he hadn't been able to help noticing her tan, and how small her bikini must have been. When he blushed and looked at the floor, she had simply squeezed past him and into the bathroom.

"I just met Sarah," he had said as he crept back into Isla's room. "I think we left the flat door open. I thought she had gone out."

Isla had moaned and turned over pulling the duvet over her head. "She'll tell her mum. Oh god!"

"Where has she been to get a tan at this time of year?"

***

Wednesday 30th November 1977

After another chemistry practical, Dacre walked back to the Central Ref chatting with Bill, who he knew had grown up in Reading. Bill had seemed friendly and interesting a few weeks ago but was now becoming tiresome. Dacre had begun to notice small details about him. He carried his notes in a briefcase, and when he had opened it in the Ref one lunchtime, there had been a *Daily Telegraph*. Dacre had no interest in politics, or, if he admitted it, current affairs. Bill, on the other hand, in between sprayed gobs of a soggy, homemade Dairylea sandwich, made it clear his opinions mattered. Amongst other things, he thought those around the low, round table shared his dim view of the evil TUC.

"What's a union, anyway?" whispered Ronnie. Ginger and freckled, he was from Thurso.

"Who cares?" grinned Dacre, rising to escape to the toilet in the foyer. As he strode past the glazed outer doors, he was dazzled by low winter sunshine reflecting off the window of a parked car over the road.

"OK, then! Ignore me!"

He spun round at the sound of Isla's mocking voice. "I wasn't expecting you. I don't usually see you during the day. Anyway, what are you lowering yourself for, coming in here?" He smiled, and she wiped crumbs from his cheek before kissing him. Not many arts students used the Ref which was surrounded by the brutal, concrete science buildings and stood a few hundred yards away from the leafy cobbles of ancient, sandstone Kings College.

"I just wondered if I'd find you here. I want to come to Hillhead with you."

"I know it's Wednesday, but I said I'd check over some stuff in the botany lab. I'll meet you after—"

Pulling his hand, Isla whimpered. "You like your plants more than me! I wish *I* was a pretty flower." As she looked up at him through her lashes, her other hand brushed his hip and slid a little down his outer thigh. "I'll just have to go back to my cold flat."

"I could get Ronnie to do it."

Hurrying through Seaton Park purposefully, they held hands. "I'm going to find your gloves!" said Isla. "Your hand feels cold even through mine!"

***

"Oh, turn that off!" They lay warm together. Dacre had been nearly dozing, and now reached out to silence Radio One. Sleet lashed at the window, melting downwards, and the floodlight under the eaves cast orange light. Black branches farther away formed a waving backdrop. Turning back he stroked the back of her neck. "In this light, your hair looks red. I can imagine you as a sexy redhead."

Isla's green eyes sharpened. "I'm not dyeing my hair for you! Especially red. Yuck!"

He giggled and nuzzled his face into her neck, inhaling her scent. "What's wrong with red hair? I thought Mary Queen of Scots was a redhead?"

"What's that got to do with anything, Rizzio?" Dacre had dropped history at school and was out of his depth.

Isla sighed. "Oh, god! I've got to go back to Crown Street, and look at the weather! It's my turn to make the dinner." Dacre still thought dinner was a midday meal. He watched her pull the curtains over and begin dressing. He was suddenly hungry.

"What are you making?"

"Macaroni cheese."

"I'll come with you on the bus. Make sure you're OK."

Looking down at him as her head squeezed through the sweatshirt top, she grinned.

"Is it food you want or another look at Sarah?"

Before they left his room, Isla stopped. "Get your gloves!"

"I'll manage," he said, reaching for the Yale.

Isla put her foot out and stopped the door. "Where are they? I'm going to find them."

"Ach! They're in the bottom of the cupboard under a load of stuff. Come on, we'll miss the bus."

Slipping past him, Isla pulled both doors of the wardrobe apart. "You lazy devil! You haven't even unpacked all term!" On the floor of the wardrobe, there was a pair of new gloves, still in a Draffens Department Store bag. Redundant hangers rattled in the space above. "But where do you keep all your things?" Still at the door, Dacre slowly looked up from the floor. His eyes flicked automatically upwards and Isla looked up behind her as he had unwittingly indicated. Elinor's old suitcase lay at an angle on the top of the wardrobe. There was a single, striped football sock hanging out.

"I, err, just use the same stuff, mostly. The grip carries enough." He pointed sheepishly to the canvas RAF holdall which she had noticed was always at the foot of his bed.

"I thought that was just your washing."

"It is, but that's what I dress out of."

"For god's sake! Get the case down now and let's see what else you've got."

"But the bus—" She was having none of it. He had to lift down the case, and she arranged his remaining clean clothes into the wardrobe. She sniffed each item from the grip to assess it: dirty, or clean enough for her to tolerate. Closing the wardrobe doors, she shook her head and looked down at Dacre, who had sat apparently in disgrace on the edge of the bed, staring at the floor. Keen to catch the bus, he now stood and reached for the flat door, but Isla gripped his wrist, laughing, "We forgot the gloves!"

"Oh, it's OK, I'll manage."

"No, get them, you idiot."

Dacre stood still, staring at the floor again. "I can't."

"What?"

"It's OK. Let's go."

"No. What do you mean? What's wrong?"

Turning sharply away and heading for the main door, Dacre pulled away, muttering, "I … I don't like the wardrobe."

He went out without her, and she had to run to catch up with him on the path to the Central Building. "Dacre! Come on, please, tell me what you mean?" On the bus, he managed to tell her he had been having nightmares about the wardrobe since early in the term. He would wake in a sweat, sitting up, sure he had been shouting.

"I don't think I do it when you are there. Do I?"

One of Isla's friends came up the bus stairs and sat across the aisle, chattering and unaware she had interrupted anything.

***

Tea was taken with Sarah, who was fully dressed. Dacre was pleased to tell Isla afterwards that she wasn't nearly so attractive with her clothes on. Isla was quiet, though, and thoughtful. When they were alone, she hugged him. "You've sorted the acrophobia and the thing about your parents, and even that awful murder stuff. But you've developed another problem. I've been thinking, it must be what happened with Miles."

Dacre told her that was exactly what it was. Fleeting images of the tied polythene bag, concave over a silent mouth, its choked scream drowned by the buzzing insects; staring eyes pleading through a milky layer of plastic and munching maggots. These pictures sharpening into focus each time his dream replayed filled his head with the stench of decay and faeces. One night, he had woken to find himself scrubbing at an imagined stain in front of his wardrobe. Now it was coming back to him even in the daytime.

"Why didn't you tell me?" Isla had tears in her eyes when she let him go.

"I was scared I'd lose you again. I had the dreams under control at first, y'know, by doing my wee ego-strengthening thing in the morning. But that stopped working, and the new dreams about Miles got even worse. And then the ones about my fucking mother came back. It's all my fucking mother's fault! And I even hate Miles now, 'cos I got him to help me, but he couldn't help himself. I know it's stupid and it wasn't his fault and I ... I ... feel guilty. Oh, fuck! Fuck! Fuck!" He was crying like a baby. "And anyway, there's another thing, even worse. I can cope with Miles if I don't look in the wardrobe. But I'm not even sure it was Bugsy my mum was—with."

Isla's flowing tears prevented her from responding, and Dacre continued, "In that dream, I mean that one with her fucking in the bed with him, I mean in the fucking bed. Fuck! But sometimes I think it's ... it's ... oh fuck, I don't know! It might be Dod Lambie in the bed."

"Who?" Isla sobbed.

"It doesn't matter if it's Elvis Presley. I've proved all that murder stuff was nothing to do with anything, but something has been going on with her. Something I've *got* to know. It's *still* messing everything up."

Neither of them slept much. Discussing his problems left them both exhausted but restless. Isla drifted off eventually, but just after two o'clock she roused to see Dacre dressing quietly.

"What are you doing? Where—?"

"I'm going. It's no good, I'll never sleep. I'm going home tomorrow after lectures. I've got to sort it out. I've got to know. I don't even know who she was with any more, but I'm going to find out what's caused all this. Even if I never see my fucking mother again afterwards!" He was pacing the cold bedroom as he buttoned his shirt.

"But Dacre, come back, how will you get back to Hillhead?"

He was able to force a smile, and kiss her lightly on her forehead, before saying as bravely as he could, "I'm going to sort it out."

"Don't wake Sarah."

He walked the three miles back to Hillhead, barely aware of the cold. In George Street, a police Cortina slowed to pass him. Satisfied he was sober, the two big men drove on.

***

Dacre was surprised to wake to his dinging alarm clock, having slept soundly. After a shower, he shook out one of the T-shirts Isla had consigned to the dirty pile. The wardrobe could wait. And he could miss lectures. This was more important.

Part III

Chapter 38

Thursday morning. By half-past nine, Dacre had caught two buses and reached the Bridge of Dee. For half an hour, he stood wishing he had money for the bus or train, and then his luck changed. A van stopped, the driver heading for Perth, but with a drop off in Dundee. By lunchtime, his thumb was out on the Tay Bridge slip road, and by two o'clock, he was dropped in Cupar, only a twenty-minute bus ride from Auchmoor. He would be home before his father finished work, which would make tackling his mother easier. His dad would probably feel he should defend her.

His neck prickled with anxiety, but he was determined to face the drama of confrontation. He'd rehearsed his lines enough times, and on the walk from the bus stop he allowed himself to note minor changes to Auchmoor: the shop that had changed hands, a house for sale, and new double yellow lines outside the post office. In first year, on his first trip home after an extended period away, he had been shocked and offended by alterations to his childhood kingdom. Now a mature and worldly-wise nineteen-year-old whose horizons had stretched, he could accept that Auchmoor might not stay the same forever. Nonetheless, it was reassuring there had been no changes in Rothes Drive to upset his composure.

The front door of No. 22 was locked. His carefully chosen words left him, along with his confidence. His mother was never out, and this was not in the script. Suddenly feeling conspicuous, Dacre looked next door at No. 24. The front doors and gardens of the two semis were separated by a low privet hedge, clipped only on the neighbour's side. No car in the drive meant Miss Crockett was out. Throwing an anxious glance over his shoulder at the familiar homes over the road he scuttled over the grass in front of the living room window and round to the back door. He found the key under the dustbin and let himself into the kitchen, closing the door quickly and remembering to lift it as it swung. Alun still hadn't repaired the grating draught excluder. Where the hell was his mother? And why did *he* feel guilty?

Half-day closing meant Elinor wasn't at the shops and he couldn't imagine where else she might go. He sat at the red drop-leaf table with a dry mouth, picking angrily at the grimy hinges. The house was unusually cold. The Auchmoor house had always been warm, but today felt more like Isla's flat. The hook for his father's overnight bag was bare, meaning he was working away. Even if it was delayed, at least that meant the confrontation was unlikely to be interrupted.

Where is the bitch?

"Mum!" he shouted, to make sure. His voice echoed in the cold, unwelcoming house. He crept out into the hallway, still trying to remain inconspicuous in the empty house. A draught through the letterbox followed him upstairs. His parents' room door was half-open, and a tatty green Dundee Equitable shoebox lay on the bed. The room was dim, and rather than flicking the light switch, Dacre squeezed round the bed to open the winter curtains, with none of his old whirling fear. He stood, colder still near the window, and squinted down through fading daylight at the empty street. The bare birch tree next door whipped in the wind and the feeble street light reflected in a puddle on the muddy stripe over the grass, the shortest path to Alun's van.

There was no sign of his mother approaching, and he stood fighting off the temptation to feel relieved. But looking back at his parents' bed, the scene of the adultery he knew he had witnessed, fanned the flames of his anger once more, and he let out a deep growl. He fell forwards onto the mattress, punching deeply into the squeaking bedsprings.

His teeth were furred from biting the bedspread when he opened his eyes. The shoe box was now on its side, its contents spilled onto the pink candlewick. Pink in winter, blue in summer, changed with the curtains, he thought. The box too was familiar. Always in the bottom of the wardrobe, it had held old knitting patterns Elinor's mother had given her. He couldn't recall her knitting since he was at primary school.

Dacre pushed himself up and rolled onto his side, muddy feet on his parents' pillows. He struggled to banish thoughts of Redbond in the bed. Or Lambie. Papers, hand-addressed envelopes, old recipes and some black-and-white photographs were randomly mixed with a few Sirdar cardigan patterns. There was the tiny monochrome image of his mother as a child. He remembered laughing with her when they found it in his grandmother's effects. An ancient buff document, folded and frayed, caught his eye. There was gothic script on one face, and on unfolding it he saw inside:

Extract Entry of Birth

Underneath, written in navy, longhand ink, he recognised the names of his grandparents, John Gray and Ethel Gray (formerly McPheat). One neat word in the first column stood out: Eleanor. His mother's name misspelled on her birth certificate.

Weird. Misspelled or did she change the spelling?

Tossing his mother's birth certificate aside, he ruffled through the assorted paper, selecting an envelope addressed in clumsy capitals to:

ELINOR DACRE, PERSONAL

He extracted a sheet of lined paper, and a coldness prickled up his back and nape.

DEAR ELINOR,

I HOPE YOU ARE WELL. I'M SORRY WHAT HAS HAPPENED AND HE KNOWS AND HE

HAS BEEN PHONING MY WORK I AM AT THE COUNCIL GARDENS AGAIN ITS THE BUSY TIME. HAS HE BEEN UPSET AGAIN.? I MISS YOU AND WISH IT WAS DIFERENT AND I COULD STILL COME AND SEE YOU AND GORDON HOW IS HE. IS HIS ARM MENDING AND DOES HE KNOW.? IF YOU WANT CAN COME HERE I HAVE ROOM HE CAN COME TOO GORDON I MEAN.

LEAVE HIM.

YOURS TRULY

YOUR BUGS

PS I MEAN IT THERE IS ROOM HEAR FOR YOU X

Shaking, Dacre looked again at the envelope. The address was in what could have been a child's handwriting; above it, a postmark: 26-MAY-1967. The buff envelope bore smudgy fingerprints.

He rolled onto his back, tears forming, fists tight. He felt sick.

It was Redbond. And the dirty bastard wrote to her. And she kept the letter. I didn't imagine it!

Restless, Dacre jumped up and paced the space between the wardrobe and the bed. When angry curiosity had overcome rage, he sat back down and flicked through the assorted letters looking for the writing he could now associate with birthday gifts from long ago. There was one more letter from Bugsy. The date read 13-JAN-1968. Steeling himself, he drew the lined paper out and held it like a nettle.

DEAR ELINOR

I AM SORRY I CALLED AT THE HOUSE I JUST WANTED TO SEE YOU AND GORDON AT CHRISTMASS SO I BRUOGHT THE PRESENTS I HOPE YOU LIKE THEM. HAS GORDON GOT THE MOSQITOE AIRFIX I HOPE NOT HE COULD CHANGE IT. ARE YOU OK I NEED TO KNOW AND IS IT THE SAME FOR YOU? YOU KNOW WHAT I MEAN I DREAM ABOUT IT LIKE YOU DO TOO.?

I WANTED TO COME AND SEE YOU BEFORE BUT ALUN SCARED ME OFF I AM NOT A FIGHTER AND I THOUGHT HE HAD BROKEN MY RIBS THAT WAS WHY I GAVE UP THE JOB AND NOW I'M IN PARTICK. THAT TIME I SAW YOU ON THE BUS WHEN I WAS COLECTING TOOLS TO TAKE BACK TO GLASGOW I WANTED TO HOLD YOU AND MAKE YOU HAPY THEN I DEECIDED TO GET THE PRESENTS.

I WAS NOT FORGETTING. ARE YOU OK.? COME AND LIVE WITH ME HERE AND GORDON I MEAN IT THERE IS ROOM IT IS A BIG FLAT AND AWAY FROM HIM.

YOUR LOVING BUGS

So, Alun did know. He had fought Redbond off and sent him packing. Pride and pity whirled as Dacre pictured his father fighting for his wife. He remembered Alun's clumsy comments on their trip to Crianlarich. 'Moody bitch.' 'Kept in line.' He had been bravely trying to protect his son from his own misery.

Next was an envelope with neat handwriting, his Aunty Janet's. On crisp blue paper he read:

16, Cedar Grove
Currie
Midlothian
EH14 5ZP
29th November '68

Dear Eleanor,

I have thought very hard before writing to you but I have not been able to rest after seeing you last weekend. I am very concerned about you. I tried to ask Alun about you when you were washing up but he wouldn't speak to me. He looked so upset, and I could tell there was something terribly wrong.

I know you told me there was nothing going on between you and Mr Redbond but from Alun's reaction when I asked him I could tell that you had been lying to me. I was always uneasy about how much time that Bugsy spent in your home when Alun was away. How can you do that to Alun, and put your marriage, your whole family, at risk? I know I didn't approve of Alun when you married him, but he is the father of your only child! Perhaps things would have been better if you had had another child. My two are just perfect. Please think of the effect on Gordon, who is clearly having problems and becoming maladjusted.

Since Mum died there has only been the two of us, and as your Sister, I feel I must try to stop you making a terrible mistake. I do so wish our father hadn't died so young. I feel sure things would have worked out better for you if you had had a proper male role model. I was so lucky to meet Douglas.

Eleanor, I had to write. Please consider things very carefully.

Your sister,

Janet

Reeling, Dacre fell back on the bed again.

Christ! Janet did know. Fuck! Maladjusted? What a cheek. Snobby bitch! And fucking Campbell went after Isla! Bastard! What did he say that night in King Street? He fucking knew as well! He said so, the night of the crane! They all knew. About Redbond. Laughing at my dad! 'Had it off with "Uncle" Bugsy!' he said.

The next letter he found had no envelope. Unfolding the lightweight sheets, he recognised his mother's writing. Somehow, he knew it was written on paper torn from the back of one of his school jotters. His mum kept them all at the end of each school year. He could smell the classroom.

7/1/69

~~*Dear Janet*~~
~~*Janet*~~
~~*Jan*~~
~~*Dear*~~ *Janet,*

I trust you enjoyed your Christmas and New Year.

~~*Keep your nose out of*~~

I am sorry I am late in replying to your last

letter. I was too ~~angry at you for interfering again~~ busy.

We had a lovely good time at Christmas, just the three of us. Alun was off work because there was no work for him to do, so his boss, George, made him take his holidays. We won't be going away in the summer, anyway, so it doesn't really matter. ~~We're not all as lucky as you and your rich husb~~

I must reassure you that there is nothing going on between me and Bugsy, and there never has been. I don't know where you took that idea from. If Alun made you believe that you must have misinterpreted what he said. He gets moody at times, that's all. Don't worry, I am fine.

I too miss Mum terribly, and since she passed on I have also thought more about our childhood. I have no regrets about giving up my education to look after Mum, though. You took a different path ~~even though I did so much better at school than you ever did~~. Alun has been a good man, really. He just gets moody, and I put up with it. We are fine, the three of us. Alun had absolutely nothing to worry about with regard to Bugsy, but in any case I don't mention him now at all. Alun fell out with him and warned him off over a year ago, anyway, and I doubt very much if we'll ever see or hear from him again. The poor chap was harmless, I promise you. He was a good friend but nothing else. Thank goodness Gordon is too young to have ever thought anything like that. Thank goodness children are innocent and pure of thought ~~unlike you~~. I know Gordon will miss him a bit, but he doesn't seem to mind not getting his Christmas presents anymore. I didn't want Alun to be upset.

I do hope we see more of each other this year. The time passes so quickly.

Warm wishes,

Elinor

At that moment, Dacre wondered if he could hate his mother more. She had kept a draft of the letter she had sent to her sister. The letter denying what he knew she had done. She must have kept the draft to make sure she could keep her story straight, he thought. She didn't know he had seen her with Redbond. Contact with Aunty Janet and her family had almost stopped around that time and Dacre now guessed the two sisters had fallen out badly.

When his tears dried up, he lay silent, brooding, exhausted. Eventually, he slept.

Chapter 39

"Do it again! Do it again!" The humpback bridge was the best thing ever. He screamed in delight as his racing car veered to the left, then the right, passing through the bends in the road. "Do it again!"

His mum laughed beautifully behind him, but called, "Slow down a bit! You'll tip him out." The little wheels whizzed round over the compacted, grit surface of the racetrack. He had never gone so fast, and his excited squeals echoed under the massive chestnut tree, leaves like huge fingers spreading to filter the sunbeams. They were approaching the humpback bridge again!

"Wheeeeeee!" The pushchair took off on the brow. Its wheels spun and the cracked white leather strap strained at his waist, until the buggy crumped down again, expertly brought back on course by the strong hands behind him.

"That was a good one!" exclaimed his dad, as they accelerated along the straight.

"Do it again!" Gordon loved the racetrack, as he thought of it. A few yards of pinkish tarmac laid out in the park, it had bends, road signs and a traffic light to teach children road safety. A few more circuits and all three were tired, Gordon from excitement and laughter, his mum from trying to keep up in case there was a fall, and his dad from pushing. As they slowed down, Elinor caught up.

"Let's get an ice cream," she said, smiling at her son.

"Ice cream! Ice cream!"

Straining in the strap to turn round, Gordon looked up pleadingly to his dad.

"OK, let's get ice cream, I could do with a breather!" said Bugsy.

***

Dacre was aware he was screaming. His head pounded, and his neck was twisted as he peered over his shoulder trying to make sense of what he had seen. The pink bed cover was tangled round him and the muddy, white pillows were on the floor. The brown and orange circles on the wallpaper made him feel sick.

What a nightmare! As if Redbond was my father. He couldn't be?

Flopping back down on the bed, he looked at his watch. Ten past two. It was pitch dark outside and the street light was swaying in a gale. He was shivering, and sweating, and realised he had slept for hours. Lost, alone, and perplexed, he lay for a while trying to banish the fresh doubts his latest nightmare had inspired, until he could bear the cold no longer. He rolled off the bed and trudged downstairs to the kitchen, suddenly ravenous. He hadn't eaten since yesterday's hurried Hillhead breakfast roll.

He had two glasses of milk and a dozen rich tea biscuits in the cold kitchen, the windows lashed by volleys of water blown from the bare branches. Miserably, he made his way along to his old bedroom. There was a dirty boot print on the carpet, he noticed, and his bed was unmade. His back copies of *Sounds* were still piled under the bedside table, but on top was a *Penthouse* magazine and an open socket set. Dacre sat on the edge of the bed, no longer his own it seemed, and flicked through the magazine. At other times he would have felt youthful arousal. Tonight, he felt sadness, pity and guilt by proxy. His dad had been expelled. Sent to sleep downstairs. Reduced to this.

He lay back on the bed, the light still on. No tears flowed, and his eyes felt parched as he fought not to blink them closed. His nightmare remained vivid, with its cruel ending threatening replays if he slept again. He tried to distract himself by opening his old scrapbooks which he pulled out from under the bed. One was devoted entirely to the 1970 World Cup, and Dacre shook his head at the cruel irony when one of the tabloid newspaper cuttings fell out. On the back was a crudely drawn image he recognised. Carol Hosie's body with a thick, zigzag line indicating where her right hand had been sawn off. It was the sick cartoon from his dreams, the missing link explaining his knowledge of the third murder. He threw the scrapbook at the wall, furious that he'd ever suspected his father.

Something else was wrong, out of place, nagging. The changes to his room were superficially minor, but something was missing. The old wire for his aeroplanes was still there, crossing below the ceiling. And the wardrobe, safely closed.

A new space gaped at him from above the wardrobe, the magnolia a little less bleached by light. His grandmother's suitcase had gone. For as long as he could remember, at least from his move to the downstairs bedroom those years ago, it had lived on top of the wardrobe. Its contents had been a gripping, child's mystery until it had eventually blended into the background, forgotten. Its absence now brought a sinking realisation that his dream had distracted him from the obvious: his mother had not returned last night.

His thoughts raced: she had left and gone to Redbond; it was still going on. The letters made that obvious. Fury propelled him back upstairs, and let him throw open his parents' wardrobe without fear. There was the old wedding dress he had made her show him once, long ago. A sky blue rain jacket purchased for the holiday to Wales, never worn again. Empty hangers, and his father's suit, a sleeve button still missing.

Dacre slammed the wardrobe shut and turned. The letters still littered the bed, and he lashed out at them, dashing the box and its other contents to the floor. He snatched at one of Bugsy's scribbled notes, and read it again, his rage rising. If he couldn't have it out with his mother, he would have to face both of them. Partick. He would go there now.

One envelope poked clear of the pile. The word 'Hospital' was visible through the window in the front, and 'CONFIDENTIAL' along its top edge. Dacre snatched it out and unfolded it. A handwritten note on a piece of plain paper fell out. 'DEAR ELINOR, I AM SORRY TO SAY I SHALL NOT BE ABLE TO SEE YOU AGAIN. I AM TRULY SORRY. GOODBYE. GRANVILLE SUTTON. 17/9/70.'

Dacre read the letter.

Department of Psychiatry

Royal Dundee Liff Hospital
Dundee

Ref. GBPS/ED

Mrs E. Dacre
22, Rothes Park
Auchmoor
Fife

14th March 1969

Dear Mrs Dacre,

Thank you for your letter, which I collected from Dr Mackie's secretary last week.

I can assure you there was no need for you to be concerned or embarrassed. I hear a great number of sensitive details about my patients' lives. Indeed, before I specialised in Developmental Psychology in Children, I worked for several years with adults who displayed a variety of psychiatric and psychological problems. At no time has my patient's confidentiality been less than foremost in my mind.

When I met with Gordon last month, it was most helpful to have your assistance in helping your son. The complex background relationship problems in the family and with others are, I am certain, very pertinent to the origins of Gordon's difficulties. Without knowledge of the relationship you described I would have found it very much more difficult to formulate Gordon's problem and devise a plan for therapeutic input.

Please let me reassure you further that none of the details you disclosed was entered into any clinical records, and will remain between yourself and myself only.

I trust Gordon is making satisfactory progress and I expect him to recover fully by following the advice I passed on to you. I enjoyed our talk and I do hope I have helped you. If there is any more I can do, or if, indeed, it would help for you to see me again about Gordon, please do write to me again.

Yours sincerely,

Dr Granville B. P. Sutton

So she'd told Sutton what she'd done and then wrote to him afterwards to make sure he kept her guilty secret. And she must have gone to see him as well.

"Very pertinent to the origins of Gordon's difficulties," he said out loud. "I should fucking say so! Look what you've done to me, you bitch! And you, Redbond! Bastard!"

Chapter 40

Hitch-hiking would have been too risky when getting to Glasgow mattered so much. Dacre caught the early bus to Kirkcaldy, and then the train, changing at Edinburgh Waverley. The letters between his mother and Bugsy Redbond seemed to prove her infidelity. Dr Sutton's letter to her mentioned 'relationship problems in the family' and 'the relationship you described' as the cause of all Dacre's problems. Now that knew this for certain he was going to let her know it.

When the train drew into Glasgow, Dacre felt he was sucked out of the carriage and swept along the platform on a tide of forging bodies. When he emerged from the blackened, sandstone station, green and yellow double-decker buses filled the road.

His confident rush to Glasgow to confront Redbond and his mother had been impulsive, but now he was disorientated and uncertain. "Watch yersel, son!" A tiny woman in shiny white boots pushed past him. He found safety against a damp, stone wall, feeling cold and small. To his right, a man in a donkey jacket was shouting and selling newspapers. Dacre made his way to him.

"Excuse me, where is Partick?"

"Seven pence." A *Daily Record* was thrust at him and the seller pointed back inside. Dacre tried asking at a ticket office.

"Doon there. The inner circle, fae Buchanan Street." The man pointed to an escalator that seemed to disappear down a tiled corridor into a tunnel. Dacre suspected the man was pulling his leg and walked off.

Buses in tunnels?

Back outside, he finally noticed a bus with Partick on its destination sign. He followed the road the bus had taken. By ten o'clock, he was well along Dumbarton Road, checking over his shoulder the front of every bus to ensure Partick was ahead. His legs were weary and he was hungry. On a busy street corner, a woman was washing a pub window. A swinging sign above the ornate door told him it was the Rosevale Tavern.

"Excuse me, can you tell me how to get to Partick?"

The woman continued her work, but said cheerfully over her shoulder and round a cigarette, "Aye, son, yer in it."

"Oh, right, thanks, where does Darren Redbond live?"

She paused, and turned, grinning. Her smoke mixed with the steam rising from her bucket of brown, soapy water. "Ehh ... let me think? Which Danny Redbond would that be?" With a gap-toothed smile, she continued, "Jeezo, son, Ah dinnae know aw the men! Ah've nae idea. Partick's a big place, son."

Embarrassed, Dacre walked away, mumbling, "Sorry."

"Hang on, son. D'ye nae know his address?"

"No, but he's a gardener, I think," Dacre said, turning. She seemed friendly. His mouth was dry, and it was the most he had spoken since he got out of the fish van that had dropped him in Cupar the day before.

"Hang on, ah'll see if Gerry knows him." She swung the big door open and shouted inside, "Gerry, a lad here's looking for a fella called Redbond. D'ye know him?"

Dacre couldn't hear the muffled reply, but the woman turned and said, "Gerry says there's a van goes past here with Redbond on the side; that's aw he knows. Says try the Yellow Pages. Sorry, son, ah'll need tae get on."

"You no finished they fuckin' windaes yet?" came from within.

A phone box nearby had no Yellow Pages, but a directory was lying on the floor. It was damp, and smelled of urine. Gagging, he flicked through to R, and his heart leapt when he saw:

Redbond, D 96c Esmond St ... 732 4325

An address and a number. There can't really be more than one D. Redbond, he thought.

The pub cleaner gave him directions, but the closer he got

to Esmond Street, the more uncertain Dacre became. His resolve to confront his mother and her lover was now melting away. What if he was wrong? He leant against a crumbly red brick wall and closed his nippy eyes. Clear pictures floated in front of him: his mother embracing Bugsy, the paintbrush and cream, and the moving bedclothes concealing his 'uncle'. The familiar scenes faded in and out in front of each other and his wrist ached. The pain roused him and restored enough determination to continue looking for No. 96. He was going to confront the bitch.

A neatly painted word leapt out at him from the side of an old but gleaming white transit van:

DUNLOP and REDBOND
Landscape Gardeners
041 732 4325

Redbond. Dacre felt an ache in his chest which dropped into his bowels, then rose with a nauseating rush to squeeze sweat onto his brow. He had to sit on a low, damp wall, the chill seeping into his thighs and buttocks as his heart gradually slowed, and some strength returned to his legs. He pushed himself up from the wall, his hands cold and slimy with moss.

The main door to No. 96 was wedged open and Dacre walked in. Flat C was on the first-floor landing, and above a *Welcome* coir doormat, the deep red door had a large, curly brass knocker. He stood hoping no one would be in, but he could hear Santana playing inside.

Dacre felt his fists clench and his teeth grind. He tapped on the door lightly. The music continued. He looked at the brass lion with the heavy ring in its mouth, sighed, and made five loud raps. He heard footsteps approaching on the other side of the door, and wanted to run.

The door swung open, and a man in a pale sweater and fair,

permed curls looked out curiously, and then smiled at him in recognition. "Hello, Gordon! Gosh! What a surprise!" Dacre froze. The man was familiar, but it was not Bugsy. "Come in. Come in. This is nice! Does Darren know you're coming? He didn't say." Lost for words, lost even for thought, Dacre followed the man into a carpeted hallway. "He's not in, I'm afraid. He will be sorry; he talks about you a lot."

"But ... err ... sorry, I'd better go. I'm in the wrong place, sorry." Dacre turned, confused.

"I don't think you've recognised me, Gordon, have you? I'm Roy. Roy Dunlop, from Auchmoor High."

"Mr Dunlop? What?"

A rush of realisation confused Dacre even more. This was Mr Dunlop, Randy Roy, the PE teacher and heartthrob the boys had looked up to and the girls had longed for. He couldn't for the life of him work out why Randy Roy was here, or how he'd managed to get Bugsy's address wrong.

"I'd better go. I'm sorry, I made a mistake."

"Now, Gordon, you mustn't rush off. Darren will be so sorry if you do. He's only painting a gate in Kelvingrove. I was going to go and pick him up in about an hour. You can come with me; it'll be a lovely surprise for him. He does miss you, even after these years. And your poor mum." He gasped and put his hand to his mouth. "Oh, no! Is your mum OK?"

"But how? I mean why, I mean, how did you know I was looking for Redbond? Sorry. What's going on?" Dacre's mind was galloping, his heart thumping and his mouth dry as a stick. Nothing made sense. "And what did you mean about my fucking bitch of a mother? Did you know what was going on? Did you have her as well? You bastard! You were another of her lovers!" The word tasted awful as he spat it out. He looked down on Dunlop: he was now three inches taller than his once-feared but respected teacher and role model. Impulsively he moved forwards, chin out. Dunlop shrank even smaller and backed away, arms lifted in defence.

“Gordon, you’ve got it wrong. My only lover is Darren.”

Dacre froze, fists ready, but knees wobbling. “What?”

“Oh, Gordon, you’re old enough to know now. We had to get away. It was getting so hard to carry on living like that. I left and found a job here until Darren could join me when we found a flat.”

“What? You and Redbond? You mean you and him? Poofs?” Dacre slumped against the wall, and slid down to a crumpled heap, his head feeling like a burst balloon. He was exhausted and confused, all his pent-up fury and determination draining away with his strength.

Chapter 41

"Gordon! Are you awake?" A loud whisper.

Another voice hissed, "He's slept for two hours. He looked awful, lying on the floor."

Dacre's eyes slitted open against low winter sunshine flooding in through a tall, narrow window. An ornate cornice threw wavy shadows onto the ceiling. Two black silhouettes moved to his right, filling with colour as they left the window's glare. Morphing into view nearest him, the taller one loomed in close and smiled, the white teeth and high brow familiar and soothing. Dacre stifled an excited giggle, as he readied himself for the big hairy tickling arm to reach into his cot. But the permed head leaning out from behind Uncle Bugsy was not his mum, and Dacre sat up quickly in alarm, reaching out in vain for cot sides. "What? Where? Uncle Bugsy?"

"Shushhhh, Little One."

Rubbing his eyes, Dacre stretched and yawned, still not able to fully escape his dream. Bugsy was still there, but where his mother should be was Roy Dunlop. There were no cot sides, and he pushed himself up on a chocolate brown couch, looking at corduroy ridges imprinted on his arm. He felt a jolt as Dunlop's revelation came back to him, and he looked sharply at Redbond, incredulous and suspicious.

"You and him?" was all he could mumble.

"Oh, Gordon, I'm so sorry; I couldn't have explained why I had to leave. Your dad—"

"Leave my dad out of it! He's the only innocent one! And my name's Dacre."

Redbond turned away and looked at Dunlop. His shoulders dropped, and he sat on the arm of the couch. "Gordon … sorry … Dacre, Roy and I want to help you, but you don't understand what's happened." Dacre thought he might be crying.

"I don't want your help. You've caused enough trouble. And now him! Why am I lying here? Oh, for fuck's sake! I don't know what's going on." He lay back, rolling his head with his fists pressed into his eyes.

"You're exhausted. I had to drag you along here to the couch."

Dunlop had spoken, and with horror, Dacre sat back up. "You touched me? I don't want you to touch me!" He looked at Redbond and said bitterly, "He tried to tell me you're a ... you know ... one of them! Like him. Fucking nancy!"

"Gordon, it's true, Roy and I have been together for years. Before you were born."

"But you were shagging my fucking mother!" He stood up quickly and advanced on Redbond, who didn't move from the end of the couch. As Dacre prepared to swing, Dunlop sprang between them and caught his right arm, effortlessly pinning it behind his back.

"Roy! Leave him, don't hurt him!"

Dacre shrunk back, grudgingly respectful of Dunlop's power and agility. Released, he sat back down on the couch and rubbed his sore wrist. Dunlop stepped back, massaging his left knee and shrinking back. Redbond stayed at the other end of the couch, and turned to Dacre, looking him in the eyes. "Elinor knows all about me and Roy. She's my ... was my friend; I always wanted to help her, until your father forced me away. Nothing more than friends. She knows me. Your father is a bastard. A thug. A bully. Oh, Gordon! You should both have come here with us."

Dacre remembered the letters.

There's room here for you. Bring Gordon. It's a big flat.

And he remembered about the smashed ribs. "But my dad beat you up because he found out about you being with my mum. That's what happened, isn't it? Or are you going to try to tell me it was Dod in the bed? But I read your letters ... it was you! That's why you think he's a thug. He was just looking after us."

As Dacre paused, his voice drying up, Dunlop spoke, "It

wasn't only Darren he beat up."

"You as well?"

Dunlop looked to Redbond uncertainly, who looked away. Neither spoke.

"What do you mean? What? Who? What the fuck?" Dacre was becoming anxious. He was suspicious that he had misunderstood something, or had been kept in the dark. He was still reeling from the idea of Redbond and Dunlop being homosexual, and unsure whether to believe it. He couldn't cope with the idea there might be something else.

"Oh, Gordon! You were too wee. It wasn't Roy he beat up. Your mum protected you from it all." Bugsy was now staring at the floor, talking quietly. Dacre noticed black paint on his hands and a smudge on his left cheek.

"What do you mean? Protected me from what?"

"He broke your mum's ribs one time."

Fury rose in Dacre once again.

The bastard's trying to blame my dad!

He stiffened, ready to respond, but Redbond went on. "I could always tell when it had happened again. She would be wearing a scarf to hide the bruises." Dacre pictured his mum, the scarf in summer, the dark glasses, puffy eyes, the days in bed. It had meant nothing to him at the time, but now he felt a sickening rumble deep inside, like an earthquake shaking his world.

"What are you saying?" Dacre's voice trembled.

Still without looking up, Redbond spoke quietly. "Your dad gave your mum a lot of awful beatings. I'm sorry, Gordon, but it's true." He looked up with tears in his eyes.

Disbelief drained out of Dacre, and he filled with searing rage. "You're trying to tell me she is the victim? Really? My dad? No!" He strode to the window and stared out.

"It's true. Ellie, I mean your mum, thought you might have known, 'cos you walked in on us once when I was helping her put make-up on the bruises. She was terrified you'd seen. I told you it was a game we were playing. You were only about four."

The little paintbrush! The jar of brown stuff!

Dacre couldn't speak. Clouds had filled the cold wet sky and dull yellow light fought through the net curtain on the window opposite.

Redbond went on. "And she said you saw Alun hitting her once, or just after. He hid in the bed."

His shoulders heavy, Dacre sighed and muttered with resignation and defeat, "I thought that was you, under the blankets, in my fucking dream." His eyes were moist. "It wasn't a dream ... was it?"

Bugsy got up and stood behind him, a yard away. Dunlop said, "I'm going to make us a drink of something", and went out closing the door quietly. Dacre turned slowly from the window and saw Bugsy watching him gravely. It was dawning on him that he had got everything wrong. "But why the fuck did no one stop him? If he did that?"

"Ellie, your mum, she wouldn't tell anyone. I only knew because there was one time I had to help her lift you, when you were a baby, she was too sore. She broke down, told me what was happening."

"That thing with the make-up ... it was bruises? That was ... real?"

"Oh, Gordon, I'm sorry!"

Dacre's tears overflowed, and he leant back against the wooden shutter. His hands picked at some cracked paint. Uncle Bugsy had been ever-present in his childhood, and his earliest memories featured Redbond in the place of his real father. Now it seemed his guilt about that was misplaced and undeserved. And that his dreams had very different meanings. "He really hit her? My dreams were real? Oh, fuck ... the scream in my dream! It was—I mean not dreams, I mean ... it was her screaming?"

"I'm sorry." Bugsy turned and sat down on the couch. "I

tried to help her as much as I could, Gordon. I was the only one who knew. She asked me to help but she wouldn't let anyone else know. She was worried for you, didn't want you to know anything." He looked up at Dacre. "I was there when you fell out of the window. You saw us, we saw you fall. You were looking right at us."

"In your letter, you said my dad knew about you. You mean it was about, you know, he knew you were ...?"

"I don't remember the letter exactly, but I know it was when he found out I knew he was bashing Elinor that he turned on me. He always knew I was gay, I mean, that's why he let me spend time with Elinor. Oh, he's an awful man, Gordon. I only stayed in touch because he used to threaten to tell everyone about me. I wouldn't have got a job, after the RAF, you know. He had a sort of control over me. But then when she told me what he was doing, I stayed to try and help her."

Dacre was staring at Bugsy, choking sobs. "It wasn't her being ... with you ... that she told Sutton about, it was that. Him. Fuck!"

"Sutton?" Redbond looked at him quizzically but went on. "Oh, Gordon, this is awful for you. I wanted to get you away from him, but Ellie wouldn't. He just controls everyone. He's a thug, a rotten thug, a bully." Bugsy's eyes were also moist.

Dacre struggled to stay calm. He flopped onto the couch beside Bugsy, who turned to him and reached out to touch his shoulder. "Just don't touch me! I don't know who to believe. I've been lied to all my life. By everyone."

The door opened quietly, and Dunlop carried in two mugs of tea, setting them down on a glass coffee table. There were neatly placed cork mats and a spider plant in the middle.

"And you!" Dacre blubbed. "Even you were a lie. You play rugby!"

"Roy and me—"

Dacre stood up and waved his hands. "Don't say any more. I can't stand it!" Dunlop went to leave, but Dacre shouted, "No!

I mean … stay here. I want to know what you know about my dad."

His former PE teacher hesitated at the door, then turned and stood still, looking with pity at Dacre. "Gordon, it's true about us. And although your dad has never known about me, I know what he did to your mum."

"But if he knows about him," protested Dacre, pointing at Bugsy, "how come he doesn't know about you?"

Bugsy said, "If he did know, Gordon, he would have told the school and Roy would have lost his job. We had to keep everything secret. He knew I was gay, but never who I was with. That's what it's like for us."

Dacre's shoulders dropped. He rose and shuffled back over to the window and raised his arms to stand, eyes closed, his hands on either side of the frame. He rocked back and forward, tears dripping onto the floorboards.

"But where's my mum?" he sobbed. Sniffing and tasting salt, he opened his eyes to the blackened tenement opposite. Way down below him, the street was flowing and eddying through his mucoid tear film, the parked cars and pavements gathering to form a whirlpool. He forced his eyes shut again before the vertigo worsened. Turning unsteadily, he staggered a few steps until the welcome arms of his Uncle Bugs steadied him and lowered him to the couch.

"Oh, Gordon, you never knew any of it and we couldn't tell you."

Dacre managed to mumble, "Please call me Dacre."

"You could call me Darren. I haven't been called Bugsy for years. It was another of your father's tricks, changing people's names. Gave him power."

Dacre looked at him sitting on the other end of the couch, Roy standing at his side. As his sobbing subsided, he remembered the green shoe box and the birth certificate. "I read letters my mum had kept, and her birth certificate had her name spelt differently." Wiping his tears he looked at

Bugsy, the trust he remembered from his childhood beginning to rekindle.

"The certificate was correct, Dacre; it is Eleanor with *e-a* really."

"But?"

"Alun insisted. He wanted to make her more Welsh, like him."

"She spelt it Elinor herself, though! Why did she let him?"

"She knew not to cross him, or—"

"Don't say it! Fuckin' bastard!"

Roy Dunlop walked towards the door and turned. "I'm going to make us something to eat. You must be hungry, Gordon, and I know Darren hasn't eaten for hours."

"It's Dacre, remember," said Darren.

Dacre managed an exhausted smile.

***

"This is brilliant! What is it?" Dacre was scraping sauce from his plate with his fork.

"It's a crab risotto. Roy's a great cook."

"Crab?" Dacre had only had trout from the river, haddock from the chip shop or kippers. He looked at Roy. "Are you still a teacher?"

"Yes, across at Whitecart Academy. I'm assistant head of department now."

"How come you aren't there? And the van says you're a gardener." Dacre was still suspicious.

"I've been off this week after a heavy tackle, strained my collaterals." Dacre had noticed the limp.

Darren, now washing plates at the sink, said over his shoulder, "And we had to both be in the business to set it up and get a loan for the van. Roy drives me about sometimes and helps with the heavy stuff. I'm the gardener."

Strong coffee made in a filter machine was better than any Dacre had ever had.

"Have you thought where your mum might be, Gordon ...

sorry, Dacre? If she wasn't at home."

"I thought she had come here. I've no idea where else she could go."

"What about her sister? Janet."

Dacre didn't know whether to be glad or not that Janet and Campbell had got it so wrong about his mum and Bugsy. "No, she wouldn't go there. Aunty Janet is a snobby bitch and my mum would never visit her. I think they had a big falling out." Dacre put his teacup down. "You don't think my dad's taken her somewhere? I mean ..." A sickening fear was rising in him. Maybe his mum hadn't thrown Alun out and made him sleep downstairs. Maybe his dad had hurt her even more this time. Maybe she was in hospital. "I've got to find my bastard dad." He stood up.

"Oh, Dacre, he's a brute. You can't tackle him." Darren looked up at him and went on, "Anyway, you don't know where he is. Doesn't he work all over the country? You'll never find —"

"Is there a phone box here? I'm going to call Dod Lambie. I know he was working away this week, his bag was gone. I need to find out where. Yellow Pages."

"It'll only be the Glasgow listings in the phone box, but the library has all the Yellow Pages, they'll have the Fife one; maybe you could find his work there," Roy said.

"Oh, Roy, he can't go to Alun!"

But Dacre was already pulling on his jacket.

"Where's the library?"

Chapter 42

Dacre found the library in Dumbarton Road and realised he had walked past it between the Rosevale Tavern and Darren's flat. It was just before three o'clock, and the reference section was quiet. He soon had the Fife Yellow Pages open and found George Lambie Specialist Engineers, but he had no pen or paper. Having already been scolded by a severe woman at the desk for talking too loudly, he was scared to ask her. He deftly tore out the page, slipped it in his pocket and calmly returned the heavy, yellow volume to its shelf. He smiled apologetically at the scary librarian as he left.

In a telephone box, he took his money from his pocket, four two-pence coins, one ten-pence, and one old florin. Expecting to hear Dod's voice, he was surprised when after just a few rings a woman answered.

"George Lambie Specialist Engineers, how can I help you?" The pips started and he quickly pushed the florin into the slot.

"Sorry, who's that? Is Dod there?"

"I'm afraid Mr Lambie is on holiday; can I help you? It's his secretary speaking."

Secretary? Dod?

"Where is he? I'm looking for my dad. Alun. He works there. What do you mean, Dod's 'on holiday'?" If his earlier suspicion had been correct, his mother might have been with Dod, but he knew now the moving shape under the covers had been his cowardly, brutal father. There was no reason to suspect his mother at all.

"I know Mr Lambie takes a lot of holidays, but as he always says, 'Live to work, or work to live'. I like that idea, don't you?" Dacre's sigh emphasised his impatience. "Sorry. You wanted to know about Mr Dacre: our Chief Engineer Mr Dacre is working away all week, I'm afraid; may I take a message?"

Things had certainly changed for Dod Lambie. Business must have picked up. "It's his son speaking. I need to contact him; where is he?"

"Let me see, oh, yes, here's his work schedule. Yes, as I thought, he's in Glasgow all week, due to finish there today. He phoned earlier to say he was running late."

Glasgow! He's here!

"Can you tell me where in Glasgow?"

"It's one of the hotels, let me look. Why did you want to know again? I'm new here, and I'm not sure what I can tell you."

"He's my dad."

"I'm sure that's OK. He's certainly been busy since we got the new contract. That's how I got my job, the expansion, and —"

Dacre interrupted, "Can you just tell me where it is?"

"Sorry, yes, I know, I talk too much, it's ... sorry, I'm doing it again." Dacre was silent until the pips in the phone went and he had to load the ten-pence coin. "Oh. I forgot you're in a telephone box. Sorry." Dacre waited, an ache building in his clenched jaws. "Here it is. The Royal Northern Station Hotel. He's been there since Tuesday."

Dacre put the phone down without replying and ran back the few hundred yards to Esmond Street. Breathless, he walked back into the flat, and demanded of Darren, "The Royal Northern Hotel, or Station Hotel, where is it?"

"That's in Edinburgh."

Roy came out of the kitchen. "There's one here too, on George Square. It's near the station."

"Queen Street station?" Dacre asked.

"Yes, just beside the entrance to the station. Why?"

"Is that where your dad is?" Darren looked worried.

"I fucking walked past it this morning! He was there! Fuck!"

"Oh, Dacre, what are you going to do?"

"How do I get there?"

"The Underground, or a bus, but you can't just go there; what are you going to say?"

There's an underground train! That's what that guy at the station meant

Dacre didn't know what he was going to say to his father, and shouted impatiently, "Just tell me how to fucking get there!"

Roy walked forward and held out two pound notes. "A taxi'd be quickest. It's not the busy time yet, and the traffic'll not be too bad."

Dacre looked at his watch, the Timex his parents had given him on his twelfth birthday, and cursed. "Shite! I forgot to wind my watch. What time is it?"

"It's twenty to four. But you can't just go and walk in." Darren was shaking.

"Thanks, Roy," Dacre said, grasping the notes and opening the door. He ran down the marble stairs, almost colliding with a woman with a headscarf and cigarette.

"Haw! Pal! Watch it. Ye nearly had me over—"

He pushed past and ran to the street, not stopping until he was on Dumbarton Road again. He had never hailed a taxi before and was surprised how easy it was, just like in films. "Northern Queen Street Hotel, please."

Through the glass partition, the driver, who had already moved off in the direction of the city, asked, "Is it Queen Street or the Royal Northern you want?" Dacre was puzzled, lost for a moment. "The station or the hotel, son?"

"Hotel." It seemed like several frustrating hours later the taxi dropped him outside the hotel. He gave the driver a pound, and asked, "Sorry, what time is it?"

"Just five to four, son, Friday the 2nd of December. In a hurry? Everyone is at Christmas, an' it's great for me." Without replying or waiting for his change, Dacre turned and ran up a slight slope on the pavement towards the entrance to the station, dodging amongst the same throng he'd fought through that morning. Two steps led up to the main hotel doors, where a uniformed commissionaire stood under a canopy.

"Checking in, Sir? Luggage?" His way was blocked by the man in the shiny buttons.

"I'm visiting my dad," he said.

"What room number, Sir? I'll have reception inform him for you, and you can wait in the lobby."

"No, he's working here. On the lift."

"Working on the lift? Sir, our lifts are automatic, we haven't had lift attendants for years. You must have—"

"No, fixing the lift, I mean. He's the chief engineer." He hated giving his father status.

"Sorry, son, both our lifts are working fine. Been busy today, and if the lifts were out, it would've been hellish for us. Anyway, they were replaced last year, and the new ones get serviced by the supplier, some sort of contract."

"But his work said he was here!" Dacre was cursing the secretary.

I bet it's the Edinburgh hotel he's at! Stupid wee cow!

"Is it important, son? Have you come a long way?"

"Aberdeen."

"Ahh. Fit like, loon?" Dacre was not impressed, but the commissionaire nodded him to stand at one side of the entrance, and whispered "Wait there, son" while he assisted two elderly guests out of the hotel. Dacre watched him through the glass door, talking to a man in a grey suit at the reception desk and pointing at two lifts in the lobby. The man in the suit pointed behind him, and soon the black coat with brass buttons and medals was back beside him, a smile under the narrow grey moustache.

"Yer in luck, son. It's the old service lift he's at. Boss says you'll have to go round the back, though, if you want to see him."

Chapter 43

When he'd found his Auchmoor home empty the day before, Dacre had felt almost relieved he might not have to tackle his mother. Now it was relief that he wouldn't be prevented from confronting his brute of a father. In less than a day, the focuses of his anger and pity had swapped targets. He had no idea what he was going to say or do when he found his dad. Walking slowly but purposefully round the hotel he found a wide alley behind it. The drumming pulse in his ears quickened when he saw his dad's van with its back doors open.

This really is going to happen!

He leant against the wall and pushed himself hard against the cold sandstone as if he could hide behind the cast-iron rone pipe. His throat was dry but his mind was clear, his limbs strong and ready.

It was now dark and the street light didn't reach far into the lane. He could see no sign of his father near the van and, inhaling deeply, he forced himself along the alley, hugging the wall. As he approached, he caught the sound of his father humming 'Take Five'. It had always seemed the only tune his father knew, and hearing it again released surges of emotion: yearning nostalgia, childish love and bitter loathing. Images of his mother wearing a high scarf and flinching painfully from his touch fought with memories of time with his dad, the rained-off camping trip and the brief luxury of the Luib Hotel with its log fire.

Creeping past the van he passed a sliding metal door, opened wide to reveal a storage area lit by a flickering strip light. Boxes were piled on shelves and on the back wall a cream-coloured, concertinaed lift door was two-thirds pulled aside. The lift was in darkness, its floor raised to waist height in the gap. On the wall nearby he could see a hinged flap had been swung open exposing a large red switch labelled 'Fireman'. Two wires emerged from the switch box and trailed down into the void below the lift floor, where a bright light flickered around in dark shadows. The tuneless humming became louder as Dacre moved silently into the storeroom. There was no one else around.

He leant forward to try to see beneath the lift. Intermittent cursing and scraping noises interrupted the humming, and the light was moving to and fro as, he imagined, Alun was trying to do something to the underside of the lift while holding a torch in one hand.

"Dad," he called out tentatively.

The humming ceased and Dacre held his breath. There was muttering, then the torchlight and the two trailing wires moved again as the scraping resumed.

"Dad." Louder this time.

"Who's there?"

Dacre's skin was crawling and cold sweat gathered. He knew he had to say something. "It's me, I was looking for Mum, but she wasn't at home."

Alun was silent again for a moment then said, "Gordon?"

"Aye."

"What are you—?"

"I came to ask you something."

"Come to see your old man? You must need money, eh? Let me finish here and we'll go for a pint. I've been at this all day. Bloody knackered."

"Should you be working down there with the power on?"

"Telling me how to do my job now, eh?" The voice echoed under the lift floor. "It's okay. I've disabled the motor at the Fireman's switch. I always do it so I can run a light down here. Saves me messing around with torch batteries. If I switched the power off altogether I'd have to keep going up and down to the main switch box when I do the test. Bit dodgy if you don't know what you're doing, but I've learned a few shortcuts in my time, see?"

Dacre couldn't hold back any longer. "Where's Mum? What

have you done to her?"

"What do you mean? She's at home. What are you doing here? She was there when I left this morning. What are you talking about?"

"You bastard. You're lying."

"What the fuck?" As ever, Dacre was shocked to hear his father swear. Alun's face appeared in the gap below the lift, thick brown grease on his forehead and in his hair. In the grimy shadow and with the torchlight behind him, his pale face was split by a wide gap-toothed grin, his eyes reflecting the flickering from the strip light. Dacre was at once terrified and furious with hatred.

"I know what you've been doing to her, you bastard."

"What do you mean? I never touched her. Ask her, she'll tell you. She wouldn't—"

"Shut up! Shut up! You're lying, you've always lied; I know now, you fucking—"

"Ask her, she's at home. We spoke about you just this morning at breakfast, how worried we are about you and your problem."

Dacre's blood surged at the repeated lying and denial. His anger had intensified into burning, overpowering hatred, now it was correctly targeted. His fury overflowed, and he drew back his right foot to swing it at his father's head, shocked at his violence. Alun dodged backwards and banged his balding head on the lift floor above him. Missing his target had unbalanced Dacre, and he had to steady himself against the corrugated lift door.

"You fucking wee twat! How dare you? I'll fucking teach you." Alun was trying to scramble out of the bottom of the lift shaft, and Dacre shuffled to his right in retreat, terror and rage bursting his forehead. "Got you!" Alun was half out, his weight balanced on the sill, and a flailing arm made contact with Dacre's left ankle. He gripped tightly, and Dacre tried to kick out backwards with his right foot but felt himself topple forward as Alun pulled at his leg. As he fell, Dacre's face crashed into the switch recess, and he heard a loud crunching as his nose hit Bakelite. The impact sent a wave through his head as if he could feel his brain colliding with the inside of his skull. A momentary searing pain was replaced by diminishing waves of warm water washing over him, soothing, calming and relaxing. His conscious level sank into a familiar state of blissful peace. He slid down the wall to lie on the floor, motionless.

***

Billy was frustrated. He'd arrived on shift late with a hangover, and had spent the day trying to dodge heavy work. The head porter had picked on him all day, though, by giving him extra luggage runs. This was the last straw. The laundry delivery hadn't arrived, and Billy had been sent up to the sixth floor to fetch four boxes of towels. Until the sixth floor was refurbished it was housing a temporary linen store. *On the top floor! And today the bloody service lift isn't working!* Billy was going to have to make four separate trips down and up the stairs, one box at a time. And he was supposed to be off duty at six.

Just as Dacre's nose hit the Fireman's switch in the basement seven floors below, Billy decided to try punching all the lift buttons a few more times. Cursing, he was about to give up when the lights above the lift door came on and he heard the familiar grinding sound of the old wheels turning.

"Thank fuck! It's fixed. There *is* a god!"

Alun smirked out at his unconscious son's bleeding face. Serves the little bugger right. He struggled to pull himself out of the void below the lift when a sudden bright light above and behind him spilled out and lit the storeroom. *What the—?* Then the grinding of the motor, screeching pulley wheels. He froze, as the gap he was trying to escape from narrowed. *Big, useless idiot hit the switch!* The lift was coming down. He scrabbled harder to climb out, but his grease-covered boots started to slip behind him. He tried to grip the smooth storeroom floor as the noise got louder and his feet ran nowhere behind him. He forced his elbows down hard trying to hoist himself up and out.

"Yes!" he cried as his right boot gained purchase at last, and helped to push him forwards. His torso balanced on the concrete floor edge, and he tried to pull himself forwards, but the axle grease on his hands meant they only slithered uselessly on the green-painted floor. The lift kept descending, the gap narrowing.

"Yes!" he called out again as his fingernails bit into the paint and he slid forward and away from the closing vice. "I've done it."

His left foot trailed behind him and his boot caught on the concrete lip. He felt pressure as the lift made contact with his ankle. He pulled himself further forward, just squeezing his ankle out as the gap continued to narrow. His foot was gripped, though, and he felt his toes being crushed. Kicking the door with his other foot, as hard as he pulled he couldn't free himself. The pressure kept increasing and his toes were bursting with searing pain. The noise as bones snapped and crumbled was sickening, and his heart and head pounded. Sparks of electric agony fired up the length of his leg. The force concentrated on his distal extremity held his whole body in a vice. The crunching stopped and started as the motor tried again and again to force the lift down. Each attempted turn of the motor cranked up the pressure on his foot. The weight of the lift was beating it like a jackhammer. Finally, the lift stopped, jammed on the thick rubber sole of his safety boot. Alun could see the ragged end of a foot. His foot. Soggy red flesh and bones among shredded, useless leather. Minus his toes. Pressure escaped through his larynx with a high-pitched, deafening scream.

***

"Bastard thing's jammed again!"

Seven floors up, Billy harrumphed the first box of towels

towards the service stair.

***

Dacre floated upwards, his ecstasy leeching away. Something wasn't right. The silent, smooth conveyor belt he normally rode was juddering. And that noise echoing around his head. Cri du chat? Banshee? Moving shadows floated over his blood-red eyelids, mixing with grainy, black-and-white images of the pitiful child in David Thom's textbook. Despite his congested nose, there was a familiar smell and he tasted blood. As his conscious level rose, so did unease. Cracking his eyelids apart unsettled him more. More red. And light. Bright, screeching, blue and white light. Light that hurt. Unease made way for pain centred in his face. And the noise. Screaming.

I'm on the Hillhead refuse trolley again, he thought. He could smell dustbins.

"He's coming round." The porter guiding the front of the buggy wore a blue uniform like his dad's old dress RAF suit. Another pair of blue serge sleeves stretched down to handles on either side of his head. The man behind him moaned as he pushed the trolley.

"Christ! The alley's blocked by a fuckin' van, we'll have to carry him all the way to the street."

He was moving, jolted over cobbles, the back of his head sore but his nose worse. He tried to lift his hand to his head but his arms were tied by straps. The taste of blood took him back to childhood nosebleeds: the smell was Betadine. His mother always kept a bottle in the bathroom. As his eyes cleared, he was able to see past the porter in front of him. For some reason, the two men seemed to be carrying the trolley. And he was in some sort of narrow alley, lined by overflowing galvanised dustbins and lit by oscillating bright blue lights. Behind his father's van (*what was that doing there?*) was a red fire engine. Its blue light was competing with another on an ambulance behind it. The high-pitched squeals became fainter as Dacre was carried along the alley, weaker and interrupted by deep moaning. From above his head, he heard a wheezy voice; it wasn't Davey the Adam Smith porter.

"Did you see the poor bastard? Squealing like a stuck pig!" After a pause for rasping breath, the man continued, "This one's OK, just a broken nose. But the other one! His foot's fucked. Still conscious too. Jeezusss! Fucks sake, this guy's getting heavy. I'm knackered." The stretcher Dacre now realised he was on paused while there was more heavy breathing.

Memories of the Glasgow flat and Redbond began to come back, and his mind flashed through the revelations, the library, the taxi, the hotel and the alley. He realised the two men were talking about his father, and he tried to sit up.

"Lie there, son, there's nothing you can do. I don't know what happened in there, but you were the lucky one." The man in front was quite young, and fitter than the bigger wheezy one.

"My dad?" he muttered, spitting blood.

"That was your father in there? What happened?"

"What's wrong with him? What did he mean about his foot?"

From behind him, he heard, "His foot's done for, son; it'll have to come off. If he survives."

"Shut up, Ally. That's his dad you're talking about. He'll be upset."

But Dacre had passed out again.

Chapter 44

Something wasn't right, and he realised he must have drifted off again. There was the unmistakable smell of the clinic room at the cottage hospital, and he had been dreaming about Dr Mackie. Suddenly a lancinating pain pierced his right eye. White-hot light flooded his brain, relieved briefly by a red kaleidoscopic film show until it was the turn of his left eye to be forcibly opened and stabbed by the blinding flashlight. Then pressure was applied to his right ear lobe.

"Oi! Get off!"

"That's good, son, if you carry on like this, you'll not get shifted to the Southern for one o' they funky new EMI scans they keep wastin' time on. Ah know yer alright, an' you're nae needin' that nonsense. See you again in fifteen minutes."

A younger voice he recognised broke in, "Listen to *you*, Doctor ... umm ... I mean Sister!" Dacre had responded more readily whenever the wee dark-haired nurse approached him to do the checks, despite the pain her torch caused.

The older, authoritative voice came back, "You're too cheeky for a student! But when you've seen as many heid injuries as me, Hen, you'll nae need a scan tae sort them out, either!" The soft footsteps receded, and he went back to piecing together what had happened to him. Their tests with their torches and pins had been making him respond from the word go. He had spoken to the nurses throughout the long night, but still, they kept coming back four times an hour to stop him from sleeping and to fill their chart. He had little idea of what had happened and nor did the nurses. The boy doctor wearing the 'SHO' badge ... grimy white coat, acne, and wispy facial hair ... had been evasive.

He remembered arguing with his dad at the back of the hotel, and that Alun had tried to get out of the lift shaft to grab him, but nothing after that until sirens were blaring and someone was screaming behind him. There had been a fire engine in the alley and he wondered if someone had set off a fire alarm. The nurses had said the police wanted to see him when he was fit, and he thought his father must have been arrested. He wondered if the screaming had been a hotel worker. Alun had probably attacked whoever interrupted the fight. It would be typical of him, he now knew. He looked forward to informing the police about the attacks on his mum.

The Sister returned, and he braced himself for the torch, but she said, "Gordon, would you like to see a visitor?"

"Is it Mum?" When he sat up quickly his head quivered with pain, forcing him to lie back on the hard mattress.

"Try not to sit up, you need to stay still. If you promise not to move I'll fetch your visitor. You need to be calm."

Dacre's mind was racing with fear, and palpitations beat the inside of his head. "Is she OK? Is she badly hurt? Oh god!"

"Ssshhhh, your mum's OK, and she'll be here later."

"What? Who's here, then?"

The Sister left and before the door swung slowly shut he looked out at the row of beds stretching into the distance under tall windows. Strip lights suspended from the high ceiling threw glossy patches on the linoleum. A chart was hooked on each bed and a man lay coughing or snoring in each, some with a bottle of fluid hanging over them. It reminded Dacre of M.A.S.H. He had a glimpse of the student nurse writing on a chart and remembered the smell of her hair when she had leant in close to test his pupils.

He waited, wondering if it was Bugsy who would be visiting him. It was getting light outside, and through the draughty window behind him, he could hear pigeons coo-rooing. When the door cracked back open, he heard the Sister's voice, quiet but firm. "Just a few minutes, mind. He needs to rest. In you go, don't be scared, he's going to be fine." She then called out to him, "G'bye Mr Dacre", as the crack widened and Isla's anxious face appeared. Dacre felt a lump in his throat and tears filled his eyes. She rushed to his bed and crouched down, flushed and welling up. She took his hand.

"I've been so worried!" She leant in and kissed his cheek. "You look awful! I mean … I mean … oh, Dacre!"

He managed to smile through his brimming tears. "What are you doing here? How did you know where I was?"

"Your Aunt Janet."

"What? How?" Dacre became suspicious. "How the hell did Janet know?"

Isla explained. "I was frantic all day Thursday, and when I phoned home, my mum mentioned she had bumped into Janet. Your mum's staying with her.

"She's staying with Janet?" Dacre's headache was making him feel sick.

"You can see why I was so worried. I knew you'd gone to see your mum. I didn't know where you were. I got a train from Aberdeen on Friday morning. Oh, Dacre … your poor mum!" Isla was whimpering and reached for a tissue.

Dacre looked down at the starched sheet. 'Glasgow Royal Infirmary' was printed in green lettering along the seam. "You know about my dad?" he asked softly.

"Your mum turned up at Janet's asking to stay there. Oh, Dacre, she told Janet what your dad—"

"I know! My fucking father! And everyone knew but me!"

Isla was crying and squeezed his hand. "But how *could* you know? It's only just happened, that's why she left him. He must have just flipped. She was right to leave as soon as he did it. My mum said once a man starts that sort of thing …"

Dacre was silent, looking at the ceiling above him.

She thinks it's the first time he did it.

"I still can't believe it, either. I went to Bugsy's. Looking for her. He told me about the bastard."

Isla was silent for a moment. "Your mum's with the police now."

"Police? My mum? Why? Is she OK? Where? I mean … she's not trying to help my dad, is she?"

Isla was now crying freely. Through her tears, she burbled, "Oh, Dacre, your dad's dead. I'm sorry … it's so … awful!"

"Dead? No, I saw him, in the lift, at his work, I mean. We had a fight, that's how I ended up in here."

"It's true, Dacre. I'm so sorry! The police told your mum. They came to tell her at Janet's, at half five this morning."

"But how? I mean, how did they know where she was?"

"They didn't, but there was a letter from Janet in your dad's van, and they came to ask if she knew where your mum was. They told your mum what had happened and that you were injured. Janet phoned my mum."

Dacre was struggling to take this in and said nothing.

"The police have taken your mum to see your dad. They won't let her see you until they've spoken to you first, I mean. But your da …" Isla stopped, and covered her mouth, sobbing.

Dacre suddenly sat up, ashen-faced. "How? Did I … do it?" He felt like a pile-driver was trying to break through his skull. As he collapsed back on the bed, two nurses he hadn't seen before entered the room.

"You'll have to go now," one said to Isla. "It's time for Obs again, Mr … errr … Dacre. It's the ward round soon, then we'll see when you can get home." A new team of nurses had taken over.

"No, you didn't do anything," was all Isla could say before she was ushered out.

Dacre stared at the ceiling in silence as the staff nurse took his readings. When she shone the torch into his eyes, she was too busy to notice he had been crying.

Dacre slept restlessly through the next few sets of observations. He barely noticed three white coats discussing him from the end of the bed. Through his fug, he worked out that the decision of the ward round was to keep him for a few more hours, allow him something for the headache, and discharge him if he woke and stayed responsive. Another white coat came and looked at his nose, holding an X-ray in his hand

and muttering, "Aye. Straight enough." Either the sleep or the codeine dulled his headache, and by lunchtime, he was wide awake and sitting up. He'd enjoyed Isla's visit, and he smiled when he thought about the dream he'd had. As if his dad was dead! He had seen him yesterday.

The police had requested updates on Dacre's condition and his readiness to give a statement, and he kept pestering the nurses until eventually one of them phoned the police station. A short, stout nurse with blue shoulder flashes came in. "Your mum's on the way here, Mr Dacre. A police car is bringing her because they need to speak to you first, but after that, you can get away. Neuro's happy with you and ENT said your airways'll be fine when the swelling goes down. Now your mum's identified the body you'll be able to get on with the arrangements." The staff nurse looked pleased with herself for updating him so sensitively. She turned away, ready to get back to the hubbub of the ward.

"Body?"

The nurse looked back over her shoulder.

"Yes, but the desk sergeant said everything's fine. All an accident, but the police just want to hear what happened, 'cos they didn't know you were working with him."

Dacre collapsed back onto the pillows and gripped his head with both hands. "No … Noooo …!" His horror told the nurse there had been a communication breakdown.

"Oh, my! You didn't know? They said … oh, god, I'm sorry …" She covered her mouth.

Dacre slumped back on the bed.

It's true? He's dead?

The nurse sat down on the end of the bed. "I'm so sorry, Mr Dacre. I thought from what they said that you knew all about it."

***

"It's all right, son, we've worked out what happened. When the screaming started, two cleaners came down the back stairs.

Terrified. They're still upset, I can tell you!"

The man speaking wore stripes on his shoulder, while the younger one was looking out of the window. A strong smell of cigarettes now filled the hospital room. Once Dacre had told them he'd just arrived at the lift to talk to his dad the sergeant was satisfied and didn't want to ask more.

"They found you lying face down, out of reach of Mr Dacre Senior, who was well and truly trapped, and as soon as they saw your dad, they ran back upstairs. Reception called 999 at 4.47 pm. His foot was in a right mess, your dad, Fergie said. The surgeon at the Royal, Mr Ferguson that is, he said by the time the firemen freed him, he had lost so much blood ... well, y'know, it was a right risky operation, they had to amputate. He died on the operating table, heart gave out, y'know."

Dacre thought the policeman was never going to stop.

"Now we know you had just arrived out of the blue to talk to him that clears up the last bit. We thought you were working with him ... that would have been a different matter, of course. Fiscal would've been right on to that one, what with the rules and all. Must have been a right shock to you. Seems Mr Dacre Senior hadn't disabled the lift properly, and someone upstairs used it, right at the same time you slipped on grease and banged your face. You knocked yourself out. And your da' was trying to get out to help you. All just an accident. That's what we'll tell the Fiscal, nae need for messing about with paperwork. Not nice for you an' yer ma, though, eh?"

"Can I see my mum?"

"Aye, son, we're finished with you. I'll let her in."

***

Eleanor Dacre came in, plaster cast first. She had yellowish bruising under her right eye.

"Mum! That bastard! He broke your wrist?" Dacre's fury built quickly again and his guilty grief for his father evaporated.

Eleanor was crying when she hugged her son. "I tried to

protect you, Gordon, I really did."

***

Dacre had been allowed out of the hospital a short time after his mum visited. Janet drove Eleanor and Dacre back to Edinburgh in her Mini and made Douglas come over from Edinburgh to collect Isla, and Janet's shopping. Isla deftly occupied the passenger seat to avoid sitting with Campbell, who sulked in silence.

That Saturday night, the Bishops were at a dinner party, and Campbell and his sister also went out. Isla was at home with her parents. Dacre and his mum spoke little, restlessly watching television until eventually he had to speak.

"Why did you put up with him?"

He stared furiously at the leafy wallpaper in Janet's precious lounge. He knew already that Janet had refused to believe her sister when she turned up out of the blue saying she'd broken her arm falling downstairs. She couldn't look after the house on her own while Alun was away.

Even now she remained reticent and defensive, insisting Alun's drunken assault had been the first-ever, and out of character. She tried sticking to the same story with Dacre.

"Mum, I know what's been happening. Bugsy, I mean Darren, told me it all."

Eleanor's fragile defences began to give way. She wept silently, then began sniffing, before beginning to shake. Her shoulders shrugged involuntarily with deep sobs until the dam broke and hoarse, deep wails escaped. She lay back on the sofa, screaming like a wounded animal. Dacre was helpless, and weeping himself.

"Mum." He tried to put his arms round her and she stiffened, shrieking more, and he drew away. "Mum. Oh, Mum."

Minutes passed and Eleanor calmed a little, exhausted, breathless and swollen-faced. Her voice was shaking as she told him a little of what she had been through. "He started it when you were a baby. It was my fault."

"But it can't have been your fault. The bastard!"

"Sometimes I couldn't get out of bed, I was too sore. I couldn't look after you properly, lift you even." Dacre worried she was going to collapse back out of control again, but she managed to blub, "Darren came round to pick something up one time and found me limping about. He guessed what had happened." She looked at her son and went on, "He's told you about him being gay, hasn't he? You know now?" She paused, wiping her nose. "Alun really bullied him."

"I know, Mum, and I know now why you wore a scarf in the summer."

With a lot more tears and exhausted silences, they had a mutual counselling session.

"I was terrified that you might find out it was going on. I tried to hide it. I couldn't stop myself screaming one time, you were about four, and you woke up and wandered in." She looked at him through her tears. "But you didn't seem to remember anything the next day. Alun, the fucking coward, had hidden under the bedclothes!" Her swearing shocked Dacre.

His dream about the squeal and the scruffling bedclothes flashed before his eyes. "I remembered it in one of my dreams and thought it was Bugsy in the bed." They both managed a rueful smile at that. Dacre didn't admit he'd also wondered if it had been Dod Lambie.

"But Mum, why did you let it go on? For years, it must have been!"

"Why? I don't know. Fear of being alone. I worried what would happen to you, I couldn't bear it if they took you away. You know? After what happened to Ewan and Sheena Robb." Dacre looked blankly at her.

"Robb? James Robb's parents?"

"Yes, I mean, you probably don't know it all but after—"

"After what? I've been dreaming about James Robb. What's

he ...?"

"Ewan, I mean young Ewan, you never knew him, their first boy, he jumped out of a window and died. He had the measles, the fever got to him. They think he thought he could fly."

Dacre fell silent. The bleeding boy on the slabs. Dreams had been showing him the scenes he'd pictured when Spake had told him about it when they were prefects. He was still burying horrors away, saving them up for the future.

Eleanor squeezed Dacre's hand and went on. "When he did it, jumped, you know, Sheena told James he had flown away to live with the angels. Big Ewan started drinking even more, and for a while James and Billy had to go and live with Sheena's mother, or they'd have been sent to a children's home. Because Sheena couldn't cope."

Eventually, Eleanor cried herself to sleep. Before the Bishops returned, Dacre roused her and helped her to the spare bedroom. He spent a restive night on the dining room sofa bed, exhausted but his mind racing and whirling with anger. He was glad his father was dead, or at least that his mother was out of danger. He wouldn't have to confront his father again, but he should have done something sooner to protect his mum. He couldn't take revenge now. He pretended he was sleeping when the various Bishops came home.

The following morning, he was surprised to see Eleanor smiling and chatting breezily with the Bishops over breakfast. He wished he had some of her composure.

"Janet, I need to pick up a few things from home. Do you have a train timetable?" Dacre didn't know how she could face the house in Auchmoor. "You've been so good to me, Janet, but I can't go on borrowing your clothes. Especially when I go to arrange the funeral tomorrow."

"Nonsense! You're not going by train. Douglas will drive you."

Douglas, in his golf sweater, looked up angrily, but meekly agreed. His planned Sunday foursome became a threesome.

***

Dacre noticed his mum's confident manner on the drive over to Auchmoor but thought his uncle looked uncomfortable. He gripped the steering wheel tightly and looked straight ahead, only speaking when he had to. He said he had case notes to read, and when they arrived he stayed in the car.

"Uncle Douglas is a bit quiet," said Dacre as they closed the door and shivered.

Eleanor went straight to the heating control, saying, "Douglas is all right, really; he's always been a fish out of water when he comes here. He knows he married beneath him."

Dacre grinned at her latest comment, blurting, "You mean Janet?"

Switching on the fan heater in the living room, something Alun had always forbidden, she smiled back at him. "You're old enough and experienced enough to know the truth now. You've taken on a lot in the last few months. Come through to the kitchen where it's warmer."

Dacre was quiet, and sat at the grimy drop-leaf kitchen table again, briefly recalling the last time he had done so, three long days ago. Eleanor sat down facing him and stretched to take his hand in both of hers. He felt the fraying plaster edge against his palm. "Gordon, you know about the abuse, and you found out about Darren and Roy for yourself, but there's something more." Dacre didn't want to know any more, and felt prickles on the back of his neck.

Eleanor went on, "It's me you should blame. I started it ... Oh, god ... how do I start?" She let go of his hand. "Gordon, I had an affair." She started crying again, but she was crying for her son. He sat stock still, his face white, staring at the red Formica and the mess of biscuit crumbs he'd made on Thursday.

"But Bugsy ... I mean ... he's ..."

"Not Bugsy." She paused between sobs, and he wished she

wouldn't tell him more, but her determined stare told him she was going to. "When you were about eight months old, I was really low, I kept crying all the time. I felt I couldn't cope. Your dad was always away on shifts at the base, and it was cold in the old cottage ... we were renting it ... it was freezing, damp, awful." Dacre had heard that his first home was on a farm near Cupar, but had no recollection of it. Eleanor rushed on, barely stopping to breathe. "Janet came to nose around one day, you can imagine." Dacre couldn't believe his mum was able to smile through her tears. "She volunteered Douglas to help move some furniture and paint the bedroom. He came the next weekend. Alun was away, of course. Douglas was nice, kind, you know?" She looked at Dacre. He didn't know what she would say next, but he was dreading it. "He came a couple more times and sort of fussed over me."

"Mum, I don't want to know!" Dacre stood up and paced, his hands over his ears.

Eleanor stood herself, followed him to the sink, and put her arms round him. She'd stopped crying. "I've got to tell you this. Listen. I'm sorry it happened, but it did, and you've got to know. He came most weekends, for a few months. Janet thought he was golfing." Sniffing at times between sentences, she went on, telling her embarrassed son it had been fresh and exciting at first, but that when she'd begun to feel guilty, she'd tried to end the affair. Douglas got angry and forced himself on her, threatening to tell Alun. Dacre stiffened and turned to face his mum.

"He forced you? You mean ...?"

"Oh, Gordon, let me tell you it all, I've got to! He had told me he felt trapped into a marriage by Janet. Called her a social climber! He said if she was going to do that to him, he was going to have me, a sort of revenge. He tried to tell me he had always fancied me. I was stuck. I couldn't stop him or Janet would have found out, so I just let him keep coming to me."

Dacre went through to the living room, crying. He wanted

to escape, but Eleanor followed him. "It's warmed up now." They sat down on the couch, and she went on hurting her son with the painful story. On one of Douglas's visits, Alun had been sent home from work early, an unexpected shift change. Finding the couple half-dressed on the couch where she and Dacre now sat, Alun had grabbed his brother-in-law and dragged him into the kitchen, leaving his terrified wife crying in fear. She described hearing muffled voices, pleas and some gagged screams. The back door slammed and Douglas's car drove off. Alun had then taken her upstairs and kept her trapped in the bedroom for three days, brutally forcing himself on her twice. Then suddenly he'd let her out, treating her kindly and giving her treats and new clothes. The beatings had started a few months later.

"You see, it's not all Alun's fault. I started it."

The journey back to Edinburgh was awful for Dacre. Eleanor explained their tear-stained appearance to her brother-in-law, her former lover, was a result of them being overcome by grief. She managed to make small talk with Douglas, who was unaware his secret had been disclosed. Dacre fumed in the back seat. He guessed his uncle would be relieved at Alun's death. He guessed Janet knew nothing about the affair, and it occurred to him that perhaps Alun had been blackmailing Douglas ever since. 'Your bloody Uncle Douglas comes in handy,' his father had said.

***

Dacre couldn't bear to stay in with the Bishops that evening. He phoned Isla and they walked together to a pub in Colinton. It was quiet, and they sat in a booth as he told her everything his mum had been through.

"Oh my god, your poor mum! Your uncle? And then your dad. Oh, no! Your poor mum!"

"I'm sorry. I had to tell you. I'm sorry."

"I'm *glad* your dad's dead."

"And I was blaming her," he said, shaking his head.

Chapter 45

The funeral had been given the go-ahead when the procurator fiscal saw the police reports. Eleanor had to admit to herself that she couldn't have coped without Janet, who had struggled to restrain her glee at the chance to take over the arrangements. Eleanor had to remind her it wasn't another pre-Christmas social gathering. Boxes of decorations waited in the hallway.

Monday had been taken up with funeral arrangements. Eleanor couldn't face having it in Auchmoor with its tittle-tattle, and a small service was arranged in Edinburgh. Janet agreed to keep it private but couldn't resist inviting a couple of her friends 'for decency's sake'.

On Monday evening, Dacre and Eleanor were alone for a couple of hours. Dacre was drained but knew he wouldn't sleep again that night. Janet's leather sofa creaked as Eleanor sat down. Dacre cleared his throat.

"I keep wondering. Did Janet know about … you know … the …"

"No. She never guessed and I never told her."

Dacre looked at her. "I … I … wonder if she does. She wrote to Dad. The police said there was a letter in the van."

"No. He took that from me. It was a letter to me. He found some old letters I had kept. He'd told me not to contact her." Dacre pictured the shoebox on the ruffled bed. Looking down, and cradling her plastered arm, Eleanor went on, "That's when he did it. The last time, this time." She held her broken wrist up. "I told Dr Mackie I had fallen, but he saw bruises when I had to undress for the X-ray. I knew I couldn't hide it any longer, and even though I wouldn't tell him who did it, he guessed it was your dad. He said I should leave." She looked up at her son. "Oh, Gordon, don't cry. That's when I decided to go to Janet. I had nowhere else to go. I didn't even go home from the cottage hospital."

"So why did he take the letter? What was in it, I mean?" Dacre wiped a tear away.

"Janet had written asking why I hadn't been in touch. Trying to make up, I suppose. We hadn't spoken properly for years. But I replied. To her letter, I mean. That's what set him off. When he found them. The letters. When I ran away, the police think he took the letters for the address. To come and get me ... they think he was going to come that Friday afternoon. The day you found him. He had Janet's letter open on his van seat."

"He was going to come here? I mean ... Janet ... Douglas ...?"

"I had to tell Janet what Alun had done. Just once, I said."

Dacre managed to look at his mum. "It all started after you ... Douglas ... the ... you know what I mean." He had to look away again, embarrassed. He was torn between pity for his mum, anger at her, and fury at his father and uncle. "They both did it to you, I mean ... forced you ... the bastards."

It was Eleanor's turn to weep, silently. Dacre stood up from the sofa and went to part the curtains. It was snowing. "Another thing: d'you think Dad was blackmailing Douglas?"

"I was frightened to ask in case it set him off."

"The bastard!" said Dacre, to the freezing darkness.

Wincing, Eleanor pushed herself up from the low sofa and stood beside him. "I did wonder about it, though. He spent enough on gambling. He thought I didn't know, but he left betting slips in his pockets. I wondered where he got the money. We were always hard up but he seemed to be able to do that as much as he wanted." Dacre knew his father had liked following the horses, but not that he'd been a regular gambler.

"And Janet? I mean, she *definitely* doesn't know about you and Uncle Douglas?"

Eleanor managed to smile. "Definitely." Dacre wondered if he would ever know truth from lies. He began to understand his mother's awful situation, but not how she continued to take some of the blame.

The next morning, after Douglas had left for work, Eleanor announced to her sister, "Janet, I have to finally tell you some of what has happened." Dacre, who had been trying to eat some bacon, was horrified. Coughing, he stood up quickly and made for the hallway, but Eleanor stopped him.

"Gordon, stay here, you need to hear this as well."

Dacre froze. Surely she wasn't going to tell Janet everything?

"It has happened before. Alun has been, I mean was," Eleanor paused only briefly, "beating me up regularly. Since Gordon was about a year old. I'm sorry I hid it from, well ... everyone. I'm glad, I mean not glad he's dead, but really ... I'm glad it's all over. There's nothing more to tell, but it's over now. I had to tell you. But there's no more ... nothing." She sobbed, and Dacre breathed out, relieved she'd stopped there.

After a short silence, Janet turned from the hostess trolley holding a plate of bacon. There were tears in her eyes. "I knew it. I knew something was wrong. You should have married that lovely Bugsy when you had the chance!" Dacre caught his mother's eye and they were able to share an ironic smile through their tears.

***

The next few days dragged by. Isla had gone back to Aberdeen until the weekend and once the funeral arrangements were in place Dacre was at a loss. He escaped to Janet's dining room when he could. The Bishops had two televisions. On the Thursday Eleanor insisted on taking the bus and train back to Auchmoor again, but the next day Janet still made her go shopping for a new outfit for the funeral. Something that would hide the plaster cast. That night the Bishops were all out again, and Dacre and his mum sat watching TV in the lounge.

"You're quiet."

"Sorry, I just keep going over it all. I told you all about the dreams about you and Bugsy, didn't I?"

"Yes, but honestly there's never been anything else about him you don't know."

"I know, I know. I know that now." Dacre was restless. He made trips to the kitchen for glasses of water and kept shifting position on the settee.

"Can't get comfortable? Will I change the channel? There might be something on BBC2."

"No, it's alright." After a pause, he went on, "it's just I had all sorts of other dreams, about Dad and stuff." Eleanor walked over and turned the TV off.

"What sort of things? Did you know about what he was doing?"

"No. Other stuff. Weird stuff." He couldn't bear to tell his mum he'd thought his dad was a murderer, but he needed to know what the other awful dreams were about. "Did Dad used to work for a butcher sometimes?"

"A butcher? No, why?"

"Ach, it's nothing, just mad dreams. Now and again there's all sorts of stuff about dead animals, and meat hanging in a butcher's shop. Dad's van, as well. I don't get it."

Eleanor smiled. "I didn't know you knew anything about that."

"What?"

"That was your dad and Mr Younson."

Suddenly Dacre felt hopeful. "The man with the stuffed animals?"

"That's him. Ex-RAF. I didn't like him. He used to steal RAF stores. Alun got involved and I hated it, but …"

Dacre felt excitement growing as his mum helped him remember. "He was a poacher! And he borrowed Dad's van!" Dacre could smell the van after Mr Younson returned it. He was shaking his head, a grin of realisation widening. "Domestos!"

"That's right." Eleanor was smiling but looked puzzled.

"You used to go out in the van with Alun sometimes. I remember you coming home in an awful state one time. You'd been sick and Alun was furious. I told him it was the smell of Domestos, and he just laughed."

Dacre could almost have said Eleanor's next words for her: "And he needed somewhere to keep the animals he killed. I think they stored the animals in a freezer somewhere. They made money selling venison to butchers."

"The lock-up! Perth!" Dacre was up on his feet, pacing excitedly round the room. It was like when he used to do difficult jigsaws. When you'd completed most of the picture and thought you were stuck, you found one piece that made all the difference, and the rest all seemed to fit.

***

His dad's funeral had been arranged for Monday, and over that weekend Dacre struggled. He had gone to bed on Friday night delighted that he finally understood the graphic dreams. But they replayed vividly, and all day Saturday he was disturbed by visions of the three dismembered girls. Saturday night was worse still and by Sunday he must have looked and sounded awful when he and Isla went for a walk.

"Oh. Dacre, I wish I could help you! But the funeral will be OK, it'll be over tomorrow." She gripped his hand and he wiped tears away, trying to smile.

That evening he asked Janet if he could use the phone to call Isla. From the extension in the dining room, he called Dr Sutton and told him about his dad's death.

"That's awful, Gordon. Is your mother OK? Are you OK?"

Dacre found himself able to speak, and told Dr Sutton about his mum's injury, and that the funeral was the next day. Sutton asked where he could send flowers.

"Dr Sutton, can I ask you something else?"

"Of course. Can I help?"

Dacre explained the recrudescence of his gory dreams.

"I'm not surprised, Gordon. You have absorbed a huge

psychological blow. Your mind can be seen like a library of books, and a big trauma is like an earthquake. Some of the books are shaken out of their shelves, and it can take a long time to close the books and file them back in order. You've seen pages from some of the most awful chapters, and closing those books is hard."

Dacre was listening carefully and picturing Sutton in his little study. He wondered if he had been at the whisky, but if he had he was making perfect sense.

"But remember, Gordon," the soothing voice went on, "there is a clear explanation of why you put those TV reports and things together to invent a connection to your dad. Now that you know about his abuse of Ellie, I mean your mother, perhaps you will find it easier to forgive yourself for inventing some guilt for your father. I can tell you now that I knew your father was an awful man, Gordon. And it's permissible for you to think that way of him, even though he is dead. You are allowed to hate him."

Dacre was glad he had called Sutton.

Chapter 46

"It must have been some whack your face took! You still look like a fucking panda with those black eyes!" Spake grinned, stifling a laugh. Dacre's hand went to his face. He had forgotten about his yellowing bruises now that his nose didn't hurt so much. "I still don't believe the bit about Randy Roy, though. I can't get my head round it." Spake loosened his tie. "I can't bear wearing one of these again." He grinned, wickedly. "Better take it off anyway in case your Uncle Bugsy ties me up with it, eh?" He winked at Dacre, who shook his head, smiling for what felt like the first time.

"You'll see later if Roy comes here after his work." Spake had heard from his mother about Alun Dacre's death and had appeared at the funeral, to Dacre's surprise. It was good to see his pal, and Janet had been glad to invite him to join everyone at the little gathering she was hosting afterwards. Leaving Spake picking at the buffet, Dacre looked thoughtfully around the lounge. Dod Lambie had asked where Eleanor was when the police questioned him about Alun's accident. He had called and spoken to Janet, who invited him to the service. Dacre was surprised to see Charlie Younson had come with him. He smiled to himself that the arrangement between Charlie and his dad had been a secret kept from Dod. He wondered if Dod knew about the RAF stores thefts his mum had told him about. Isla had briefly caught her boyfriend's eye when Eleanor introduced Dod. She'd smiled and Dacre knew she understood the irony: only a few days ago he had suspected his dad's boss might have been his mother's lover.

Dacre moved towards his mum, who was talking to Isla and holding a cup and saucer. "I'm going to sit down so I can drink my tea," she said, turning towards the black leather sofa and sitting down carefully. After putting her saucer down on the brown tiled coffee table in front of her, and struggling awkwardly to pull her black skirt down as far as she could, she picked up the cup and sipped the cooling tea. "I'm getting used to doing things with one hand," she said to Isla, who sat down beside her. Dacre joined them and Isla took his hand.

"Are you OK?"

"I'm fine, just glad it's all over. I still can't believe people turned up saying they were his friends, though. Bastard didn't deserve it."

"Gordon! Your dad was very popular in his RAF days. And they didn't know what he'd done." Dacre struggled to believe she was still trying to defend her dead husband. Blaming herself. He noticed that one-handed or not she could apply make-up like an expert. Her bruised eye was invisible.

"But after what ..."

Isla broke in over her boyfriend. "It's nice some of his friends remembered him; they didn't know," she said, looking Dacre in the eye, meaningfully. He took her cue and changed the subject.

"Here's Bugsy. He's looking smart. I've hardly ever seen him out of dungarees." He pointed out of the window where the van he had seen in Partick had just drawn up.

"He's a good man, Gordon. Oh, Janet, thanks for doing this, I couldn't have—"

Janet had marched in with another tray. "Not at all, I love entertaining. Well, you know what I mean." Dacre stood to let his aunt pass, and Isla did likewise, offering her seat to Mrs Bishop, as she called her. "Thank you," she said, smiling brightly at Isla, "it's such a shame Campbell couldn't make it, you two get on so well, I hear."

Isla took Dacre's hand enthusiastically, and ushered him away, whispering, "Don't react. My mum says she's always been like that. Anyway, her son's a real diddy." Dacre smiled again. Cracking his grim mask was becoming easier.

Darren Redbond entered wearing a checked jacket and desert boots under his slacks, followed by Roy Dunlop. As they approached the sofa, Janet squirmed and hissed into Eleanor's ear, "Who's that with Bugsy? He's lovely—!" Eleanor's elbow dug into her sister's ribs, and her plaster cast knocked a plate onto the beige carpet, scattering crumbs and pieces of pink icing.

"Oh, Darren, don't you bother, Janet can manage," said Eleanor. Her old friend had quickly crouched down and started to tidy the mess. Bugsy stood back up and introduced Roy to Eleanor.

"Eleanor, this is Roy, you never met him, but you'll remember me telling you about him."

"Of course I do. Roy, it's nice to meet you at last. I feel like I know you somehow already, if you know what I mean. Or at least I know what you were like years ago." Eleanor spoke quickly, almost boldly, and went on, "Janet, would you mind letting Roy sit down, and fetching him a cup of tea? He's driven from Glasgow after his work."

Janet looked shocked again at the change in her sister's confidence and stood to make for the kitchen. She paused after a few steps. "What's that van doing in the avenue? It'll have to move. Douglas parks there before he puts the car into the garage." She drew the heavy drapes quickly, hiding the van before anyone could read the Glasgow phone number on its side.

Raising her eyebrows, Eleanor said quietly to Roy, now at her side, "Don't move it, he's got a driveway to park in. He's just a show-off like her."

Roy Dunlop looked amused, uncomfortable, and uncertain. "Thank you for inviting me here, Mrs Dacre; I am so sorry to hear what happened to your husband."

Eleanor shrugged but looked down as she said, "One of the policemen said I should be glad. But I can't." She looked up at Roy, cleared her throat quietly and went on, "How's your new job? Well, it's not new now, is it? A few years, I suppose. Different from Auchmoor?"

Roy Dunlop was sensitive to Eleanor's need to change the

subject. "Nearly three years now. It was this time of year I left Auchmoor, end of term, Christmas holidays. Darren had been moving around all over the place, but now we're very settled. My job's good. Kids are kids, but they're a different group at Whitecart Academy."

Loud voices from the direction of the kitchen were quickly muffled as the door closed firmly. The room hushed for a moment and Janet's shrill could be made out, over a duller, deeper voice. "I wonder if that's Douglas home from work," Eleanor commented. Dacre steeled himself. All week he had struggled to stay calm in Douglas's presence, and he had been relieved that the man had chosen work over the funeral.

Isla was looking out of the side window. "There's another big car just parking." A few minutes later the doorbell chimed, and shortly afterwards Janet opened the lounge door.

"Yes, of course, Dr Sutton," she said, "you are most welcome, and thank you again for the lovely flowers! Gordon, it's your psychiatrist! Isn't that nice of him to come all this way?"

Granville Sutton looked helplessly into the room as Janet whooshed off to find a vase. Dacre felt his face reddening and could see Spake stifling more laughter. Eleanor excused herself and followed Janet to the kitchen. As Dr Sutton approached him looking unusually smart in a dark suit, Dacre's discomfort increased. The room seemed to have gone quiet.

"I'm sorry to arrive uninvited, Gordon, but I did want to pay my respects, and it was too late to have flowers delivered ..." He sounded awkward, but Isla rose and shook his hand.

"Let me introduce you to everyone, Dr Sutton. I'm Isla, and this is Darren; Roy; Mr ... errr ... Younson; I'm sorry, I don't know everyone's name."

"Thank you, Isla."

The chatter picked back up and Janet insisted Dr Sutton had a meringue. When Dacre returned downstairs after using the toilet, Dr Sutton was in the hallway. "I'm sorry, Gordon, to take you by surprise, but after you called last night I wanted to offer to help you. In any way I can, as a friend. And your mum, if I can." Before Dacre could respond, Dod Lambie came out of the lounge. He grinned at Sutton as he squeezed past them on his way to the bathroom. Sutton looked away and lowered his voice. "Sorry, I need to get back to my goats. Say sorry to Ellie."

A short time after the blue Volvo pulled away, Eleanor came out of the kitchen. "I thought I'd have a go at doing the washing up. I've made my plaster a little wet."

It felt heavier, somehow, when it was disconnected. A shiver of delight tickled through him as he pushed her gently out from the edge before letting go.

Off you go, he whispered, as he cradled the severed leg and watched the film of blood drift downstream on the gently flowing river. Flowing water was always best. His mind flashed back to the oily, still blackness he had had to leave Right Hand in, poor thing.

He had come a long way since then. Always learning. And they had thought he needed a cure! He would remove the foot and the ragged bits later. Now he had a working knee! He had chosen well this time. The girl, this dell, this river. And all done with his new knives.

Chapter 47

'Police in Edinburgh are eager to trace 17-year-old Sarah Kibble, missing since she left her weekly dance class in Oxgangs on Monday 12th December. A spokesman said concerns were raised when she failed to arrive at her father's home for a pre-Christmas visit. Now over to George with the sport—'

"Oxgangs. That's quite near Janet's house. And she disappeared on Monday. How awful." Eleanor rose awkwardly from the couch and went to the kitchen. She called through to him and Dacre couldn't hear what she was saying until he'd turned the TV down. "I said, would you like another sandwich. I'm sorry I've got nothing else in."

It was Wednesday evening and it had seemed to take forever to get back to Auchmoor. The train had broken down and they'd missed the early bus from Kirkcaldy. Janet's offer to have Douglas drive them had been declined.

On Thursday morning Dacre woke late. His bedclothes were disordered and his pillow was on the floor. As he floated out of sleep, he had a familiar queasiness. He knew to expect a bad day, and sure enough soon the Fraserburgh road sign, the policeman with the red beard at his dad's van window and the drawing of Carol Hosie's severed wrist began to flash before him. And there was a new, fresh image: the girl in the leotard from the TV report. For some reason, in his mind, a clear picture of The Mount hung on the wall behind her. He heard the echoing reporter's voice, "Sarah Kibble ... Sarah Kibble ... Sarah ..." He had gone to bed with barely a thought for the missing girl, other than noting distractedly the coincidence that she had disappeared on the day of his dad's funeral.

He ran a bath, pleased that his mum was now leaving the hot water on all day. He smiled to himself as he let his head submerge. The Mount? That was a new one. The tall monument that stood on a hill near Cupar was visible from much of North East Fife, and a familiar feature of his childhood landscape. Most boys at primary school claimed to have climbed it at some time, though the rumours of ghosts and past suicides meant no one had. But he could dismiss the return of his crazy dreams. Like Dr Sutton had said, it wasn't surprising given all he had been through.

***

"Are you thinking about your mum?"

Dacre had left his mother in Auchmoor. He had been keen to visit Isla and Eleanor said she would be fine on her own. They were now walking on a wide promenade beside the Forth estuary after Isla's mum had driven her to meet him at the station and taken them across Edinburgh. It was a grey Friday afternoon, and the wind was biting his ears. "Sorry, what did you say?"

"You've been very quiet." Isla pulled him to sit on a low stone wall. A dog walker passed them, and he could smell the muddy estuary behind him. "Are you all right? Please talk to me, you've hardly said anything all day. Is it your mum you're worrying about?"

"Not her, she's OK." He looked at the tarmac between his feet and mumbled, "Fucking dreams", half-hoping Isla wouldn't hear him.

"More dreams? About your mum and dad, and Bugsy? Oh, Dacre ..." She squeezed his shoulders.

"Not about him. About that girl."

"Dreaming about a girl? How could you?" She was trying to make him smile, and he wished he hadn't spoiled things again. Since they had got together again he hadn't dared mention last summer or his dreams about murdered girls. But he had to tell her this. "It's since that girl went missing, the one the police are looking for now. I'm sorry, but I've been dreaming she's dead. Two nights in a row."

Isla looked shocked. "That's horrible!"

"I know, I'm mental. It's like all that mad stuff I made up about my dad." He gazed out towards Fife hoping Isla would believe he had dismissed his sick notions, and wiping away tears with his sleeve. "Sorry, the wind is making my eyes water."

"Maybe the dreams aren't surprising. After everything … your dad and …"

Dacre was silent, but took her hand and squeezed it. "I don't want to put you off me again. With all that mad stuff."

Isla tightened her grip on his shoulder and kissed his neck. He could smell her hair again now the swelling in his nose was clearing. "You won't, Dacre, I'll help you." She took her hand back to wipe her own tears away.

They didn't mention dreams again until they were on the bus back to Colinton. "*Are* you still dreaming about your mum, and I mean … well, your uncle? And … you know?"

"Nah," Dacre replied almost nonchalantly. "It's like that's all sorted. Since my mum told me everything, and how my dad took it out on her. I'm almost pleased she had an affair. It sort of serves him right, although it happened before he started hitting her. He must have been a bastard all along. I can sort of think straight about all that now. And no more problem with heights, either." He smiled for a second and then slumped. "But, fuck! Now this new fucking dream!"

They sat in the bus shelter before he walked Isla home. It was getting dark and the street lights cast an orange light. Bus and car tyres hissed on the wet road. He told her about seeing the girl in the leotard.

"I saw that too, on the TV report. They'll find her, she'll turn up."

"But the weirdest thing is The Mount is in the dream."

"The Mount?"

"It's a tower on a hill in Fife, someone's memorial or something. You can see it for miles. But it's in my dream. The Edinburgh dream. I'm mad, eh?"

"No. It's what Dr Sutton said, your mind can't cope with it all. Maybe you're having new dreams as a way of trying to explain it to yourself?"

He hugged her tight to him. "I'm glad you are listening. Taking me seriously, you know. All the shite I'm talking again." He loosened his arm around her and sat back against the wood of the bus shelter.

After a moment, Isla stood up, pulling his hand, and they walked in silence towards her house. They kissed at the gate to number 37. "I won't come in, I'd better get back to Aunty Janet's. Rescue my mum."

"I wish my parents were out," she said. Her hand was on his bum as she held him close.

"We'll soon be back in Aberdeen," he said after a minute's embrace. "Don't give up on your mad boyfriend."

"I won't, Dacre, I'm keeping you forever."

Before he left, she said, "You should speak to that Dr Sutton again. He seemed nice. A bit weird, but he *is* a psychologist."

He walked in cold drizzle towards the Bishops' house. He was glad he'd spoken to Isla but relieved he hadn't blurted out what was upsetting him most. He was doubting everything, and even himself. He'd started wondering if he might have got the dates in the work diary wrong, and Alun could have killed the girls after all. And because Sarah Kibble disappeared on the night of the funeral he'd begun to think he had unconsciously abducted and killed her himself. In some hypnotic fugue state, he was continuing his father's work.

"To hell with Sutton," he said out loud as he passed a couple walking the other way. He walked on past the end of Janet's road and turned right towards Oxgangs.

Chapter 48

"That search is being run from St Leonards, sonny, you'll need to go down there. And join the queue."

"But you didn't listen to me. I think I know what happened to Sarah Kibble. The one in the paper."

"Listen, I just told you, that's being handled by HQ and I don't have time to listen to your shite. Dreams, other old murders, hypnotists! Fuck, you can set yer watch by it! Weekends before Christmas are always a nightmare. And a missing person means the place is filled with even more headbangers. I'd rather be working on a bloody Edinburgh derby. I mean it, son, take it to St Leonards if you want to, but they'll not believe you either." As the huge man behind the desk turned away towards a door, Dacre heard him muttering, "Another fuckin' nutter! Always the same."

A younger policeman looked up from the desk at the back of the small office and smiled, shaking his head at the older man, but catching Dacre's eye. He stood up when his senior had moved into a back room, and pushed a notebook over the counter towards Dacre. He saw 'PC Masson' on the front before it was flicked open to a fresh page.

"Don't mind Sgt Wardrop, Sir. Put your name and address down here, Sir, in case we need to contact you." His big ears distracted from his smiling ruddy face.

Dacre was dejected as he walked back from Oxgangs police office towards Colinton. It was the second time he had been ridiculed by the police. The three deaths he had reported in Auchmoor had been in the past, and he could see why he'd been dismissed as mad when he turned up out of the blue. But this one had just happened. They thought the girl was missing but he knew she was dead, for god's sake!

He couldn't face sitting through a meal with the Bishops and bought a bag of chips. He sat in a bus shelter for an hour, pretending to be asleep when anyone approached. One man shook his shoulder in case he missed his bus.

***

"Oh, hello, Dacre. It is nice to hear from you again already. How are you and your mum? I've been thinking about both of you."

"Can I ask you something again? I don't know if I believe it myself. Do you really believe I have this power? The one you talked about, the super-susceptibility. I mean, how bad is it? I mean how much … I mean … what can it do to me? And I've been having the dreams again. About the dead girls. And my dad. And I think—"

"Stop! Slow down, take some deep breaths … slow it … slow yourself … breathe slowly."

When Dacre had composed himself, he managed to give some details from his recent dream, and say he was worried again his father had been a killer.

"But this is all explicable, Gordon, given the trauma you have been through. And we do know there are very good reasons why your subconscious invented those associations. Give it time. I'm sure this will pass."

"But what if hypnosis has made me … I mean … you know about that girl that's missing? In Edinburgh?"

"The girl who was on TV? I expect they'll find her soon."

"But maybe I killed her. If the hypnosis sort of made me act out what I thought my dad did!"

"No, no, no, Dacre, that can't happen. You remain in full control of yourself when you self-hypnotise. You can be induced by an unscrupulous charlatan into following his instructions, like I think you have seen on stage. But you cannot make *yourself* do something against your will."

"There's another thing. There's something to do with The Mount. You know, The Mount outside Cupar. There's something important about it. I know there is."

***

Dacre lay on the sofa bed going over his conversation. He had been reassured by Sutton's words, delivered in his usual calm, considered way. He had been surprised, though, at Sutton's reaction when he told him about The Mount. He had ended the call quite abruptly, wishing Dacre all the best for his future. It seemed Sutton had run out of patience with him.

He felt miserable and tried to empty his mind of his confused ideas. *At least I'm not a killer … I hope. But if Sutton's giving up on me I'd better wise up, or I'll lose Isla again.* He stared at the ceiling and started his trance induction, desperate to sleep.

Chapter 49

When Dacre woke early on Saturday morning it was still dark. He was sweating and soon realised that, despite Sutton's reassurances, the same dream had played. Visions of Sarah Kibble in her leotard smiling for the camera in front of The Mount had alternated with the cartoon Carol Hosie. And for only the second time Dacre had also seen his own small fists holding up an ice-cold severed hand.

He wondered again why Sutton had abruptly ended their conversation. He tried to tell himself the psychologist was scared of revealing something his mum had discussed in confidence, but it had seemed more like Sutton was hiding something. He remembered Sutton's handwritten note to Eleanor. 'I am truly sorry. Goodbye.'

Rolling over on the sofa bed he pulled the blankets over his head.

***

"Gordon! Wake up! The police want to talk to you!"

Dacre thought he was dreaming, but Campbell's gleeful calls to him continued.

"What?"

"He's on the doorstep. Says he needs to speak to you. Haha! They've caught up with you."

Piss off you prick!

"I'll be there in a minute."

After his dreams, he'd eventually gone back to sleep and it was now past eleven o'clock. Coming out to the hallway he saw Janet peering through the frosted glass inner door. "Thank goodness! No uniforms or police cars. What's this about, Gordon? Is it to do with your dad?"

"I've no idea. It's Saturday morning, isn't it?"

Closing the inner door behind him, he found a shivering, wet figure on the doormat. He recognised the profile framed against the grey sky: PC Masson from Oxgangs. There were drips of water hanging from his ears.

"What, I mean why, I mean ...?" was all he could think of to say.

"I'm sorry, Mr Dacre, I shouldn't have disturbed your hosts, I thought this was your home address."

"I'm just visiting."

"Yes, your aunt told me you're from Fife. Can we talk? I have been giving a lot of thought to what I heard you tell Sergeant Wardrop yesterday."

"You can't come in, Aunty Janet would drop a brick."

"I'll wait in my car, come out when you are ready." The policeman, wearing flared jeans, training shoes and a Harrington jacket, turned and walked down the short path to the open gate, and ran through the rain towards a red Ford Escort parked opposite. Dacre quickly washed and dressed, overtaken by the urgency to return to the police station. PC Masson had been sent to collect him.

"Gordon. Don't you want any breakfast?"

"Sorry, Aunty Janet, I'd better go." He slammed the front door and ran across to the steamed-up Ford. Masson was writing in his notebook, holding it against the steering wheel. The door was locked and Dacre knocked on the window. The policeman unlocked the passenger door without stretching across.

Central locking!

Dacre put his seatbelt on. When PC Masson had finished writing, he looked to his left and said, "Sorry, I keep thinking of more questions and possibilities. Where do you want to go?"

"Well ... the police station? I mean, isn't that why you were sent to get me?"

"Sent to get you? Eh? Ah, right, I see. No, I'm not working, I'm off today."

Dacre was confused, and a little suspicious. He started to open the door. "What are you? Some kind of poof? Fucking cheek!"

"What? No! No, listen, I just want to talk, I need to hear what you know about those murders. From what I heard you say they're too similar not to be connected. Or two of them are, at least, I couldn't remember all of them. We found the Perth one, the girl in the harbour, and the one in the ditch, the Grampian one. Where was the other one again? There's got to be a link to one man."

"We?" Dacre got a word in edgeways.

Masson was flicking through his notebook, barely pausing for breath. "I phoned Jack, he's my friend in Dundee, and he ran what he could through the PNC. Didn't you say something about your father? What did he have to do with it? I didn't hear that bit. It wasn't until after you had gone I had the idea. This is exactly what we wanted. I stayed late after my shift until Jack phoned me back. I can't claim the overtime because the gaffer doesn't know I was there. Shut the door, it's freezing." Dacre could see the policeman was excited. And very young, probably no older than he was. He could also see Janet watching the car from her living room.

"I don't know what the PCN is but can we go to the police station now? My aunt is going to be out here with us if we don't."

Masson laughed, and said, "PNC. I can't take you to the station, I'm off duty and this isn't official." He started the car and drove off without fastening his seatbelt. "I'm Craig, by the way. Craig Masson."

"I'm Dacre."

"Right, Dacre. Let's go."

"But … what? I mean why have you come to see me? I thought we were going to the police station. I don't like this. Let me out."

"No, honestly, it's OK. It's just, what you said about three murders in different areas, we can link them all up now. That's what the PNC does. You need to tell me again so I can write it all down, then I can get back on to Jack and Phil."

Masson drove fast and soon they turned left at traffic lights onto what Dacre saw was Lanark Road. Masson continued to talk excitedly about his discoveries with his friend Jack. They had used the scant details of dates and locations Masson could recall from overhearing what Dacre told the sergeant, and identified the cases of Inga Sabiston and Carol Hosie. Both murders remained unsolved, but no apparent connection had been made between them, despite the glaring similarities.

"I mean, it's amazing. Two young girls having limbs removed, three in fact if you're right, and each one treated as if it's a one-off! Where was the third one again?"

"Glen Dochart. On the way to Crianlarich."

"That'll be Stirling's, I think, so that's three different force areas. Four now if this Sarah Kibble does turn out to be dead."

Masson suddenly pulled into a rough lay-by on the right and stopped the engine. "What has your father got to do with this?"

"Nothing. He's dead."

"Oh, sorry. But why did you tell Wardrop about him?"

Dacre quietly told PC Masson about his dreams about the murders and how he had proved that his father wasn't responsible.

"You mean you dreamt about these murders before you knew they were real. How is that possible?"

"I had some problems when I was a kid and had to see a psychologist. But it didn't work and in the end, I tried hypnotherapy, and it made my dreams mental, about murders and stuff." Pleased that someone seemed to be listening to him, Dacre continued quickly. "When no one believed me I went back to Dr Sutton and he told me hypnosis had reached into my subconscious to sort of dig up old stuff I had heard somewhere, about the murders I mean. But I'd forgotten it, you see?"

Dacre stopped and looked away. His palms began to sweat.

He'd told Masson's boss that he'd killed Sarah Kibble. Masson was going to arrest him.

"Why did you go to Oxgangs yesterday? And why did you say you knew Sarah Kibble was dead?"

Dacre looked at the floor between his feet. The rain on the roof of the car drowned the pulse beating his ears. "I had another dream. After I heard she was missing. A dream about girls with limbs missing, I mean. I thought my dad had killed them after all."

"But you just said you had proved your father didn't kill them. Are you wasting my time?"

Dacre thought he was in so deep he could only carry on. "But I'd begun to think he might have changed the dates somehow, to hide it, you see. And then after he'd died the hypnosis made me go out and murder another one to continue his work. But Dr Sutton said that's not what happened. But now I keep wondering if Sutton's got something to do with it."

"You *are* just a headcase. Hypnosis making you kill someone, for god's sake. I've heard enough. I thought we might get something good from you for our PNC stuff. But Wardrop was right. Another time-waster."

Masson started the engine and set off back towards the city. He said nothing until he had driven quickly through Currie, where Dacre remembered the Bishops had once lived. "You are a nutter. Your detective work linking the old deaths was impressive, but this dream stuff, I can't believe that."

Dacre climbed out of the car in Colinton Road and walked dejectedly back towards the Bishops'. The rain had stopped, at least, and he walked slowly. He realised he was muttering to himself when a passer-by gave him a nervous look.

Chapter 50

After an awkward 'brunch' with Janet and Douglas, he was glad to escape to meet Isla. He told the Bishops that Masson had just been an old friend from Fife.

Walking slowly towards Isla's home, Dacre told himself he needed to get a grip. In the last two days, he had started to believe his father could have been a killer, moved on to suspect himself, and confessed to the police twice. This was despite Dr Sutton's patience with his crazy ideas and simple explanation of them. He needed to wise up. He was pleased he had called Dr Sutton as Isla had suggested, but it would be best if he didn't say anything about having spoken to the police.

He rang the bell just after two o'clock ready to tell Isla he was feeling much better. She opened the door immediately and pulled him in, and ran up the stairs, calling behind her, "Come on, we might not have long". She was in her dressing gown. He followed her up, looking behind him to see if he could see Mrs Alexander through the open kitchen door.

"Are you sure I can come upstairs?" On his one previous visit, he had stayed in the living room receiving the condolences of Mr and Mrs Alexander while Isla had readied herself for a trip to the cinema.

"Yes, there's no one in. I said I had a headache and couldn't go to Gran's. They'll be back in an hour or so." She pushed a white door open and pulled him into her room. The unmade single bed, plush carpet and Bowie posters were all he could take in before he was on the bed with her as she rushed him out of his clothes.

***

"Mmmm."

"I know, but we'll need to get up and dressed before they come home. Put your shoes and jacket on. I'm going to say you just arrived."

"You planned this well," he said, grinning.

"We haven't been alone for weeks. Sorry if it took you by surprise. I won't do it again." She was up and pulling her head through a sweatshirt, and Dacre stood up quickly to grab her around the waist.

"Surprise me like that anytime you like!"

"Come on, get dressed. I don't know when they'll be back."

While they waited downstairs, Dacre told Isla about his call to Sutton. She smiled "I told you that's what it would be. Your mind tricking you again." She'd just filled the kettle to make tea when her parents returned.

"Are you feeling better?" said Mrs Alexander as she entered the kitchen. "Oh, hello, Gordon, take your jacket off, we must have just missed passing you in the road."

"Yes, Mum, the aspirin seems to have worked. Will I make enough tea for you and Dad?"

"No, thanks, we had tea at Gran's. Could you unpack the shopping? I must go to the loo. Terrible about that poor girl isn't it, her parents must be frantic." As Dacre removed his jacket again, Isla pulled a bottle of tonic water, some onions and a newspaper from the bag Mrs Alexander had left on the table. The paper's headline screamed at Dacre.

PLEASE FIND MY SARAH

City Mum's Plea to Police and Public

Underneath was a different picture of the blonde girl. In this one, she was smiling at the camera, again dressed in a gymnastics leotard. A dance class was practising behind her.

Dacre felt sick and sat down at the kitchen table. While Isla put the shopping away and continued making a pot of tea, he quickly read about the girl's disappearance. She had last been seen when she left her weekly dance class on 12th December. She had been due to spend time at her father's house to allow her to see him before Christmas, the paper went on. The parents had separated two years before. Her mother was quoted: "When she didn't come back to me on Tuesday evening I phoned him and he said she hadn't ever arrived." The police had been called and all attempts to find her had been in vain. Her father and his girlfriend were both quoted, below a picture of Sarah Kibble's parents on their wedding day.

"What's wrong?" Isla sat down beside him and scanned the paper. "Oh, no! The missing girl my mum was talking about. How awful!"

"No, it's good!" Dacre smiled up at her. "It wasn't me. Her friend saw her getting into a van. Thank god!"

"What do you mean? That's a terrible thing to say." Isla looked angrily at him as Mrs Alexander came back in.

"Mum, we're going for a walk. Come on." Isla was walking towards the back door beckoning Dacre to join her, and still glowering.

"But you've just made a pot of tea!"

By the time they had walked to the end of Kinlockhart Avenue Dacre had apologised. He had to explain about suspecting himself, and that he'd taken her advice and called Sutton. "He told me it was impossible, I mean for hypnosis to make me do it. I thought I'd got it out of my head, but the newspaper rattled me again. When I read she'd got into a van it was like I'd just been found not guilty."

She slowed a little. "I don't care, it was horrible to be glad, smiling like that. And for god's sake! As if you could have done it! You're getting out of hand again." After a silence she let him take her hand.

***

In the evening they sat in Isla's kitchen while her parents entertained friends in the lounge. Occasional laughter came through the wall, louder as the evening progressed. The Two Ronnies were on TV in the kitchen when Isla turned the volume down.

"Listen, promise me you're going to stop all the murder nonsense. I thought that was all over last summer."

"I ... it's the dreams ... they came back and—"

"That's just it, Dacre." Isla's voice rose and she turned the volume back up. "They are just ruddy dreams! And they're making you impossible again."

"But they're true. I found out about all of them and—"

"Stop it! Believe the specialist, you made things up to cope with your mum and dad."

Dacre's chair screeched on the tiles as he pushed his chair back and stood up. He yanked his wallet from his jeans pocket and found the old newspaper cutting David Thom had posted him. "See! This one's fucking real!" He threw the folded paper on the table between them and a second cutting fell with it. Dacre grabbed it, unfolded the *Perthshire Advertiser* article the librarian had printed for him. "And here's another one! I'd forgotten about that!"

The kitchen door opened and Mrs Alexander walked in, laughing back over her shoulder. "Oh, hello, you two, I'd forgotten you were here. There's another bottle of wine in the fridge."

"I'll get it, Mum, Dacre's just leaving."

Chapter 51

Sunday 18th December 1977

As Dacre put the phone down on the hall table he heard the toilet flush then footsteps on the stairs. It was Campbell in a dressing gown, yawning himself awake.

Dacre bristled. *Fucking speccy git!*

"Help yourself, why don't you!" said Campbell, pointing at the telephone.

"Oh, hi Campbell. Sorry, just letting my mum know what time I'll be home. Aunty Janet said it's OK if I call her. I didn't mean to wake anyone." He couldn't resist adding, "I'm going to call in on Isla before I catch a bus."

He'd had another night of roiling images of Sarah Kibble and The Mount, and the wardrobe. Miles's hand felt as cold against his leg as the small, frozen limb he held in his hands. Fingers protruded from the stiffened cloth wrapping. At one minute he was furious with himself, and at the next with everyone else for not believing him. He didn't know who to blame and had decided to go home to Auchmoor. He would try to use hypnosis to banish the visions, or at least make them unthreatening. That had worked before.

He walked towards Isla's house. Before catching the bus he was determined to apologise and let her know he was going home to leave her in peace until he had sorted himself out. He was expecting her to tell him to leave her in peace for good. He wandered the quiet Sunday streets until it was nearer nine o'clock and not too early to ring her doorbell. When he approached though, he looked up and saw her waving to him from her bedroom window. She opened the door seconds later. "Thank god! Campbell said you'd gone back to Fife."

"Campbell?"

"I phoned looking for you."

"It's OK, I've come to say sorry. I'm going to—"

"No, it's OK, listen, come through here." She headed to a room on the other side of the hallway and took the two news cuttings from her cardigan pocket to spread them out on a dining table. "Look! The ring!"

Dacre was bemused. "Listen, it's OK, I mean it, I'm going to forget about all that—"

"Dacre, your mum was wearing that ring at the funeral. I know she was."

"Ring?"

"Didn't you read this? The special ring the girl was wearing. It says it was missing, but there's only one like it. It's got to be the one. Your mum's ring!" She looked at him, beaming and pointing to a picture on the cutting. It was unique, made by Carol Hosie's grandfather. There was a quote from Carol's mother that her daughter had worn it ever since her grandmother died.

"See! In the picture. Your mum had it on. On Monday."

Dacre looked closely at the picture. It had been blown up large to show the ring was etched with a tiny rose.

"I told your mum it was lovely, and she said she'd never worn it before. It's the same ring ... I'm sure it is!"

Dacre sat down at the table, unsettled about something connecting his mum to Carol Hosie. It was getting too much. And far from dumping him, Isla was suddenly interested in the murders.

She was insistent. "Don't you see? There's got to be some connection between your family and the murders. Or at least that one! Maybe you were right, and it *was* your dad."

The newspaper cuttings were swimming in and out of focus. Dacre had been trying to dismiss any connection to his family. He had to force himself to speak. "I proved it wasn't him. I went and checked the dates. I know I got them right. They didn't fit with any of the murders. He wasn't there."

"There's got to be some connection."

He tried to resist her logic. "Now I've infected you with my madness." He forced a smile and kissed her cheek. "My bus'll be here in a minute."

***

Craig Masson arrived at Isla's house half an hour after she had seen Dacre off at the bus stop. She opened the front door to a young man in jeans and trainers holding a police badge. "Sorry, Miss, I'm looking for Isla Alexander's house."

"What? Who are you?"

"PC Masson, Craig. Is Mr Dacre in? I need to speak to him urgently."

"He's just left," said Isla, peering at the badge suspiciously. "And how did you know he was here?"

"His aunt told me he had come here. He's travelling back to Fife today, I think?"

"Yes, but—"

"Miss, I'm sorry, it's urgent, and I can't tell you what it's about, but I need to see him. Please. Tell me where he is going and then I'll leave you alone."

"Is it about the missing girl? Have you found her? The one he said he knew about?"

"You know about that?"

"Yes, but it's nothing to do with him. He made a lot of things up when he was upset. His dad dying, and his hypnosis and phobia and—"

"She's dead, Miss, we found her body. And, I shouldn't tell you this, but she's had her leg sawn off."

Isla held on to the doorpost.

"Are you OK, Miss?"

"But ... the three other murders ... they're not connected, right?"

"Since you seem to know at least as much as me I'll tell you this: he was right that she'd been kidnapped, and that she was dead. I don't understand how he knew, but ... anyway he seemed to connect it to murders in Grampian, Perth and ... where was it again?" Masson was scrabbling in his back pocket for his notebook. “Christ, I’m not supposed to have this with me, I’m off duty, and the boss said to leave it to St Leonards.”

“Glen Dochart, Crianlarich.”

“That’s it. Listen, do you know where Mr Dacre lives? Where in Fife, I mean. I should have asked his aunt.”

“Auchmoor, 22 Rothes Park.”

Masson turned to go. “Thanks, Miss.”

“Wait. I’m coming with you.”

“No, sorry, Miss, you see—”

“I’m coming with you or I’m phoning the police now to tell them you’re breaking the rules.”

***

He’d been lucky with the bus and train times and was in Auchmoor not long after eleven o’clock. Rothes Park looked different. Instead of his dad’s van, there was a red car in the driveway. A fleeting pang of grief for his dad quickly made way for curiosity. Then anger.

That bloody cop! He’s pestering my fucking mother now. What the fuck?

He opened the front door and strode in. “Mum? Are you OK?”

Isla appeared out of the living room, and Craig Masson was behind her.

“What? How?”

“Is that you, Gordon?” his mum called from the kitchen. “You have visitors. I’m making tea.”

He was struck dumb by confusion.

“Listen. You were right about the girl.” Isla spoke quietly while Eleanor was still in the kitchen. “We drove over, Dacre. PC Masson needs to speak to you.”

He managed to stutter, “But ... you came with him? How? And what do you mean about—”

“Craig, PC Masson, arrived at my house just after you had gone, and we set off more or less straight away. They found her body in Colinton Dell.”

Dacre looked past her towards Masson who nodded. “It’s true. And the injuries were like the others you know about, Sir.” They were still whispering to each other.

“Will you stop calling me Sir. You said I was a nutter. What’s changed now?” On the journey from Edinburgh, Dacre had been trying to dismiss everything, but now fucking Masson had dragged it all up again. And involved Isla.

“I can’t believe this.” He walked past Isla and sat at the kitchen table with his head in his hands. “What the fuck?”

“Gordon! I heard that!”

He looked up at his mum who had a tray of cups balanced on her plaster cast as she walked out past him to the living room. Isla came in and put her hand on his shoulder. He could hear the loud ticking of the kitchen clock.

“Get off.” He shrugged her away, then grasped her hand. “Sorry, I just don’t know what’s happening.” He looked up at her. “What’s happening?”

Craig Masson stood at the kitchen door. “I’m sorry I didn’t take you seriously. When they found the body and she’d her leg removed I had to speak to you. I asked Wardrop to get Lothian to use the PNC but he was just furious with me for speaking to you behind his back. He sent me home and told me to stay off work.” Masson was staring past Dacre and out of the kitchen window. He appeared to be voicing his thoughts as they occurred. “Bastard Wardrop will take the credit if they link all those other cases you mentioned. He’ll be straight on to Force HQ at St Leonards now, but he doesn’t have details, so we’ll be ahead of them.” He turned back to the room. “And Isla told me something about a ring. I didn’t really follow that bit, but if there’s a physical link, evidence, I mean, it’s got to be someone you know.” He was looking back and forth between Dacre and Isla.

Dacre shook his head, and shouted, “Fuck! Fucking hypnosis! I wish I hadn’t started.”

“Gordon! What’s got into you? I’ve put the tea out through

here." Eleanor was calling from the living room, but Masson came into the tiny kitchen and closed the door. Isla stood aside to lean against the draining board and Masson sat down opposite Dacre. Bright winter sunshine was shining through his protruding ears when Dacre looked up.

"I wanted to ask you more about the other murders. Background, I mean. What you discovered. Did you say newspaper reports? And a library? I'm sure there's a link, all one murderer. A serial killer." He had his notebook out and was barely pausing for breath.

Dacre sighed. "As long as you don't turn round and call me a headcase again." He quickly related how he had found out from Big Alick about Mhairi in Glen Dochart, and from David about Inga Sabiston. "So I knew I'd seen TV reports on those two, and for the Perth one I had the cartoon, on the other side of the World Cup stuff I'd cut out, I mean. In my scrapbook, when I was a kid."

"And do you mean hypnosis made you remember all that? Really?" Isla still looked sceptical, but rapt. "How come you started dreaming about it all?"

"At first, I didn't understand any of it. But then I began to wonder if there was some connection, something about me, if I seemed to know stuff about all three girls. I managed to prove my dad wasn't responsible, but even that didn't help, and it all just got more mental." He looked at Isla and managed to smile. "You said to me, 'you need help'. That's why I went to see Dr Sutton, and he said I'd put old memories together to blot out my mum's affair. Because I'd seen her with Bugsy. I thought ..." He paused. "But she wasn't. And nothing was linking me or anyone to the murders. Sutton said I'd made a connection up. A defence mechanism, he called it."

PC Masson was writing screeds in his notebook. Dacre was staring at the red table. "And then the dreams about my mum got bad again, sort of got in the way, but then the stuff with the wardrobe, and Miles, and that fucking frozen hand!

Something about that hand is important, but I just don't know what!" He looked up at Isla.

"You're not mad, Dacre. It's making sense now, somehow. It's the ring. The ring means there *is* a link." Isla had lowered her voice. "I haven't said anything to your mum about it."

Masson said, "Tell me about this ring. What did you mean, a 'unique' ring?"

Isla related how she had seen Eleanor wearing the one-off ring described in the *Perthshire Advertiser*.

Dacre stood up. "I can't keep all this from my mum. I'm going to tell her what's going on." As he made for the door, it opened.

"Aren't you bringing your friends through? The tea'll get cold. Come and tell me about yourself, Craig, are you at university in Aberdeen as well?"

Masson looked at Dacre and then back at Eleanor. "I'm sorry, Mrs Dacre, I should have told you. I'm not really a friend of Isla and Dacre. Mr Dacre, I mean. I'm a police officer." He was shuffling his feet.

"Police? You? Why, what's he done? Isla, what's going on?"

"We said Craig was a friend instead of upsetting you. I'm sorry. We didn't expect to get here before Dacre."

"What on earth is going on?"

Isla said, "Let's all go through and sit down."

Masson said, "Mrs Dacre, would I be able to make a phone call?"

"Yes. If someone promises to tell me why you're all here."

While Craig Masson spent some time on the phone in the hall, Dacre and Isla sat on each side of Eleanor. Dacre told her he'd started hypnosis when his acrophobia worsened, and then about his dreams, suspecting her of the affair, and then thinking his father might be a killer.

"He was awful, Gordon, I can say that now. But he wasn't a murderer! I can't believe all this. And you've been going through all this? And hypnosis? All this and you didn't tell me." Despite his mother's tears, Dacre knew he had to continue. He went on to explain about his visit to Dr Sutton.

His mum's sobbing slowed. "I was so surprised when he appeared at the funeral." She put her hand to her mouth. "Oh, Gordon! Does that mean you discussed everything with him? I had no idea you—"

"Dr Sutton didn't tell me anything about the beatings, Mum. I found that out from Darren."

"He didn't tell you anything else?"

"No. Why?"

Masson came back in with an excited expression, but after looking at Eleanor he stood quietly. She was wiping tears away and Isla had come across to sit beside her. "It must be awful for you to hear all this, Mrs Dacre."

Eleanor managed to smile at her, then looked at Dacre, sniffing. "And you have learned all that, about the murders, through dreams? It's hard to believe that's possible."

Dacre looked at his mother and said, "But I didn't learn it, I knew about them already, I'd just sort of buried the memories away. The hypnosis dug them up." He looked across at Isla. "But I can see why you thought I was mad."

"I don't now. And we know where the ring came from."

Dacre shook his head, and with his eyes, he apologised to his mum.

Masson took over. "Jack has confirmed enough details from the PNC to show the deaths are all nearly identical. And now you telling me about the ring, that clinches it. There's some reason that ring is here. And your poor dad was dead by the time Sarah Kibble was abducted, so he was innocent." Masson looked towards Eleanor. "I'm sorry, Mrs Dacre. This must be awful for you. And so soon after you lost your husband." Dacre, his mother and Isla shared glances. Masson didn't know about the beatings.

"Ring?" Eleanor was shaking her head. "I don't know how to follow this."

Isla took out the news cutting and showed Eleanor the picture of the ring. When she had read it, she leant back on the couch. She held her left hand up and looked at the ring on her pinkie. Dacre hadn't noticed it at the funeral, and this was the first time he'd ever seen it. "I found it when I was looking for clothes for the funeral. I'd forgotten all about it, never worn it. Alun brought it home from the Ladybank auction one Friday. He'd gone there to buy a freezer for some reason—no, it was a TV that time—he said he bought the ring for me on the spur of the moment. It was the only nice thing he had ever given me. But then things ... went on the same, even that same night." She looked away, out of the window, before continuing. "That ring made me sick and I put it in a drawer. But it didn't seem so bad when Alun was dead. Is that awful? I can't believe I am saying these things." Eleanor was crying freely again.

"It's OK, Mrs Dacre." Isla had her arm round Eleanor's shoulders. Masson was looking at the floor.

Dacre was thinking about the freezer, the lock-up in Perth, the 'secret meat'. Suddenly he knew why he had dreamt about holding a severed hand. He could remember sneaking into the lock-up and lifting the frozen girl's hand out of the freezer. And that hand wore a ring. Now he knew why he'd been so ill in his dad's van. It was another memory he'd buried deep, and this one had come to the surface now, while he was wide awake. The ring on the hand in the freezer had to be the key to everything. The hypnosis had dredged up a lot, but this was the only thing definitely linked to a murder. The hand he had lifted was Carol Hosie's.

Masson spoke before Dacre could say anything. "I'm sorry, but I have to do something. Someone's killed a girl and we know something that links her death to three other murders. I've got to do something. I'm in enough trouble with the sergeant as it is."

Isla cleared her throat. "We know it wasn't Mr Dacre." She looked directly at Dacre, "and we know it wasn't you! But there's some link to the ring. Who else could be connected?"

Dacre felt a lump grow in his throat that threatened to stop him from speaking. He raced to beat it. "I think Sutton knows more. He's been strange. He's not letting on about something, I know it."

"Is that the psychologist?" Masson was writing in his notebook. "I could find out if he has a police record. I'm in up to my neck already, I could ask Jack to look at the PNC."

Eleanor had been sitting staring out of the window. She turned to the room. "It's not Granville. Dr Sutton, I mean. He's kind. I know he's not like that. He was so good to me, to us. I mean to Gordon."

His mum looked embarrassed, and Dacre remembered the handwritten note. Sutton had already told him he knew Alun had been beating her, and guessed that after she had confided in him he had offered to continue counselling her unofficially. His note to her presumably indicated he had decided it was no longer appropriate. But Dacre still thought Sutton was hiding something.

"Do we know where Sutton lives?" Masson was on his feet. "If he knows something, anything, it might help."

"I've been to his house," said Dacre.

Chapter 52

"You bastard! You fucking ..." Dacre lunged at Sutton, who made no attempt to defend himself.

Masson's hands gripped him. "Leave him, Dacre. Who is this 'Dod Lamb'?"

Sutton was sitting in his musty study, cleaning his glasses and shaking his head, his eyes red and moist.

They'd surprised him when they arrived at Motray Den. He'd just come home after taking his mother to catch a train, and when he heard Dacre's friend was a policeman he had become edgy and evasive. Masson had asked rapid questions, and the policeman's suspicion that he knew something about a series of murders had made him own up.

To Dacre's horror, for nearly two years Granville Sutton and Eleanor had an affair. It had started after Dacre's first appointment in 1969. Eleanor had disclosed her history of abuse and Sutton had comforted her and agreed to see her again. After several appointments, a tenderness had developed between them and they had met in secret. It ended when Dod Lambie had called unexpectedly at 22 Rothes Park, interrupting the half-dressed couple.

"He was a brute. Leering at us and threatening to tell Alun. He wouldn't go away. Ellie was worried you would come home from school, and Lambie deliberately stayed until you did."

"So it was you driving away?" Dacre had said. "That time I came home and Mum was crying. Dod Lambie was just leaving? I remember that." As Dacre had come along the street, a speeding car passed him and Dod's van was outside his house.

It was at that point in Sutton's confession that Dacre had tried to attack Sutton. He was furious that yet another man had taken advantage of his mum. Did *he* rape her as well?

Dacre felt numb but heard himself answering Masson's question.

"Dod Lambie. Just my dad's boss. He was always appearing, picking stuff up, dropping things off, giving his orders. He used to let himself in."

"I know more about him." Sutton's voice was weak.

"You shut up! You've done enough harm—"

"Wheesht, Dacre," said Masson. "Let him speak. He knows something."

Sutton explained that early in the counselling, before the affair started, they had been discussing Alun's violence when Eleanor disclosed that she had discovered Alun was involved in the theft of fuel oil from the RAF. Charles Younson was the source and Alun's van the transport, while Dod Lambie moved the stolen oil into the market. Eleanor was too scared of Alun to expose the scam, and Sutton had agreed it would be too dangerous for her. "That was advice I always regretted giving. But after Lambie had caught us together, I became foolish."

The besotted Sutton had confronted Dod Lambie in his workshop, threatening to expose the thefts if Lambie told Alun about the affair. "It was a boyish, romantic gesture, I saw that straight away. Lambie, of course, immediately threatened to expose my affair with a patient to the General Medical Council. The GMC would have struck me off the Register. Ended my career. My wife would have found out. Not that she was innocent." Sutton was staring at his untidy desk, still cleaning his glasses. "I had to tell Ellie it was over."

Dacre had no sympathy for him, but now understood the handwritten note his mother had kept.

"Does this Lambie have any connection to the murders? Who was the other one you said was stealing? Youngson?" Masson was impatient.

"Charlie Younson. He was a friend of my dad's. Bit of a weirdo. He liked collecting animals and stuffing them. Taxidermy, you know. It was odd he turned up at the funeral, I hadn't seen him in years."

"He was in Edinburgh on the day Sarah Kibble

disappeared?"

"Aye but ... no ... but ... maybe ... wait a minute! Younson was a poacher, fucking hell! The freezer! The frozen hand I thought was another dream. It was him!" Dacre was pushing his fury at Sutton aside. He explained quickly about the recurring dream about the iced hand in its linen wrapping, and that he now remembered seeing it when he'd sneaked into the lock-up.

"So this bloke knew how to butcher animals, and you say you found the girl's hand with the ring on? And they stored animal parts in the lock-up? That's got to be it!"

Granville Sutton spoke. "It could be Mr Lambie."

"But he was just my dad's boss. And a thief, not a killer. It's Younson!"

"There's something else you should know." Sutton rose stiffly from his chair and went out of the room, returning a minute later with a buff file.

"When I made my silly visit to Lambie's workshop the shed door was open and no one was there. I was going through his papers when he came in." Sutton had found a child's diary in a drawer. He hadn't had time to look through it but he remembered the name on the front in clumsy capitals. "Harold Pitcher, and his address was a hospital in Surrey. I always remembered that. I wondered why Lambie had it. When I saw him at your dad's funeral, I became angry all over again. About what he had done to break us up, your mum and me. I think seeing Ellie again had stirred my emotions."

Dacre was bristling, but Sutton continued. "I always felt guilty for putting my career ahead of protecting Ellie from Alun and the abuse. After the funeral, I couldn't get Lambie off my mind. I still wanted to get him back, to get him in trouble over the thefts." He looked up sheepishly. "Silly, adolescent revenge, in an old man! I remembered that hospital in Surrey, where the Pitcher diary came from: a colleague of mine had worked there. He's also a child psychologist."

"Is there a point to this? Where do we find Younson? Dacre, do you know where he lives?" Masson was jangling his car keys.

Dacre was startled when Sutton raised his voice. "Listen!" He held up the file he had brought. "This arrived in the post yesterday, I asked a contact down south to send me it. Harold Pitcher's old archived file, I'm surprised it still exists. I shouldn't have it, but I'm retired now and the GMC can't trace me, I hope."

"For Christ's sake!" Masson was heading to the door.

"I said listen!" Sutton shouted, and had their attention. "Dod Lambie and Harold Pitcher are the same person. I'm sure of it. Harold Pitcher spent years in a secure hospital with a history of animal mutilation. He was a psychopath. That long ago they thought they had a way of 'curing' him. But now, we know a psychopath can never be cured. Dod Lambie is a psychopath."

Masson sat down, looked at his watch, and stood back up quickly. "Twenty past one. Dr Sutton, can I use your phone? Quick!"

"Yes." Masson ran out to the hallway and pulled the door shut. Dacre sat trying to suppress his anger at Sutton, who was drumming his fingers and staring straight ahead.

When Masson returned he was beaming. "Jack checked the PNC and Lambie has no criminal record. Normally that would mean we couldn't get any info on him, but Jack said his name came up on another list. Top Secret or something. Wait 'til you hear this! It was a list of people who had officially been given a new identity. George Lambie officially didn't even exist before 1952. But in 1952 his address was care of RAF Lossiemouth, and he was described as a 'boy entrant'."

Sutton spoke. "Boy entrants were about 16 or 17, I think."

Masson rushed on. "It must be him, I mean he must have been Pitcher, the psychopath boy. I asked Jack to look for Pitcher's records but he wouldn't. He said he'd taken too many risks already."

"So we're not really any further forward. It could still be Younson." Dacre remained sceptical. And he didn't trust Sutton.

"There's something else, Dacre. When I phoned Jack earlier, from Auchmoor, I asked if he could find out anything about that ring." Masson was now pacing the little study. "Jack found police notes from Perth, the Hosie investigation. The ring was unique, like the newspaper said, made by the girl's grandfather. And it had an inscription on the inside, 'My Darling V.H.' Dacre, could you ask your mother? Get her to look at the ring, see if that's written on the inside? Just to make sure."

His mind was in a whirl, but Dacre went to the phone. A few minutes later he reported that Isla had helped take the ring from Eleanor's finger and that just visible on the inside was the exact inscription the police had described.

"That proves it's the ring from Carol Hosie's finger, but nothing else," Dacre said. "And my dad said he bought the ring at an auction."

"It's linked to your family, though. And you saw the ring on the frozen hand in the shed, in Perth, right?" Masson was still pacing. "We know the ring links someone to the killing of Carol Hosie, Dacre. Even if we don't know how your dad got it. Your dad's not the killer, so it has to be either Younson the butcher or Lambie the psychopath."

"Or both?" said Dacre, starting to feel lured in by Masson's enthusiasm. "They came together to the funeral."

Sutton cleared his throat. "No. One thing I know about psychopaths is they don't work in pairs. They are too egocentric to share their pleasures."

Craig Masson smiled. "You're a handy man to know, Dr Sutton." Dacre glowered as Masson continued, "It's got to be one of them. Do you know where they live? Either of them? We can go to the nearest one."

"No idea. Charlie Younson used to live in Glenrothes, but that was when I was wee. He could be anywhere now."

"What about Lambie?"

"Sorry. Might be anywhere. I only know his office."

"We might find out something there. Come on." Masson was on his feet, his car keys back in his hand.

"But what if he's there?"

"It's Sunday lunchtime. Anyway, it's our only move."

"We said we'd go back to Mum and Isla. I promised my mum. Can we go back there on the way?"

"No time. Dr Sutton, can you go back and sit with Isla and Mrs Dacre in Auchmoor?"

"No! That bastard's not going near my mum!"

"Dacre, see sense! He knows where we're going next, and he knows as much as we do about Younson and Lambie. It'll be useful to have him there, he can tell them what's going on. And it'll be backup when I get in trouble for doing this. Wardrop's never liked me."

Granville Sutton was pulling his jacket on and didn't see Dacre's warning stare.

Chapter 53

"Falkland with the palace? That's not far from here is it."

"It'll take us about twenty minutes."

Masson accelerated. "It's two o'clock already. We can do it quicker than that, just tell me where to turn." He was banging the steering wheel with the heel of his hand in time to the radio.

They were pulling out of Auchtermuchty when Masson spoke next. "Listen. I know Dr Sutton said psychopaths don't work in pairs, but did you say Younson and Lambie arrived together at the funeral?"

"Aye. They left together as well. Hang on! They were in Dod's van!"

"So?"

"Sarah Kibble was last seen getting into a van. That evening."

Masson turned to look at Dacre, grinning. "Hey! Who's meant to be the polis here?"

"Watch the fucking road!" An oncoming truck driver blasted the horn as the Escort barely made it round a tight bend near Dunshalt. Masson laughed as he sped on.

Dacre gripped the closed police notebook on his lap. "There's bad bends up ahead."

"OK." They didn't slow down.

Dacre tried to think of something else. "You keep talking about the PNC. But what exactly is it?"

"The Police National Computer."

"Computer? Like in 2001? Space Odyssey? Wow!"

"It's a massive machine that keeps crime records all over the country. They started it a couple of years ago. I got Jack to access it for me today, off the record."

Dacre gave more directions as they approached Falkland. They pulled on to the gravel outside the Nissen hut, in the exact spot his father had used on the morning they went to

Crianlarich. He had another momentary pang of sorrow before telling himself, *He deserved it.*

"How are we going to get in? It'll be locked."

Masson smiled. "Leave that to me." He took a crowbar out of the car boot and quickly split the bolt away from the wooden door. He swung the door open on its noisy hinges just far enough to let them in and ushered Dacre ahead of him. "Be my guest," he said with a grin.

Dacre slid through into the dark of the workshop and found a light switch. He felt a prickling up the length of his spine, his pulse quickening, and his mouth sticking like glue. As Masson followed him in, Dacre turned and said, "I don't like it here. What do you think we might find?"

"Anything would help." He moved into the workshop under the bare lightbulbs. "You've been here before, right? Is there an office?"

"That's it at the back." Dacre pointed at the scrawled sign at the back of the hut. But when they opened the door the tiny space had been transformed. An office chair and a small typewriter had been added, and the desk was tidy. Next to the phone lay a ballpoint pen with a pink, fluffy gonk on its end, and Dacre remembered Dod's chattering secretary. Masson squeezed into the office and tried the drawer below the desk. He came back out and took a large screwdriver from a bench, and had soon forced the drawer open.

"Should you do that?"

"No."

"What are you looking for?"

"Anything that connects with him. Sure you don't know where he lives?"

"No."

Masson removed the drawer completely and tipped it on the floor outside the office. "Here we are." From amongst the bills, receipts and letters he held out an envelope bearing an Inland Revenue postmark. It was addressed to George Lambie at Windygates Cottage, Luthrie. "Where's Luthrie?"

"Not that far from here."

Masson was back in the office. The old wooden frame containing the mounted insects was on the floor against the wall. Its place on the wall had been taken by a calendar, a picture of the Bee Gees for December. Picking up the frame, Masson said, "What the hell is this? Bits of insects?"

"He told me it was a hobby he had when he was wee."

Masson brought the frame out. "Look, the sick bastard has removed one leg or wing from every one of them." He turned it over. "Yes! This has got to be him!" He showed Dacre a faded label in childish handwriting. 'Harold Pitcher 1947'.

Dacre was confused, but Masson was already dialling a number on Dod's phone.

"I don't like this. I'm going outside, I feel sick." He left Masson talking quietly into the black phone. The car was locked, and he sat on an old wooden cable reel. Ten minutes later Craig Masson emerged, smiling and waving Dacre back into the Nissen hut.

"Got him! Come back in, I want you to listen to this."

"What?" Dacre followed reluctantly. Masson was already back in the office, picking up the phone.

"You won't believe me unless you hear this for yourself. Jack's going to read out what he's just told me. Hurry up, before he gets caught, he shouldn't be on the PNC." He spoke into the phone. "Jack, read out the important bits."

Dacre took the phone. "Hello?"

In hushed tones, he heard, "Harold Pitcher, date of birth 17/2/35, Bonstead, Essex. Offences: animal cruelty, animal cruelty, animal mutilation, animal theft, animal theft, animal cruelty, animal cruelty, animal mutilation, animal mutilation, animal mutilation. It goes on for a few more of the same. The dates are between 1943 and 1946. Forensic psychiatric diagnosis: Psychopath/Sociopath (fixed obsession with animal cruelty and mutilation) Disposition: Secure accommodation,

The St Isaac Juvenile Hospital for the Insane, Surrey. Admitted May 1946. Then comes the important bit. Discharged 1952. NOTE: New name assigned prior to relocation George Lambie. All childhood records archived."

Dacre listened intently, his eyes fixed on the framed picture of The Mount which still hung on the wall, next to the calendar. He could almost picture Sarah Kibble in her leotard.

"Christ! Why did they let him go?"

"I'm sorry, I need to go." The man named Jack ended the call.

Masson slapped Dacre in the middle of the back. "Got him! Now I'll tell you the rest. The best bit. The shrink who passed him fit to be let out and given a new identity thought he had cured him. Psychotherapy he called it. He said Pitcher had started cutting limbs off animals in retaliation for a surgeon having removed his left testicle when he was seven. The guy's a complete nutter."

"But why is he killing girls now?"

"Maybe he's always been doing it. Maybe you only know about some of them. Jack said he's only on the PNC because he was on that old list. The list of people who were given a new identity. It was so he could be monitored. What a joke, eh?"

"Can we go to the police now? I think we should."

"What a cheek! I am the police." Masson was grinning, and rushed on excitedly, "Anyway, they'd never believe us. There's still nothing to link Lambie to anything except the insects with missing bits. And that's historical. He was 'cured', remember?"

Masson was heading back through the workshop. "Come on."

Dacre followed him out. "Where are we going?" Masson pushed the door back into its frame and lined up the displaced bolt.

"Luthrie. We need evidence. Come on, you're the navigator." He had the engine running and started moving before Dacre closed the door.

"What about Younson?"

"My money's on Lambie. If it's not him we can look at Younson, but come on!"

"But—"

"If he's there we'll deal with it. He's probably out Christmas shopping. Or at the butcher."

"That's sick. Fuck, I don't like this."

After fifteen minutes of fast driving, while Dacre held on to the sides of his seat and gave directions, they slowed at last. "Is this the turning?"

"Left here. I don't like this."

They drove past Windygates Cottage twice. It was on its own behind a high hedge and they passed it slowly from both directions checking for vehicles or signs of activity.

"I really don't like this." It was all Dacre could say.

Masson pulled in onto a worn, grassy driveway between the gable of the cottage and another hedge. They both sat silently when he switched off.

"Not a sound. He's not in. Brilliant!"

"I don't ..."

Masson opened the car door quietly and disappeared round the back of the house. When Dacre followed slowly, he found him with the crowbar. Soon they were inside, Masson creeping about and Dacre standing in the back passage, glad to be out of sight.

"Bloody hell! Come and look at this!"

"What is it?" He stood still.

"In the room off the hallway. Come on!"

He found another broken door jamb and splintered wood on the floor outside. A padlock swung loose on its mounting.

"Bloody hell!" Masson's voice was raised, and as he pushed the door open Dacre saw an open wardrobe. His anxiety became revulsion and he vomited on the bare floorboards.

"Gruesome, eh!"

The wardrobe had been shelved and held no clothes.

"There's legs, feet, eyes, hooves, ears. Jesus Christ! There's a sheep's head here!"

Dacre couldn't look again. "Are they all animals?"

"Yeah. They all seem to be coated in layers of varnish. Some of it's peeling off. They're hard, solid. Preserved I suppose."

"You touched one?"

"This is bad enough but there's still nothing to link him to the girls. What's in here?" He pulled a drawer at the bottom of the wardrobe, continuing his gruesome commentary. "Papers. A key. More insects in cases ... eeeugh! Aw, Jesus!"

"What is it?"

"Hair. Long hair. Loads of it. Hang on ..." He turned round after a moment. "There's a receipt. McEwens of Perth. Didn't you say something about that?"

Dacre meekly took the piece of faded paper. It was a receipt for a men's leather belt. Price 15/6d. The date was 5th June 1970.

"Carol Hosie was last seen on that date, and she was strangled with a leather belt. She worked in McEwens."

"Got him!" Masson crossed the room to a large chest behind the door and inserted the key. The top wooden drawer screeched as he pulled it open. Dacre couldn't help himself and walked over to look. He could see a human leg, hacked off through the knee, the ragged flesh dried and shrivelled. Beside it was another foot, severed at the ankle. The hand he was familiar with was lying on the patterned piece of linen it had been wrapped in when he lifted it from the lock-up freezer. Underneath some of the body parts were yellowing press cuttings.

"Fuck!" Masson had pulled open the next drawer, and now retched. "This one's fresher. It's not been varnished."

Dacre leant forward to risk another look. Another human leg. The bone ends stood out neat and white against dark red flesh where they had been precisely cut through above and below the knee. He could imagine the labels on Dr Sutton's poster. There was a sudden, dull thud behind him and Craig Masson fell backwards, unconscious. As he turned he heard a familiar voice.

"Welcome! Enjoying my little museum?" said Dod Lambie, as the crowbar hit Dacre's temple.

Chapter 54

He was moving feet first, slowly rounding the whorls of a steep helter-skelter. On and upwards.

Upwards? And my head keeps thudding. And who bandaged my hands and feet together? I'm going to sleep again.

***

It was cold, windy. The back of his head ached and when he cracked his eyes open ahead of him was a grey sky overlain by vertical black lines rising from the top of a curving stone wall. A circle of railings. He was slumped on a hard, damp surface, his head and shoulders propped up against cold stone. He could now see and feel that the ties he had thought were bandages were loops of red bailer twine, tying his bare ankles together. His legs were cold and white, and he was naked from the waist down, his buttocks chilled by the damp stone flags. He tried to move and found his wrists were still bound, but now behind him. As he surfaced from his stupor he realised it was his shoulders that ached most.

Around the curve of the wall he was leant against he could see a pair of boots. He strained to his right and by craning his neck, he could see knees in green trousers. Someone was sitting on an oil drum bearing an RAF symbol. He could hear a rasping, rhythmic metal scraping.

The noise stopped, and he saw the knees straighten. A dull steel blade was laid on the top of the drum, and the pasty face of Dod Lambie appeared round the curve. He was in the same green overalls Dacre's dad had worn.

"You've come round. Delicious. You're just in time. I was about to start without you. It's much better when they are conscious." The grin loomed into Dacre's face and despite the wind, he could smell decay on Lambie's breath. "Now you are here, I'll show you around. Welcome to my sanctuary."

"Let me go you creep." It was all he could think of to say. To his horror, Lambie picked up the long blade and advanced towards him. “Fuck off! Don’t come near me!”

“My! My! You have grown up!” He was staring at Dacre’s genitals.

To Dacre’s surprise, Lambie swiftly sliced through the tight binding round his numb ankles and stepped back. Dacre tried to move, but with his hands bound behind him, he fell prone. Loud laughs were carried away on the strong wind. Facing the curved wall, his left cheek was on the wet stone and his temple felt bruised. With a huge effort, he drew his knees up under him and managed to lift his body upright. Lambie grabbed his tied wrists from behind and hauled him up off his knees, twisting him round to force his face against the spiked iron railings.

“Still scared of heights? How do you like this?” The sneering voice was loud, the face near his ear. Ahead of him was more grey sky, and below it in the distance the misted grey-green outline of undulating low hills. Looking down, the ground stayed still, not rotating at all. A fleeting acknowledgement that his acrophobia was well and truly cured flashed through his mind. Turning he now saw Lambie had withdrawn backwards and was round the curve, out of sight. He moved his cold feet forward to approach his captor but a searing pain in his shoulders stopped him as the twisted twine pulled his wrists behind him. He was tied to an iron ring six feet away.

“Help! Help! Help me!” he screamed into the sky.

Cruel laughter approached from behind him. Lambie had completed a circuit of the narrow platform. He leant in close and Dacre felt the foul breath in his face again. “No one can hear you. You’re one hundred feet in the sky, and there’s no one for miles around. I have you to myself.”

“We’re at the top of The Mount?”

“Well done! Go to the top of the class!”

“But how? It’s been closed off for years.” Everyone knew all access to the Hopetoun Monument had been stopped years ago after numerous suicide jumps.

"A simple exercise even for a poorly trained engineer like me to saw through a padlock and replace it with my own. I've made it nice, don't you think? Everything in its place. Everything has a purpose. I keep my varnish in the RAF drum. I kept it for old time's sake, it makes a nice chair, here in my little den. Just for me and my little friends." Lambie indicated behind him. Low cages lay in the lea of the outside stone parapet. Dozens of brown mice chewed, scampered and burrowed in clean dry straw.

"You're fucking mad! They should lock you back up like before."

The laugh again. "You know about that? Well, you ought to also know I'm not mad. They cured me! Or so I led them to believe. They thought their drugs and hormones had fixed me. And their stupid '*psychotherapy*'. What a joke that was! No, I'm not mad, and anyway, you are in no position to criticise! All marked out for surgery and displaying your wares!"

Dacre looked down and shivered, now in fear. A thick blue line had been marked out horizontally above his pubic hair, and two more lines descended into his groin, around his scrotum.

"Fuck off!" he screamed. "Get away from me, you pervert!"

"Haha! Pervert? If only! That would be good."

"I know what you did to those girls. You're not doing anything to me!"

Lambie opened his palm to reveal a live mouse he had been cradling. He threw it over the side and bent down to pull another one from the cage. He took up the knife again and swished cleanly through the tiny rodent's body before tossing the two bleeding pieces into the wind. "Yes. Sharp enough now." *The rasping sound ... he was sharpening his knives.*

Lambie looked at Dacre now, smiling. "I wasn't going to start on males until I had a full set of female specimens, but since you volunteered yourself, you can be first ..." He walked forward with the blade.

Dacre was beginning to accept he would never escape. “What do you want? My left ball, so you get a full set again? You had one removed.”

Lambie paused. “That’s when they started all this. It’s why I need revenge. When that stupid surgeon got it wrong. Bastard. I had to get them back somehow.”

Dacre didn’t know what he had said to start Lambie off but he was glad to delay his mutilation.

“What did they do wrong? Take off the wrong one?”

Lambie took a step back. “That’s just it. They took the correct one off, or out. It hadn’t come down, you see. But after the operation, I kept telling them the other one was sore. But they didn’t believe me. Told me I was being a silly boy, and it would go away when the wounds healed. But he’d done something wrong, the surgeon, see, the bastard got the blood supply caught up in his stitches. Strangled it. And the pain didn’t go away. Not for months. Not that they cared. And then it did go, the pain just faded away. But so did my other testicle. It shrivelled away. Strangled.”

“So you’ve got none?”

Lambie ignored him and was in full flow. He seemed to be enjoying himself and Dacre realised his gaoler and executioner might never have told anyone his story.

“When I got in trouble, they examined me and told my parents I had to have hormones. They didn’t care about side effects, they just wanted to try it out. I was only pulling off birds’ wings and things anyway for god’s sake. I didn’t need locking up. I just liked collecting. But I fooled them. In the end, I made that stupid shrink think he’d cured me.”

“But why the change of name?” Dacre was interested, but mostly in delaying Lambie’s next crime.

“My fucking, loving, caring bastard parents didn’t want me back. And with my history, the experts thought it would be a good idea to give me a new identity. A new start they told me.

But no one adopted me anyway so they turfed me out into the RAF." He was staring out over the Howe of Fife, and Dacre thought he might be crying. But when he turned, he showed a wide grin and bore down on Dacre holding the knife. "Yes, you'll be a good male to start with, especially with that trollop of a mother you've got."

Dacre rushed forward in fury, knife or no knife, but was arrested by the rope and the tearing agony in his shoulders. "You bastard! Did you rape her as well?"

Lambie stopped, laughing ironically, leering at Dacre and pointing at his own groin with the knife. "What? A eunuch? That's a good one. No, I didn't do her but stupid little Alun told me about your uncle. I was the perfect coach for Alun. I taught him about revenge, told him how to keep the bruises where they wouldn't show. Poor, stupid Alun! I was able to keep him on a low wage or I would expose him as a wife-beater. I made him grateful to me, gave him the idea of blackmailing your uncle to supplement his wages. Stupid bastard fell for it, and didn't realise he was providing me with opportunities to add to my collection and stay undetected."

"What do you mean? Providing opportunities."

"I sent him all over the place on business contracts, remote places where I knew I might be able to find bits for my collection." He looked at Dacre with a sneer. "You're not likely to be seen taking a girl in out of the way places."

"But what did my dad have to do with it?"

"I see you are stupid as well," Lambie sneered. "In the remote possibility that some smart alec made a connection between the bodies that were found ... they are always found, eventually ... if someone clever investigated, tried to make the link, they would find your stupid father had been in all the places the girls disappeared. So I could keep adding to my set of specimens, and he would be the suspect."

Despite his fear and being resigned to his upcoming fate, Dacre felt a tickle of satisfaction at being able to point out a flaw in Lambie's stratagem. "But the dates were wrong. They didn't tie in with the girls disappearing. I saw those dates in the work diary."

"You have been a busy little detective! Yes, the dates were wrong. But not the dates on the timesheets I made him sign every month. Whenever I needed to hide one of my operations I changed the dates. He didn't notice once. It worked every time. And stupid Alun was happy as long as he got his little pay packet. And my next piece of genius was giving Alun the ring. I told him I had found it and he should give it to his little whore of a wife."

Lambie smirked and Dacre lunged angrily at him, but fell to his right, against the parapet. He saw a blue car was parking behind his dad's old van. Fleetingly he wished it was a red car and that Masson had arrived.

"The police know about you, by the way. All about you. They are on the way here. That's who you hit with the crowbar."

"Him? That one with you in my house?" Lambie was laughing again. "It doesn't matter who he is. He's safely ... err ... pre-medicated. In the van. He's next on my operating list."

Chapter 55

Dacre was dejected. Defeated. But, looking up at Lambie, he had one last try.

"How are you going to explain it when I'm found?"

"You are going to get special treatment: you aren't going to be found. Ever! Your body ... or what I don't keep ... will disappear. There are some nice new concrete foundations about to be dug at the new workshop I'm building. It's a shame I won't be able to show you the plans sometime. Business is good!" he said with a cruel grin. "Anyway, what they *will* find is this letter you are going to sign." He waved a typed sheet of paper. "I typed this out before I brought you here. I'll not read it all out, it's pathetic, the ramblings of a madman. But it explains you couldn't live with your guilt about having killed your father and the girl, that you are going to kill yourself by jumping off the Forth Bridge. They'll search for your body for a while then give up. They always do, they wait for a dog walker to find it. I'll think of something else to explain your policeman friend's disappearance, but you'll be together in the concrete. I might keep his car, I think. Quite nice. I'll get it resprayed and scrape the numbers off." Lambie was becoming animated, speaking very quickly, drooling. Dacre interrupted him.

"What do you mean about 'the girl'? What girl?"

Lambie seemed to ignore him. "Yes, this is good, starting my male collection with you. It's time to move on from girls for a while. After Alun died I thought I'd never get any more without having him to cover my tracks. But the funeral excited me and I just couldn't resist one more. It was that night, in fact. I kept her in the van overnight. I had to get that idiot Younson out of the way, first, of course. I did the girl at dawn. Beautiful. And your letter admitting you killed her will cover my tracks perfectly. Even if it does lead them to find the body when your letter makes it clear she's not just still missing.

Perfect, don't you think?"

Dacre suddenly realised that Lambie didn't know Sarah Kibble's butchered remains had already been found. Masson had said they'd only discovered her this morning and the newspapers wouldn't have put anything out yet.

"You mean the one in the Water of Leith? In Colinton Dell. The one whose right leg you removed. The one whose knee you kept?"

He hoped to god he'd remembered the details. It was very soon evident that Lambie was as shocked as Dacre could have wished for. He doesn't like not being in total control, thought Dacre, the freak looks like he's been kicked in the guts. Lambie now looked over the parapet and appeared to be listening intently. Dacre could hear a siren in the far distance.

"Sign this fucking letter. I want to get on, then I've got to get your friend dragged up here. Quick, sign this now." A pen was thrust under Dacre's nose. Whether it had been Dacre's revelations about Sarah Kibble or the sound of the siren, Lambie now seemed to have become anxious. Dacre grinned at him and shrugged his tied hands behind his back. His shoulders hurt but it was worth it to see Lambie's frustration.

"I'd be glad to."

"Fuck!" Lambie spun Dacre round and bent down to pick up the knife from the ground beside them. Dacre heard heavy footsteps and a loud grunt before Lambie fell forwards into the back of his legs. He buckled, falling backwards to sit heavily on Lambie's back, very confused by Lambie's sudden collapse.

"Dacre! Stay there, hold him down." It was Craig Masson's voice, and craning his neck Dacre could see he appeared to have rugby-tackled Lambie to the ground and was gripping his legs. But Lambie was writhing under him and without the aid of his arms, Dacre lost his balance, falling onto his side. He could hear Lambie roaring and saw him thrash, twist and push up with his arms. He stared triumphantly into Dacre's eyes as he managed to shake Masson's flailing arms loose and kick the policeman hard in the middle of his chest. There was a loud grunt from Masson who lay still, and Lambie rose to his knees and quickly crawled round the central column and out of sight. The wind picked up and whistled through the high railings. Masson was still lying flat, the only movement his chest heaving.

"Are you OK?" Dacre whispered into the wind. He tried again louder.

"Just winded. Give me ... ooyah! ... a second. Christ!" Masson moved painfully onto his knees and Dacre saw him point with his thumb over his shoulder with a questioning expression on his face. He nodded in reply, and Masson crept towards him and took a pen-knife from his back pocket to begin sawing at the ropes.

"Where's he gone," whispered Dacre, "back down the stairway?"

"I hope not, Sutton and your girlfriend'll never stop him."

"Sutton? Isla? What?" Dacre's mind cleared of everything else. The blue car, the Volvo. They must have let Masson out of the van. "Get these ropes off me! We've got to stop him."

The wind stilled momentarily and they heard scuffling and muffled cursing before the next whirling gust. Dacre ripped the last strands free and started to stand up, but Masson held him and gestured to keep quiet. He whispered close in Dacre's ear, "He's still up here. You go that way", before turning and creeping tight against the inner stone wall, gripping the pathetic little knife. Dacre heard the siren again, much nearer now. He leant against the cold sandstone and edged himself round, his free hands roasting with prickles as the numbness receded. He hoped Lambie wasn't descending the stairs but didn't want to meet him on the platform either. As he passed the opening to the spiral stairway he listened for sounds of footsteps but heard only the squeal of the wind through the slit windows.

Further, nearer, the scuffling louder, the tin drum scraping on the stone flags. Slowly onwards until he saw wary mice venturing from now-open cages. Into view came Lambie silhouetted against the light grey sky, crouched, perched on to the top of the railings. Masson was walking very slowly towards him, his mouth appearing to say "Don't do it" into the wind. Dacre stood motionless.

Lambie stretched up to stand, balancing on the rail, facing in towards the centre column and grinning madly. He screamed over the howling wind, "Never! They'll never stop me!" He stretched his arms out high, the long knife in one hand. Looking upwards he leant back against the wind, toppling, teetering, taking forever to fall.

But his feet slipped off the wet, mossy railing and his weight threw him forwards, all balance and control gone. His arms flailed as he fell, his face screaming into the howling gale. His bulging eyes were fixed on the railing spike he knew was going to kill him. His scream was cut short as the rusty iron arrowhead pierced his neck and forced on upwards through his tongue before it exited through his left eye socket. The railing took his weight and his body whumped heavily against it to hang in its green overalls, blood and eye-jelly blowing off the spike in a slimy streamer.

***

Partway down the stone spiral, Dacre shouted ahead to Masson.

"Hey! Craig, stop a minute. Give's a loan of your jacket."

A few steps down he saw Masson holding on to the wall, panting and wiping his mouth. There was sick on the shallow sill under a slit window cut into the thick stone wall of the tower. He looked up at Dacre as he spoke.

"I needed to stop anyway. Need to think of what I say to the boss," replied Masson, turning to look at Dacre. "I'll be in deep shit for—what the fuck? Christ, he stripped you? Did he bugger you? What's that ... those lines around your ...? A tattoo?"

Dacre couldn't help grinning. "You mean you didn't notice

until now? The bastard had me ready for surgery. Was going to cut off my bits."

"Fuck!" Dacre realised Masson's swearing was rougher than usual.

Masson reached the bottom of the tower first and pulled at the heavy metal door. "Thank fuck he couldn't lock it from the inside!"

With Masson's Harrington jacket tied round his waist, Dacre followed his rescuer into the fading daylight. Isla ran towards them and gripped Dacre tightly. She didn't speak. Behind her, Granville Sutton ambled from the Volvo with an anguished look.

"Are you injured, Gordon? Oh, thank god! I had to tell the policeman I was your doctor and you were probably already dead. They still didn't believe me, I don't think."

A bright blue police transit van with a revolving blue light on its roof appeared bumping up the overgrown track between the trees. It pulled into the small clearing beside Dod's van and like Sutton's Volvo, it had brown bracken hanging from the mirrors and radiator grille. A man with a chevron on his arm emerged from the passenger side. A much younger policeman was driving. Adrenaline flashed over Dacre's mind, a realisation that police everywhere must be organised in similar pairs ... except for the young pair who had been first on the scene when Miles killed himself, and they couldn't handle it. That must be why they try to have an older one there ... experience.

Experienced or not, the sergeant looked shocked and unfit, only managing to utter raspingly, "Reports of a death ... suspicious ... young man ... where?" Craig Masson stepped forward.

"I'm PC Masson, Sir, Lothian. The body is at the top of the tower."

"Don't give me that, sonny. Davies, cuff those two, leave the old one and the girl. Christ! We'll have to go up to the top.

Bloody jokers! If you're wasting our time—!" Looking at Masson he said, "And you could do time for that, sonny, impersonating a—"

"Just look up there." Masson was pointing towards the top of The Mount, as the young constable reached for his handcuffs.

The sergeant stopped, suspicious, and glanced up, peering. The grey sky was split by the towering stone monument. "What's that on the railings? Not another jumper, surely. There's not been one of them for years."

"I think it's a body, Sarge." The constable had binoculars and held them out to the sergeant. He dropped the handcuffs and started to run towards the door to the tower.

"Davies, don't go up there. Call for an ambulance! And the Fire Brigade." The sergeant had focused on Lambie's remains. "When we've got these two cuffed I'm calling the Inspector. He'll want the CID on this." He gestured to Isla and Sutton, who had backed away. "You two! Sit in the van and don't move." Isla still hadn't spoken a word.

Chapter 56

"I'm alright. Really, I am. I've told them everything I know. But how did you know where to come?" Dacre was still wrapped in a tartan blanket Dr Sutton had handed him before the police bundled him into their van.

Isla let go of Dacre and they moved aside to make room for Masson who had come in after having also finished his statement. Granville Sutton sat motionless in one of the two upright chairs in the bare, windowless room they had been asked to wait in.

"Mum? What are you doing here?" Eleanor was sitting in the other chair, just a few feet from Sutton. Dacre looked back and forth between the two, his expression darkening.

"It's OK, Gordon. The police sent a car to Auchmoor to get me, I'm only just here. They want another statement tomorrow. The CID, they said." She rose from her chair and smiled through tears as she took her turn to hug her son.

Isla stood behind Eleanor and turned to look at Sutton who was looking at the floor. "When Dr Sutton came to your house we got worried waiting to hear from you. Your mum suggested we should come and look for you. We knew you'd gone to Lambie's workshop and Dr Sutton knew where it was, so we went there in his car."

Dacre glowered at Sutton, but Eleanor said, "It's alright, Gordon. It's alright." She let go of Dacre and turned and smiled at Sutton, who looked up meekly. Dacre rubbed his wrists and noticed Masson, still standing in the room doorway, was doing the same.

"But Mum! He's another one who ... who ... another one!" He slumped against the wall, and the pain from the lump on the back of his head was almost welcome.

"Oh, I know ... Gordon ... you shouldn't have to know these things." Eleanor was still looking towards Sutton. "But he's the only man who's always treated me well." Sutton's eyes were turned down again, and the room was silent for a moment. It was Isla who spoke next. "Your mum told me about Dr Sutton while you and Craig were away. She was worried you would find out and I could tell she was upset."

Dacre closed his eyes, exhausted. Isla stood close and took him by both hands. He winced when she brushed his bruising wrists. "Oh, Dacre! When they took you away in the police van …"

His mind returned to the top of The Mount. "I think the police believe us now. About what happened, I mean. I think it helped when they came down with the knife, the ropes and stuff. And the letter he tried to make me sign."

"Letter?"

Dacre's mind was racing with images of Lambie and the knife. He was pacing. "I think he dragged me up that stairway, by the rope round my feet, I mean. The back of my head's all sore as well as where he hit me." He was gingerly touching his temple as he looked at Masson. "Did you see those mice?"

"Mice?" Dr Sutton looked up. He was polishing his glasses on a handkerchief.

"He was sick! Breeding mice to test his knife on. It was bloody sharp!"

"Oh god!" Isla covered her face with both hands.

Dacre looked from Isla to Sutton and back. "But, how did you know where to come for us? The Mount, I mean."

Isla calmed herself. "When you weren't at the workshop and the door was hanging open we went inside. The letter with Lambie's address was lying out. We guessed you had gone there."

"You went there? To his house?"

"We were frantic about where you had gone. When we saw the door broken open, we thought you were inside. That stuff in the wardrobe! Those girls! He …" Isla sat down on a chair and gagged into her hands. Dacre sat down beside her. The exhaustion began to overwhelm him.

Sutton took over, still not looking Dacre in the eye. "I looked out of the window of Lambie's kitchen and saw The Mount. I remembered you telling me it was prominent in your dreams. I've never liked The Mount since I saw the picture of it in his office when I went to see him and he threatened to destroy my career. I even look away when I drive past it. He saw me looking at the picture and said it was his 'happy place'." He raised his head. "Sorry, I'm rambling. The Mount seemed to be the first place we should come to look for you. That's when I phoned the police and told my little fib about you being my patient. They certainly took some convincing."

Isla spoke again. "And when we got to the foot of the tower there was a van, and we heard Craig banging. And moaning. He was gagged. Tied up." She looked at Masson. "As soon as we untied him he told us."

"I don't want to think about this any more. I want to go home." Dacre stood up and walked to the door. Isla was able to laugh when Dr Sutton's tartan travelling rug fell away leaving Masson's jacket barely concealing his bottom half. Before Dacre could reach the door, Masson interrupted.

"We won't be able to leave until they're satisfied. They've gone to Luthrie to check on his house."

Opening the door anyway Dacre saw opposite him PC Davies standing guard. Nicknamed 'Davy' at school, Dacre had never known his real first name.

"Davy, can we go now?"

Davies stepped forward. "Sorry, Sir. They want you to wait. The CID is coming. You'll have to stay here."

It felt strange to be called 'Sir' by Davy who had been three years ahead of Dacre at school.

"It's OK, Davies. I'll handle this." At the sound of the booming voice from along the corridor, Dacre shrank back into the interview room.

The sergeant strode along and filled the door frame with his bulk. "Things have moved fast. Some new computer or something seems to be stirring the CID up. You can go, but you've not to leave your home, Mr Dacre. The CID want to see you tomorrow.

"Mrs Dacre, they'll also want to see you. They're too busy today at the Luthrie house. They found a man's body in a freezer. His wallet said his name was Younson.

"And all hell broke loose when they checked out what PC Masson said, what with the link to the Edinburgh girl and everything. And apparently there are more old cases all over the country. This is going to be big."

***

The police had said Masson could collect his car from Luthrie, and they set off in Sutton's Volvo.

Dacre held the back door open for his mum and sat in the front himself. Masson squeezed into the other back door beside Isla. Even before they were out of Cupar he was talking about the PNC. "Imagine if police in every area put everything unsolved on the PNC. All the other forces could see if similar things were going on outside their own patch!

"They'd have caught Lambie long before this. I'm telling you, this is the future! Wardrop and his like will have to just get used to it. Computers are going to take over policing. And it's not just policing. One day everyone will have a computer and they'll all be linked up like a great big road map, except it'll all be wires I suppose, linking them all together. Communication! I'm going to make it my career if Wardrop ever lets me stop doing stupid paperwork.

"Oh, Christ, I'm in trouble. I hope they let me off with doing this. And Jack. But still, without us, Lambie would still be carrying on!"

Dacre guessed Masson's adrenaline levels hadn't slumped yet. He just wanted to sleep and forget about it all. But Sutton had been listening.

"I think you should remember the human brain may retain some usefulness. Hypnosis was the key to unlocking memories

Dacre had hidden miles away in his subconscious. His mind then played out their importance to him in his dreams, and he began to remember."

Dacre sighed to himself.

Maybe that's right, but please! No more dreams. Now, I might sleep in peace.

THE END

Acknowledgements

Thank you to the 'SWFers'—the graduates of the Start Writing Fiction course run by The Open University—who have been immensely supportive to me throughout the years it took to write this story.

I'd also like to thank the Local History Office at A K Bell Library, Perth who advised on libraries in 1977; Sue Leckie who freely shared with me her knowledge of Edinburgh; and John Harkin for his help and especially for the valuable insights into 1970s police work and Glasgow in general.

A big thank you to my beta readers who have helped me with several versions of this book: Jeanette Everson, Melissa Levine, Steve Kaprelian, Debbie Coverdale, Marlene Pitcher, Ellen Kirkman, Dave Speck, Elizabeth Coby, Caroline McAleer, Sally Whitman and Jan Brown.

And lastly, I wouldn't have been able to complete this book without the support and forbearance of Helen while I drove myself to distraction.

Lightning Source UK Ltd.
Milton Keynes UK
UKHW010743090822
407056UK00001B/15

9 781739 63670